Doctor Lisa A. Johnson comes from a very close-knit family of four girls and no brothers. Lisa was one of the youngest and without a doubt the scariest of the sisters. This fact and their own love for sitting together to watch horror stories and challenge each other about who can be the most entertaining gave rise to this story. The family hopes you enjoy it as they all did.

This book is dedicated to my parents Gene and Vera Johnson.

Lisa Johnson

A VIEW OF THE MEADOW

AUSTIN MACAULEY PUBLISHERS™
LONDON * CAMBRIDGE * NEW YORK * SHARJAH

Copyright © Lisa Johnson 2024

All rights reserved. No part of this publication may be reproduced, distributed, or transmitted in any form or by any means, including photocopying, recording, or other electronic or mechanical methods, without the prior written permission of the publisher, except in the case of brief quotations embodied in critical reviews and certain other non-commercial uses permitted by copyright law. For permission requests, write to the publisher.

Any person who commits any unauthorized act in relation to this publication may be liable to criminal prosecution and civil claims for damages.

This is a work of fiction. Names, characters, businesses, places, events, locales, and incidents are either the products of the author's imagination or used in a fictitious manner. Any resemblance to actual persons, living or dead, or actual events is purely coincidental.

Ordering Information
Quantity sales: Special discounts are available on quantity purchases by corporations, associations, and others. For details, contact the publisher at the address below.

Publisher's Cataloging-in-Publication data
Johnson, Lisa
A View of the Meadow

ISBN 9781638291282 (Paperback)
ISBN 9781638291299 (Hardback)
ISBN 9781638291305 (ePub e-book)

Library of Congress Control Number: 2023912707

www.austinmacauley.com/us

First Published 2024
Austin Macauley Publishers LLC
40 Wall Street, 33rd Floor, Suite 3302
New York, NY 10005
USA

mail-usa@austinmacauley.com
+1 (646) 5125767

I want to thank my cousin Shari for allowing me a vacation in her home in Germany's Black Forest, my Aunt Shirley for faithfully reading early versions of the book and critiquing them, but most of all my late big sister, Attorney Iris Johnson-Bright and her good friend, who must remain anonymous. They both were entertainment attorneys who challenged me to 'write something really scary'.

It is a beautiful morning when Charlotte awakens. It almost always is in Mendocino. The California seasons or the weather never seem to matter. Just being in or near the estate that Charlotte's parents had purchased, shortly after arriving from Germany, is always comforting.

The Von Shillingsfurst home is nestled along the Mendocino coastline, a total of ten acres if you include the stables and the run down to the sea. While its beauty soars unsurpassed, it is a lot to handle for a twenty-eight-year-old woman alone. Even with the generous assistance of the trustees, it still could be trying at times.

These very thoughts occupy Charlotte's racing mind as she dresses. It is of paramount importance that today her appearance be perfect. Meeting with the Chamber of Commerce and several other city officials is no small venture, especially while carrying a request for permission to open and operate an art gallery, one of her lifelong dreams.

A knock at the door interrupts her train of thought. It is Megan's knock, firm but unfailingly polite. Megan Hampton has been Charlotte's nanny since her parents died in a car crash when Charlotte was two years old. "Good morning," says Megan. "You had better hurry if you wish to make the meeting on time, Charlotte. Your breakfast is ready. Mr. Leopold called to say that he has acquired the services of an excellent architect to renovate the property as you requested, with your approval, of course."

These last words are spoken brightly but with her characteristic sly smile. Megan knows all too well that Charlotte is too frantic about the acceptance of her art gallery proposal at city council to worry about the architect. "Hire him," Charlotte replies over her shoulder, climbing into her Volvo. "I'll see you at dinner."

Charlotte drives directly to the office she is temporarily renting to pick up copies of the proposal. Jennifer, her newly acquired secretary, has it all ready. Charlotte often has to marvel at Jennifer's enthusiasm for the project. Charlotte is showing great appreciation for Jennifer's good attitude and her tendency to sustain support for Charlotte and the project. *I hope your attitude is contagious*, she thinks silently.

As they proceed to city council, both feel lucky that they don't have to address an open meeting with all its pretend pomp and dragging confusion. Instead, today's gathering will be a closed session. As they slipped through the giant oak doors, Charlotte immediately took stock of the boardroom. Present were the mayor, the vice mayor and five or six other formal-looking committee members that normally review these types of projects. Charlotte was comforted knowing that this gathering would suffice. Winking at Judy, Charlotte was elated that they didn't have to call a full session.

As Charlotte prepares to address the assembly, Jennifer takes a seat close enough to assist her with anything she might need. Charlotte holds up some graphics of the building she is proposing to buy, and Jennifer fastens them to the chalkboard. The person who owns the building has already agreed to sell to her if the rest of the project will fly with the city council. With a frank air, she calmly displays pictures of how it looks now and, quite proudly, what it will look like when she has finished with it.

In a clear and steady voice, Charlotte addresses the vice mayor and the assembly, first identifying herself as Charlotte Von Shillingsfurst, a long-standing member of the community. Since she had been away at school, Charlotte silently chuckled, all present were most likely totally unaware of who she really was. Realizing their attention was now deep in her pockets, she informs the collective that she is very well suited to run an art gallery. Displaying the framed Bachelor of Art Science degree that she earned from a well-known private school and two master's degree scrolls, one in art and the other in business administration, Charlotte hoped the assembly was impressed. Feeling buoyed by the twinkle in the eyes of the vice mayor, she explains that she doesn't think the project could possibly fail for several sound reasons. Her unlimited funding was probably the only reason she needed to mention but she continued by reminding the collective of the heartbreak that befell her family some thirty years ago. The tragedy that has, in a way, brought her such good fortune at such an early age has now allowed her return home to live at the estate as a full-fledged active citizen of Mendocino.

The assembly applauds her.

She is a little shy. She has never had to do quite so much talking before. This reception gives her confidence to go on.

She smiles and acknowledges the applause. She goes on to tell them, "I have traveled extensively throughout Europe and the United States. I have several people that are lined up ready to exhibit. And I personally do sculpture and watercolor, should it happen that I not have someone to exhibit."

Charlotte draws their attention to the business plan that Jennifer is now distributing to all the members of city council that are present.

She tells them, "Please turn to page eight. You will find that I only intend to use the art gallery seasonally. I understand that Mendocino is quite a seasonal city and that people come to the wine country in general during certain seasons. Those are the seasons that for right now, at least, I plan to exhibit. The rest of the time I will be sending back the exhibits and contacting new exhibitors and cataloging their new art objects to exhibit for the next season. That takes up quite a lot of time with the staff that I have right now. As I grow, and should the project and my staff grow, then I will advise the city of the difference. I am hoping this will bring even more people to Mendocino, and, of course, more dollars. People might stay a longer length of time than they would normally stay. It would bring more culture to the city."

Once again, she gets applause. They welcome her back. The mayor goes on to say that they don't have too many questions to ask her. "I don't think that your project will do anything but generate good will in the city. It's not the kind of project that should bring about hooligans, or things that are negative. I wish you well." He understands that she will probably have no trouble financing it and keeping it afloat. "Just be careful that you are penny wise." He congratulates her on being very well educated and turning out to be a beautiful young lady.

Some of them, from time to time, have had a glimpse of her growing up, when she has come home from school, but they haven't seen that much of her. The mayor says, "I can see nothing that will stand in the way of your project. We have had ample time to review your proposal. We will take a vote and you will be notified by mail. But I can almost assure you that you will have no problems. I thought your presentation was very well organized. You will probably be just as organized with the rest of your business and in everything else you do."

She is dismissed. The city council goes on with the next person who has a business proposal. She leaves the town hall with Jennifer. By the time they are out in the hall, they are plastered against the wall. They are so relieved.

Charlotte didn't realize that it was taking so much out of her and that she was so nervous. But this was very important to her, and these were the only people that could stop her. She could finance it herself. She had already received approval from the gentleman who owned the building. She already secured another architect who could set it up properly for the lighting and all things needed to exhibit artwork in it.

Charlotte says to Jennifer, "I hope this all goes off as well as we've planned. But we can't be too overconfident because the best made plans of mice and men don't always go off well."

Jennifer says, "I don't think we are going to have a problem. I think we could just go back and start putting things together from the business plan so that your art gallery will open in two or three months."

That is what they decide to do. She drives Jennifer to a restaurant. At lunch, she tells Jennifer that she is really noticing that this has taken an awful lot more out of her than she thought, so she suggested that Jennifer return to the office alone. "I'm going to take a walk through the city and get a better feel for Mendocino because I have always been in and out of Mendocino. I want to walk around a little, especially if it's going to be a place that I'm going to call home."

Jennifer says to Charlotte, "I understand you need the time by yourself. It's no problem with me. I'll be happy to go back to the office. I can start reviewing the names of the people who have said they would like to be in the grand opening. I must contact some people to cater, hostess, and do various other things at the grand opening." Jennifer knows she has a lot of things to do. Charlotte has made out a list of things that they both have to remember to do, including contacting the man who owns the building to tell him that they have completed their proposal in front of city council, that the ownership of the building should be changing hands within forty-eight hours and soon they can begin the alterations that will transform it into an art gallery.

She calls the owner of the building to let him know that this contingency had been removed and she was signing and sending the check in now. She also must contact some people to cater and to hostess and to do various other things at the grand opening. The owner is already prepared for this because they assured him, ahead of time, that he will be receiving a check. He knew that escrow had already been opened and this was the only contingency they needed to remove.

Charlotte is walking around the streets of Mendocino greeting people and speaking to them. Some of them know who she is and some of them do not. Mendocino is quite small. She goes down to the docks, sits down and watches the ocean for a while. She realizes that quite a bit of time has passed, and it is time to go home. She goes home. When Charlotte returns home, Megan is waiting for her. She is eager to know how the proposal went. But in her mind, she knows that Charlotte was successful.

Charlotte tells her that they had just about given her a guarantee that nothing will interrupt her plans. "I'm very excited about it. I have to wait at least one day, maybe two, to get it in writing. As soon as I get it in writing, I'm going to be able to move on it."

Mrs. Hampton tells her at that point, "I know you are very excited. But in the library, waiting for you, is the architect that Mr. Leopold has hired. He would like to speak with you and meet you to see exactly what you have in mind."

Charlotte puts down her portfolio and takes off her coat. Mrs. Hampton takes them up to her room. Charlotte goes into the library. Waiting for her is Jasper Smythe. He is not quite what she expected. She doesn't know exactly what it was that she expected in an architect. Maybe she was thinking that because she was such a young artist, he would be slightly younger. But actually, he is about fifty-five or sixty, graying but very congenial.

He has such a friendly smile that she immediately relaxes. The first thought is that, if he is an older architect and I am a young woman, I'm going to have a hard time getting him to do what I want him to do. But he is so respectful, so friendly and so congenial that she dismisses this thought from her mind immediately. She introduces herself, "I'm Charlotte Von Shillingsfurst, and I understand that you are the architect that has been recommended by one of my trustees, Mr. Leopold."

He says, "Yes. I am Jasper Smythe. I hope that I'm acceptable to you for your project. I was wondering if Charlotte Von Shillingsfurst existed because all I kept running in to were trustees. And I was wondering if I was going to have to do the house to their specifications or to those of a nice young lady."

Then that same feeling came back to her, that this will be a little difficult. She is again realizing how much the trustees have done for her in the past and how little she has had to think about very major occurrences in her life. But this she wanted to handle herself. "No, to my specifications and very much so to my specifications." She is a little sterner than she normally would have been, but it is only because she has this inner doubt that he's going to run all over her.

He says, "Exactly what are those specifications? Have you got them in mind? I understand that you have quite a background in art and a little in architecture because of it. Tell me, do you have definite plans for each room? Are you going to expand the house? Have you thought much about the exterior? The grounds?"

Again, we have a slightly awkward moment because Charlotte is insisting upon the specifications. She realizes she doesn't know what specifications she is insisting on and that she should have something in mind before she decides to take charge. She says, "In all honesty, to be frank with you, I haven't. I haven't thought about all these things. I haven't seen most of the house. I have been away at school most of the time, and I would return in the summer, until recently. Some of my summers have not been spent here but have been spent in Europe or other parts of the world. So, your suggestions are very welcome. I would like you to think about this and to return with some suggestions. If you haven't already done so, please walk around the grounds, in all the rooms, and come up with some ideas for me. I'm not very displeased with the decor as it is. It is very elegant. It is very pleasing. It's just that it is thirty years old, and it needs a little updating."

When he saw it, he said that he was also very pleased, and it seemed that someone was taking very good care of the grounds, but it definitely hadn't been professionally landscaped. She says, "As a child, I used to horseback ride in certain areas. People were hired because we liked flowers, but it hasn't been professionally landscaped. There has been some gardening done. There's gardening done constantly."

He says, "I'll take care of it. It is a very beautiful estate, and because you are in between the redwoods and the ocean we must take full advantage of that. We want to make sure that we use all the different shades of light that are possible, because this is the best possible setting, a romantic home." Then he asks her, "It hasn't been mentioned to me, but you're not married, are you?"

Somehow, he realizes that maybe he has said the wrong thing. But it is too late, it has come out.

She says, "No. I'm not married."

The memory of Jean still hurts after three years knowing that he didn't care for her then, he doesn't care for her now, and everyone in their circle, at that time, knew that he didn't care for her. She always thought that she would return to this house and be carrying on this conversation with him at her side, and that was very foolish, very, very, foolish. She didn't have time to explain that. She didn't want to have to explain that to Mr. Smythe. She was hoping that she could cover it up. He was too perceptive. He had seen too much into the remarks. Fortunately for her, he was sensitive enough to let it drop.

He says, "Well, I am very happy to meet you and I will spend the rest of my time here, as you say, looking around and getting ideas. I don't think I'll be back within the week, but I'll probably be back from time to time with suggestions for different parts. I'll probably start on the landscaping first. Then I'll move in toward the house because that's going to take a lot more thought from both of us, because, once that is done, you'll have to live with it."

She says, "I fully agree that this should take place." He asks to be excused.

Mrs. Hampton arrives at the door and tells Charlotte that she will be more than happy to show him around the grounds and any other parts of the house. Charlotte thinks this is a great idea because she is very tired after her day, and she needs to get a little bit of rest before dinner. While Charlotte is bathing before dinner, her mind goes back to France, about three or four years prior. She can see the introduction. She recalls meeting Jean at a small party that Yvette gave. Her good friend Yvette introduced her to Jean at this party. She remembers how wonderful he was, how polite he was, and how he had swept her off her feet.

Next, her mind goes to the chalet in France where she was snowed in, the embarrassment she felt when she discovered he was married, coming down the stairs, going to the fireplace where everyone was gathered around, seeing everyone that she already knew, and everyone she thought were friends of theirs. They were all there to have a small vacation away from their everyday lives. A woman entered the room and was very comfortable. Her coat was taken. She was well received. All the people that were sitting at the fireplace moved toward her to greet her as she was coming through the door. They greeted her as Mrs. Jean Duvall.

Charlotte is frozen on the stairwell. She tells herself this woman looks too young to be Jean's mother. She noticed that she was wearing a very large wedding ring. There must be some mistake. She can't be Jean's wife. She could always go upstairs and ask Jean. That was her thought right before she saw who was behind Mrs. Duvall in the doorway. It was Jean helping her carry in her bags. Now Charlotte was realizing that] she was in a room with people who were not friends of hers and Jean's, but who were friends of Jean's and his wife, and Yvette wasn't there. She turned to go up the stairs, but not before she realized that Jean had seen her, and she had seen Jean.

Jean realizes that she had taken in the whole scene, and he was not concerned in the least. She thought that he would follow her upstairs. From their room upstairs, or what she thought was their room upstairs, she could hear the commotion of the arrival of Mrs. Duvall and various other people who all apparently planned to spend the three-day weekend in this same lodge. She was wondering if she could get a sled out or any other kind of transportation out.

Then she realized that she was in front of the mirror. The mirror was telling her that there were tears running down her face and that her bra was wet. She could not be seen in that condition. She had to pull herself together before she could go downstairs. Somehow, she knew she was going to have to spend the rest of the entire weekend with all those people.

When she went downstairs, the wife was introduced to her by Jean as simply Charlotte. They were left to talk. The wife, whose name is Marie, says, "I have been aware of your affair through various sources, and I don't have to mention how I know." Marie goes on to say, "It doesn't matter who told me or how I found out because Jean does this all the time. I only find out about it when he is ready to end the relationship. I am aware that you have quite a bit of money, but Jean would not leave me risking the loss of funds that I provide him with. I have seen this happen before, and I am very sorry for you. But it is just one of those things that happens to you. He's just that sort of man and I have accepted it. I hope you can continue to have a good time. I plan to spend the rest of this holiday with my husband. Of course, Charlotte, you are welcomed to stay because, as far as I know, there won't be any other people able to get in or out because of the weather."

Charlotte stood and listened to this conversation. It took every bit of training and every bit of her inner strength, will and composure not to show or reflect any emotion. She simply says, "I'm very happy to meet you Mrs. Duvall. I'm sure I'll being seeing more of you." These are her thoughts as she is taking a bath now three years later in Mendocino. She is still crying. She realizes that she's still crying. A knock at the door tells her that she should go downstairs for dinner. It breaks her train of thought.

She calls out to Mrs. Hampton that she is still bathing and that she'll be down shortly, as soon as possible, and not to wait for her. She will get there in time.

She comes back downstairs after she rests for a little while and proceeds with dinner.

The next day, in the mail, she receives a letter from city council giving her the full go ahead. She is elated. She hugs Mrs. Hampton. She tells her, "We've got what we want!" She runs upstairs to call Jennifer. She tells Jennifer, "Go ahead with it." Jennifer, of course, is jumping up and down in the office. She does her job in that she goes right down the business plan. She tells everybody that they can go ahead and writes the necessary checks. Things begin to roll, and Charlotte hasn't even gotten there yet.

By the time Charlotte gets into town, the building has been bought, the architect has already arrived on site with his men and he's starting to take things down and put things up. He tells them that it probably won't be safe for them to come into the building for at least two weeks. This is fine with Charlotte. "We have been working out of the address that I gave you earlier, and we can stay there for at least another month."

He says, "After that, you can move and work out of your office here because I've got your office ready. But it still might not be safe to walk around the construction areas until I get them set up and ready, redo the walls, put the windows where you want them, add the lighting and have the electrician come in and do some of the wiring, so that everything is just right. We wouldn't want you young ladies to get hurt while that is happening."

She says, "Fine. I understand perfectly."

He says, "I will follow the blueprints that we've agreed on. You have picked a building that we don't need to do an awful lot of alterations to. But we will do the alterations as you say. It will probably take less than a month to get finished with this." Jennifer has already given him a check for fifty percent of the job. The rest he will receive when the job is completed. He says, "Thank you very much."

Charlotte and Jennifer go back to the office. They spend the rest of the day trying to contact the exhibitors for the grand opening. Charlotte knows that this is the most important thing because initial impressions are usually the most lasting. They spend their entire day talking on the phone with the two exhibitors that they narrowed down prior to this to show at the opening. They want to make sure that they have all their accommodations just as they require. They want to know their flight times, any other problems that need sorting out and how they can make this more comfortable for the exhibitors since it might go from a two-day stay to at least a week. The exhibitors should always be present at the grand opening.

Everything seems to be falling into place, and neither she nor Jennifer can believe their good luck. They just hope that it keeps working just the way it has. This is the way the rest of her two weeks pass. She is planning things that she can plan outside that don't involve actually being in the art gallery.

She and Jennifer are very excited when the architect calls in two weeks and tells them they can now come in to use the art gallery office. It is a loft type design overlooking the marina below. She had already decided to leave the temporary office. Since she had given prior notice to the landlord that she would be leaving in a month or so, he was prepared and not the least bit angry.

Within two to three days, they have movers move their furnishings to the new office site which is above the art gallery floor. It takes two or three days to get settled. They watch the construction. They have another entrance to come into the back of the art gallery where they don't have to walk in through the main entrance. The street entrance has been locked so that people passing on foot and in cars won't get in anyway get hurt.

She is working very hard. She has very little time to be at home. When she does get home, after two and a half weeks, she runs in to Jasper Smythe. He has gone full speed ahead on the landscaping. He says to her, "We're at a place where I want you to decide on some things." He shows her, again, some graphics of choices he thinks are best for a house that is located within this kind of soil content and a place that has experience with these kinds of weather changes. Fortunately for her, she could do almost anything she wants. He knows she is very busy so, he opens the conversation by saying to her, "I purposely narrowed your choices, Mrs. Von Shillingsfurst, because you're in a perfect spot to do almost exactly whatever you want. It might be difficult for you to ever decide, so I'm giving you these four choices for your twelve acres.

All of them involve not touching some of your twelve acres. But the ones nearest your house and on the drive to your house should be a little more scenic than they are. These are your choices."

She reviews the choices. She picks the fourth choice which seems to give a little bit more beautification to the area immediately around her house and to the drive coming in. His layout is also designed to give a person objects to look at and things to do while either sitting or walking in this area of her grounds. It is already naturally beautiful, but he wants to add a few things to improve its beautification like certain statues and plants. He has incorporated a couple of freshwater pools, some statuettes and different kinds of trees and plants that he doesn't think will take away from the beauty of the trees seen in the distance. She is happy that he has kept in harmony with what nature has already put there. She expresses this to him.

He says, "That was always my intention. I am very flexible. I know when you first met me you didn't think that I would be, but I'm very flexible. I'm very open to suggestions. But I have always given credit to nature, and I try to do anything I can to remain in harmony with it, while using the natural beauty that is already there." She thanks him. She tells him that the fourth choice would be the better of the four and he could begin working on it. Mr. Smythe proves to be very prompt because the next morning she awakens to the sound of workmen doing all kinds of things all over the exterior of her home.

After breakfast and conversation, she weaves herself through what is literally a mess on and around her grounds just to make it to her car. She goes to work. When she arrives at work, she finds that she is now permitted to go down to the art gallery floor. She couldn't remain there for long since the architect and electrical engineer want her to approve some of the important wiring and lighting blueprints. He wants to make sure she has some flexibility in her exhibits as exhibits will be changing from time to time, year to year, month to month.

It is at this point that she meets David Sellers. He is in Mendocino, he thinks, for a short period of time. He is staying in one of the inns after arriving in town the night before. He had read about an art gallery opening and, because he was a photographer, he thought this would give him something to do in a town that was a little less boring than he had anticipated, even though he knew that he had too much going on where he had just come from.

He had photographed the victims of an organized crime slaying. That was a new job for him, but he will never take that kind of assignment again. He didn't realize exactly what he was getting into, but he had made it clear to the publisher that he would not take any job from him again. Because he freelanced, and because he had acquired a little wealth through his photography profession, he could turn down a person politely. He didn't appreciate being misled, so basically, he could tell someone to go to hell.

He is not usually temperamental because he realizes that temperament in this industry gives you less opportunity for work, no matter how good and how reliable you are. It is just that he has never wanted this kind of an assignment and he has made that very plain. When he took the assignment, he had no idea that this was the subject of it, even though he's basically the kind of person who doesn't want to lead a dull life. Being in the middle of the action is where he likes to be because there, he feels he is somewhat in control of it. But now, he came to the west coast looking for someplace where he could just cool out.

He is somewhat familiar with the west coast, mostly the southern part of it, so he decides to go north to find something different. This morning, as he is flipping through the newspaper in a bed and breakfast inn while eating very stale croissants, he is thinking that this atmosphere has got to be the other extreme. But his eyes fall on an article in the newspaper that details the opening of an art gallery, and it seems that this is the only thing going on in this town, so he decides that today, maybe he will investigate it. After all, it will give him something to do today, since he will probably leave for Los Angeles tomorrow.

The architect, again, brings Charlotte down to the main floor of the art gallery. She is asked specifically, by the electrician, where she wants the lighting and how much flexibility she needs in the placement of her exhibits. His questions fall on the height and width of the exhibits and whether they will always be in the same places, even though they are not the same size. Understanding the problem, Charlotte tries to help him with the information that she has. She suggests that perhaps his idea of track lighting with electrical mobility would be best suited for this area since she would hate to have to hire someone just to help her reset the lighting whenever the exhibits are changed. She asked him if he could keep things simple so that she, Jennifer, and perhaps someone she hired could reset the lighting from a diagram, whenever moving exhibits was necessary for esthetic purposes. The diagram had to be easy to understand for her now and in years to come.

Both the architect and the electrician say they understand the problem and will do their best to accommodate her. She again points out that some of the exhibits, depending on what she is exhibiting and its age, have more sensitivity to heat than others. What they are doing about that situation is her next query. While she acknowledges that she is not familiar with their field, she tells them that these points are just reminders. The architect replies that he had already considered that because, as he told her when she hired him, he had done other art galleries and that she wouldn't have to worry about that.

With that, she turns her mind to every other possible problem that she could have with the set up as it is now. Jennifer is off making some of the arrangements for the caterers and some of the people that they need to host the grand opening. This is going to be a formal event. They plan to serve champagne. She is also giving out some very definite invitations. Even though it is going to be advertised, there are some very specific people that are going to be invited. As more things come to mind, she continues to express them to the architect. The architect and the electrician continue to discuss them.

In the background, she sees a very nice young man, about six feet two and about two hundred pounds with dark hair and blue eyes trying to get in the front door. At first, she is a little taken back. Then she starts wondering if he is someone the architect knows. She asks the architect, "This gentleman that is trying to get into my front door, is he someone you know, or is he someone that can easily get hurt?"

He says, "I've never seen him before, and I don't think any of the other staff has either. I'd better tell him that he shouldn't be near the door because he could get hurt here."

She says, "Actually, I should probably talk to him and find out if he is looking for me for some reason or other. I better go with you." They go to the front door and ask him what he is doing.

He introduces himself, "I'm David Sellers. That may not be a name you are familiar with. I am a freelance photographer. I was reading in the newspaper that your art gallery was having an opening, and I think I'm going to be in town long enough for it, so I thought I would come down and see if anything was happening here right at the moment." She suggests that he come around the back to her office. She tells him that he can't get in this way because the construction work makes it too dangerous as she points to the warning signs. He says, "That's apparent to me now. If you don't mind, I really would like to come to your office and talk to you."

Charlotte is taking David around to the back of the art gallery so he can view it from another perspective. While she talks to him, thoughts of him being an exhibitor in disguise pepper her mind. After all, he does freelance photography. But most of the time he has done the kind of photography that has ended up in magazines or books, not in an art gallery, though he has made quite a living from it.

While she is not aware of this, she takes him upstairs. He is very impressed with the activity on the lower floor. He asks her if she is doing this alone. She responds, "Yes, I am Charlotte Von Shillingsfurst. This is my art gallery." Then he realizes that she is very attractive, and she seems to be barely thirty years old. His demeanor changes into one that is slightly flirtatious. She is not responsive to this since she has seen it all before. All she wants to do is explain the art gallery to him, well knowing that every contact is potentially a business contact or a good contact. She is gracious about the situation.

He realizes that she isn't receptive to this, so he turns his path back to business. He tells her that he really didn't mean to be deceptive, he is a freelance photographer, but he doesn't do the kind of work that he has ever thought anyone would want to exhibit in an art gallery. She says to him, "I, personally, am not as familiar with photography even though I have an extensive background in art. My personal medium is watercolor, and I did some sculpting. I did my apprenticeship in Europe after graduation. I'm not as familiar with photography, though I have had some classes in it. I am impressed by people who seem to have mastered it in any form." He is happy. At least she shows some respect for his line of work.

Charlotte says, "Well, Mr. Sellers, I would like to see the other portfolio you have put together."

He says, "You can call me David, and I'd like to know if I can call you Charlotte."

She says, "Of course you can call me Charlotte. I hope you will be here for the opening."

He asks her, "Exactly when is the opening?"

She says, "We are projecting a month, maybe a month and a half, to make sure we have everything just right. We don't really want to invite people here and not have all the places for the exhibits filled. We want to give the very best impression we can and, we want to continue exhibiting throughout this season."

David is wondering. His thoughts begin to see Charlotte as very reserved. He is wondering if she is engaged or if perhaps, she has a significant other. He can't believe that she is just not interested. The best way to find out, he thinks, is just to go ahead and invite her to dinner. He decides that the invitation would be a good way to approach the subject. David informs her that he was raised near the northeast coast and, because of his freelancing activities, has developed some valuable contacts on the west coast. These are contacts, he explains, that he hasn't used himself, but will gladly inform them about her grand opening.

She replies, "The invitations aren't ready yet and they probably won't be for at least a week." Deep inside, this news pleases him because it gives him a viable excuse to come back. With the requisite courage mustered, he asks her if he could take her to dinner where they can discuss invitations, the guest list and anything else under the sun. His goal is to get to know Charlotte Von Shillingsfurst better, much better.

She thinks that this is a reasonably good idea. While not overwhelmed about the dinner idea, she does see it as a legitimate way to conduct business. With a smile of agreement, Charlotte tells David that she will meet him for dinner when the invitations are ready. He still has no answer to his question, the question that is in the back of his mind, is she involved with another man? He knows he is very attractive, and she hasn't even indicated in any way that she is aware of this. She can't be that involved in her business that she doesn't notice that he is attractive, and that she hasn't noticed that he is trying to talk to her about something other than her business.

He decides that he won't go any further now. He won't try to pressure her and ask her if she is seeing someone else, if she is involved. He will keep it on the level of I'm trying to help you with your business, because something tells him that if he doesn't do that he won't get to dinner. He decides to say, "Here's my number. I'll let you know when I get another number because right now, I'm staying at a bed and breakfast inn, and I'll have to move to more permanent accommodations. I'll let you know when I'm moving and how I can always be reached so that you could give me the invitations, and I'll know how your project is going."

She says, "Thank you." She is very happy that he has taken such an immediate interest in it, but she is also wondering what has made him decide to move from a bed and breakfast inn to something more permanent, because obviously he had intended to be here a shorter time and now something has made him extend it. She doesn't voice these questions. She simply says, "Fine. My secretary and I will be more than happy to meet you for dinner on Tuesday, a week from now. We should have the invitations ready by then. If they are not ready, I will give you a call as soon as I find out that they are not ready. Then we can change our dinner engagement."

He is very disappointed that she is going to bring her secretary, especially a secretary he hasn't seen. He expects that she is probably fat and not too attractive. She is a third leg, and he has never really wanted to go out with a third leg. But he doesn't say this because one contact can always lead to another contact, and he already knows that she doesn't appear to be engaged.

He excuses himself. He decides that he is not going to press too hard because he is much more drawn to her than he expected he would be. He tells her, "Have a nice day. I'll be calling you."

On his way out, he passes Jennifer, who is not working today but drops by to see how things were going. Jennifer wants to know. "Who in the world was that?"

Charlotte says, "He is a photographer. His name is David Sellers. We stopped him from coming in the front door because he would have hurt himself. I brought him around the back because he told me he was a photographer, and I was thinking that he might be a potential exhibitor. But it turns out he doesn't do work of that nature."

Jennifer says, "Who cares? What happened next? Did he ask you out or what?"

Charlotte says, "I don't know. Why do you always think in those lines? Yes, of course, he did ask me out. We are going out to dinner, the three of us, as soon as I get the invitations because he says he has some contacts back east. He comes from Canada. He wants to make sure they have an invitation to the opening."

Jennifer has already decided in her mind that she is not going to be there. But she doesn't say it to Charlotte. She says, "That's just fine. What are you going to wear? Are you going to dress up for this because, you never know, every potential business contact is very important?"

Charlotte says, "Yes, I know that. That's why I accepted the invitation in the first place. I think if I had permitted him to do so, he would have been more flirtatious than I wanted him to be. I am a young woman in business, and I am serious about this business. Photographers can have very mysterious backgrounds. You're probably too young to know this Jennifer, but I just need to be a little bit more cautious."

Jennifer says, "I just dropped in to see how you were doing. I'm going to go back because this is my day off. I'll see you later." She leaves Charlotte there.

Charlotte is upset with herself because she does not want to go to dinner with David. She cannot get David off her mind. David is very, very attractive but looks to her like trouble. But she knows that she shouldn't avoid these kinds of situations. She knows that she should put herself into these positions and learn to control them because she is going to be meeting nice young men all her life, and she just has to handle the situation right. Besides, he is a photographer, and he may not have a mysterious background. He may have some good contacts back east, and she should avail herself with that if he is willing to help her. She still spends the rest of the day thinking about David and thinking about what it is that she is going to wear to dinner a week from now.

In the meantime, Jasper Smythe is overseeing the landscaping of the exterior of her home. As some digging is being done, he heard someone hit something. It didn't seem right to him. He asks them to back up a minute because he doesn't know if it is a water main or what. The workmen went off to take a break.

He always carries tools with him even though he's overseeing and not actually working. He pulls out his case and pulls out a brush. He brushes down to what looks like something that is made of metal, but it doesn't seem to be round like a pipe. He keeps brushing and removing the dirt. It starts to show a picture to him. He tries to loosen it from the dirt, and it comes out in one piece. It is about six by eight and about two to three inches in depth. He decides that he is going to zip it up in the case with his tools because he doesn't know exactly what it is yet. He thinks that it might be important. It is not an Indian relic. It looks like it is European. It is too refined. It is not primitive at all. He's going to have to clean it up better before he can see exactly what it is.

At this point, he decides to take it to Otto Weinberger, a friend of his that teaches at a university on the outskirts of Mendocino. Otto Weinberger is an archaeologist and has a Doctor of Philosophy degree in theology. He thinks that he should take this over to his friend Otto. He doesn't think he should necessarily mention it to Charlotte. He doesn't know why. It may be significant, or it may not be. It might predate her parents buying of the grounds, which he knows happened in 1950s. It is hers since he found it on her grounds, but she may not have an explanation for it, so he'd rather quietly take it over to Otto to see what Otto thinks about it. He thinks it will be a good thing for Otto because it would be like a puzzle, and they could work it out together. He feels nothing sinister at all about it. He thinks that it would be good fun, and that they can tell Charlotte that they found something interesting on her grounds. She should be very pleased with it too because, after all, she's interested in art, and it seemed to be a piece of art. It doesn't seem to be made from a mold. He zips it up in his case and holds it until the end of the day.

Jasper Smythe calls over to his old friend, Otto Weinberger. After three rings Otto Weinberger picks up the phone. He immediately recognizes Jasper's voice. He asks Jasper how has been doing since the last time they were together, and it was on some nephew's or niece's birthday, he couldn't remember the name, but he just simply says, "The birthday party of that nice young man of yours."

Jasper said he had been doing fine, the whole family was doing fine, and he asked how Otto was. Otto says he, himself, has been doing fine, and the university was proceeding as usual.

Jasper says, "Nothing new, huh?"

Otto says, "No, nothing new to date."

Jasper says, "Well, I thought that might be the case. I have something that I think you might find very interesting. If you have time for it, I'd like to bring it over today because it is very intriguing to me. I'd like to show it to you."

Otto Weinberger says, "I have been slightly bored, and if you say it is interesting, I am sure it is. Please come over, and we'll have dinner together. It should be ready about seven."

Jasper says, "Fine. I'll be over about seven, and we will have plenty of time afterwards." He shows it to Otto after dinner. They proceed to carefully clean it up and get it so they could look at exactly what it is. It appears to be a coat of arms.

There are unusual things on the coat of arms. Coats of arms usually have animals on them. But the animals on this coat of arms are not the gargoyle type, nor a lion or wolf. Somehow, they convey the ferociousness of an animal that could almost be a wolf, but not quite. The reason you are not sure that it is a wolf, or you can't be one hundred percent sure, is because the most pronounced feature of the wolf is his upper fangs rather than his lower fangs, and the upper lip is drawn back in a harder smile. There is also something that seemed to be a bat present. It is a stylized bat, and you couldn't be one hundred percent sure it is a bat. It has a definite kind of strength about it. Something about the bat suggests intelligence immediately when you look at it, but you are not sure what it is.

These are the two things that Otto and Jasper could agree upon. Then the usual things that you find on a coat of arms like weaponry, shields, and swords are present. Otto and Jasper take it as German. They are not quite sure what it is. There is some characteristic that lets them know that it is clearly German. Jasper says, "Well, what do you think about this? I found this around Charlotte's house. I told you about this new job that I've been hired for. This doesn't seem to be Indian in character. This doesn't seem to be Russian. And Charlotte's family is from Eastern Germany. You remember the story about thirty years back? You were here then, weren't you, Otto?"

Otto says, "Yes, I was here. I remember the Von Shillingsfurst estate and the tragedy that took place where the parents burned in a car crash, I believe, a young wife and mother and her husband. They left a two-year-old child behind."

He says, "Yes. This is the very same estate. This girl has now grown up and she is back to open an art gallery. She has hired me to renovate her house because while she was away at school she left, apparently, just a nanny named Megan Hampton and a skeleton staff. She would return home on her vacations, but she went to school back east. Since the staff was apparently hired by the parents before they died, then just given duties and paid routinely by the trustees that had also been hired before the parents died, nothing was done to the house. They didn't have the authority to redecorate the house, which was one of the things the parents were going to do before they died, as I understand it.

"She is giving me a pretty free hand on it because she is so occupied in opening the art gallery. The place does need work. But her room, the kitchen, the formal dining room, and a few other places have been livable since they have been used all the while during her childhood. It is a very big house. It has about ten to fifteen bedrooms and several bathrooms. It has two wings and a main entryway. So, a lot of areas of the house have not been used, and she wants the whole thing renovated."

Jasper continues, "Anyway, I found this on her grounds today. What do you think of it?"

Otto does not say anything. He voices that he agrees that it seems to be Eastern European, and it comes from the area which he himself also comes from. In his mind, his first natural response is that this is definitely the emblem of nobility. This is the coat of arms for a family that has been knighted, a family that probably got their title not through heredity, or through a means that you would think would be more congenial, but through fighting. This is probably a family that has either worked their way up through the ranks of the king's army or was maybe the actual king's guard before it was knighted. He comes to this conclusion because everything on the coat of arms suggests nobility. He voices this first impression to his friend, Mr. Smythe. He has no idea why it has been there for thirty years in this area.

He tells Jasper that he is not quite sure what it is, but he sure would like to have it so he could do a little research. He wants to take it back to the university to see if it is as old as it appears to be, and to see if he could place it with any known families or any other people from that area.

Jasper says, "You know, I basically didn't tell her that I had removed this from her estate. I doubt that she even knows it is there. So, I am going to give it to you, and you can do with it as you choose."

Otto is inquisitive. He is excited about it. His life is rather mundane now. He basically goes to school and teaches. Every now and then he takes a sabbatical that takes him out of the country. This is the first real excitement that he has had for quite some time. He's just about Jasper's age. He has gotten the same kind of excitement for the same reason that Jasper does since they are armchair investigators. That is what he is anticipating, an armchair investigation. He tells Jasper, "Fine. I'll take care of it, and I'll get back to you when I know something." That is where he leaves it. They spend the rest of their evening doing what they normally do, playing chess.

Otto Weinberger, unlike Jasper, who always seems to be very congenial and very easy to get along with, is not difficult to get along with, but he has a certain stubbornness about him. He seems to be somewhat introverted. He is not unattractive, but he's a lot leaner than Jasper is. He seems to be a more serious 'down to business' person who gives you looks straight in the eye, looks that sometimes can almost burn through you.

But Jasper has gotten used to that. This is one of the looks that he gives Jasper now. Now Jasper knows that there is something more to this than Otto Weinberger is voicing, but he continues to play chess with him the rest of the night. Then Jasper goes home.

David has made this date for a week away from now, but Charlotte stayed on his mind quite a bit too. He thinks that Charlotte is very attractive and there is something different about her than most of the girls he meets in America, even though he has traveled to Europe. She just has kind of an old-world quality about her. He can't put his finger on it. He finds her very attractive. He is saying to himself, "I hope I'm not being sucked in by this concept of a challenge, but I think there is more to her. She seems to have a lot of things very well in hand, and I don't think I'm wrong about that."

So, he continues to call her from time to time to see how she's doing.

She is glad to have someone to bounce problems off because she often talks to Jennifer and Megan Hampton about different things, and this is a person who is more experienced in the world than either of those two. He provides her with a good listening ear. She tells him various things that are happening to her during her day, and he gives her advice on how to handle things.

This goes on for the week. He calls her every day. He must refrain from calling her twice a day. She is very pleased about the attention, but warning lights come on for her because she doesn't want to get too involved with someone who might cause her a great deal of pain because he is extremely attractive.

She thinks an awful lot about going to dinner with David. She thinks more about it than she would like to think about it. She is very anxious about it. She can't put it out of her mind. He stirred a lot of emotions in her that she had tried to smother because of her relationship with Jean in France. She is hoping that dinner will be strictly business and Jennifer will be there, and that will help to distract a lot of the things that she is feeling. As he continues to call, she knows that he is elevating thoughts in her that she doesn't want to bring to her conscious mind. She knows the thoughts are there. She is really counting on Jennifer to be there and to be the best distraction possible.

Jennifer knows that she is not going to tell her until the last minute that she is not going to be there, because Jennifer suspects that Charlotte will find somebody to take her place. She waits until the last minute.

It is about five o'clock. Dinner is scheduled for eight thirty, enough time for her to get out to her estate, to get dressed, pick up Jennifer and meet him at the restaurant. She doesn't want him to come to her home. They are running a little behind schedule. Jennifer says to her, "Don't worry. I'll finish things up here because I can't go with you tonight anyway."

Charlotte says, "What do you mean you can't go with me tonight? It is almost five-thirty, and you are telling me you can't go with me?"

Jennifer says, "No. I cannot go with you tonight. I am expecting a call from San Francisco and that person hasn't been able to reach me all day. They called me earlier this morning. I must be there just about this time tonight for them to call me back. I'm sorry. I just can't make it. But I'm sure you're going to have fun. He seems like he is a lot of fun, and he has been calling you every day. I know because I have been answering the phone."

Charlotte says, "Well, I just don't think that it's fair of you to leave me like this at the last minute."

Jennifer says, "Something personal has come up. I can't explain it to you. I just cannot be there."

Then Charlotte feels a twinge of guilt because she is requesting a babysitter, and both know it without saying it. She backs off the issue. She decides to pack up her portfolio and go home. She is driving home, and she is wondering if she could show up gracefully with her nanny. She decides that she cannot show up gracefully with her nanny, and she has got to go out by herself.

She drives all the way home wishing that her friend from France, Yvette, were with her because Yvette would not have left her like Jennifer has. And she could always go to dinner with Yvette and another person, and Yvette would understand exactly why this would be a good thing for her.

She greets Megan Hampton in the hallway. Megan already knows that this is the night she is going to dinner with David Sellers. The nanny has already perceived that this man has more than the usual effect on her, so she is a little closer at hand than she normally would be. She draws Charlotte's bath, and she helps Charlotte select clothing and perfume.

Charlotte is relieved because she knows that she is nervous. Megan is telling her to calm down, "After all, you said it wasn't quite a date, it's just a business meeting, and he might have the right contacts that you need. Just look at it from that point of view."

Charlotte tells her, "Jennifer isn't going, and that takes the business edge off it for me."

Her nanny tells her, "There is going to be many times in the business world that you are going to have to go out and handle things by yourself. You know that I shouldn't have to tell you that. So just go ahead and see where it leads you, and don't be disappointed if it doesn't lead you in either direction." She doesn't have to say any more than that because she knows that Charlotte is not willing to admit that she hopes David likes her the way he seems to be suggesting that he likes her.

Charlotte drives off to meet David at a French restaurant. They sit down. She lets him order. He notices that she reads the French menu in French. He is very much impressed by this. She tells him that her roommate at school was from France, that she has been to France several times, and that she is fluent in French. He lets this go. He says, "Well, I do, in all honesty, probably have some business contacts so you can give me those invitations." She promptly opens her portfolio and gives them to him.

He noticed that she is carrying her portfolio. He says, "But I do have an ulterior motive for asking you out to dinner. That is, I, of course, find you very attractive. I extended my stay in Mendocino for that reason." She is taken aback by his frankness. She is trying to keep her composure.

He is noticing that she is blushing. This is interesting to him. He did mean for it to have a shock effect on her because oftentimes she switches the situation so she can always stay in command of the conversation. He begins to sip the wine and pretend to make menu choices. David informs Charlotte during this dinner that he wished permission to continue to call her and to date her because he had planned to continue his stay, that he needed more rest from his previous assignment that he had estimated, and that he found her company very pleasant. He also found himself taking a much more formal tone with her because somehow it seemed to be called for.

She didn't have a good excuse for severing this relationship and it might prove to be fruitful in a business sense. She could think of no reason to be hostile, so she agrees to be available for phone calls. She begins to rely on his phone calls. She always finds herself looking forward to his phone calls and wondering if he is going to ask her to do something. She still hasn't invited him to her home. She is basically dating him. If he wants to take her to dinner, if he wants to take her to a play, or if he wants to take her to the movies, she meets him there. She hasn't even taken the long drive into San Francisco, which is what most people do, or into Santa Rosa or any of the surrounding areas with him.

The relationship is developing. She is finding herself talking to him a lot more about everything. She realizes that there is something about his personality that pulls this out of her. She doesn't think she has had enough time with him. So, she proceeds with it. When she goes to work during the day, it is a source of amusement for Jennifer. Jennifer teases her about it.

She and Jennifer are working on getting the caterer in from San Francisco to cater the grand opening. She has compiled her list asking some people that David Sellers knows. He sent some invitations back east to several of his publishers who have used him on a free-lance basis. Although he is not aware of it, he sends the invitations back east and they fall into the hands of the organized crime ring. He tried to do as much as he could for her so he sent them to as many contacts as he could.

He attracts the attention of the organized crime ring. They were wondering where he was. It came from the address of his mailbox. David's previous job was photographing a gangland murder. He had never done anything like that before and he was sure he didn't want to do anything like that again. He didn't have a choice. He was the best person for the job. So, he went ahead, and did it because he thought that he needed to round out his experience anyway and that it would be educational. It is not that he really wanted to leave and go to the other part of the country, he wasn't sure that wanted to go home. He wasn't ready to go to his immediate family, meaning his brother or father. So, he went to the west coast looking for a small place. He was familiar with the California coast but mostly the southern part of it, so he thought that he might as well look at the northern part of it.

When the invitation is intercepted by the organized crime members, through a leak from an employee of one of the newspapers, it leads them to David. They send two people that have a contract out on his life. They think that he is more involved with the murder investigation than he is. They think that he has more information about the murder investigation than he does. It is an on-going investigation going deep into organized crime.

They decide that one of the things they could do fast is to get a hold of any negatives or see if he can tell them where the negatives are. They are sure he still has the negatives because they know he freelances. They figure he is probably hanging on to them, and they would like to get a look at that.

They also plan to kill him. They send two of their best hitmen. Because they are such good hitmen, they have cased the town. They know that he doesn't come from this area, and they are wondering what brought him here. They have done nothing to make him suspect that they are interested in him, so he doesn't seem to be running from them. They are aware of that, so they are wondering what brought him here since he sent some invitations back. He is obviously not trying to hide. He is trying to bring people out here to the opening of an art gallery. They figure she must be important to him because he is calling her every day, sometimes twice a day, and he is obviously not new to the relationship because he is making what is considered definite moves toward her, and she seems relaxed with him.

They are trying to determine from the information that they have if this is a new relationship. They conclude that he couldn't have just stumbled on this lady since this area is too small. He must have come here looking for her, so she must be important to him. They begin to watch both. It appears to them that she is an easy target. They decide that they are going to kill her or scare her badly, then she will either go back and tell David, or he will find out that she died there. They will let him know they killed her. He will be willing to talk then, and they can get this information out of him, maybe they will kill him too.

In the meantime, Charlotte's art gallery is very near opening. It is about two days before the art gallery opening. The caterers have come into town and set up at a local kitchen, in order to ensure everything goes right. The exhibitors are here also. The town is pretty much more involved in this than they would have been because the opening has brought quite a few people to town. Even local newspapers were there to cover the different artists that were in town to cover the opening.

It is much more an item than she expected, but she is very happy about it. It makes her more relaxed, a lot more vivacious, and a lot more open to David. And from all appearances they are getting along well. They have always gotten along well. It is developing into a very intense relationship. Even though he does not go to her home, he wants to keep in contact as much as possible. But she is so busy. She is submerged in the art gallery opening.

She is wondering what her relationship will be like. The relationship is different. It could be more involved. She is trying to get things going.

The hitmen, Frank and George, are trying to get close to her estate. But they haven't been able to get as close to her as they thought because whenever they go in during the day it is covered with workmen. They don't go at night because of the landscaping. They are not sure about crawling around or near places that have gaping holes or that are fenced off. It would attract too much attention to go around with flashlights. So, they decide not to approach her at home. The want to keep silent because they don't want to have to kill any more than those two people. They decide that it is better to catch her coming out of the art gallery because for the most part it seems like she just has one girl working with her, and they don't always leave together. She seems to be very relaxed. It appears to them that she has no fear and no suspicions, so they are sure that they will be able to get her in the street. They plan to end her that way.

They know exactly where to find David. He just rented a small house in an apartment type setting just outside of town. They are sure that they will be able to take care of him very quietly with no problem. They think the best opportunity will be after the opening of the art gallery because the spotlight is very much on her and him, him only because he is with her right now.

They approach things this way. She is not talking to him, and she is not talking to Jennifer. She must greet visitors. She is very much a hostess in that she wants to make sure that they have proper accommodations in town, and they all do. She is exhibiting some sculptures. She also has some oils. Those are the two basic mediums that she is showing. She doesn't want to overload herself. She knew that returning those objects would be difficult. Besides the artistic temperament doesn't need to have too many cooks in the kitchen. She is exhibiting two artists. One is a sculptor, and the other is doing period oils.

She permits David to accompany her on this venture. He admires her. One reason is that she has two American artists, both of whom, as far as he is concerned, are nonchalant. They just sit there waiting to proceed. She must be careful and tactful in her conversations with both of them because basically both of them are used to having whole showings to themselves. Right now, neither one of them have enough work to have a whole showing to themselves. Also, she is not sure exactly what is acceptable in Mendocino, so she chose the more conservative choices out of the choices available. She wants to attract people that are more conservative or their art, not necessarily in their lifestyle and in their demeanor, but in their art. She realizes that she is in Mendocino and not in San Francisco. She hopes to attract people from different places, and she still wants it to be a success.

David, when he is at dinner with her currently, he is more enamored with her because she seems to handle her conversations very well, and she knows the field. He admires her because she could have sat at home and done nothing. He is aware now that she has quite a bit of reserves. But she has gone out and is learning different things. She can deal in what is apparently pretty much a man's world and handles it very well. He is very proud of her.

When he gets alone with her between desserts, he tells her that he is very proud of her. She says, "I am glad that you are proud of me." Then she says that she is kind of embarrassed. She says to him, "You're probably not used to women functioning this well, are you?"

He says, "Well, actually I'm not used to watching this. It's a joy to watch. I hope you continue with it."

The other two men look up and smile. They go on with their desserts.

The evening has very nice overtones, but it is significant as there appears to be onlookers that they are unaware that they have. The two men go back to their hotel rooms. The next day is going to be the opening.

Of course, it is black tie. Charlotte is extremely well dressed. She has jewels, conservatively but expensively. Jennifer is perfect in her role as the secretary.

Megan is permitted to come. She also is appropriately dressed. Various city officials are there. It is a full house. Everyone is sipping champagne being served by waiters and waitresses in traditional attire. David feels more relaxed and more in command because, after all, he has been in her company for almost the past two weeks. He is hoping that she is more relaxed and a little more comfortable. This is what we have all been waiting for, and maybe this is his chance to get a little closer to her tonight because a lot of the questions will be off her.

It is an obvious success. The room is packed. She has placed her exhibits well. She has chosen her exhibitors well. Everyone is congratulating her.

He manages to take her aside to ask her if she would mind spending the rest of the evening with him. This is the wrong thing for him to say. First, she is annoyed that he pulled her away from all the people she has been spending her time trying to attract. She doesn't know what lead him to believe that after a two-week interval he could ask her that.

She tells him that she is in the process of trying to accomplish something, that this is her life dream, if nothing else than she is in the middle of her business event. She says, "This is very important to me. I have worked very hard for this. I thought you would understand this better than anyone because I did permit you to accompany me. And you saw a lot of this stuff. But a lot of the stuff you have witnessed as an ending step. You can imagine what kind of work went into setting is up. How is it that you think I have time even to be away from my guests and to have this conversation with you. I just think that you are a very thoughtless person, and I would rather not have too much contact with you for the rest of the night. That is not what is on my mind. What is on my mind is making sure my guests are happy and my show goes well."

She is very irate about it. She doesn't give him any chance for an argument if he wished to make one, and he's not used to having to make one, so he doesn't. He leaves her there. He tries to leave as if he has not been scolded. He attempts to leave as gracefully as possible. But he knows that he is leaving right then because he is quite upset. She is upset, but she has had enough training not to make it visible. She puts on her best face. She comes out and continues with what she must do.

Jennifer pulls her aside because Jennifer knows her a little bit better now, and she knows that something is wrong. She asks her, "Is something wrong? Is there something that I can do? Everything seems to be going smoothly. The food is wonderful. The champagne is fine. All the guests are happy. Just about everyone we have invited, and some we didn't, seem to be here. I'm sure that the exhibitors are going to be happy because I have heard several offers. What could be wrong?"

Charlotte says, "It's personal. It's nothing that I want to discuss right now. I don't mean to put you off, but I really must think about it myself before I can talk about it. I've got to get back to my guests." Jennifer agrees that they both should get back to the guests.

Also, the nanny notices that she is a little pushed out of shape. She approaches her about it. Charlotte says, "Everything will be fine. You should go to bed early, as you're used to doing, and I'll be home after I get things closed and cleared away. Most of these caterers will be here until right before I leave and Jennifer also." That night, Jennifer's friend from San Francisco came down for the opening, and he had planned to take her home. She asks if she could leave early because she had been up almost fourteen hours, and he needed to take her so that she could rest. It was obvious to everyone that she was having a good time. But she was tired since she had put a lot of work into it. Charlotte, not wanting to be the slave driver, says, "Yes, Jennifer. I was going to suggest that you go home early."

Jennifer left shortly after David. After Jennifer leaves, so does the nanny.

Also, in the art gallery is Otto Weinberger and Jasper Smythe. Otto Weinberger had asked Jasper Smythe to get him invited, which was not difficult to do, so he could observe Charlotte. He had researched the coat of arms, and it seemed to be the coat of arms of someone either involved in the king's guard or somehow in the defense of the king. He came to that conclusion because of the hostility that was exhibited on the coat of arms. He is sure that it was Eastern German, but he wasn't sure that it began there.

He had been, in the last two weeks, tracking every place that Charlotte had lived. It was a very easy thing to do. He was relieved to find no unusual occurrences, nothing that would fit into any of these categories. He wanted to meet the young lady and congratulate her on being able to do this and tell her that she had hired a good man to renovate her house. He is there really enjoying himself with his friend Jasper, who was also enjoying himself. Jasper is the kind of person that it is not difficult for him to enjoy himself.

Jasper makes the introductions to Charlotte. She is happy to see him coming. He is very congenial. He is smiling. He has a smile that almost bolsters and supports your energy. She found herself smiling back. He says, "I won't take much of your time because I know you've got to get around to all of your guests, but this is one of my friends, Otto Weinberger, and he is a professor at one of the local universities. He teaches archaeology and theology. We share ideas and knowledge because being an architect he has called me about things from time to time, and I have called him about things. We've run in to each other at seminars. We've been friends for almost thirty or forty years. We have been in this area almost longer than you are old."

They both thought that was interesting. They all laugh at that. Then Otto, being formally introduced, says, "I'm also congratulatory because I understand that we both come from the same area, and primarily I come from the eastern part of Germany also. I have roots there also."

She says, "Oh you do? Well, I don't know too much about Eastern Germany."

He says, "We all know. We are very sorry at what happened when you were two years old, and both of your parents died."

She says, "Yes."

He says, "But I also thought that probably during your lifetime you have been back to visit some aunts or other relatives that you have there since only your mother and father came over."

Though she was a little nervous saying it, there was an inner feeling, a twinge. She says to him, "I have no other known living relatives. I thought that that was one of the things that the newspaper accounts made clear."

Then he realized that he hit a sore spot. He says, "I'm sorry. That was very tactless of me. No. I didn't know that. I still have some relatives there, and if you should ever go back there, I will give you some names that you could contact. You have such a very rich heritage, and you should be aware of that."

She says, "Well, I have been through Europe extensively. I studied there. After I got my degrees, I apprenticed under a sculptor, and my best friend in Europe is French and I visit her often. But I haven't been very far into Germany except for a couple of times we crossed over into the Alps."

He found that interesting, but he also found that very agreeable, if she was telling the truth. Jasper slaps him on the back, and they drink to that. He tells her, "We better let you go. We've had a nice time here."

She says, "Yes. I should be getting on to my other guests."

Charlotte mingles with her guests throughout the night. It seems like everybody is having a very good time. She is relaxed leaving the art gallery after it has closed. A lot of the cleaning up had to be done, and she couldn't leave the caterers with the exhibits. Though they were licensed and bonded, she just couldn't take that chance. So, she had to wait until they left. The exhibitors had already started their long drive to the airport to catch their flights out. They knew that their exhibits would have to be shipped to them sometime over the course of several months. They were also happy it was a success.

She has given them their goodbyes. She knew that she would have no problem at this point generating a reputation and getting people to come all the way over to this small town to exhibit.

She had a premonition which related to the exchange that she was having with David, and it was better that she does not see David anymore. These were her thoughts when she was coming down the steps after locking the door to the office part of the art gallery. She goes down the steps and over to the car. The two men that have been hired to carry out the contract on Charlotte and David are waiting for her. They watch her as she approaches her car. She is really nervous and a little anxious, but she thinks it is just probably the excitement of the night.

Their silenced weapons are drawn. They are relatively comfortable and confident because they think she is one of the easier kills that they have been sent out to do, this should be easy money, and they could finish David off and go home and collect it. As she is coming out onto the street through the back entrance of the art gallery, they begin to draw their weapons. They take aim to fire at her. She turns because she senses something at her back. Her keys are in the door of her car, but she has sensed that someone is around her. She sees the two men. They appear to be about the same height, dark haired, nondescript clothing, and they both had weapons. She doesn't know why, she doesn't know them, but she is certain they are going to kill her. Maybe they haven't seen her, it is very dark, there is no lighting. These thoughts are running through her mind as she stifles a scream. She is trying to be very quiet with her keys.

The men now have her, one at a time, in their sight. The first man has her in his sight, and he is ready to pull the trigger. He is trying to focus on her in the dark. He focuses on her clearly. Then he begins to lose focus. Then he starts to regain focus. As he begins to regain focus, he now realizes that he is focusing on an old wooden wagon with wooden wheels. It is creaking past him. It is, of course, bigger than life. In the wagon are bodies with runny sores and bruises. They are bleeding and have discolorations. They are very definitely dead. Various parts of the bodies, arms and legs are hanging over the side and end of the wagon. The man is dressed in tattered clothing. He is hooded, but you could still see his face. He is missing two or three of his front teeth, and the others are blackened with decay. He has a lantern on each side of his wagon. He is demanding that the hitman, who he is now in focus of, stand back because he is carrying plague victims. He is asking him, "Are you crazy? Don't you know these are plague victims? Stand back!"

The hitman backs up because he has no other alternative. He realizes that he is on cobblestone streets. He starts to move back as quickly as he can. He turns because he notices that his heels are starting to slide down, and he is almost going into an open grave. Terror begins to mount in him. He turns in the other direction because there are shadows in most places and the light on the wagon is slowly leaving, slowly going ahead of him. He is tapped on the shoulder. He turns, he is afraid to turn, but he turns.

There is a very well-dressed gentleman there. He is very attractive. The gentleman doesn't seem to be at all diseased. At the same time, the hitman is noticing this, the gentleman is calling the hitman by his name. He is saying, "Frank, may I help you at all?"

The hitman, whose name is Frank, says, "Well, I don't know where you are."

The gentleman, who is very well dressed, says, "Yes, I know you don't know who I am or where you are. You must wonder how it is that I know your name."

At this, Frank attempts to leave. He turns in the other direction. In the other direction is a man who obviously has contracted the plague but has not died from it yet. He has open running sores. He is just walking down the street. It is not even obvious that he can see where he is going, but he is heading in their direction. He is begging for help. Frank is nauseated. He turns back to the gentlemen who seems to be aristocratic and asks him if he can help him. He says, "Yes, of course, I can help you. My carriage is coming up the road. You can hear it now."

Just as he is saying that, Frank can hear carriage wheels coming up the road, a different sound now than the wagon wheels that were leaving with the lantern. The shadows are starting to fade slightly because this coach, which is certainly a coach, which he can see it in the distance, now has very proper lanterns and very good lighting. There is a coachman and a footman. He knows that there is a coach and that there is a footman. He knows that this must be possibly the fifteenth century. It is very warm, and the man's speech is clearly not French. Maybe he is Italian. He turns to him and says, "This is your coach?"

The gentleman says, "Yes this is my coach, and my name is Count von Shillingsfurst. Would you like to come into my coach?"

At this point, the coach has stopped in front of him, and the footman has gotten off the top of the coach where he was seated. He has let down the footstool and opened the door. Frank could clearly see that there are two other occupants in the coach. One is a man. One is a woman. The woman is exquisitely beautiful. The man is very well dressed. They appear to be either married or very closely related. He sees that he has no other opportunity but to accept this ride. He thanks the Count and says, "Yes I would like to accompany you in this coach."

He gets into the coach, and the Count entered behind them. They are all very well seated. He is opposite the lady who has been introduced by the Count as the Countess. The gentleman opposite her has been introduced as her brother.

They begin to travel. He notices that the coach is moving. In his mind he cannot understand what is happening. He is saying to himself he must be dreaming, he must be asleep, something must be wrong. But the Count continues the conversation with the other two people who he also has introduced now as von Shillingsfursts. He says to him, "Frank, don't you remember that you just left Mendocino?" At this, Frank is shocked because Frank did remember that he just left Mendocino. But he thought it was a dream, and he thought that this man would go along and be some person in his dream.

The Count tells him, "No, this is not a dream, Frank. And you did just leave Mendocino. And we are Von Shillingsfursts. Do you remember what you were doing in Mendocino just before you left it?"

Frank says, "Yes, I was going to—"

The Count finishes the sentence for him, "You were going to kill Charlotte, weren't you?"

Frank begins to grab for the handle of the coach door. The Countess extends a very long, very beautiful arm. The right arm is slightly jeweled. It doesn't have a wedding band, but it does have a very distinctive diamond bracelet. She just holds his arm. He looks up at her face, and she is the most beautiful thing he has even seen. She has the most beautiful eyes that he has ever seen on a woman. He cannot look away from her. Her eyes just pull him in deeper and deeper. He knows that the right part of his neck has been ripped away. He hears his cervical vertebra snap. He hears the bones in his neck snap, and he doesn't mind before he finds nothing but blackness.

His partner, the other person, is also focusing in on Charlotte. His focus sharpens and he has her in his sight. Then his focus blurs. Now he is seeing a candelabra. The candelabra seems to be seated on a piano. Then he realizes that actually what he is focusing with are his own eyes, so he doesn't have a gun, there is no Charlotte, he is not in Mendocino, there is no car, there is just a man and a group of people there playing a piano. They are in powdered wigs, and they seem to be in tights. It is maybe the seventeenth century, and the speech seems to be in French.

They call to him, "George, please come over here. Sit with us and have something to drink." He has no other choice but to walk forward. He realizes that he is now in a castle. The castle is not too brightly lit except for in what appears to be a living room or a library. There are four or five guests. A man is at the piano.

He says, "You know my name," and he's a little hardened. So even though he is not in Mendocino, and even though he is looking at people in powdered wigs, he still has enough gumption to ask them, "You know my name and you seem to have the advantage on me. Who are you?"

They say, "We are Von Shillingsfursts. We're the Von Shillingsfurst family."

He says, "The Von Shillingsfursts?"

They say, "Come on in and have a drink."

One of the gentlemen that is standing puts his arm around George and tries to bring him closer into the circle. George also feels the muscles tear away from his head. He feels something scrape against the bone in his neck. Then he sees no more.

The next thing she knows, there are mangled bodies lying on the asphalt. Most of their clothing is still intact, except for the clothing around their necks. A lot of their musculature and veins are pulled off their necks. Both of their necks are exposed to the bones, and the bones have been snapped.

She begins to scream. She doesn't even remember what happened, but she knows that she has seen this. She also remembers hearing firing. Then suddenly it starts to go gray. It goes grayer. Then it is black to her.

Charlotte's scream brings some residents to the scene because, as said before, Mendocino is a very quiet town. She didn't realize that she was screaming so much before she lost consciousness. The first people on the scene were Mendocino residents who are, of course, horrified. The police come immediately, and they call the ambulance. By this time, Charlotte has been revived. She sees the bodies. They tried to prevent her from seeing the bodies, but they were unable to. She has seen the bodies before she is taken away in the police car.

The police psychiatrist knows that she is past hysterical, and he knows that she should be immediately sedated if she is going to retain any sanity at all. He recommends that they postpone any questioning just by looking at her. He gives her a shot to sedate her. She is taken to her home and is guarded there. Upon inspection of the bodies with the coroner and the other policemen, he recommends that they simply leave her alone because they all agree she could not have put these two men in that condition. They turn to her male companion, who is not quite her boyfriend, David Sellers. They want to question him. They want to know what he knows.

By this time, he tells them everything that he could ever think of that he has ever been associated with because he is as horrified as everyone else is. They make the connection that possibly it is the photograph that he has taken of murders the mobsters were involved with. They get in contact with the police department that was in control and involved. They fly out immediately and said that they would work with the FBI to try to find out who is paying for these hitmen. They have a pretty good idea. They don't have any indication or any idea that they might be sending some more out after her and after him.

Then, of course, they question him repeatedly because they can't get anywhere with her. They decide that it is safer because they know the men that have come from back east have been involved, and they know she doesn't know anything. They want to get her some place far out of town. So, they ask her where she would like to go, if there was some place she could go out of town where she would be safe. Naturally, she just says, "I want to go to Europe. I want to go visit with my friend Yvette a while and stay two or three months. I don't know if I will ever come back." But she doesn't tell David Sellers, they allow her this right to privacy, so he doesn't know where she has gone. She takes off and goes to Europe. The art gallery is simply closed for the moment.

Otto Weinberger is trying to work himself into police circles so that he can get some more information as to exactly what happened to these bodies. He wanted to see autopsy reports and any other data that he could pick up because he had decided that she couldn't be involved. He had decided that he must had been mistaken about the relics. He was celebrating at the art gallery because he thought he was wrong that she had any connection with nobility or Eastern Europe. He thought from the time he was first shown it to the time at the art gallery that he had been wrong about her, and that she had no connection with nobility, she had just been very rich. But now, he has come to equate these murders with the supernatural or something that had to have the mark of a vampire. He began to re-picture the symbolism of the coat of arms in his mind and realized that that was what was bothering him the most, not that it was Eastern European, not that it had come from Germany, and not that is was misplaced, but that it was probably the emblem of a vampire, somebody in the practice of the supernatural, or witchcraft. He was so happy that he was wrong, that this was not in any way connected with her, even though he knew about her European background.

He was, of course, still curious about the relic and still cautious about it. He was going to examine it some more. But he did not want to associate it with her. Even though her European background, it was obvious though not clearly understood. He is thrown for a loop. He is trying to get closer to the local police department because the people in New York have cleaned up. They are very efficient. They think that they have gotten the target out of town.

They are still watching Mr. Sellers and they are also watching the people that they know to be responsible for it. They lay back and observe them from their distance. But they didn't bother to include the local police. They didn't tell them any more than they needed to know. The Chief of Police is very unhappy about this. He is a little boy where his ego is involved. He decides that he can't really talk about it to his men because he didn't solve the case, he doesn't know what happened to these people, and he is not sure that he will ever know. It is one of the biggest things that has ever happened in his town. He was never permitted to have access to a lot of the information, so he has gripes.

Otto Weinberger makes sure that he has his easy listening ears on so that he can talk to them. As this goes on, they kind of develop a relationship based on this. The policeman gives him, in conversation, every little bit of information he knows. Then, when he realizes that Weinberger has a little bit of detective experience, he decides to let him in on what is left in the police lab and the coroner's office, and what specimens they had left. He wanted to see what Otto could make of it. Otto Weinberger uses this material to further his research while Charlotte is in Europe.

What Otto Weinberger discovers in the criminology lab in the city of Mendocino, after the FBI had finished their investigation, is that the two dead bodies not only were mangled at the neck and most of their musculature and all the soft tissues and the veins were removed down to the level of the bone, but in one instance the cervical vertebra was snapped, forcibly snapped. In the other instance, there appeared to be a gouging of the actual bone at the neck, though the neck was not snapped. There is no, and never was any, blood either on the victims, in the victims' bodies, or at the scene of the crime.

The FBI decided that this is just another creative method that organized crime uses to horrify and instill terror on anyone who should come across another one of their victims. He, himself, has never seen anything like this in a vampire murder, but he takes notes and acknowledges the fact that this is what happened.

David, in the meantime, follows her to Europe as soon as the police let him go. That is rather quickly because the police have decided, once again, that David had nothing to do with it either and that he was probably the object of the hit. They have no idea who killed the hitman. They just draw the conclusion that it was a rival crime organization because of a cross into the wrong territory. They didn't have any idea of anyone in the Mendocino, Napa, or Sonoma area who would have this kind of organization. So that is the only conclusion that they can draw. They know David didn't do it, and they know that Charlotte couldn't have.

David, on the other hand, is feeling very guilty. He is horrified. He knows that he is responsible for this. He knows she almost lost her life. He knows that these people were here looking for him, and the last thing he had to say to her was how fast could she make it into bed with him. Her disappearance without explanation is not unusual to him. He understands why she might just want to go away for a while, but he doesn't want to leave it at that. He feels a certain amount of responsibility to make sure that she is all right. He also has a personal interest in her. He wouldn't have discontinued the relationship had this not happened, and he did not want to discontinue the relationship because this had happened. He went home and decided that he had better work on a different approach. He knew that he had moved too fast. He wants to smooth things over so she would talk to him again and he could continue to date her. Obviously, her art gallery was a success, and she didn't need any tips from him.

He hires a private detective who is a reference that he has used before from one of the people that he free lanced from. It takes the private detective about a week to track Charlotte to Perpignan. He finds out she is with Yvette. He relays this information immediately to David by phone from Perpignan, and he continues to watch her to make sure she doesn't leave the city.

David, on the other hand, gets on a plane for Nice and decides to drive into Perpignan. On the plane, he has lots of time to think, and while he was looking for her, he had lots of time to think. He knows that she is sensitive, and he shouldn't go over there and tell her that he loves her if he doesn't, and he shouldn't go over there and try to make more of the relationship than really exists. But he should tell her that he knows he has some responsibility, and that he wanted to try to build a relationship with her, and that he would like to be permitted to talk to her.

He obtains Yvette's number, which is publicly in the phone book, from the private detective. He calls Yvette when he is in Perpignan. He explains to her who he is, and that he would like to talk to her about how Charlotte is doing.

Yvette says that the situation is confidential, and she would like to know how he found them. He said he would have to be frank and tell her that he found her through a private detective. She says, "That means that Charlotte didn't tell you where she was, and that Charlotte didn't give you my phone number."

He says, "That's quite true. Charlotte left town and I had no idea where she was, and I was concerned enough about her that I tracked her down."

Yvette says, "And you couldn't wait until she got home to finish the conversation with her?"

David says, "No. I feel very responsible for whatever is happening to her, and I would like to be with her so that we could talk. I want to talk to Charlotte. I don't want to have to talk to anyone else but Charlotte."

Yvette says, "I'm a friend of Charlotte and I just cannot get involved in this."

David takes total responsibility for what has happened to Charlotte. He decides that she is very important to him, and he has got to see to it that she gets on her feet. He is a little taken away at being in France, close now to the Spanish border. He is in a much more romantic setting than he has been in the past. He is trying to rationalize out that yes, they both have been through a horrible experience, and yes, she is a very attractive female. But he shouldn't make her promises that will go away in the light of day. It is not fair to do that to her and that is exactly what Yvette is trying to tell him. He realizes Yvette is right. But he stills finds himself overwhelmed and wishing that he would never have to leave her, and he could always see her. He is hoping that she will permit a more intimate setting, a setting without Yvette.

He requests that he be able to speak with her without Yvette present, no reference to Yvette. He tells Yvette he needs to see her, he hasn't seen her, he just wants to talk to her, and he wants to hold her and make sure she is all right.

Surprisingly enough, Yvette is a lot more receptive to this than he expected her to be. She tells him frankly that she hopes that he is as up front as he appears to be because Charlotte does need someone. She goes on to relate to him the experience that Charlotte had had previously. She says to him, "It is all too recent for Charlotte. Any other person that it had happened to it would have found it difficult to handle. But they would have let it pass, and they would have gotten over it. But it is harder for Charlotte because she is alone. And when she makes relationships, they tend to be more important to her than when other people make relationships because she has no other family. This is what I am trying to make you understand. So, if she is just, I'd hate to say another pretty face, leave her alone because she has had enough."

He wants to know exactly what it is she means because he has had some idea that he has exposed her to a side of life that most American women don't see on any strata. He is sorry for having done that, but he was unaware that he did it. He has found out now that the invitations he sent out in an attempt to help her were actually what brought the whole house down on them, and that the people who tried to kill her thought that she was more important to him than she was. He had to examine that. He had to realize that their actions and their movements, as they were being watched by these very trained killers, were true and that she is very important to him.

Yvette says, "If that is the case, and I understand that you cannot commit yourself to, I guess, say that you are in love with her, but maybe she is the kind of girl that you would like to fall in love with, you should know why I protect her so much. The reason why I don't want it to be me, once again, is that in the past I have been in your shoes. I introduced her to someone who was devastating for her. I can only tell you that he turned out to be married and it was a very bad situation for Charlotte. Charlotte was never very aggressive when it came to men. If you look at her, you can see that she never really had to be. But she had finished school and she was starting to relax a little bit, let her hair down a little bit, because that's what everyone always teased her about is not being able to let her hair down, and now she was ready to do it because she had done all the various serious things.

"Then along comes the man who seems to have the right attitude, the right amount of confidence, the right amount of courage, and he sweeps her off her feet. She's willing to be swept. She is ready to be swept. This is life for her. But he's the wrong man. And he's the man that I introduced her to. So, I want to make sure that never happens again. And I am one of her best friends. She came to me to rest, and I want her to rest. So please don't interfere unless you can say something more than how are you doing Charlotte, because I can tell you how Charlotte is doing. I will write you letters if necessary. I can call you in America. But don't come all the way over here to inquire about her health."

David says, "On the way over, on the plane, I realized that I should have a better explanation than this. I also realized that I had hired a private detective to hunt down a free citizen. So that says that I have more interest than I probably should have in Charlotte."

Yvette says, "You're concerned about her safety? You know that the police will only go so far in protecting a citizen, and that the police are often wrong when they conclude that someone is no longer the object of a manhunt or the object of a murder plot. And she is safe over here unless you have led someone else to her. I've been cautious, somewhat cautious, when she explained the situation to me and I assure you she is very horrified, and she knows nothing about anything like this. But the other thing that I need to point out to you that you may not be aware of is because Charlotte has no parents, she has trustees, and her trustees are fully aware of this situation and they will do everything they can to see that she is properly protected. So, if your only concern is for her physical safety and or her mental stability, we'll all work on that. And for you to come in and lend a certain kind of emotional support and then withdraw it could be disruptive."

Once again, he says, "Yes, I guess you've gone and taken away every superficial reason that I could have for being here."

Yvette is standing there with her arms folded, and she is looking at him from under her eyebrows. She is nodding her head. "Yes, that's why I met you and I didn't let Charlotte. It's none of my business, but she did come to me. She is aware that you are here, and she does not want to see you at all. I don't think that that is a healthy posture for any woman to take, so I have taken it upon myself to have this meeting with you. But I am still going to keep you under scrutiny because I don't want to have happen to her again what happened to her before.

"And I know that you can't assure that all is fair in love. I can't assure that to someone who may be more in love with me than I am with them. But she has explained to me a little bit about her perception of you and to be frank, because there is no way else to be under these circumstances, she has said that you are extremely attractive, that she finds you extremely attractive, and she knows that you will get over this. We are more concerned about her now. She is not used to seeing people drop in front of her like that. And she's starting to feel guilty because of it.

"We are told that this is a normal and a natural response, but I think she has taken it beyond that. She just tells me that somehow, she feels that she's more connected, or she's more responsible, and she is having nightmares about it repeatedly.

"So, this is the situation that I am willing to deal with, and her normal support system that has always been there since she has been a child is willing to deal with it, and we probably will be able to help her through it. If you should intervene for reasons other than the ones we have mentioned before, then I guess we welcome you. I am not sure that Charlotte could handle you strictly platonically, and that would be nice too. It is always nice to have a good friend.

"But I am not sure that Charlotte could handle you strictly platonically, so I would say go away for two or three months, cool out, and come back when she maybe can take you on platonically. You seem like you are a very interesting person. You're a very nice person. You are very intelligent. You seem very well traveled. And she needs to be exposed to more people. I fully agree with you on that."

David is feeling kind of bad about now. Everything that Yvette has told him is true, and every argument that he could have made to have a reason for being there has been stripped. Now he has got to come out and say, "She is more important to me than anyone I've ever known, and I don't know why. I've never been in the position to have to explain why. I don't think I should have to explain why. I know under these circumstances; things are a little bit more critical. But I cannot explain to you why. That's just how I feel. I really don't want to let her out of my sight, and I don't want to rely on anyone else to take care of her. I want to take care of her myself, and I want her to trust me to take care of her."

Yvette says, "You know that's she is not going to do that. That's why she is here with me. And you know that that's a good thing that she is here with me."

He says, "I know that it's a good thing that she is here with you. I believe that you are her best friend, and that you have her best interests at heart. But please just let me through to talk to her so that I can tell her my feelings, and I can explain to her that there are feelings that I don't understand, and that she shouldn't force anyone to have to understand right away. That is as honest as I can be with her."

Yvette permits the meeting. She says, "I will talk to Charlotte. I will do the best I can to arrange for Charlotte to meet you. I'll call you and tell you where and when the meeting is to take place. If you come anywhere near our home, my home that I now have Charlotte in, I'll have to do something because she's just that upset."

He says that he knows that he has come across the United States, across the Atlantic, looking for someone without an invitation, and he does not want to force himself on her, he just wants to talk to her and see that she is all right. Yvette says, "I hope that she will face this. Charlotte is the kind of person who is strong enough, the Charlotte that I know, to face most things. It's just that the murders were so devastating for her. She would try to do it just out of shear strength to talk to you and get it over with. And it may end up that way, that she just faces you now and gets it over with, instead of facing you in three months which would probably be easier, or four months, and getting it over with, or it may be that you both come to a compromise. Either way, it is none of my business. I just hope that you have understood me very well."

David says, "Yes I have understood you very well, and now I would like you to go back and ask Charlotte if I can speak with her."

Yvette says, "No problem." She says her goodbyes. He promises to go in to Nice and stay out of Perpignan.

Yvette goes home and talks to Charlotte. She tells Charlotte, "David is in town. He is in town! He knows exactly where we are. He has hired a private detective, and the private detective followed you from America to Nice to Perpignan. Then upon reaching Perpignan, the private detective called his boss, who was David, and told him exactly where you could be found, and that my phone number was listed. I agreed to meet him to keep him from coming here and upsetting you."

Charlotte is happy, in one sense, because she missed him. But, in another sense, she associates him with those people that died in that tragedy. She is wondering, Nice is a playground, so why has he followed here? Why does he insist upon talking to her now? Can't he wait until she gets home and better rested?

Yvette says, "He is concerned about your welfare. I told him that we could take care of you, we've been taking care of you for a long time. Then he told me that he was concerned about your safety. I told him that you had trustees, that the trustees were aware of the situation, and that you would always be fully guarded. Then he said that he just needed to see you because he misses you too."

Charlotte says, "Oh, yeah."

Yvette says, "So I told him I would tell you this because I really think you should see him. I think you should face the issue and deal with it, whatever comes out of it. If you just talk to him and tell him that you don't want to handle it right now, you are at least facing it. I'm not trying to push you too hard because I know you've been through something that is really, bad, but I think you ought to talk to David. I think you ought to meet him up in the Alps. I'll go with you and have a little privacy and just talk to him for a while. I'll arrange it. I'll talk to him, and I'll just have you there, and he'll be there. Then we will leave."

Charlotte says, "Let me think about it."

Yvette says, "I'll give you all the time in the world because I told him I didn't want to be the one to have to do this. But since I am the one who must do this, my advice to you would be to face your fears because you have a much greater fear than this. Get this one out of your way."

Charlotte sleeps on it. The next morning, she tells Yvette she is right, that she does have a much greater fear than this, and that she had better deal with David now, especially since he has come so far. Yvette calls David at the number where he tells her that he can be reached and tells him the plans and arranges a rendezvous between he and Charlotte, though she will be close at hand. They meet and they talk in a private café. Yvette is not too far.

She has agreed to meet him there because she really doesn't want him to come to Yvette's home. He is starting to explain how important she is to him, and how he doesn't know exactly how important to him she is, but he doesn't want her to just disappear. He makes it clear to her that he wants to be sure she is all right and at least know that mentally she is all right, that she is stable, and that she can resume her business at the art gallery. He mentions that he would like to see more of her. He is not ready to make this all out commitment, but he knows that she has been more important to him than most things in his life, and so he should be permitted to see her.

She responds with something that he really doesn't expect. She tells him that she is aware that she is avoiding him because she doesn't want those emotional ties. She also suspects that she had some involvement in those murders also, and that is what she can't resolve in her mind yet. That is one of the things that has her more panicked about than anything, though she has no rational, logical, or concrete fact to support that. She is just horrified. Because she cannot really voice this to him or to Yvette or to anyone else, it internalizes itself. She is telling him this in not so many words but not really clear enough for him to pick it up.

He is talking to her, but he is not listening to her very thoroughly. She agrees, "I'll go back home, and I'll see you from time to time." It is almost in a daze that she responds to him because there is so much on her mind. She says, "OK if this is what you want, I'll go back home with you. I'll see you every now and then, and we will see where things go. I won't make you commit yourself any more than I'm going to commit myself."

The three of them spend a little time in Europe. Charlotte and David return together by plane. Charlotte goes to her home in Mendocino. Her nanny, who she has been in constant contact with, is very happy to see her. They are happy to make things as homely as possible.

In the meantime, the architect has drawn up some fabulous plans. He has hired an interior decorator. He has a lot to show her to make the house a lot cheerier, so she can occupy herself with looking at that and making decisions about exactly what she wants to do about the landscaping and the interior.

In the meantime, David goes off on some more freelance assignments. He keeps in constant contact with her. He is never gone for longer than a month.

This gives Charlotte some time to think. She also keeps in contact with Yvette by phone. She is starting to calm down a bit for two reasons. One of the reasons is that the murders are very far removed, and the visions of the mangled bodies in front of her are starting to fade. The other reason is that the vampires, her ancestors, have started to communicate with her more telepathically, not only when she is asleep as they did when she was a child, but also when she is awake and alert. They have tried to teach her not to fear them and not to fear what is happening.

That is calming. It is starting to be reasonable to her. One of the reasons that it is starting to be reasonable to her is because she has always had a psychic part of them, they have never left it. She is truly a vampire; she just never practiced it. She is starting to function again. She is starting to be able to think about the house, the art gallery and all the other different things that she thought about at one time.

On the other hand, they are starting to show her more of their life style as they lived it throughout the centuries, the legacy that she has, what she has to be proud of, why it should not discontinue, and also her obligation to make sure that it does continue. This also is beginning to seem reasonable to her.

In the meantime, Otto Weinberger has decided that there is some vampire connection. He has kept in contact with the house. He is permitted to come to the house because of Jasper Smythe.

He approaches David Sellers and tells him that he has tracked her in every place that she has been since she was two years old, and that there have been no murders. He tells David that he can't blame her for that, but with the information that he has gotten from the local police and from the coroner, these people have not been killed by accident, by a car running over them. They were killed by vampires, but he can't really substantiate it. He explains to David that he felt he needed to tell him now because he wasn't sure what other people's position in town would be, or how fast he would have to act if something like this would happen again because he still doesn't understand the object.

Otto has had Jasper Smythe looking around for coffins and different things like that. He hasn't found anything like that. He is thinking she has no problem coming out in the daytime, and she has none of the normal characteristics that you would apply to a vampire. He is stumped, but he does know that two people died there recently, and he is afraid that it will happen again. He approaches the person that he thinks is closest to her and who he feels is still totally human and, therefore, may be in more danger than anyone else. He tells him, "I think she is a vampire."

Of course, David is furious. He tells him to get lost. He tries to be respectful because he realizes that the man is a very learned man, that he comes with university credentials, and that the man is dead serious when he makes this allegation. He also considers the way it is presented to him. Otto says that he really can't back it up, but he wants to put the thought there so that if anything should go a little wrong that he can't explain, at least he would be thinking maybe in this direction. David doesn't beat him or anything, but he tells him that he really doesn't want to hear from him again. David tells him, "I already hired a private detective, and he has done some investigation himself. I know that there is a something different as far as her parents go, but that doesn't bother him. I am ready to accept whatever happened. I know that she has gotten whatever money she has legitimately, and that she has gone to school. I think that she would probably make somebody a good wife someday. Why go and tell her of being a vampire?"

Otto Weinberger backs off. He really didn't have a position to take. He backs off, and says, "All right, but remember if you need to talk to me any time during the day or night, I am available." He goes off and he decides to go to Europe and pick up the trail of her ancestors because he knows that her mother and father were truly vampires, and they would have tried to cover that trail. He goes off to do that.

In the meantime, David Sellers also sends his private detective to Europe to find out anything that he could find out. He decides that he made enough money, and he has enough money in reserve that he could spend a little bit more time in Mendocino, and she could spend it with him. It just so happens that she has no one to exhibit right at this moment. She has been exhibiting a few artists, but it is part of a down season for Mendocino in general and it's not really the tourist time of year. She really doesn't feel like creating or motivating a big publicity campaign to get some people up there. She takes this opportunity to rest and work on her own art. Her medium has usually been watercolor.

This is the time he takes to visit her. He has dinner at her home a couple of times. He comes several times during the daytime, and they go horseback riding and swimming and different things like that. He gets closer and closer to the house. He asks questions like why there are no pictures of her parents. She says that she really doesn't know. She has asked these questions of her trustees and they don't know either. She tells him, "I have wanted to take the time to look, but the way my life has been, I have been in school. Then I started this project. I thought that when I had settled down and started to renovate the place, I would run across some things. But so far, I haven't. I really don't know why. I don't know where to look."

He says, "Well, they didn't leave you any messages, any notes, anything in the will?"

She says, "No, nothing particularly pertaining to me, just maintenance and taking care of me."

They think it would be fun to look through the house and see what they could find. So, they begin to look through the house over the course of several weeks. They don't really find anything pertaining to her parents. It is there, but they just don't find it. But they do find the paintings that she did during her life. These paintings are nothing but scenes of either vampires being murdered, vampires murdering, or the normal daily life of her ancestors, either in their courtyards, inside their castles, having balls or even shifting shapes. These are different things that they communicated to her, and she painted it in her waking normal daily life. It wasn't in her conscious mind. She showed it to him.

Even as she showed it to him, it was not really in her conscious mind. It was, what she thought, some of her best work, though she didn't know what it meant. She was not the kind of person to take it out and show anyone else. She was considering exhibiting it, but she would rather really involve herself with the business side of things right now and really get a good reputation so that artists would want to come to her gallery. That is what she was trying to do. She figured that she could put her stuff in the back and just keep working on different pictures until she had enough of a reputation where she didn't have to worry about people coming to show all kinds of sculptures, paintings, and photographs. David is horrified at what he sees, but he manages to camouflage it. He talks to her to see if she remembers it and if any of this is bothering her. She just shows him the pictures and goes on about it.

The pictures are all very well done. They are beautiful. They depict reality.

David is very much alarmed. He knows the pictures are old and that the pictures span her lifetime. Now he must go looking for Otto Weinberger in Europe on sabbatical. David's private detective is also in Europe. He calls his private detective home because he doesn't know why Otto Weinberger is on sabbatical, and he would like to get in touch with him right away. David doesn't want to ask Jasper because he is not sure of Jasper's relationship with Charlotte and with Otto Weinberger. He thinks that it would be better if he just sticks with his private detective.

The private detective has learned very little. David brings him back home and tells him to find Otto Weinberger as soon as he can. His private detective has means of tracking Otto Weinberger. He finds Otto Weinberger in Germany on sabbatical. The sabbatical is not at all related to his studying at the university.

The private detective tells him who he is and tells him what he wants. Otto Weinberger is relieved because he found certain things, but he still hasn't put it together yet himself. He is willing to come home because he knows he could always go back. But if there is something for them to look at, they would want to see that now. That might give him some clue as to what is going on and what happened in Europe. It might also give him a better way to trace it. He immediately returns with the private detective.

The private detective, Otto Weinberger, Jasper Smythe and David Sellers are discussing this vampirism as a very real possibility. They are even wondering maybe she should go to a psychiatrist and find out why it is she dreams, why she sees this, if this something she made up in her mind. David Sellers throws in the idea that this could be because she never knew who here real parents were, and she never has had any family. He suggests, playing the psychiatrist, that this is Charlotte's way of keeping her parents around, and this is a continuation of a childhood fantasy. Otto suggests a test using David's full cooperation. He knows David might view this as a deception. All parties involved agree to this action.

He breaks a trust by getting Charlotte out of the house long enough for Jasper Smythe and the private detective to show the paintings to Otto Weinberger, who is very upset. But they don't know that all of this is known to the vampires. As usual, they never act until they feel they absolutely must. They have no other choices and no other way out. They are just watching the situation to see where it is going to go.

He decides that maybe he should do a more thorough look himself. If they could get her out of the house with her nanny, distract the servants a little bit, and if he could have access to the premises, maybe he knows a little bit more about what to look for in the house. He knows he can't really walk up to her and say, "I think you are a vampire and I think I should look through your premises." He tries to try to find more evidence.

There are mirrors there. He even tried to bring in certain plants that are supposed to bother her, but they don't. He is at quite a loss for how to handle this. Otto Weinberger now has everyone's full attention, everyone being Jasper

Smythe, the psychiatrist who saw Charlotte briefly after the murders, and the private detective. They have not brought the nanny in on it yet.

He decided to continue with their method of getting the nanny out of the house. He takes it one step further by sending her a fake telegram from one of her aunts. This information has been obtained by both him and the private detective.

Megan Hampton goes back East to visit this aunt knowing that she would keep in telephone touch with Charlotte. The other servants are easier to get rid of because they could just be given the day off (the ones that stay all night). They could be given the day, or a good portion of the day, off. What he proposes to do is to lock her in a room with objects that are harmful to vampires (certain plants and various other objects). Charlotte doesn't know why she can't leave. She knows why the nanny has left. She really doesn't understand why the servants are gone when she wakes up. The servants are gone, the nanny left her a note, she can't leave by car because her car is not working, and she is too far from town.

She doesn't know this because they are in constant contact with what is happening to her. She is virtually locked in. She can't go anywhere or do anything but sit around these objects that she doesn't know are there.

That terrifies her, along with the fact that she has already been the target of murderers. She doesn't want to call the police because she doesn't have anything to say, nothing is wrong. She doesn't have any real friends in the community to call. She does have a secretary, but the secretary is also out of town on a small vacation. As far as she knows, David Sellers is out doing a little freelance work. There is no one she can really call. She just must sit in this house.

Sitting in the house does produce an affect, but it doesn't produce the desired effect in that she doesn't show any more vampire characteristics. It doesn't weaken her in the sense that she's going to need blood, she's going to want to stay out of the daylight, or she's going want to take a victim. But it does work on her mentally. She is very stressed out about it. It was the last thing she needed after what she had been through.

When someone finally shows up, she is furious first and confused second. She knows that the nanny had a legitimate reason for leaving, and she trusts the nanny. She doesn't think the nanny is involved. She is not quite ready to trust these four men as well as she had done before. She had to be sedated by the time they found her. The psychiatrist was more than willing to do this because he felt like the whole operation was under his control. He went ahead and sedated her, and she slept for two or three days. David Sellers came back and forth to visit her.

Jasper Smythe and Otto Weinberger were at a loss about what to do. They agreed that Otto Weinberger could look down in the wine cellar to see if he could find any remnants of a coffin or anything that might belong to her parents. Off the wine cellar is where her studio is located where she used to paint. It also opens to the greens and the ocean. She has a view of the greens, the ocean, and most of the estate.

The vampires are very upset at what happened. If they had not been with her most of the time, she probably really would have snapped, maybe possibly have a nervous breakdown. They decided that they needed to slow Otto up. They don't want to kill him because the murders that are taking place have already been explained and filed away. They like murders that have been explained away because it doesn't throw suspicion in her direction. They decide that they don't really want to kill him or maim him since he is too prominent of a figure. They just want to slow him up a little bit so that he is hesitant to try this again, or at least give him some glimpse of what he is dealing with.

They decide to put him into one of her paintings for just a few seconds. For him, when the episode is over, no real time has elapsed. They pull him into one of the paintings, one of the open scenes in the meadow. In this scene that she has painted, the vampires are being hunted. They are being chased out of their castle by villagers. They are being staked, decapitated, spilt open and various other things. They are dressed very elegantly in their ball gowns because they were having a party. It is of night, and they are being chased by people who have torches, picks, axes, and knives. There is this terror on both sides. There is terror from the people who were chasing them, and there is terror from the people who are running. He is in the middle of it, and he can see some of them. In their attempt to escape they are shifting shapes, going to dogs, to bats etc. But a lot of them are still being caught, burned, and decapitated.

He realizes that this painting is not static, it is dynamic, it is changing. As he turns to look, he can see a girl who more than likely is Charlotte. She is about sixteen or seventeen years old, and she is there painting. He sees that he is not clothed. As she begins to paint, she dresses him as a vampire. Now he becomes a target, and he must run. He stops one of the vampires and he asks him what he could do, what is going on. The vampire answers, "It all depends on your perspective," and he keeps moving.

While he was inside the painting, aware that he must be inside the painting, he was watching what looked like a sixteen or seventeen-year-old, Charlotte, paint the picture and draw in the creeks and the trees. He was on the side of the vampires. He began to feel all the lust for blood, all the power that they have, and the ability to change. He knew exactly what side he was on. He was being chased by villagers. These people surrounding him seemed to be his relatives. He was watching female members of his family, very well dressed, satins and jewels, being dragged from their castles and their homes, staked and decapitated. The ones that had time, either fled in various ways by changing shapes or attacking themselves.

He starts with all the emotions, all the intimacy of someone being in that position. He also felt whatever terror you would feel if you could experience mob violence, if you could be the center of mob violence, or the target of mob violence. He felt it fleetingly, momentarily, but intensely. He was sure of it, very sure of it. Once again, he was outside the picture looking in.

He decided to leave immediately to catch up with the other three who were upstairs. No real time had elapsed during his experience. He was getting nervous, very distracted, and incoherent. He was ready to go home. He got home and decided that maybe he should go back to his books. This seemed to be a little bit near the supernatural and her family history. But at this point, it didn't seem to be as critical as what had happened to him, what had altered his reality. He began to go through his books at home. He tried to put together what information he had dreamed about, he was in the black forest in Germany, in the Carpathians with the Von Shillingsfurst family.

Otto Weinberger, in his research of the clan that comes from the Carpathians, determines that the Von Shillingsfursts come from the part of the Carpathians that run through Poland. He thinks that part of the name, Schilling, comes from Schlecha which is Polish for Gentry, and that the clan came to power in 900 A.D., and they began to be knighted about 1000 A.D., but they were Schlecha by then. As they moved toward East Germany, they become Von Shillingsfurst, which he feels is possibly an attempt to change the name, Von simply meaning from, and an attempt to keep their identity as Schlecha. This is how he thinks they derived the name Von Shillingsfurst. When he was in the Carpathians, he was fully informed that the people in the Carpathians felt that there was supernatural activity going on with these people who had a name Scheknava, and they had a coat of arms like Charlotte's.

The clan at that time was a large family group of very strong, very athletic and beautiful people. But they had no real time and no real land. They were somewhat nomadic. They later found favor, or very well-earned favor, with the king of the land because they could eliminate completely whoever they took on in battle. There were a lot of young men in the family. They did engage enemies in battle. But they always engaged enemies that were truly their enemies, they didn't just fight for the king. They fought these battles at night. They only took members from their family to be on their side. At that time, they didn't have people to chronicle what happened. They took no prisoners. The other side, whoever the other side happened to be, never returned alive. So, with a complete and total victory which made the king happy at the time that it happened, the king decided to knight them initially. He gave them some of the riches that he had and bestowed various jewels and other gifts on the family as the family began to blossom and multiply. The king also began to bring them up in rank. They begin to maintain their fortress, also his land.

No one ever knew why they won their battles so completely and so thoroughly. They didn't really care to find out. They just knew that the area was safe, in some ways, from most attacks. As time went on, they had various titles, and they obtained wealth and land. They had begun to teach their children culture, arts, and sciences. People began to suspect that there was something supernatural to them always having this and always having that.

When Otto Weinberger was in the Carpathians, he heard a rumor, or a legend of this clan of people described previously. He found some fragmented documentation after they received their titles later. He didn't find any history on them dating back to the earlier stages before they were knighted. He also found, once again, something that could be the coat of arms or close enough to it.

What other people weren't realizing is that they weren't dying. They were being born, but they weren't necessarily dying in the same life span that other people were dying. They could live on for three or four centuries. They changed their dispositions quite extensively. That is how they think of the habits where they only kill when it is necessary. They are very thorough when they do it, and they are very efficient. They learned to hide their habits in that they are vampires now and probably vampires all along. This is the heritage that she came from.

They put him into the picture to give him a feel of what they could do to him and to give him an understanding of their side of things. And then to have him slop bothering Charlotte, not to try to exclude them from Charlotte again because it terrified her, and it didn't serve any real purpose. If nothing else, he could go back and study it and get it right so he can approach her again with some new way to prove that she is a vampire. They know that he will not be able to prove it until she gets to Stockton.

They know he will not be able to prove it until she participates in the blood feast. They know that she hasn't and probably will not participate in the blood feast and that all he has succeeded in doing was making her a nervous wreck and continuing to destabilize her thinking. She was trying so very hard before to get on solid ground after the first two murders.

Otto Weinberger sits at his home and starts to go through books on the supernatural, witchcraft and demonology. He is trying to understand how a vampire could be there and yet not be there. He thinks that this is now the best trail to follow. How they can do these things intrigues him because even vampires by the nature of their condition have certain laws that they must follow like humans such as gravity and sunshine rising in the east and setting in the west. He is aware that they are not following any of their natural life that he has known them to have, that he has ever heard of them having. He wants to know how they manage to escape this. He has not located any bodies or any persons, and he hasn't seen the massive need for blood because there was no massive need for blood sustained on the victims that were mangled there. But he needs to justify what he knows is going on, it must be going on.

He spends two or three days at home where he doesn't answer the phone. He just ponders what is happening. He reads a little of what is already at his house, the normal vampire lore. He decides that even though it is not written anywhere, and even though he has never heard of it, that possibly the people in the painting are dead, have always been dead, and there is nobody to find. What he is finding is a spirit, and a spirit in more than the sense of a malicious ghost. A spirit that has carried its supernatural powers that it had when it had a body with it, but for some reason has not chosen to or is not permitted to take another body.

As he begins to toy with this idea, it starts to lead him in the direction of what they could possibly want with two normal healthy people, because they have done nothing to discourage or harm or get rid of David Sellers. In fact, David is very comfortable there, and you would have to really show him that something is wrong because he would see it otherwise. He would think there is absolutely nothing wrong with her. So, he arrives at the conclusion that if these spirits are still hanging around, and they have made themselves known in mass, he still doesn't know to what extent they are present. He considers that possibly they have some use for Charlotte and David. The only thing that he can think of would be a rebirth.

The reason he thinks they want to have a rebirth is to keep the same blood line through Charlotte because they have never been the kind of people to take another body. It has not been their pattern. They have also liked to stay clannish and in their family. This is how he arrived at the conclusion that actually what they must need Charlotte for, even though Charlotte is very much one of theirs, is to help with new generations, not all at once but gradually and slowly. She must learn to hide and to cover what she knows and what she doesn't know.

Once he hits upon that idea, then he must decide would they be like Charlotte in that they are not going to use blood, or they are not going to have blood lust? Are they bringing Charlotte to the point where she would exhibit a blood lust? And as the generations come and she has more children and more grandchildren and aunts and uncles, will they start going back into their own practices? These are the things that he is thinking about while he is at home. He is turning it over and over in his mind. Even though he thinks that he is really right about this, he still is at a loss to find out how to stop it because, once again, he has no bodies, and the vampires can shade themselves and communicate to him when they choose to. He suspects that they have not begun to fully materialize, as they may be able to, simply because they haven't chosen to.

He also has noticed a weakening physically in Charlotte, though he hasn't established a need for blood. He has decided that when they do some of the things that they do, they are drawing on her energy. Charlotte is still somewhat sedated. The vampires have decided that she needs a little bit more support, and that they need to bring her a little bit closer into the fold. So they take her into one of their safest centuries for what is two or three normal weeks (though time hardly passes for the servants, her nanny who is back home, or any of the other people that regularly come to the house to visit).

They know Otto Weinberger is pretty much out of the picture for the moment. They used some of their European contacts which they had to establish a long time ago when they couldn't do things in the daylight. They contacted them telepathically and suggested that they call David Sellers over for a freelance job on the way to Europe to photograph Monaco's rulers.

He takes the position because, frankly, Charlotte won't let him in the house. She is very angry at what she thinks has occurred even though she hasn't put his part in it all together yet. She would rather just not deal with him right now.

He jumps at the chance to learn more about royalty because, though he has had many, he has not come close to this before, especially European royalty, and it is a short assignment. It is not difficult to get him to go because he stops to talk to Otto Weinberger who assures him that nothing human will ever hurt her, so he doesn't have to worry about her physical safety. Also, Otto Weinberger, at this point, gives him the relic. David goes off to his assignment in Europe. He does what he is supposed to do and rubs elbows. He is an excellent photographer, so his work comes out well. He returns to America to attempt to get someone to examine it.

In the meantime, she is there with all her ancestors in a very nice mansion in Italy in the summertime. She is in the century prior to revolutions, the century where people were affluent, and royalty was above question. She realizes that she is dressed, she is in this beautiful home, and she is dressed as the people are in that time period. They greet her. Some people walk by her and just nod and smile. They expected her to be there, and they know her. She is family, and she immediately starts to feel this way. They show her to her room where she will be staying. They tell her that she will probably stay two or three weeks, and that they really think she needs to rest. As it is called for, they introduce themselves on a first name basis. They tell her who her cousins are and where her ancestors are from. She is very comfortable and falls right in line.

During the daytime, they draw very heavy curtains. Their movements are also dormant. There would be very little activity. They entertain her with needlepoint or a concert with a grand piano, harpsichord, flute and harps.

Different members of the family will entertain. Time passes away. She learns to talk with the women. The men walk with her and talk with her and falter her, but it is all in a brotherly, cousinly, sisterly way. They are very supportive of her. They are supportive that she is not pushy, not rushed. She starts to calm down. In the meantime, she is aware that there is very little verbal communication going on. A lot of what is happening is going on telepathically.

The servants that are present are controlled. They have free will and they are not harmed, but generally they ask no questions because they are in kind of telepathic hypnotic state. They think that other people would notice, or it would alert other people. They just pass right by.

The food to her, for instance, is delicious; but none of the other relatives are eating. They don't want to alarm her with that yet. She doesn't notice it either. She does begin to take on this telepathy, this control, this interaction, this sixth sense. In the evening, she spends her time in beautiful gardens. It is warm. She enjoys the terrace and the lovely flowers. She is escorted by various people, either older generations or younger generations. They take her to play lawn games. She goes horseback riding. She has just a wonderful time. She relaxes. She is not afraid of anyone there. But what she doesn't realize is that she has picked up a certain habit of living.

Jasper shows up within a few days after they return her to her own home. He has the decorations that he wants her to choose from. She immediately chooses the heavier drapes, the tapestry. She chooses the ones that won't let light in during the daytime. She selects marbles, paintings, and scrolls. She just wants to be consistent with the style, which was prominent in the thirties, almost oriental. She explains it off that way. She wants satins, silks, and bouquets everywhere. He agrees. He orders what she says she wants.

She begins to control the servants. She doesn't ask them to do anything to harm themselves or her, but she eliminates a lot of questions that they might put to her. A lot of the conversations are totally telepathic. But they don't realize it, even the nanny. She is amazed, but she is somewhat happy that she can do this. She also realizes that the people who locked her in, and god knows what else they would have done to her, liked her better than anybody in town with the exception of the nanny, and if what she is beginning to suspect is true, that she is a vampire, the town might tunnel her in mass hysteria and do away with her. She takes the attitude that had better learn how to use these things and shut up about it.

By the time David Sellers returns, she realizes that he does care for her, she does care for him, and he is a legitimate mate. She welcomes him back into the house. She is almost a whole different person. She is relaxed. She is radiant. She is very confident in her surroundings. Her servants obey her completely. She is the mistress of the house, instead of being the little girl who grew up in the house. They make suggestions to her which she follows pretty much. They are now definitely controlled.

Her interaction with him is also drastically different in that she is not promiscuous, but she is not reserved. She had definite goals. She wants to now start defining them, whereas before she didn't want to think about them. He doesn't mind this, but he knows that something more is going on. He is very alarmed because this is not the women that he knows. He has panicked. He notices the heaviness of the drapes. He knows that she is almost dormant and won't really receive him in the daytime. She schedules him mostly in the nighttime. They go out for dinner, for a drink, to play a game, they watch something on television, or they might go out to a movie. But all of these are nighttime activities, and she tells him that she is either relaxing during the day, or she is working on new paintings. Since she doesn't have any paintings to show him, he believes now that her activity during the day is limited. He has put that together because he has seen the decorations go up. So, he thinks, *I better act fast.*

He goes back over to Otto Weinberger, who still has nothing to offer him. He decides in a mad panic that the only thing he can do, but he can't do this legally, is to exhume her parent's bodies. He thinks just maybe they have pushed her to the edge where now she is starting to believe something that is not true. He figures they could just exhume the parent's bodies since everybody knows where the graves are. What a simple thing. Why didn't he think of it before? He didn't think of it before because he couldn't get a court order to do it. But he knows enough people that would do things just for pay and, he has got a list of people to ask. He gets in touch with a few people. They go in and dig up her parents using some information from old newspaper clippings, which are very sketchy. The obituaries mostly lean toward sympathy that a young child would be left parentless, left an orphan. The articles focus on how the people came into town elegant, with lots of money. They didn't ask anybody for anything. They gave money to the town by asking various people in this town to do things to help them, then paid for it. The town didn't have any hostility toward them. It was a nice obituary on the surface.

He goes in at night, and he digs up both parents. He opens the grave. He finds that both bodies are there. Both bodies are charred. The bodies are not totally and completely burned, as he was led to believe by the newspaper clippings saying that there was almost nothing left, but they are badly burned to the point of probable death. They died of smoke inhalation. He looks at the hands because everything else seems to be normal. As he looks at the hands, he is startled because one of her father's hands pops out, and it is not a human hand. It is a claw. It has hair and extended nails.

After he overcomes his initial shock and his initial tendency to run, which takes him quite a bit of time, he asks the other people to take a few steps back so that they cannot see this. He knows that since he has gone this far, he might as well go all the way. He takes a good look at the faces and everything else. Everything else is charred, but it is human.

He had brought a big bag of scissors and other small tools. He clips the hair on the hands and clips a little bit of nails. There appears to be metal and upholstery under the fingernails. He takes all that with him, but he puts the metal and upholstery in a separate bag. On the wife's hand, he noticed a wedding ring, but he also notices another ring that looks an awfully lot like the relic Otto Weinberger gave to him because Otto wanted to get it out of his house. To make sure that it looks like the relic, he pulls it out of the knapsack he is carrying. When he does this the bodies come to form. The hands become human hands. The bodies are no longer charred. There are just two beautiful people there who appear to be sleeping. They have no signs of decay. It is as if they were driving down the road at 30 or 35 at the time of the accident and nothing ever happened to them.

David is awed and again horrified. He is showing revulsion. He decides that he had better just pack and close things up because he can't let them see this either. He wanted to just close the casket and hide the bodies. He puts away the coat of arms and gets them to cover the bodies up. They do it to make it look like the graves were undisturbed.

David goes back to Otto Weinberger. He says, "Listen to me. I want you to understand this thing that I saw happen." In the meantime, he drops the hair samples and nail samples off at a veterinarian, explaining, "You know, I found this animal and it tried to attack me. I just wanted to know if it was a cat. I wanted to know what it was. I'll be back in a couple of days if you let me know."

The veterinarian says, "Fine. I should be able to identify it from what you have given me here." David relates the experience of the transformation of bodies to Otto Weinberger. Immediately, Otto Weinberger says, because he doesn't think about it at all, he must come up with something. He says, "The relic is probably the curse that was placed on the family, and when it was in the presence of the bodies that were dead the curse was over for these people. Then the bodies could resume their normal shape." He doesn't quite buy it, but he takes the relic because he thought that the relic was going to be his for some time. He goes back to the newspaper clippings and looks at them again. The newspaper clippings noted that the roof was ripped opened from the inside, and the highway patrol could not explain some skid marks and catching onto a tree. They didn't remark on how it could have happened. But it was noted.

David went to the veterinarian to get an opinion on what kind of hair it was. Did this man just have long hair and long nails? What is going on? The veterinarian tells him, "It's a wolf. The wolf is very old. It has been dead for at least forty years. I can't believe that this wolf attacked you yesterday. I'm not even sure it is an American wolf. But it is certainly a wolf. Maybe perhaps you were drunk. Maybe you ran into some stuffed animal. This could be an animal off a wall. This one could not have been alive and moving yesterday."

David thanks him. He is very embarrassed about the whole incident. He, himself, didn't sustain any scratches, but he just wanted to make sure. He couldn't remember what happened and maybe it is just better that he leaves things just as they are. He is saying this as he is backing out of the door of the veterinarian clinic. He doesn't really want any more questions asked of him. He comes to the conclusion that the parents are doing some of the things that he had seen in the picture, and that was to get out of the car, and they are panicked, and they tried to rip the roof off in the form of a wolf.

This is very horrifying. David is very repulsed. He is disgusted. He doesn't know how he is going to deal with it. He knows that he doesn't need to go and get his woman right now, though he knows that he still loves her. He collects his items and puts them in his dark room. He had also taken photographs of the claws and of the people after the transformation. He tries to track down the person who did the autopsy, if there was an autopsy done. At the time, there was no autopsy done because the death was from all these causes. There was no alcohol in the bloodstream, so they left the bodies intact and buried them.

He did find the old coroner who was now at his ranch by the Ell River. The coroner tells him he had handled it. He adds, "Well, did you notice anything unusual about the hands?"

The coroner says, "Oh no. They were just in a normal posture of a person who has been in a severe fire. The tendons retract. The muscles retract. They call it the boxer's posture. They were just gnarled up a little bit. We noted that, but that is nothing unusual. No autopsy was done because everything was straightforward." That was all the coroner would say about it. He didn't make any more comments.

David thanks him for his time. The coroner asks him what he wanted to know. Of course, he didn't tell him that he had seen the bodies. He just said that he had read the clippings, he was interested in the girl, and he just wanted to know a little bit more about her background because he was very wealthy. The coroner says, "Well, I'll just have you know that she is fairly wealthy too, and I don't think if her parents were alive that they would appreciate you digging around. Just hold on a minute, maybe I've said too much. I probably shouldn't have even told you that."

He says, "Don't upset yourself. Don't upset yourself. It will be all right." He is hoping that the coroner will not call anyone down in Mendocino and relay this conversation. So, he leaves as soon as he can.

By this time, David spends a little bit of time by himself. He decides he could not tell what he knows because they will kill her. He knows that either Otto Weinberger will kill her, or have her killed, or anyone that finds out about this in the town will go off and kill her. He has made up his mind. He has chosen the side that he is going to back her no matter what. He returns to her house.

She knows that he has made this decision. They go horseback riding together at night. Her horse finds every one of these symbols that are buried in the ground. He just shows them to her. Her horse takes her on a path of where they are. She is aware of what her horse is doing and where everything is. She is making a mental note in her mind. She also thinks that David Sellers doesn't know this. The vampires know that he is extremely depressed. They want him to stay alive. They want him to become a mate. They let his horse follow the other one. His horse follows the other one, but not in the pattern so you could recognize the trace back to any of the other ones. He doesn't think that she has seen it, and she pretends that she hasn't seen it. So, he covers it up right away. They continue with their horseback riding.

After he comes home, he mulls it over. He decides that it couldn't be a curse because no one has followed them from anyplace or else Charlotte wouldn't still be alive. The only friend that he knew that she had was her parents, so it must hold some significance to the family, some protective power for her family. He knows that he had better keep it to himself. With David Sellers' resolution to stick by the side of Charlotte, and also the significance that he found in the relic that he now knows must hold some protective power for her, he decides that the only other step that he could take is he is going to have to marry her and show her that he doesn't intend to hurt her. And he knows that he should take this step immediately. It is obvious to him that she has a certain amount of strong will herself and she is certainly a vampire. But he knows the vampires have more influence over her than anybody. David knows that he must marry her in order to have a voice in it. He wants to bring her as close as he can back to the person that he knew before all this started. In some ways, even though he knows that these victims were victims of vampires, he knows that he triggered it, and it might have come to fruition anyway. But he didn't mean it to happen then, and it might have happened at a time in her life where she had chosen another path.

He decides that he is going to propose to her. He has a very nice ring prepared. She is very ready to accept his proposal. She is going to accept the proposal because this is pretty much in line with the plans that she has and with the plans her family has. She does love him. There is no reason why she shouldn't go ahead and marry him. He has demonstrated his commitment and his loyalty to her family, and he is the person who could be trusted not to expose her because exposing her could very well mean not only her death, but both of their deaths.

While David and Charlotte are in Mendocino getting to know each other better in now a much more intimate way because they are planning to be married, the private detective that David has hired, who has been very closely involved with whole subject from the start, has returned to his home state of New Jersey. He is a bachelor. He lives alone at home. He has a housekeeper that comes and goes as she pleases because his job is a job that keeps him irregular hours and irregular days. One night, he is at home sleeping. He too is having nightmares, not the same sort of nightmares that Charlotte is having, and not nightmares that are particularly directed. He is having nightmares because he has been so close to this incident, and he has seen photographs of the murder victims. He awakens in a bad frame of mind. It is not totally light yet. He imagines movement in his house. He gets weapon which he keeps very close to him. He goes down the hallway looking for movement that he thinks he has seen. He is still not fully awake. The upper part of his body, just about mid shoulder, gets hooked by a coat rack. He is thrown to the floor, but the coat rack is firm and is still standing there. He begins to fire shots. He is sure he is not in the house alone. He gets up and turns on all the lights. He can't find anything, and he can't find anyone. He feels like a complete idiot. He has drawn the neighbors to the house as well as the police. His only explanation is that he was sure he was being burglarized.

The police know that he is a private detective and that he should know pretty much if he is being burglarized, so they go with him to examine the premises. They decide that they could see no signs of forced entry, but that doesn't mean he hasn't run up against someone who is pretty good at getting in and out of houses. The cops on the beat are rather familiar with him because of his line of work. They notice that he is unusually tense. They suggest that maybe he should take a vacation away because he seems to be just a little jumpy, perhaps a little bit trigger happy even. They look at his gun and suggest that he be a little bit slower about using it next time. They really didn't think anything was in the house with him.

He is still not satisfied with this. He is very shaken. He is not happy with the results of his investigation. He is also not happy with the fact that he was simply dismissed after being privy to all the occurrences, going into eastern Germany and participating in an exhumation of a body and opening a grave. He has never done anything like that before. He has seen lots of dead bodies, but he has never gone in after they have been dead forty or fifty years to look at them. He is just rattled. He finds that he is unable sleep. He doesn't really want to say that he is afraid, but he doesn't want to turn out his bedroom light. He decides if he hadn't taken on this job with David Sellers, he wouldn't be in this position. He knows he has made a fool out of himself in front of the neighbors and in front of the police. Once more, he is still not sure that there was nothing in the house, so he decides to go back into David Sellers' apartment and find out what it was David Sellers photographed.

Now he is fearful. He thinks that he should have gotten more money for what he really turned out to be doing, which was vampire hunting. He had never bargained for that. He is pretty much afraid for his life. He breaks into David Sellers' studio in Mendocino and goes into the dark room. He finds the veterinarian report which describes the hair clippings from the bodies as wolves. He finds the blown-up pictures of the people that they had exhumed. He sees that the hands are paws. This is what he didn't see when David Sellers asks them to stand back. He also sees the relic, their jewelry, a repeat of the relic and the transformation that took place. He has pictures of the bodies uncharred and beautiful, the clothes are not tattered, the hair is not disarrayed, the people just look very peaceful and at rest. These are still photos. They are well done because David Sellers is a very good photographer.

This all must have taken place in a crypt, and he is horrified and very frightened. He is beginning to wonder how far away he is. He is thinking of all the very strange and weird things that have happened in California. He decides that this is sick, extremely sick. He doesn't know why David hasn't recognized that this is sick and bringing in the psychiatrist isn't enough. He decides to kill them both. There is no other solution. They are not even human. He doesn't know how far David is involved, but he knows that David is in love with Charlotte and is protecting her to the fullest. He assumes David is no longer human either. He doesn't want to have to wonder how this could happen. It is just easier for him to kill them to make sure that he had no one visiting him at his house in New Jersey again.

He confronts David at his house. He is just sitting there when David walks in. "I know what is in the dark room. I know what you wouldn't let us see on the crypt. These things are monsters. The two that are dead should stay dead, and she should go along with them." Immediately, they have a fight. He initiated the fight. He comes there pretty much with the wrong state of mind. He is perfectly willing to beat David Sellers to death, and he knows how. Though David Sellers is no lightweight, he is not a professional by any means. He is not a private detective who is used to sometimes even doubling as a bodyguard.

He beats David Sellers badly and leaves him for dead in his own apartment. All David Sellers can do is think that he has got to get to this woman, because he is going to her next and she is not going to be able to even stand this one. He has probably got a concussion and contusions. He is just really messed up and messed up to the point where a big person who is trained at looking at dead bodies is pretty sure he was or will be dead. He gets in his car, and he follows the guy out to her house.

All the while he is thinking, I opened her up for this because I was the one that invited him in on the incident we had when we closed her in, he knows the complete layout of her house, he knows exactly where her bedroom is, he knows how to get into her bedroom windows. He is thinking this over and over in his head, blaming himself, as he is driving ninety miles an hour down the highway to try to catch the man who beat him. He can't do either because he couldn't even see when he sat up, so he is at least fifteen to twenty minutes behind the guy going at high speed.

The private detective arrives at her bedroom first. She has double French doors off a terrace. It is very easy for him to pick the lock. She is in a wing that is empty. The servants are far away, and the nanny is several rooms down. Charlotte is asleep. He has had this plan in his mind all along because he knew about the first series of murders. He knew that they would blame it again on the mob, that David Sellers was beaten to death by the mob and his girlfriend could have committed suicide because everybody has seen her publicly be a basket case over and over again, either with the murders or different other times when she has not had the right composure. The psychiatrist can only testify the many times he has had to come in and sedate her, and he wouldn't dare mention that he actually participated in that or there was any possibility that supernatural is involved because they would probably take his license. He is pretty sure that if he kills her there won't be too many questions asked.

He is willing to bet that David hasn't advertised this engagement because he is trying to keep everything else so private and so personal around this lady. Her room is a very large, feminine room. It has high ceilings, very comfortable, nice fluffy pillows, nice fully comfortable. He is taking all this in, it has a nice perfume smell, it must be the perfume that she wears most of the time, she is very attractive, she is very beautiful as she is laying there struggling. He is so occupied with this he doesn't notice that in the four corners of her room there are men levitating. They appear to be dressed as monks. They are wearing hoods. You can't see their hands because their robes come all the way down. They are wearing the knotted belt on the side, very simple brown robes with a white knotted belt. They are levitating about two feet above the floor, and they are in all four corners of her room. They are almost translucent, but they are there.

As he attempts to begin to violate her, her struggle intensifies, and her anger reaches the point where she throws him against the wall. He slams into the wall. She doesn't use her hands. She is unable to use her hands because he has her hands restricted. She is not in a state of complete consciousness. She doesn't know what she is doing. What is happening is that he has been thrown against the wall at her wish. He slumps back from the wall. She is now up right above the bed also levitating. The windows are open. Her gown is blowing. Her hair is blowing in the wind. She is furious.

All of this is witnessed by David. He sees the room. He sees the monks in the corner almost there, but not quite there, and not touching the ground. Then he sees her take an almost similar posture, and he witnesses the private detective's slamming into the wall. He is sure that he is knocked unconscious. David is hoping he is not dead. But before he can get to him or her, and she by now has slumped on the bed, the private detective is gone, and he thinks that she may not be conscious. He looks around the room and the four monks are gone too. He knows they must have left simultaneously.

The private detective is now clothed in the clothing of the monks, and he is standing in front of a monastery. He looks around very slowly. The monastery, like most monasteries, is set in a terrain that is almost inaccessible. He can only see one visible road out, and it looks like it is not a very easy path to take. He is barefoot. He is cold. He looks around and realizes that it is twilight. He knows that he is facing the archway, and that it is the opening to the monastery. There is a plaque on the side of the monastery. It says, "This is the year of our Lord, nine hundred A.D. The monks in this monastery have taken a vow of silence. Should you enter please do not disturb their worship."

He once again looks around. He sees that he doesn't have a pretty good chance of getting down this one road that leads from the monastery, and he can't see anything for miles. It is just bleakness all around him. He knows that he is on one of the highest points in the area and he still can't see any cities, and he can't see any towns. He doesn't see anything that looks like streetlights, or cars, or highways, or roads. He is filled with an intense fear. So, he says to himself, "Well, it's a monastery. I should go inside and ask if I can get directions home."

He knows that the monks have taken a vow of silence, but he is hoping that there is someone there who will speak to him. He enters the archway. Now he is in the actual monastery. He is still confused and very disoriented because he does have a lump on the back of his head that is bleeding. He has a slight concussion. But even if he didn't have those things, he would be confused and disoriented. He is walking down the hall. Somehow, he knows he is looking for something, but he doesn't exactly what it is he is looking for. He knows that he should go down to the end of the hall. He is being drawn to the end of the hall. At the end of the hall is a light. Hooded figures are walking past him in twos and threes with bowed heads. They are walking past him as if he is not there. He is drawn to the only room where there seems to be any kind of activity. He begins to walk toward the light.

When he reaches that room, there are several people kneeling. They are all clothed similarly in that they are hooded. As he enters the door, there is a monk by that door, there is a monk in the corner to the left of the door, and there is a monk in the corner to the right of the door. The corner immediately opposite the door is empty. There appears to be thirty to thirty-five figures kneeling in the direction of that empty corner, all clothed in this attire. He can't see any hands, or any faces, or anything. He looks around to see if there is anyone else that he can possibly talk to. Somehow, he knows he is in a monastery, they have taken a vow of silence, and they are not going to talk to him. He also believes that there should be no hostility generated here, after all he is in a monastery.

He walks further around the assembly to get into the center of the room to where attention is directed, which is the empty corner. He notices that there is nothing in the room to indicate any kind of a religion, no signs of anything, no crosses, no statues of any kind. He walks to the empty corner and asks out in very low reverent tones (he has been a Catholic man and he knows that he should be respectful in these situations), and says, "Please excuse me, sirs, but I'm lost, and I would like to know where I am." Again, he is ignored. He says, "Please talk to me. I'd like to know where I am. I need to know how to get home. Would you please look up and give me your attention? I know that you're not supposed to speak, but I don't know how I got here."

The monks answer him without looking up, almost in unison, and almost with a beauty to their voices as if in chorus. They ask him, "You would like to speak with us?"

He says, "Yes. Yes. Please. I'd like to speak with you. I need to know how to get home."

They ask him once again, "You want to talk with us?" He is thinking, my God, how could they say this in almost choir like tones, it is so beautiful.

They say, "All right. This we will permit. This will be permitted. You understand that this is a monastery where we have taken a vow of silence. But since you want to speak with us, since you want our attention, we will give it to you."

At this point, they all stand, once again in unison, and throw off their robes. They all appear to be male, or some form of male. They are horrible in the sense that they either have fangs, they are severely discolored, black and blue marks, moles, half werewolf, jackals, just your worst possible nightmare. Some were just plain vampires with fangs and claws. Some had hands that are extending, seemingly to him, out into eternity. They start coming toward him, though the movement they are making is imperceptible.

He backs up against the wall. The voices still have not changed. They are still in unison, and they say to him, "We will speak with you now." He still is backing into that corner. It is the most horrible aspiration that he has ever seen in his life. As he backs into the corner, the wall starts to part. It is not a trap door. It is not a fake door. The wall starts to part. There is a place in there for him. He backs into it. He is grateful. It starts to prick itself up, and once again he is grateful because he no longer must look at this horrible aspiration.

In the meantime, he is having a heart attack. He is suffocating while he is having his heart attack. Once again, he is grateful. The monks put their robes back on and they resume their position.

David and Charlotte are keeping each other together. They are trying to make sure that each other are all right. David has her in his arms. He is holding her as tightly as he can. He is very much aware that she is not fully clothed. The first thing that he wants to do is to put some clothing on her because he has some sensitivity to someone who has almost been a victim of a rape. Neither one of them can tell what time frame it is relative to what happened. The nanny is coming through the door. She summed up the situation, so she decides to get a doctor. Charlotte is equally as concerned about David as David is about Charlotte. Charlotte is angrily saying, "It is my house! This man has come into my house!" David was expecting her to cry, but that didn't happen yet. She was still very angry. She just sat on the bed and kind of leaned back and forth saying, "This is my house! He has come into my house! He was trying to kill me! He has come into my house!"

The doctor decides that they both should be sedated. David has some very serious bruises and contusions which the doctor must also investigate. He sedates Charlotte. The nanny promises to lock her French doors and to sit by her bedside until morning or whenever she awakes from her sleep. They decide that David could spend the night in another room. The doctor takes David into the other room where the nanny has already laid out clothing for him, clothing that belonged to Charlotte's father. The doctor bandages him up. He suspects, if he is lucky, he may only have a few broken ribs. He is asking him if he could breathe.

David said that he hasn't noticed until now, but he is having a little bit of difficulty breathing. He adds that he doesn't know if it is just because he rushed so hard to get here, or just the tension of the situation. The doctor says, "What situation? What exactly happened here? I'm not sure."

David realizes that he can't explain to the doctor, who was a local Mendocino resident, what he has just witnessed. He hasn't had time to talk to Charlotte about it himself, so he must lie. He must make up a very fast lie. He says he was attacked somewhere, and he is not sure, but somehow, he thought that he should get to Charlotte because of the previous problems that Charlotte has had. The doctor wants to know if the police should be called, if he could describe his attacker, and if he knows anything about his attacker. David says, "No. I have no idea."

The doctor says, "Well, do you think it was associated with what happened before? I think we should call the police."

He says, "No. It was probably just someone trying to rob me because I am missing my wallet, and when I wasn't such an easy person to rob, they decided to beat me up. But in the back of my mind, I guess initially it didn't seem that way to me, and now that I've had time to think about it and time to be more reasonable about it, actually someone was probably just trying to rob me and there was no association with Charlotte."

The doctor notices that Charlotte's gown has been ripped, and he knows that she is equally upset. He knows that he is not going to be able to get any more out of David, and David has deliberately chosen to lie about some fight he has gotten into. He knows that he hasn't gotten into this fight. He assumes that he was somehow protecting her, and for whatever reason he has chosen to tell this lie. Being the family doctor, he accepts it and tells David the most important thing he could do is get some rest because he is going to feel bad when he wakes up in the morning. David says, "Yeah, I think that's a pretty good idea too."

One of the servants is sent in to make sure he can find everything that he needs. The doctor also gives him an injection that he thinks will last him at least twenty-four hours. Then he leaves some pain killers with the servant with instructions for both Charlotte and David. He tells David that if he wants to talk about what happened, or if he just wants to call him again, that he should go ahead. He thinks there is more to it than David wants to talk about, but he doesn't want to call David a liar. So, he says, "I'll be available if you need anything, and there will be no questions asked."

David is relieved because he is getting a little groggy since the medicine is working. But he knows that the private detective was in the room, and now he is not in the room. He doesn't know where he is, and he doesn't know if he is alive. These are the last thoughts he is thinking as he falls off into the sedated sleep.

Both David and Charlotte awaken about the same time. David decides that he has got to talk to her. He feels like he can barely get out of bed. He knows that most of the bleeding has stopped. He is hoping that there is not going to be too much scarring. Fortunately, the punches that the private detective threw didn't land near his face. Though he has got to talk to Charlotte because this is a new element. He hasn't seen any of this from her before. He knows that she did it, and he knows that she did it consciously. But he is also very concerned about her because he knows once again, he has exposed her to something that she has never had to deal with before. She was always a little bit standoffish, and she didn't permit him to touch her as easily as other girls he knew. He was wondering what effect this would have on that now, not from a sexual point of view, but from a mental point of view. He is very concerned.

He is lying in his room. He is wondering should I call in one of the servants and ask them to let me speak with Mrs. Hampton. He decided that it is better to call in one of the servants. He picks up the phone. He calls in one of the servants. The servant tells him that the mistress of the house, being Charlotte, has suggested that he have some fresh juice and a light breakfast in his room. David thanks him and says, "Please tell her that that is very thoughtful of her.

But is Mrs. Hampton available? I need to see her as soon as possible." The servant said that he'll try to find her.

Mrs. Hampton arrives about the same time as his breakfast does. She tells him, "I don't want to leave Charlotte too long. Charlotte was awake for just a little while, and her first concerns were about you. The servants had told her you were resting quietly. So, she had given those orders about the breakfast and drifted back off to sleep. As far as I know, she is still sleeping." She suggests that he try to eat a little bit. She would wait very quietly until he finished his food, and they could talk.

He found that eating was a little bit painful. His neck muscles were sore, and he was sore around his ribcage. But he didn't think that anything had been broken. He finished a light breakfast which consisted of juice, a boiled egg, some pastries and sliced fresh fruit. It did help. There was also milk on the tray, and that helped too. He asks Mrs. Hampton how soon she thought he would be able to see Charlotte, and what state of mind Charlotte was in now because he knew that last night Charlotte was very angry. Mrs. Hampton says, "She left a message that she'll be available for you tonight. She is looking quite forward to talking to you tonight. She suggests you go back to sleep because the doctor has called this morning. He said that neither one of you would probably be too mobile before evening and if you tried to get up before that you would be too groggy and disoriented, and you might hurt yourselves. So just rest and go back to sleep. Should you awaken again, you're free to call for another meal." With that, she left the room.

David is stirring again. He can hear the ocean very loudly. Someone must have come in and opened his windows. He has windows that open onto the ocean to give him some fresh air. Now it is the sound of that ocean that has awakened him. He tries to jump up, and he realizes that that is just not the best idea. So, he just lays back down and tries to get up a little bit more slowly. He turns his head to notice that the clock says it is about seven-thirty, and there is a note at his bedside which means that the servants have been in his room telling him that they are waiting for dinner for both he and Charlotte. The note mentions that Charlotte has been up since seven, she is dressed, and she is downstairs waiting for him to join her at dinner.

He gets out of bed, and he finds that a bath has been drawn for him, and that other clothing has been laid out. The clothing was older, but it fit him. He soaks in the tub. He is anxious to get to Charlotte, but he knows he can't move any faster than he is moving. The servant knocks on the door and tells him, "Miss Von Shillingsfurst is waiting dinner for you. Not to worry, you need to soak. She knows that you need to relax in the tub. Just take your time. Feel free to use anything in there. She'll be waiting for you downstairs at dinner." David gets dressed after he has a twenty-minute soak in the bathtub. He looks around this room. Once again, he is astonished at how beautiful her house is. He gets dressed. He finds everything he needs, down to razors. He also shaves. He prepares to go downstairs. He doesn't know what he is going to say to her. Then he decided not to be overly anxious about it, just to wait until she starts the conversation.

As he arrives downstairs, it appears that Charlotte is either eating very little, or she has finished what she is going to eat before he has gotten there. He is a little confused because he has been told that she was waiting dinner for him. He proceeds to eat. He finds that he is extremely hungry, but he is very sore. He has never been in a position where he is too sore to eat, but this is the case. She just quietly watches him eat. She doesn't have too much to say. After he finishes dinner, she suggests that they go for a walk along the grounds down by the beach. This, of course, is exactly what he wanted. She sensed that. She also sensed that he feels, once again, responsible.

She starts the conversation by telling him that she was very angry and that she is not sorry about what happened last night.

He says, "Exactly what did happen last night?"

She says, "I'm not quite sure I remember all of it. But I'm not ready to discuss that. I just don't want you to feel too bad about it."

He says, "My primary concern is that you are all right."

She says, "Yes, I am all right. I have no scratches. I have no bruises. I fared a lot better than you did."

He says, "Let me see," and he begins to be a little bit playful. He turns her around because prior to this they were walking side by side. He puts his arms around her, and he pulls her into him so that he can kiss her. She doesn't fight it. She is very gentle with him because she knows that every little thing hurts. As much as he wants to kiss her, every little thing hurts. She decides to put her head on his shoulder and rub his hair back.

He realizes that too much of a squeeze, even from her, will cause him some pain for the next few days, so he is content with that.

They walk along the beach. They talk about how they almost lost one other. She says, "Though I have spent most of my time asleep, in my waking moments all I could think about is that you might not have ever come through that door. Then the private detective would have done what he intended to do which would be to kill. Then there would be someone at my door the next morning to tell me that you are dead."

He says, "I am glad that I wasn't stopped by the police because I was coming at ninety-five to a hundred miles an hour down the road to get to your house, hoping that I could get to you in time. I knew that Robert had planned to kill you." They both indicate that they have obverted that, and they still have each other.

They walk. They talk basically about how two people could attract so much violence in so little time without any good reason. At this point, he bites his tongue because he knows that mentally and physically, she is not ready for the reason that the private detective came to her home, came after her, and came after him. He doesn't want it to be perceived as a justification for what the man has done, what he has done is inexcusable. He thought that he had picked a private detective that was of a higher caliber, and unfortunately, he was wrong. He doesn't voice his thoughts. He is sure that there are some thoughts that she is having that she doesn't voice because this is the very same private detective, he used to lock her in, and it seems that she has forgiven him for that. He feels kind of bad. She knows he feels bad, bad enough that she doesn't have to say you've hired this man, and he has done this, and he has done that.

They walk along the beach and nestle up against each other. They feel the ocean on their faces, and the sand under their feet. They run away from the waves a little bit. They do this for perhaps two or three hours. She suggests that they go in because she knows that he really isn't up to this, even though she knows he wanted some privacy with her, which she was more than willing to permit. Physically, he couldn't withstand this walking much longer, and they still had to turn around and walk back. She suggested that they do that now.

He understood fully why she felt that way. He thought it was a good idea because, even though he had been sleeping most of the day, he was still ready to go back to sleep. He says, "I wonder what it was that doctor gave us."

She says, "I don't know, but I'm sleepy too."

He says, "I could have gone right back to sleep after dinner."

She says, "I felt the same way. Maybe it's best that we do just go in and rest, and you rest. The doctor is going to come back to check and make sure you have no broken bones."

He says, "I don't think I do. I've taken some falls. I played sports when I was younger. I've played football. I don't think I've broken any ribs or any bones, but I do think I'm going to be sore for a couple of days."

The next day, David Sellers gets a call at his home. It is not from the police. The police don't know because he didn't report it. He gets a call from one of his old publishers who says, "You know that private detective that I recommended to you a long time ago? You know, I just read the newspaper and they found him in his apartment. He apparently died of suffocation or cardiac arrest brought on by suffocation, or suffocation brought on by cardiac arrest. It says that he was covered with mortar dust, and they couldn't explain why. I just thought you may have wanted to know that because he is no longer available.

"But they say it must have been natural causes because they couldn't find any signs of foul play, his house was locked, and there were no signs of forced entry. So, if you need a private detective, you can't use that one. I don't know when the last time it was that you used him, but you can't use him anymore." David is horrified. But at least he knows where the body went because up to this point, he had no idea where the private detective was or if he was even alive.

Once again, after dinner they opt for a walk on the beach. It is very calming and very intimate for them. He still has the problem of whether he is going to be blamed, or they are going to be blamed for the murder of the private detective.

It is in both of their minds, but that is not what they discuss. They are walking along the beach, and they are talking. He tells her, "I still haven't changed my mind. I still want to marry you. It is even more important that I marry you. I feel like I'm losing you. I feel like I have no influence over you, I have no say over you. You are doing things that humans do not do. How far is this going to go? How far are you going to let this go? Does this bother you at all? I understand that you were in a position where you had to defend yourself, but I'm still not happy with what I saw. I don't know where the line will be drawn, and I don't know if you know how to draw the line."

She really doesn't want to think about it because she is very angry. She is furious, somebody has come in her room and has attempted to do this thing to her. The number one issue on her mind is she was almost dead again and not almost dead outside her house, but almost dead inside her house. She is not happy with that, and she is not going to let that go. That was why she sent him into the wall. She doesn't know how she was able to send him into the wall, or what would make him go into the wall, but she is not sorry that he went. And if he should happen to be dead, she's not sorry about that either.

She just wants him to leave her alone. She wants everyone to leave her alone. And if he loves her, if he understands her, and if he wants to be with her then he is going to have to take that point of view. This pattern of thought is forcefully put behind a mask of calm as she waits to see how he will approach this. Will this, once again, be an attack on herself or her family? Or will he simply pour out more guilt and concern? Either way, she knows how she will answer it and hopes that this time it will sink in.

This is how the conversation proceeds. He says, "So far, it doesn't look like the first two murders will come back to haunt us. You had nothing to do that. Since we don't know where the private detective is, we don't even have to think about him again. Otto Weinberger is in kind of a fog, where he probably should be seeking psychiatric care. He may not ever pose a problem, but he won't pose a problem until we can work this out. I'm sorry that that is the case, but that is what it is. Jasper Smythe will just keep decorating the house until it is over. Then the job is finished unless you call on him to suggest someone who will do the maintenance.

"In the meantime, we should get back to you and me and what is happening between you and me. We should start on our wedding plans. Have you ever wondered, or have you any idea if you can have children? I assume you could have children and what these children will be like? Have you thought about that?"

She says that she always wished she could have had a family, maybe two or three children. She has been thinking about it more as a possibility since she had accepted his proposal of marriage. She has some idea of what will be expected of the children, but she really doesn't want to talk about it. All she will say to him is if he is going to marry her, he has got to be loyal to her family. She believes that he understands very well why.

They walk and talk. They are getting closer and closer than they have ever been. The sun begins to rise. She says, "Well, it is time for us to go asleep. We have been up all night." Both Charlotte and David return to their rooms after their walk on the beach. Though they have a lot on their minds, they are tired. They both go to sleep for about eight hours. When she awakens, she lets it be known that she is not ready to face David. She lets this be known to her nanny and her servants who have been up and about since six o'clock that morning. She plans to take a long restful bath to give herself some time to think. There are a lot of questions that she has that she doesn't know the answers to.

While Charlotte is taking a very long leisurely bubble bath drawn by her nanny, she is thinking. There are a lot of questions in her mind, a lot of confusion, and a lot of very basic fear. She has two fears. One for her own personal safety, and the other is fear of the intervention that she is aware of. This time, she saw the interventions that came on her behalf. That is upsetting to her. Though she must be happy that it occurred, it still was out of her control. A lot of things happened that night that were out of her control. She does not know how far she will have to go to maintain her life. She doesn't know if she will have to need immortality just to live a normal life span with the kind of pressures that are being put on her right now. Because she does know what a vampire is, she has some idea what she would need to do to protect herself. How long will they keep intervening on her behalf? She has been painting about it and visiting with them, but it is still not a concrete idea in her mind. She doesn't know what she is going to have to do to stay alive, but she is sure that it is going to be, at the very least, abnormal. She has a pretty good idea that she may not like it. She knows she has only glimpsed what they can do. David put some very fair and logical questions to her, and he does deserve an answer.

She is very pleased. She is aware that he is in another room of the house. She is very pleased that her potential husband is in another room in the house resting, she hopes, and waiting for her to come out and talk to him again. But she doesn't have any real answers. She is going to have to go and tell him once again she is going to have to buy some time.

She realizes that communication has been permitted with these people who appear to be related to her and concerned about her, but they seem to always initiate the communication. She is not sure if she could ask some of these questions on her own. She is not sure that she could put herself into a position to ask them if she could call them when she wants to talk to them. She wants to tell them what she wants to know, get answers about what they want from her and where this will go. So, she is very frustrated.

She feels very helpless in a lot of ways, and it is very easy to not think about any of it and just let David handle it. But she knows, or at least she thinks she knows, that the way David is going to handle it is going to be to keep pressing her about things that she is not clear on. She decides to rest her mind. It is easier to think about wedding plans. She begins to think about what kind of wedding she would like, where she would like to have it, the guests that she would like to invite, and the guests that she knows will be present whether she invites them or not. Then she begins to wonder if David has any good friends and who he is going to invite. She knows he has parents and wonders if she will meet them. Her mind goes on a very normal train of thought. If they had children, would they look like David? Will they look like her? Will she have a boy first? Will she have a girl first? Will he be content to stay at her ancestral home and raise a family here? He is somewhat of a wandering type of man, though she doesn't question his loyalty to her. Will he be able to really settle down here? Is it clear to him he has got to be quiet about whatever is going on and whatever they are to learn in the future, and he is as much a part of it as she is? If he is not clear about that, then she knows that she cannot marry him.

David, on the other hand, has showered and has had brunch. He is walking around the grounds. He has decided that it is time to tell her what he found in the crypt because she is not addressing the issue. He has never used the term vampire in front of her. He is getting no guidance from the psychiatrist or anyone else as to what could happen if he pushes it too far. But he thinks he had better let her know this information so they could have some more in-depth conversation. He thinks maybe it will bring something out of her that she has forgotten or doesn't remember, or at least the reality, or what he feels is reality. He must deal with it every day, and he wants her to deal with it every day. It seems like her life has been pretty much a fairy tale, except for losing her parents, until the murders happened. He knows she hasn't really seen what the dark side of her family does, though she is painting it. It's not affecting her the way it should. She is horrified. He is not even sure that she is fully aware of it or that she understands that it is directly connected to her, and even possibly she could fully become one of these things and enjoy it. He must break through her façade.

He decides that he will at least bring up the subject to her when she chooses to speak to him again. She has promised that it would be later that evening. He is going to go back and do basic research in the library of vampirism because he doesn't know much about it, except for the movies that he had seen as a child. He knows that she must have seen those same movies. So, he knows conceptually that she must have the idea of vampires, werewolves, and creatures from the black lagoon. But he is not even sure that what he has seen and read before as a child and as a young adult are even accurate. What he has been witnessing here, once again, does not follow any of the normal story lines and stereotypes that he has seen before. He has lost an acquaintance that he liked, and thought was reasonably decent. He is not very happy about that, but he couldn't stop it. He realizes that the man had attempted to kill him. So, he could also see the justification in his mind for trying to kill him.

He is mixed up. He does not want to see another murder happen. He doesn't know how much control she has of herself now that he has seen her do some things. He doesn't know how much control these other people have who seem to always be there. He is not sure if they are ghosts, but he knows that he has seen them. He knows that they are not dead and buried like her parents are. So, he is pretty sure that they are not her parents. But he doesn't know who they are. But he did see them act on her behalf when they needed to help her and when he couldn't have helped her.

He has quite a bit to think about. He decides that he is going to take out a horse. He goes horseback riding, walking around the beach, mulling everything repeatedly in his mind, what he knows. It still has not occurred to him that if she should become a full practicing vampire, if she's not already, that she is going to need a source of blood. It also still has not occurred to him that he might actually no longer be human from associating with her, that he might be one of her victims or he might be one of the victims of these other entities, even though he feels that she will not permit him to die. He has a good understanding now that there might be some things that are worse than death. He is taking the point of view that whatever else there is here to offer would almost be worse than death. But he is not sure that she is looking at it that way.

So, he returns to the house. He is at another end. He showers and changes back into his clothes. He doesn't want to go back to his apartment because he doesn't know if there is any kind of investigation going on around this missing person. He is glad that she is still letting him come in because one day to the next she changes her mind. Sometimes she decides that she doesn't want to see him for two or three weeks. He thinks that he had better stay near her to protect her. He is sure that she is going to be at dinner. He knows that he shouldn't talk about it at dinner because he knows that most of the servants are local people.

They have a normal dinner, and they have small talk. They make small talk at dinner as they normally do. He makes small talk with the nanny because he has the depth of perception to understand that the nanny appears to be only a nanny and that the nanny is loyal to Charlotte. He needs that. He doesn't want to do anything to interrupt that. That is his one ace in the hole. He understands that the nanny also has known Charlotte longer than anybody, and if anyone should start to get the least bit suspicious, they take one look at the nanny and it all seems ridiculous. She is always so practical or commonplace or trustworthy, just a good homebody. This is to the good and knows better than to suggest differently. It might mean at the very least a more difficult way of life and maybe even death for he and Charlotte.

He and Charlotte make small talk at the table. There are a lot of undercurrents. He complains that she is on the defensive, she is on the defensive about herself, and she is on the defensive about her family. He hasn't even told her about the claws. There is an edge to her voice and an edge to everything he says, but he can also tell that there is a lot more depth of feeling now that is coming through. He feels more comfortable in saying things to her and even telling her things that she should do and things that she shouldn't do. Before he felt that if he showed her this, she might just tell him to leave. He feels more in command and more in control.

So, once again, he suggests that they take their sherry out on the veranda, walk around the lawn, and look at some of the work Jasper Smythe has been doing.

She agrees, even though she knows that he wants to talk, and he wants to talk about a subject that she cannot fully participate in. She is not happy that she can't participate in it because she is not the kind of person who is usually at a loss for words. But she also doesn't want to engage in an argument where she is not fully informed. She is going to go along with this, but she is going to try to hedge the conversation. He starts off by asking her, again, how she slept, how she felt about the attack, and has it changed her feelings toward him. He just comes at her from a very sensitive to an attempted rape point of view.

He doesn't try to make any physical or intimate contact. He then opens a subject that she can't emotionally let flow. He says that he senses that she is horrified, she is terrified, she feels helpless. He says he doesn't know how the private detective could have such nerve to do this. Why in the world would he want to do this? He asks everything but where in the world did the private detective go?

She blushes. She cries. She has emotions about what happened to her in her house. This goes on for about forty-five minutes. He says, "I know that it is going to take you some time to get over that, but I would like to stay close enough to you to make sure that it doesn't happen again. Though I'm not trying to shed my period of engagement or rush our engagement, but we haven't set a date yet. Have you thought about that?"

Once again, that is another subject that is very pleasant to her. She says, "Oh yes, I have been thinking about that. Thinking about it makes me very happy. Making plans makes me very happy. I was wondering if you have friends. I have never met any of your friends. You seem to be quite a loner. I have never met any of your relatives. I'm not even sure I know exactly where you come from and where you were raised. You know every little bit about me." So, they have a conversation on his background.

He tells her, "I came from a family that was middle class. I have brothers and sisters. My sisters are married, and each of them have two or three kids. They are married to people who are very upper middle class and have not done anything particularly significant. My brothers, on the other hand, seem a little bit more aggressive. Maybe it is because it is a male world. They have done a little bit better. Most of them have a sizable net worth. Every now and then, we get together, Christmas or other holidays, and talk. Or we will call each other up and help each other out. We are all in different fields. I was raised on the northeast coast, almost near Canada. I'm used to big city ways of doing things. I'm also very used to a rural setting. I could feel very comfortable making this our home. As far as my feelings on photography go, I'm sure that I can make my trips as long or as short as both of us would agree upon, or often times you might even decide that you want to go with me. That is one of the reasons that I picked this occupation. I like to have freedom."

All of this is, again, small talk. David doesn't realize that this is very important information, and they haven't bothered to get to it prior to now.

Although this is really what they should be discussing, it is still small talk. They continue it.

He says that a wedding in the spring is usually traditional. He asks her if that is what she wants, and will that give her time to get her things ready? Of course, she is more than willing to pay for it because traditionally the bride's parents pay for it. She asks him if he would like to have the wedding at the house. He avoids the subject of asking her about her religious commitment. He tells her that they could probably just go to a justice of the peace, have a nice ceremony, and a nice reception afterwards.

They talk about that for a while. Then he tells her, "I want you to sit down."

They are away from the house now. They sit on one of the benches made of nice heavy redwood, very well carved and stained. Jasper Smythe added it to the landscaping. "I want to talk to you because I have done something that I know is going to make you unhappy. You should know it now before we get married. And we need to talk about it for a lot of other reasons. But it won't keep me from marrying you." He tells her that he had found her parents' crypt and exhumed their bodies. She is horrified.

He tells her about the transformation that took place as accurately as he can, trying to cover as much of his revulsion which is still very present. He was also trying to hide his fear of what happened, what he saw about her parents, this is a reality. He tells her about the analysis from the veterinary report. He tells her also that he knows this is what stalked the attack with the private detective, but at this point, he did not know what happened to the private detective. He says that her parents must have been, from what he could understand, fully practicing vampires with the ability to shift shapes.

This is a mouthful. Everything is still. Everything is quiet. They have full concentration on this subject. It is really the first time that she has let the words formulate in her mind. It is not that she doesn't want to hear it. She would like, maybe, to feel the force of his words. Her first defense is, "Well, you don't know my people, you don't know my family. I don't know what you happened to have found. But all I can say is that you don't know any of us. I am a product of whatever they are." His response to that is, "In some ways, I don't know what you know. But in other ways, I know a lot more than you do and a lot more than you are willing to face. I think that you are uncomfortable because you don't know where this is going, and you don't know what happened in your bedroom that night. Though you realize that you did it, you don't know how you were able to do that. I think you are terrified."

She admits to this. She admits that she is terrified. She admits that she doesn't know what happened to her in the bedroom. She doesn't know how she was able to throw a man across the room without touching him, by wishing that it would happen. She realizes that the thought was in her mind. She can communicate that to him. He thinks that at least it is a good start. This is something that she desired to do, she wanted to do, she thought about doing, and it happened.

He tries to get her to tell him of some other times when she was able to think about something and it happened. She says that she has never been in this position before, she knows of no other time. He says to her, "You have been in a position before because two men were murdered less than six months ago, horribly murdered."

Once again, she is on the defensive. By this time, she is crying because she remembers what they look like, and she doesn't want to be accused of having attacked someone like that and leaving them it that position. She also knows she doesn't know what condition the private detective was in because they can't even find him. So, he must back off. She is crying uncontrollably. She is beginning to shake. He is trying to calm her down long enough to get her to the house. He is hoping that she can go to sleep tonight.

He tells her, "You know we have got to talk about this. I'm sorry that I have pushed it this far. You know that I've done the best that I can with this situation. I love you. I don't mean any harm. I must do this. We both must do this. We will have to talk about it again. It is enough for tonight. Was there anything else that you wanted to do tonight?"

She says she doesn't want to do anything else, she is not in condition, and she just wants to go to sleep. He says, "Fine. Okay. Do you still have the medication that the doctor put you on to sedate you?" She says she does. He suggests that she take it so she will truly go to sleep.

He has explained to her that he thinks that he should keep somewhat of a low profile, though he has been in contact with most of the people whom he freelances with. He explains that he doesn't know if the person is dead or where he is, and he doesn't know if this is going to be written off. He knows of the obvious connection to both, and he is not quite ready to be picked up by the police until he has gotten his story better together. Once again, he is afraid that he is going to have approach Otto Weinberger, but he will not tell him what happened because he is not going to incriminate himself if he doesn't have to. He is going to try to see what he can get out of him, and tomorrow, during the daytime, he will spend his time at the library trying to learn a little bit more about it.

At that point, she interrupts him and says, "Oh, about the animals, okay, you go to the library and you learn about the animals." She walks away and goes into the house, into her room, and gets ready for bed. He also goes into the house and proceeds to get ready for bed. Her family, once again, is aware that she is pretty shaken up. They begin their telepathic communications. They have decided that it is probably not a good idea to materialize. Again, they have a discourse with her as she is getting ready for bed. It takes place, as described before, in such a way that it is almost as if you are talking to yourself. They are suggesting ideas to her. They are making it very plain to her that these ideas are not coming from herself, that she is not generating these ideas.

They are saying things that they believe will her help her reason and will help her calm down. Together they are concluding, because they are so close to her thought patterns and her emotions, that she still is wondering if she is sane and if this communication is taking place. In the past, she has not had time to wonder this. They have also acted at a time when the situation was life threatening. All she had to think about was would she survive. Now she is wondering if she can initiate a conversation with people that she knows are long dead and who have simply told her they are her ancestors. She is wondering if any of this is reality. As she starts to wonder this, her mind begins to take on a spiral. They are perceptive of this, and they stop it. They begin to remind her that everything that has occurred to her is real. It is reality as they have learned to perceived it, and it is the reality that she is going to have to maintain. They also remind her that they have attempted to slowly bring her to these conclusions by having her paint early on in life, and that they can bring back to her full conscious memory the dreams she had that produced these paintings. They would rather not because some of these dreams are both painful to them and would be terrifying or horrifying to her. They hope she will just take on face value that she is sane and that her conversation with them is sane so that they can get on from this point to what it is they must tell her.

What it is that she needs to know is that they have been protecting her life, and that they will continue to protect her life.

They go on to tell her that she has incurred more disharmony in her everyday life because of this unforeseen threat of this contract murder, and up until then she was also sheltered, and she was not in a position where they would have to act out in the open. Had it been their choice, they would have never acted out in the open. They would have slowly brought her along to where they hope she is now and that is to know her choices and to know what their hopes are for her, but to also be aware that she always will have a choice to decide what she wants to do and what she does not want to do.

But they are also saying things to her that are coming from their point of view, "Yes you are a vampire. You have no immortality which is why we've had to guard your life because you have not taken any blood. You have not taken blood in any form. You have not chosen your own victim. Your parents have chosen victims many times in the past. Your parents have the full extent of their power. They weren't much older than thirty years old when they died." They begin to explain to her that when she has children they will be in a state of mortality or they may be in a state of immortality, and those children will still have free will just as she did. Those children though, they could pretty much guarantee they will be a reincarnation of one of her ancestors. Unlike herself, they will be born with full knowledge that they possessed in their prior life, whichever one it happened to be. They still will be under her guidance as a child and depending on her influence and depending on their free will, they will also have a choice to make that she still must make. No one can interrupt that.

This is one of the reasons she is so important to them. But they love all their family members. Her part of the family came here to try to continue the line. Her mother and father were vampires, live vampires, who had not been killed in the accepted vampire manner. They possessed a certain kind of limited immortality. When they died in the car crash that was one of the ways that they could be killed, and that is how they lost their life. If they had not died in the car crash, they would have been in the same form as she. They could have taken any age at any time they wanted to. If questions started to arise, they had learned ways to camouflage the fact that they were not dying. These are all the ways that they are ready to teach her, ways that will seem second nature to her, ways that will be almost first nature to her children, whether they choose to use them or not.

She is not at all alarmed that she has knowledge now that any child she carries will be one of her relatives and that any child she carries will arrive with probably telepathic, telekinetic and powers like immortality and shifting of shapes. In fact, she almost welcomes the company because she realizes that she is the only one here like herself.

She asks them if there is another branch of the family where there are still some remains, maybe somewhere in Europe or in another continent. They tell her that they are not ready to let her know this information because there are a lot of choices that she has not made that affect her, and if she knows every last thing about someone else then she could also endanger them. They tell her that it is possible that there are several segmented branches left and it is possible that it is only her. At any rate, they would not harm David and they will guard David as they guard her if she chooses him as a mate. They make it clear that they sanction the union, and they will be present at any form of at a ceremony that takes place.

They also discuss with her the fact that she has no obvious religious preference. She never has had one, and that David is aware there isn't one. They wanted her to understand that she could continue this tradition throughout her marriage and throughout her life, or she could attempt to break this tradition at which point they don't know what would happen to her. They are not sure how they would be able to protect her, and they are not sure that she would be able to protect herself.

They tell her that this is enough for their little girl to learn in one evening, that they admire her, and that they want to be able to give her the strength and pride of their generation because she does carry a very heavy load. They explain to her that there is nothing that they can do but be there, and also be there to protect her until she makes up her mind. They will never try to remove her free will from her, though they have the ability, they would never try to remove her free will from her. They make it clear to her that they will not choose a mate for her, they will never make her do anything that she does not want to do. They can do anything that they want to do and that is one of the reasons that they exist in that lifestyle.

Neither of them brings up the topic of the victims. One of the reasons that she is not so anxious to is because every victim that it has occurred to so far has been trying to kill her. She is not ready to even consider that she might have to go out and kill unnecessarily to support a physical need. She goes to sleep. They aid her in her sleep so that she has a sleep that is untroubled and completely restful.

David, on the other hand, is pacing the floor. He has said a lot of things that he is not exactly sure want they mean. He knows that anything he finds in the library will probably not be from anyone who has encountered a vampire. He is not sure that it is a good idea to come at her with all this information. But he doesn't know what else to do. He loves her, but he doesn't know if he loves anybody enough to become something that isn't human. He doesn't know if he will have a choice at some point. It looks like now and as far as he can see down the horizon, he will always have a choice, but at some point, he doesn't know, he may not have that choice. He is horrified with that thought. He would like to be able to think that his strength, will, his love for her, and the normalcy will keep her in a normal lifestyle. His backup for that is that she has lived one for thirty-one years.

The nanny managed it through without any problems, and that if these people would just leave them alone, maybe this sort of thing wouldn't have to keep coming up. He thinks that it is because he doesn't understand about the need for reincarnation. He thinks that her ancestors, if that is who these people are, would like to see her survive, and that they can do it. How they got it is their own cross to bear.

He doesn't understand yet that they have a use for him. This will be the thing in a few days, maybe a week, that Otto Weinberger will have enough nerve to tell him, but he won't be sure that he is right. Right now, David Sellers thinks. She has been on an even keel so far. We just had a run of bad luck, and a lot of that is my fault. She could stay out here where things are relatively calm. We have a low crime rate, so she won't have any problems. And if it looks like there is something that I could take care of I'm sure we won't have any more of these interactions. Besides, the fact that a lot of people have ESP and maybe it is not something that I should frown on. Maybe that is a very arcane way of thinking. Maybe I should be a little bit more modern about it and be happy. Maybe that the worst-case scenario would be she could tell me which horse to bet on. I don't know where this can go. Maybe I can take it in a positive direction.

These are all the things that are going through his mind with the information that he has. He also knows that he does need to get back in contact with the people that have employed him every now and then on a freelance basis. He needs to contact them if, for no other reason, than a lengthy absence of more than two or three weeks without notifying someone. He decides that he is going to rest with her for a couple more days, put a few more questions to her, and make sure she is all right. Then he will pay another visit to Otto Weinberger. He is hoping that when he does this, he doesn't set him up as another victim. Instead, he could communicate to him enough information that he won't set himself up as another victim also, and he wants to know if he is all right, and how he is doing. He knows that he won't get anything out of Jasper, who is in and out enough, but Jasper is very closed mouth about how Otto Weinberger is doing. He is just observant, and he does what he needs to do and leaves.

His plans for the rest of the next two weeks are to stay with her in the house two or three days, visit Otto Weinberger, and make some contacts with his publishers. Then maybe he should start talking to his family to let them know that he has found the girl of his dreams and he intends to marry her.

The next night, Charlotte decides that she wants to talk to Yvette. She wants to talk to Yvette basically about her wedding plans, to tell her that David has gone ahead and proposed, and that she expected it because he has been by her side most of the time. This is a special kind of friend that she would want to share this with because of the things they have been through. She must call Yvette late because of the time lapse in France. Charlotte tells Yvette, "I am so lucky. He is so handsome. He is also reasonably wealthy. He is going to be taking me to meet his family soon. And we are very well suited for each other. We rarely argue." Charlotte goes on to say, "He seems to be all consumed with protecting me. He seems to be very concerned with my welfare. All this has happened to us, and we still managed to stay together. In fact, right now he is staying in another room of the house."

Yvette thinks that this is all very wonderful. They just go on about all the different things that had happened to them, present and past, since the last time they talked. Yvette was happy. She says, "I'm very happy to see that you are so much better off than when you were here last time. It's terrible that you were mixed up in all that horrible mess. I'm very happy that you are out of it, that the police aren't bothering you, and you haven't had any more problems."

At this point, Charlotte breaks down. She says, "I have had a few problems, and there are not too many people that I can talk to about it. I really don't even want to have to talk to you about over the phone, but I don't want to run away from this. I don't want to run over to Europe and hide. I want to stay here and stand my ground, deal with my house, my home and the man who is to be my future husband, as long as he is willing to do it."

Yvette wants to know, "What is the nature of your problems?"

She tells her, "Well, things have been happening that are not practical. They are not normal. They are not logical. It seems that I am expressing more of an ESP or a telepathy, or possibly some telekinesis."

Yvette is not the least bit surprised because Yvette was Charlotte's roommate, and there were a lot of things about Charlotte that Yvette was aware of that she never mentioned. She had just put it off as a sensitivity. Yvette could pick up from Charlotte's voice that there was a lot that Charlotte really wanted to say that she couldn't say. She has known Charlotte well enough to know that this was, once again, a crisis or near-crisis situation.

Yvette is thinking now on the other end of the phone. I have got to get to Charlotte, and I have got to get to her about more than her wedding plans. I would love to go over there and talk to her about wedding plans. In fact, I'm going to come well equipped to help her, but I'm also going to bring with me a very good friend of mine who happens to be a parapsychologist. I'm going to talk to David about it. While she is thinking about this, Charlotte is trying not to break down, trying not to cry anymore. She says, "Well, how are you doing now Yvette. What has been happening in your life?"

Yvette goes on with small talk. She says, "I've met this man, and he is a very sensitive man. We spend a lot of time together. He doesn't seem to have an awful lot of money, but he has got a lot of compassion, a lot of depth and a lot of insight. If it is all right with you, I would like to bring him with me. I plan to spend a few months there while we plan your wedding. I would like to meet David's family also."

Charlotte is elated. There is another person here that she can interact with, someone she really trusts, besides the nanny. She says to Yvette, "How do you have the time to spend with me?"

Yvette says, "Well, you know I model when I choose and right now, I'm just not in that frame of mind. I've saved enough money. I have a few investments. I had been settling in talking to him. We had been developing kind of a relationship, and he has been demanding more of my time. His name is Robaire."

This is not altogether true because her relationship with Robaire is mostly platonic. She doesn't ever lie or deceive Charlotte, but she wants her to trust Robaire as she trusts Robaire, and she wants Charlotte to trust Robaire as Charlotte trusts Yvette. She is crying, and they laugh. It is almost like finishing school again. She says, "Can I talk to David because the last time I talked to David, I don't know that he got the best impression of me, and now that he is going to be your husband, I sure want him to visit me as frequently as I want you to visit me, and I want to be able to visit you. So, I'd like to smooth over a few things."

Charlotte says, "Sure, he's just in another room. He's in the library. I'll send one of the servants down and ask him to pick up the extension in the library. I'll hang up and give you a little bit of privacy."

She puts David on the phone. David is in the library. David is wondering if there are any books in the library of the family tree. He knows that he would have no such luck because they have gone over this before. He still concludes that a public library is no place for him because he is sure that the authors of the books in the public library have never encountered a vampire. He picks up the phone. It is Yvette. Yvette is gushing because she is still carrying on this act that she had with Charlotte. She wants to make sure that Charlotte is off the extension.

Charlotte hangs up because Charlotte knows that most things that go on in the house she will find out about anyway. She is basically an honest person, so she hangs up. There is no reason for her to suspect that anything will be said between David and Yvette, other than what Yvette has told her. She is mussing over Robaire and the fact that possibly he could play a part in the wedding, or maybe they will be so close by the time they get here that they will have a double wedding.

She goes off to occupy herself with other plans, the art gallery, tomorrow night's dinner, and the wedding. Yvette gets straight to the facts. She says, "I just finished talking to Charlotte and things have gotten considerably worse than the last time I saw her. But they're worse in a different way. There's one other thing that I didn't really tell you. Because so much was going on, I did not want to detract from Charlotte's credibility. But being Charlotte's roommate for as long as I have been, I have always suspected that Charlotte was a little paranormal. She always functions. She was very practical and very logical, so there was really no need to bring it up. But she has had a sixth sense about a lot of things. We used to laugh at it and play it off. But in talking to her, something very wrong has happened there. It happened more than the one time that I know about.

"Since the one time I know about, I've happened to have run across an old acquaintance who is now, possibly even then, involved in parapsychology. His name is Robaire. I have told Charlotte that we have a relationship. I had told Charlotte because Charlotte invited me to come out early and help her with the wedding. She is very excited about the wedding, and she has asked me to come out and help her with the wedding plans. She wants me to participate in the wedding. I told her that I would be bringing an intimate friend, Robaire.

"Robaire is very close to me, but we are platonic. He's a parapsychologist, as I've said before, and I think this is a way to go with Charlotte. I think we should do this as soon as possible. He is a very sensitive person. He is a very intense person, and he is a very private person. He will know to keep his mouth shut. David, I wanted to talk to you about this, and I want it to stay between you and me. I don't want to deceive Charlotte, but there are things that sometimes friends have to do."

David, on the one hand, is very happy about this because he was at a loss and was kind of embarrassed because he is man. He is supposed to be able to answer most of the things. He has done all these different things right, besides the fact that love conquers all. He really does love her, and he knows that she loves him. It is just not fair. So, when Yvette calls with this new proposition he says, "I'm elated to hear from you. I am happy to hear from you for a lot of reasons. I am glad you are all right. I am glad that Charlotte wants to communicate with you. I'm happy that you have some knowledge of this happening because the nanny seems to be oblivious to this, on any scale, even on a lower keyed scale that I've seen it happen on. I won't explain to you what I have seen until you get here. But the thing that I caution you on is that as far as I know there are at least two people dead, and there is one person that we don't even know where he is. I know that Charlotte was directly involved in that and that was paranormal, if that is the term that you use."

Yvette says, "Don't worry about the terms. I have picked up a lot of different terms hanging around Robaire. All I wanted to do was bring in someone that I think is sensitive to the situation who will not hurt her in any way."

David says, "Well, I would love to have him come and help me because I need all the help that I can get. The person who is missing is my private detective." Because he feels like he can talk to her openly, and although it puts both him and Charlotte in a position of suspicion, he says to her, "I don't know if the man is dead or alive. I don't know where the man is. The other help we had, the volunteer help, Mr. Weinberger, has been so terrified by something he didn't want to answer his phone. He doesn't want to receive visitors. The architect still goes to visit, and that's the only contact we have with him. He is not in school. He had taken a sabbatical earlier to go into the Carpathians to find out more about Charlotte's family, which he did, and he relayed the information. But something happened to him in the house, and he has almost lost his mind.

"I visit him periodically, but he doesn't seem to be doing too much better, and he does not want to discuss the subject. Every now and then, he gives me bits and pieces or clues that can help me, but not enough, not nearly enough." He tells Yvette, "There is so much that I want to say to you that I cannot say over the phone, and I cannot wait until you get here. The thing is, I wanted to make you aware that I cannot ensure anyone's safety here. I cannot ensure Charlotte's safety. I'm hoping that Charlotte and I are safe. I cannot ensure yours, and I cannot ensure Robaire's."

Yvette says, "I have loved Charlotte for a long time, and we have been really good friends. And she is the best friend that I've ever known. I don't think Charlotte would hurt me. I'm also anxious to get to her to see how she is, to see what she is doing, to see if I can help. Maybe I can simplify this whole thing. I hope it is just something that is blown out of proportion. I want to get there while Charlotte still has some mind left. They agree then that Yvette and Robaire can come to Mendocino under these conditions. He tells her, "I am trying to be as honest with you as possible. You do not know what we have been through."

But there is no keeping Yvette away. Yvette says, "Tonight I will make arrangements to get there as soon as possible. Can you just tell me the nearest airport to fly in to and have someone there to pick us up, have a car for us?"

He suggests San Francisco, "I will have a car there for you that will bring you into Mendocino. It is quite a long drive, but you will have some time to think about it. I would love to be on that long drive with you talking to you about the things that I know, but I don't want to leave Charlotte for that length of time."

She says that she understands. He says, "But there will be plenty of opportunity for us to talk, for you and Charlotte to talk, and for me and Charlotte to talk in private. I want to plan, hopefully, for the future."

Yvette says, "Robaire has some sensitivity himself, but he has some equipment that he uses. I will need a way to get this equipment in the house without Charlotte knowing that it is there. I'm not sure that I will be able to do that, but let's try it anyway."

He says, "Okay. That's all we can do." He wishes her a good flight. He tells her to call back with the information and if he is not there, or if Charlotte is not there, that the servants will handle it, and that she and Robaire would be met at the airport and picked up.

They plan to leave over the next two evenings. So that is taken care of. He says his goodbyes and hangs up.

Charlotte whisks down the stairs. She is happy and unhappy. She is happy that her friend is coming to visit her. She is unhappy because of all the things that have transpired in the past. She has mixed emotions. She gives David this big hug and sits down in front of the fireplace that is going in the library. She tells him that they will have another couple that they can go out with, they can double date with. This is something that she and Yvette used to do when they were in school. She is happy about Yvette's expected arrival.

Charlotte tells David, "Yvette has promised to bring me samples of cloth and designs from Paris for my wedding dress and for the bridesmaids' dresses. I am very excited about that. There will be someone that I know. She will probably handle the wedding dress, the bridle dresses, maybe the whole scene. I am going to talk to Mr. Smythe about arranging a special area on the grounds to conduct the ceremony. I think he is right that the spring season is a good time of year. If we put the right trellis overhead, then even if it decided to rain, we could have a beautiful wedding."

They talk about the wedding. She refuses to let her mind go on any of these other sorts of things. He, on the other hand, is thinking that he should get to Otto Weinberger as soon as possible to tell him that this parapsychologist is coming. He wants to contact him make sure he is all right, and to see if this can be of some use in this situation. But, once again, he does not want to reveal anything that will hurt Charlotte. They say their good nights.

The next day he makes a call to one of his bosses who tells him the news about the private detective. Though he now knows he is dead, he now knows there is more danger than he had expected, and it can come from Charlotte. He goes to see Otto Weinberger and leaks all this information out. He has another friend, in the meantime, who checks to see if there are any warrants out for him. As far as his friend can determine, there are no warrants out for him. He is put at ease about that.

He visits Otto Weinberger who lets him in. David tells him, "A parapsychologist is coming. He is a friend of Yvette's in France, Charlotte's friend. He seems to be very aboveboard. I don't know. If he turns out to be a flake, then he won't let him anywhere near Charlotte. But if he turns out to be more, then I'm hoping maybe he can explain the things that have been happening because she has been exhibiting telepathic and telekinetic powers. Otto Weinberger, once again, reiterates that he does not want to be involved, that that this is not unusual, her hearing will probably, get better and her sight will probably get better. This is on the side."

He also says, "I have done some thinking, when I can, about your situation. Your situation being separate from my situation, though they are inevitably entwined. My situation being my physical safety and keeping my sanity, your situation being what could be planned for you and Charlotte if we had found no bodies. The conclusion that I have drawn is that the two of you provide the bodies because you are going to have children, and your children are going to have children. These people seem to have great patience and time on their side, and they live for years and years and years. We have looked for bodies, and there are none to be found. The reason that there are none to be found is because they are already dead. They really are dead. You found Charlotte's parents' bodies because they weren't dead. They were live vampires, and when they burned in the car crash, then they became dead.

"The other people that you are running into are not ghosts. They are not malicious ghosts or ghosts of any kind. They are still vampires. They have been killed in the accepted vampire manner which has limited their mortality. But they have extended their supernatural ability in that they can still communicate with one of their own telepathically and telekinetically and remove her own natural power. I believe, but I don't know for sure, that if she takes a victim, she will attain immortality. I don't know if she has any control over that, or if they are suggesting these things to her. I think that her original statement when the first murders occurred that she saw two men walking toward her with a gun, she saw nothing, and then she saw these people come back dead, is true. And I think the reason it is true is that they are able to bring the victim to them."

He is rambling. He knows they can bring the victims to them, but he does not say from personal experience that he knows that they are able to bring the victims to them. David does not ask him to expand upon it because he also knows from personal experience that a body had disappeared in midair and ended up in another state. He wants to get off that subject because he doesn't even want to slip and tell him that the private detective is missing. He says to him, "So, you say that they want us to go ahead and get married. So that means that they probably won't want to kill me."

He says, "No. They have no plans of killing you. You haven't seen anything. They haven't done anything to you. What they would like you to do is to produce children for them. I believe that what will happen to these children is that these children will be their reincarnates. What I also believe is that Charlotte will go along with it, and something in my mind tells me that you will too."

"That's enough for today, please leave me. I'd like to rest. I'm very tired. I'm being reminded constantly that I'm a much older man than sometimes I would like to believe. I'd like to help you, but right now I need to help myself."

David leaves. As he drives back to Charlotte's house, the words are ringing in his head repeatedly, "They want you to reincarnate. That's why you have not been harmed. Charlotte is fully aware of this, I believe. I'm a much older man than sometimes I would like to believe." He realizes that he has involved a lot of people. Although Otto Weinberger volunteered, a lot of people's lives have gotten tangled in this, and some people haven't walked away from them alive. He has got a sinking feeling in his stomach because now he knows where the private detective is, and he knows that Yvette and her friend are on a plane on the way over. He knows that Otto Weinberger could not handle it.

As he drives up, Jasper Smythe is giving directions to more of the workers. He passes him by, goes into the house, and has lunch. Once again, it is apparent to him that Charlotte is not there. He knows that there is nothing he can do about it. He would like to have Charlotte be there, awake and alert. It is in the daytime, and he would like to pull back the curtains to let the sunshine in. He gets up from the table and turns around. He goes horseback riding to let his frustrations out.

Within the next three days Yvette and Robaire show up. David takes Charlotte for a walk because he knows that Robaire and Yvette are twenty to thirty minutes from the house. The chauffeur that he hired has told him that. He wants Robaire to have a chance to set up his equipment in the house. The vampires are aware of it. The vampires know that this is her friend. They are aware that she does not want her friend harmed and she does not want her friend upset. So, they don't interfere.

He walks her around. By the time they get there, it is twilight. Charlotte talks, and she is excited that Yvette is coming. She can't wait to see the samples that Yvette has brought her because Yvette has always had the better taste of the two of them. She can't wait to see the designs and to imagine that she would be able to wear a Paris line. This is just too much for her. She realizes that this is the best thing that could happen to her, that Yvette would have two or three months to spend with her again and they could just do everything together. It has inspired her to go back to the art gallery. She knows that the wedding plans will take a lot, she has got to get some more bridesmaids, and she is going to have to write back to the school to find out where everyone is. She is just rambling on. It is happy talk, very happy talk. He is smiling, kind of a sad smile. But he is smiling because he is so happy to see her happy.

They return to the house when they had been signaled to by Yvette. They meet Yvette out at the garden just outside the house. Robaire is shortly behind her.

They hug. Everything is just fantastic. Charlotte couldn't be better, and she couldn't be happier. Yvette is here. Robaire is quite handsome. Robaire is very easy to get along with. He is kind of a lowkey person. He is blond. He is six foot three. He is reasonably athletic but not over exerting. He understands that Charlotte has been told that Yvette and he have an intimate relationship, so he hugs Yvette, and he goes along with the whole charade. He is playing it up. He is finding out very well. He has got well-trained eyes. He could see that she has been through a lot, she is worn, she has dark circles under her eyes, she is obviously worried, she is obviously very frantic, and she is just not very much in control of her emotions. The sad thing about it is that David is showing the same symptoms. He decides that he will bide his time and get a chance to talk to both independently.

Charlotte and Yvette decide that it is such a good idea to go shopping and to cook for the men tonight and tell let the servants who normally cook have the night off. Of course, the nanny will stay. This is one of the things that they had talked about sometime while being shown around the house. David wanted to re-establish trust in Charlotte. He wanted her to realize that people could leave the house, she would be aware that people were leaving the house for a perfectly good reason, nothing would happen to her, and she could be in command of it.

So, he suggests she and Yvette go shopping and buy some food. He wants Charlotte to show him that she can cook because so far, he hasn't seen her prepare a meal.

She is sure that Yvette will come up with something that is very French. She is delighted that they can cook together and eat it together. The girls think it is a wonderful idea because it will give them a chance to laugh. So, they take the car into Mendocino. Yvette is trying to get everything out of her that she can while they are driving into Mendocino. She uses her form, her normal sensitivity, and her normal basis as an approach. This also is an accent on some of the things that Robaire has asked her to do. While they are out, David takes Robaire downstairs to show him the paintings on Yvette words that he could be trusted. In the back of his mind, but he hates to admit it, he knows that if he can't be trusted he will be killed. He tries to put it across to him that this is a very dangerous situation before he even takes him down there.

David says, "I would love to give you as much information that I can, as I have. But I do not wish to expose Charlotte to any harm or any public ridicule, and I don't want to be exposed to any myself."

Robaire says to him, "Well, in my line of work, we know that we have to be discreet. Also, in my line of work, if there is another entity involved then there is no person to prosecute. If there is a person who is out of control telepathically or telekinetically, basically people won't believe it anyway. So, once again, there is no person to prosecute. The main thing to do is to find out what is going on and to achieve balance again. You can trust me not to do anything else. If I feel that things are so out of control that I can no longer do this, then I will leave just out of self-preservation. But I will leave without taking any information unless I can send back someone that may better help you."

They have a gentlemen's agreement on that. David shows him all around the house. Robaire's interest is Charlotte's room. He is looking for cold spots. He is looking for any sign that there is an outside interference or a malicious presence.

David asks him, "Do you know of any telepathic powers, or have you had any telekinetic experiences?" He is very low key, low key enough for him to become interested in the subject. David also mentions to him that he noticed that after he went to Europe, the differences in her became stronger and this is one of the reasons he didn't want to go to Europe again. His only explanation for that is that she has had more communications with these other people.

He points out the decorations that she has chosen. He explains to him the history of the house. He explains to him that the decorations were elegant, the drapes tended to be heavy, but now things are such that light will not come in unless you want it there. She has reversed her schedule, she does everything when the sun is down and when the sun comes back up, she is in her room and manages to go to sleep. The parapsychologist asks, "Well, is she eating?"

"Yes, she takes her meals. She takes dinner with meat, and she takes snacks during the night. But everything seems to be somewhat in the reverse. I have chosen not to fight her on this because we started out with the premise that she was a vampire. We suggested to her that she was a vampire, and we went to go on about proving it."

So, he says, "Who is this we?" He explained to him that he didn't know if he understood of Charlotte, if Yvette had filled him in on how he met her and what had happened.

Robaire says, "Yes, Yvette did tell me about that."

David says, "Because of my interest in her, I hired a private detective. The private detective made up part of this group. Also, there is a psychiatrist who had been originally suggested by the police force. We also have a volunteer named Otto Weinberger, who had been brought in by Jasper Smythe. Jasper Smythe is still renovating the house at her directions, but her directions now seem to be toward a more, the only word I can use for it is, grueling, beautiful but gloomy. It is almost surreal. I'm not happy with it because her art gallery, before this began to take place, didn't reflect that. At the point that you and Yvette were called, three people were dead. All three died horribly, and a fourth maybe hopelessly insane."

Robaire interjects with, "Well, let's start with the fourth person. There still seems to be some hope there. You say he may be hopelessly insane. What do you mean?" David goes on to relate what he knows about Otto Weinberger's condition now and how he feels that Otto Weinberger came to be in this state. He explains why it is that he feels Otto Weinberger suggested that he could help in some way, and that Otto Weinberger initially was an uninvolved independent party. Robaire would like to know what he means by an independent party.

David says, "As far as I know, Charlotte and Otto Weinberger had not met before the art gallery opening, and for some reason Otto Weinberger took it upon himself to take an interest in Charlotte."

Robaire notes this as an interesting change, but he wants to hear more. He wants to see more about her room, and he wants to hear more about Otto Weinberger. This is something that David cannot understand. He says, "Well, Charlotte is having these problems, and Charlotte is having these difficulties. You came over here because Yvette is Charlotte's friend. And we all know that Charlotte is really in a bad way."

"Yes, I understand that, but something tells me that Charlotte will come out possibly better than most people think. A person who is really near the edge is Otto Weinberger. Do you know what happened to him?"

David says, "No, I don't. There are a few reasons why I don't. I was being somewhat selfish because I was thinking about Charlotte. Also, because I always thought Otto Weinberger was self-reliant, who could take care of himself and would work it out. Thirdly, because Otto Weinberger refused to talk about it. I don't know if he refused to talk about it because he is embarrassed, he hasn't put it all together in his mind yet, or he cannot talk about it. The thing that I think we ought to do while they are away is visit Otto Weinberger. But I would still like to see her room."

David takes Robaire up to see her room. Charlotte's room is beautiful. It is very feminine. It is a very nice deep spacious room. There is nothing in the room out of the ordinary. Nothing. There are even mirrors in the room. Robaire can't find anything. There is nothing destroyed in her room. There is nothing broken in her room. Everything in her room is in its proper place. The room is rather neat.

He says, "Well, that tells you something, but we won't discuss that. Let's go to see if we can get Mr. Weinberger to open his door. He should talk to us."

They call him ahead of time. He suggested that they come right over and not to go down and look at the paintings yet. They go right over to Otto Weinberger's house. After they check out each other's credentials, and after he is assured by David Sellers that this is someone that he could completely trust, Otto Weinberger tries to fill him in as much as he can up until now. Otto Weinberger explains to him what he could remember, what his mind will let him recollect, "Even though it seems very out of this world, I do have a solution to the murders, how they were allowed to occur, how they happened, and how these vampires can be here yet not be here." He goes on to tell him that he knows from personal experience. He begins to relate the story of her family history, the clan in the Carpathians. When he gets to the murders he reminds him, "Charlotte's story was that two people came after her with a gun, she saw the man, she saw the gun, and the next thing that she knew they were dead and mangled in front of her. Everyone accepted it as just fright, it was a time of black out. She didn't permit hypnotism, and the police couldn't make her go through with it. One reason is that they didn't necessarily believe it enough to force it. The other thing is they couldn't figure out a way where she could have been a victim. No one knows what took place in that time period."

David goes on to tell about the third victim, the one that he witnessed. This is where he thinks Robaire will come in because he knows that Charlotte did that herself. Otto Weinberger intercedes and says, "Well, I beg your pardon, she did half of it. She did throw him into the wall. She did have a panic reaction, if from what you were saying he was attempting to violate her, he had come close to her, I'm surprised that they permitted him even to come that close, but they probably knew she was ready to defend it off. She threw him into the wall. They continued out the thought pattern, her desire.

"Her desire was to see him go into a wall, and he probably did go into a wall somewhere. You say what you saw were four hooded monks standing in each corner of her room. So, you don't know what happened. But you did see figures there that are not normal members of the household. They are the ones who took him that step further. They are the ones who redeposited him in his locked apartment in another state. He probably died of suffocation or a heart attack because he died in a wall."

David Sellers is relieved to know that maybe she didn't mangle the bodies, so maybe she won't mangle his. He is also relieved to know that she didn't finish this out. His is amazed at how she unconsciously gave directions to people who would follow them through to the letter. Otto Weinberger tells his story while he is cautioning him about the paintings. He tells them, "From what I have been thinking, and I have been sitting here thinking, the paintings were their form of communication with one of their own. She was probably almost in a trance-like state when she painted them. That is why when she pulled them out and showed them to David, they seemed so very normal to her. She has been doing them all her life. I went down to look at them, and I attempted to do something that the vampires considered harmful to her. And although David looked at them, nothing happened to him."

He describes the episode where they actually pulled him into the picture, "The picture went from being a static picture to a dynamic picture. I was in another century. I was horrified. I was naked, and there was a sixteen-year-old girl painting me. She was clothing me. Then I had taken on all the feelings, the emotions, the stiffness, and the blood lust of a vampire. I know that when they did that, they were trying to tell me something. I think that I understood it well which is why I haven't been back. I have been spending my time trying to get a grip on my mind. I was, as best as I can describe, in a time warp. There are no bodies to be found. When they kill, they kill by bringing the victims to their century. So, they are still alive because they have been killed, their immortality has been limited. But they have done something that is just unnatural, and they have been permitted to do it for some reasons that I have not ascertained. Although I know the object of it must be reincarnation, and that David and Charlotte must be the object of it, as far as detecting a ghost in the house I wish you luck. I feel they can materialize as wolves. We also noticed that when they are materializing, it is a drain on Charlotte. They have no physical bodies to sustain. They have no need for blood. She, as of this moment, has not demonstrated a need for blood. She must be their energy source, and something else in that house is also their energy source."

At this point, David almost chokes because he knows the relics, he remembers the relics, and he remembers what the relics did for the parents. He knows that the relics must somehow be an energy source, but he doesn't know why, and he doesn't want anyone else to remember that. Once again, Otto Weinberger says, "I've helped you all that I can right now. I know it is difficult for you to understand the position that I am in, but I am trying to keep my sanity. My experience with them was both mentally and physically debilitating to me. It's outside of every rational thing that I know. I have no means of fighting it. I cannot stop it from occurring again. So, I'm in the reverse position that Charlotte is in. I do have a strong instinct for self-preservation, so I will have to ask you to leave again. Please!"

They are very sorry to bother him, but they had come mostly to check on him.

David says, "I came by to see mostly how you are. If there is any person, I can leave with you or get to nurse you or stay with you while you are going through this, please let me know. There will be no charge. We asked Jasper how you are doing, and all he can tell us is that you are doing well, you are doing fine."

Otto says, "He has invited me over for Thanksgiving. I usually go. That should put me somewhat in a different state of mind. I haven't attempted to contact any of my relatives. I don't know where this is going, so I'm just trying to get a good grip on myself right now."

So once again they reiterate that they are sorry. Otto says, "Before you need to be sorry, I got myself into this situation, and I have got to get myself out of this situation. I hope everyone can get out of this situation, at least as well as they came into it. I'm sorry that I'm not any more of a source of information than I am, but I believe you have most of the pieces of the puzzle. You just haven't organized them in a manner that makes sense. I also think that the wedding is a very good idea. I think anything you could do to get closer to Charlotte is a very good idea because, if nothing else, it will force their hand. Then, David, you will know if they are going to hurt you. I think right now you are strong enough that if they try and hurt you, you will know that you need to get out of this."

They leave him and return home. They are sitting around and talking. When the girls walk in, they are talking about ski season and friends. David says, "It would be nice to be on a slope somewhere skiing."

Robaire says, "Yvette and I love to go skiing together. We have now started to consider buying a chalet together." Robaire is saying these half-truths so that Charlotte will overhear it, she will feel more comfortable with him, and she will start to relax.

They cook. The kitchen is all to themselves, and they prepare a beautiful meal. She is hungry. She eats it, she eats all of it. She eats normal portions, and she drinks normal portions of her drinks. David has taken full stock of this because she had cut down to almost nothing, though she wasn't really losing any weight. He thinks this has got to be a good sign because if Yvette could show up and do this then this is wonderful.

After dinner, Charlotte and Yvette go up to her room and look at the designs and the samples of cloth that Yvette has brought from France as suggestions for the bridesmaids, the maid of honor, and the bride's dresses. The men go downstairs. They look at the equipment that Robaire has brought. They turn it on. He has been through the house. He hasn't seen any abnormal things that you would find in a haunting, no cold spots, no spots that generate any unusual energy. He moves further through the house.

Yvette knows that she should keep Charlotte in the room and show her these samples. Charlotte is excited. She is very much occupied with this, and she is happy because this is pretty much what she would have picked. She goes through the designs, and she finds a design that she thinks would look good on her, and she finds a design that she thinks will look good on Yvette which is slightly different. Then they go through which one of their classmates and other people that they met in Europe they are going to ask to be in the wedding. They decide on having six bridesmaids and a maiden of honor, Yvette. They start on the designs. They decide on the people. They make up the list. So, they decide they are going to call them at a decent hour to tell them that she is getting married, and that she has chosen a date. They also need to obtain everyone's measurements and shoe sizes so that they can get the wedding dresses and shoes.

The men are downstairs looking for protoplasm, electroplasm, and anything that would show sign of a haunting. They find none. Robaire is somewhat disillusioned because his own feeling is that there is something in the house, but he can't pick it up. He has understood the warning very well by Otto Weinberger. He wants to stay clear and not do anything that would be perceived as a threat, but he does want to generate some action. He goes over the house and over the house. He can't get anywhere. He is getting rather discouraged. David is watching him, and he is feeling kind of bad because he still hasn't told Robaire about the relics, and he still doesn't want to tell him what he knows about the relics.

It is getting late, and Yvette has stalled Charlotte the longest she can. She decides that it is time for them to take their baths, retire to their various rooms, and go to bed. They all retire for the evening.

During the night, the vampires tell Charlotte what is going on, things that Charlotte cannot sense herself. Charlotte knows that there is more to the situation between Robaire and Yvette, but she doesn't want to believe it because Yvette was the person that she could trust completely. She can trust David completely, she loves David, but it is in a different way. She knows that if David can stop her or alter her plans, he is going to try. She just didn't know about Yvette now. The only way she could see it is Yvette is in cahoots with him.

She is filled in by her relatives that Robaire has machines all over the house, and he is not who he says he is. They communicate to her that Yvette is part of this deception, and so are Otto Weinberger and David. It is the same series of people who had set her up before. They don't think that it will go this far this time, but they want to make her aware of what is going on in her house. They want her to be aware that Yvette is honest and that she did bring the samples for the wedding over, but she had much more in mind. They wanted Charlotte to know that Yvette had telephoned that over to David before she came, and she brought a parapsychologist with her who is trying to quantify, prove or locate any abnormal ability in her and any entities in reference to them.

They do have varied personalities depending on which one she is talking to. These two that are relating this incident to her when she was with in Italy when they were trying to calm her down and they introduced her to several of her relatives. There were some that she favored more than others, and these two females came to talk to her. They think that it is rather amusing at this point, but that it could get out of hand. They are very much worried about her, but they want her to take it somewhat lightly. They want her to try to take things off the cusp because David is doing everything that he can. He has exhausted all possibilities. He, unlike her, cannot talk to them, and he wants her to be a normal human being. They inform her that they will keep informing her because it might become very important very soon, things can take a very quick twist.

When she does arise, and she is dressed, she is furious. She feels betrayed again, and she feels she has been deceived. But she plays it off this time because temper tantrums are not going over very well. She is tired of screaming at David. She does not want to yell at Yvette since Yvette is her friend. She knows that Yvette has come to her out of love. She has decided to approach the parapsychologist.

While Yvette is upstairs waiting for her, she catches the parapsychologist walking around the grounds. Robaire asks her, "How was your night? Did you sleep well? Yvette is very happy to be here, and she is very much interested in the wedding plans." He continues to go on with this drivel. He also told her that he was an engineer, and a lot of times he had projects going that he couldn't stop.

Yvette says she wouldn't mind if he brought some of his equipment with him. She stopped and turned. She coldly says, "This is not true. I don't like you to come in my house and lie to me. I especially don't expect the person, who for most of my life I considered one of my very best friends, to come to my house and lie to me. I know, for one, who you are. know what you are doing. I know why you are here."

He says, "Well, tell me what it is that you know. Let's walk, and let's talk about it."

She tells him, "Your name is Robaire Decarte, and for most of your life you have been a parapsychologist. You do know Yvette very well. You are very good friends, but it's platonic. You are over here simply to find out what is happening with me and my house. I'm not happy with deception. And David was fully informed of why you came over, but no one bothered to ask me or suggest this idea to me. No one thought that I would perhaps be a little bit concerned about things that I was seeing happening in my surroundings."

Robaire goes on to play devil's advocate or somewhat of the innocent. "Well, your surroundings are beautiful. You are having things very well landscaped. You're picking the furniture, the drapes, and everything you want. You are getting married, and you seem to have a beautiful wedding setting. Things on the surface seem very normal. It there anything else you want to talk about?"

She counters with, "You know very well that more has happened here than that. You know very well that I left my home, left my country, went to Europe to talk to Yvette because a series of murders took place here that I had no explanation for. You know very well, at this point, that another murder has taken place that I, in some way, participated in. You are lying to me."

So, he says, "What this proves is either David is very untrustworthy, which I doubt, or someone can give you this information, or you are able to pick it up on your own. Do you mind telling me which?"

She says, "I'm able to pick up a lot of things on my own. I have been fully informed, and it did not come from David. I will take this up with David privately later, as I will take it up with Yvette privately later. You are a stranger in my house, and you are a stranger in my house on Yvette's good graces. I want you to remember that for your own sake, as well as Yvette's and everyone else involved, please do not do anything that will put you in danger." Then she walks off leaving it at that.

The next person she keeps her appointment with is Yvette. She takes Yvette for a long horseback ride. She tells Yvette, "I'm really at my wits end. I'm at my wits end because here I thought you were coming over here to plan my wedding."

Yvette says, "Oh, of course I am."

She says, "Yes, I know that you are, but you also have some ulterior motive. If you thought that I was near the edge and it was more than a psychiatric problem, if you thought that I had some telepathic or telekinetic ability, why didn't you come out and say so? My understanding is you always thought so, you just didn't know to what extent it would go. So, when you had that conversation that you had with David."

Yvette interrupts, "Well, how do you know all of this?"

She says, "I know a lot of things. Just let me finish. When you had the conversation that you had with David, you told him that you knew these things. You could have just as well told me. I am your friend. I introduced you to David. You met David through me."

Yvette is somewhat astounded. She tries to put herself back in a position of trust, but she realizes how hard this is going to be. The only tactic she can take is to say, "I would not bring anyone in your house that would hurt you, that would invade your privacy or make anything that takes place in this house public. We are only here to try to help you. I can see that you are very angry right now, and I think it is a good time for us both to separate because I'm angry too. I may not be able to do anything more about it than yell at you, but I am angry too. I have come a long way to see about a good friend, and if you can't take it any other way, I am very upset. I would like to go to my room to rest." So, she leaves.

Undaunted, Charlotte goes to look for David. David is on the phone with one of his bosses trying to tell him why he can't take this job. It is a really good job, and he would like to take it. He is the person who can do it because he has done this sort of thing before. But he can't take this job right now because he cannot leave. If the job could be postponed maybe five weeks, maybe two months, he would be able to do it right before his wedding; but right now, he cannot leave. His boss says, "Well, I'll get back to you. I realize you freelance. I'll get back to you."

David turns and she is glaring at him as he looks over his shoulder. She is standing in the room. The doors are open. She is coming through the garden. She has obviously been riding. She makes sure that he is out of ear shot of the servants. She lets him know that she knows everything that has happened.

She also tells him, "The thing that bothers me the most about it that I thought that there were things that I could talk to Yvette about that you would never know. Now that relationship is destroyed, and I will never have the kind of trust in her as I did before. Though I don't think Yvette will ever hurt me or anything, it's just that Yvette is talking to you about me and Yvette is my friend. How dare she do that."

He gives her the same thing. "They only have your best interest at heart," and on and on and on.

She finally says, "Wait a minute. Sometimes it's good to talk to me and not at me. I know that a lot of times when you talk to me, I am not responsive, or I'm in a bad mood, or I'm out of control of my emotions. I think you should give me time, and when you give me time you will get good solid answers to a lot of your questions, if those answers are necessary for you to have. There are some answers that are not necessary for you to have, and I suggest that you not pursue them. I don't think I need to explain any more to you than that."

He says to her, "Well, is that a threat?"

She says, "No. That is not a threat. It's just that you brought two people into this house when you know that I cannot be responsible for their safety. Have you considered that?"

He says, "I did, and I had informed them."

She says, "Well, I'm not happy about this situation and I will have to decide what I'm going to do about it. I've talked to Yvette, and I have talked to Robaire. So, I understand the whole charade. But I have got to decide what I am going to do about you bringing these people into my house. I don't know how far he will go. He seems to be a very nice, a very sensitive man. But I've already been filled in about the questions that you brought him here to answer and to ask. That happened two nights ago. So, I'm ready, and I have those answers. As you need to know, I will tell you."

He takes this opportunity to say, "Wait a minute. I've talked to Otto Weinberger. He explained to us that your friends want me for some sort of stud. That's the only way I can put it."

The argument has become heated by their standards. He says, "These are vampires, which we agree. You are a vampire. You need a mate. They want you to procreate, and that's why I haven't seen any of these horrible things happen, except for the one I stumbled up on that you did."

She says, "Well, the only two things that I know happened, had happened when my life was in danger. And you are the cause of my life being in danger in those instances where two people lost their lives." He informs her that the third one had died now, and he has gotten confirmation of that and how he was found.

She says, "Well, a third person has lost his life who was in my room, in my house, trying to kill me. I'm glad whoever was able to stop it could stop it, because otherwise I wouldn't be here to talk to you about it now. If you think that you are being used for any unnatural purpose, and that wedding me or marrying me will put you in this position, then I think you should leave right now and not return."

With that, it was almost over. Charlotte leaves. She goes to her room, and she shuts her door. Of course, she is very upset about it. He is still in the library because he is not ready to leave. He is not going to leave. He will go in his car and drive off or walk around the grounds to cool off, but he realizes what he said to her, and he realizes the only way that she could have taken it. He's hoping that he can defuse the situation and bring it to the point where if she does understand, she will share the answers to the questions with him. If he cannot locate any entities, then Otto Weinberger is right. There are no ghosts, no malicious spirits, nothing here that he can track.

So, he calls in Robaire. Robaire is, of course, not very far. He says, "Yes, I ran in to her too, and she is very angry. If there is going to be any kind of poltergeist activity, it should take place right about now." He says, "I don't even want to think about that. I just would like us to go back to our original wedding plans. I think we should wait a couple of days. We should all stay right where we are, have another private dinner, and let her tell us what it is that we didn't need to find out by bringing you here or through your machines. If she truly knows, and if she wants to share it, she will tell us. At least she owes it to me if she doesn't owe it to anyone else."

Robaire says, "I think that is a good idea. In the meantime, I will pick up what I can on my own. I'll try to not step on her toes because it is her house, and she is justifiably angry. We did come here with deceit. But because her anger is healthy, my concern right now is Otto Weinberger. I would like to spend some time with him."

He decides that it is a good idea to go back to and talk to Otto Weinberger and find out exactly what happened to him. But this time, they put him on tape. He set up his equipment in his house. As Otto Weinberger suggested before, if she is aware enough to know about them, she may be aware enough to block them, or whatever entities are possibly there might be aware enough to block them. He is not sure he is going to capture any supernatural activities, so the best thing to do is to talk to someone who has had a supernatural experience or thinks he has. He also thinks it just might prove fruitful in a lot of different ways. He calls Otto Weinberger and asks for permission to go over to speak with him.

He says to him, "I might press you a little bit too hard. But I'm hoping you are willing to do this for everyone's sake. In my experience, people who have had any encounters with the supernatural or things that they believe are encounters with the supernatural, are much better off when they talk them out. Sometimes it turns out to be nothing. That is a relief. And sometimes just sharing the experience and knowing that someone is aware of it is comforting."

Otto Weinberger agrees to have him over for a lengthy talk. He suggests that they have tea. He wants to bring Jasper into it because he feels Jasper is the reason that he originally came into it. Robaire rejects this idea. Right now, he just wants to know Otto Weinberger's innermost feelings, his emotions, the depth of what is happening to him. Then he can get the factual details later. He will be there a long time, and he can get bits and pieces and put them together.

Robaire goes over alone. He goes over without David so that David can keep an eye on Charlotte, though he knows that Yvette is going to be there to do the same thing. Otto Weinberger lets him. Otto Weinberger sits down in his rocking chair by the fireplace in his den. He is wearing a shawl. He looks like he has aged ten to fifteen years. It is difficult for him to keep his hands still.

He rocks back and forth continuously. He makes furtive glances constantly around the room. It is difficult for him to keep his eyes still. He wrings his hands. Robaire takes a seat. He sets up his taping equipment and some other equipment that he had because he wants to make sure that he is in the room only with Otto Weinberger. But he doesn't really explain that to Otto Weinberger. But Otto has been around enough to surmise this and dismisses it.

He tells Otto Weinberger, "I would like to talk to you specifically about what happened to you, the supernatural experience that happened to you. My understanding is that you taught at a university. You taught archaeology and theology. You come from a background where you are not easily shocked. You are the last person that we would expect to be in this position. You are somewhat of a veteran. We would like to know what it is that put you, and I don't mean to offend you, in this state." Otto Weinberger responds, "It is not offensive to me. I understand that something has changed, and I am trying to fight it myself. It's not something ongoing happening outside. If I can explain it to you this way, the experience itself has stayed with me so. It undermined my self-confidence. It undermined my ability in myself to determine reality from unreality, and I can't protect myself. When I first got into this, I was first brought this relic by Jasper Smythe. I thought that there were a few things that I could run into that I would not be able to deal with. I thought that there would be some danger, some harm, and maybe a little terror if this was even true, but I did not think that it would not come to this extent."

At this point, Robaire says, "I must interrupt you because no one has really filled me in on the relic. What relic?" Then Otto Weinberger is slightly alarmed, but he tried not to show it because he knows that Robaire has not been talking to Jasper, but why is it that David has kept the relic from him? He senses that there is not a complete trust between Robaire and David, Robaire and Yvette, and David and Yvette, and possibly even David in himself. Then he concludes that hopefully the only thing that is behind that is the fact that he loves Charlotte. But there is the possibility that David has discovered something else that he has decided to keep to himself. This is another thought that he puts in the back of his mind.

He relates the story to Robaire of finding a relic, of finding something buried in the dirt, on the grounds of Charlotte's mansion when Jasper Smythe was landscaping. "Knowing the history of the land, Jasper Smythe thought it was misplaced. It wasn't a Russian artifact. It wasn't an Indian artifact. As far as I know, it is eastern European, and to be sure I took it to the university. That is how I entered the picture."

Of course, this is all going on tape with Robaire. "Immediately to me, I suspected that it was a coat of arms. I was right, it was a misplaced coat of arms. Possibly, there were things about the coat of arms that led me to believe it might have a supernatural significance, or it might be the coat of arms of a vampire or a family that had somehow either needed to be marked as unusual or needed to mark themselves as unusual."

So Robaire asks him, "Well, what is it about this coat of arms that was so disturbing?"

He is not ready to explain that to him yet, but he says, "The mere fact that it was in this place that it should not have been enough to set me off. Things that I have seen in the past, I have come to learn to spot because of my family history. I was not born in this country. I was born in Eastern Europe. And my family, oftentimes, generations back, have encountered and had to kill vampires. It hasn't happened recently, but we are aware of the tradition. I was educated, of course, in Europe. When you come from certain parts of Europe, certain things are accepted and just are not spoken about. I was educated normally in Europe, and I came to America. I took a job, and I didn't think that I would ever run into this again.

"When this was brought to me, part of it I must admit was ego. I thought that this is something that I can handle, this is something that my family used to dwell the time. In addition, it coupled with my education. Besides I was well rested. I figured I could just explore it and find out where it goes. So, I took this on. I asked to be brought into Charlotte's circle.

"Also, I had a real legitimate concern for the community. I knew that if there is a vampire in the community it would be a very bad thing. I had been thinking about what would have happened if I had decided not to investigate this. I don't think that much would have changed. After my experience and because of the two murders, I felt somewhat guilty." Robaire says, "Normally in our profession, or in a supernatural occurrence, the first way you break down a person's own existing personality or their own existing resistance, is to have them feel heavy guilt or dread. So, this is quite understandable."

Otto Weinberger says, "Yes, I'm aware of that, but I must caution you that this is not a possession by any means. I will explain that you to later. I have had much time to think about it. I went into this thinking that I could do something about this. But after I thought about it, I could have disturbed some things that maybe I should not have disturbed. I, in some way, feel relieved to know that the murders were triggered by the fact that David Sellers arrived in town, and they would have taken place whether I knew about them. Possibly, if anything, my presence and my knowledge, and the vampires' knowledge of my presence, slowed this occurrence up."

Once again, Robaire stops him. He says, "Now we are using this term vampire, and we are all accepting this term vampire. I see no signs of the traditional vampire in Charlotte. I've read some accounts of what occurred in the newspaper because Yvette had them with her. Charlotte had brought them over to her when she came the first time. I'm still not sure how you are settling on a vampire."

Otto Weinberger says, "Well, we could do it two ways, and we probably should do it two ways. Then you will understand better. I can relate what my feeling is about what is going on here. Then I can back it up by recounting my personal experience to you."

Robaire says, "I have nothing but time, but don't be upset if I interject a few questions because this is new to me."

He says, "No, no, I accepted this meeting. I am permitting what could only be termed an interview or an exchange."

Robaire says, "Well, I would rather you look at it as an exchange because I hope it is a fruitful exchange of ideas that will help Charlotte."

Weinberger says, "Nevertheless, I permitted it, and I will go through with it as long and as far as I can."

Otto Weinberger relates the story of the clan that he tracked in the Carpathians. This clan was invincible, and they stuck together. At first, they just roamed wild. There were a lot of them. They were all thoroughly successful in battle. They took on every one of their opponents. They took them on at night, and they killed them thoroughly. He related the whole story to him. "They were knighted. They were granted titles. They received jewels, money, land, deeds, and everything because they also protected the king. No one would come up against them. This is the clan that eventually developed into royalty that I believe Charlotte is a descendant of.

"This tale was told to me by several old timers in the Carpathians, which I went into. There are even remnants of some of the castles that they lived in.

There is history of several purges where they have had to move. So, they moved further into middle Europe, which is where Charlotte's parents come from. It was too dangerous for them in that they were being purged and pursued. Her paintings depict this history."

"But what he did not understand and what I have come to believe now, is that the paintings are totally accurate. The peasants did purge and pursue. They did kill in the accepted vampire manner. Charlotte's parents came to America fleeing this purge and bought this house because of the solitude. They brought a two-year-old child with them and all the money that they could get up at the time. And they died purely by chance, and Charlotte was raised normally because of this. The other entities, or life forms, or personalities that you want to call ghosts, are not ghosts. It has been a long time since they were ever human. They were vampires who have been killed.

"The mistake I made was to begin to look for coffins. There are no coffins. You will find no coffins. You will find no need for blood because they have no bodies to sustain. This is my theory. But somehow, they manage or are permitted to reach out from the centuries that they have been living in, the centuries prior to the time that they died. It is almost as if they could warp time. Not only can they communicate with Charlotte, I believe now that the murders that took place did not take place here but took place in the centuries where these people were alive and had bodies."

Robaire stops him at that point and says, "And this is not a ghost?"

He says, "No, this is not a ghost. I have never heard of a ghost that was able to do this. I've come up against ghosts that have been able to make you think that these things are happening, but I have never heard of a ghost that can actually have enough power to make this a reality."

He says, "This is your theory, but can you tell me what happened in your personal experience that made you believe this is a fact?"

He relates to him, "I was downstairs without Charlotte's permission with the full knowledge of the psychiatrist, David Sellers, Jasper Smythe, and the private detective who seems to be missing. I went to look for coffins because I had sent Jasper, who I felt could do so inconspicuously during the daylight, several times. He never found anything, so I assumed that Jasper would not know enough to know where to look.

"So, I went to look myself, and I ended up down in the wine cellar. Of course, the wine cellar is very pleasant to be in. There is nothing wrong with the wine cellar. Off the wine cellar there is a room where Charlotte paints and it is open air, all glass around it. It has a view of the redwoods and the ocean. All her paintings are in there. I had seen her paintings, and I just took a little time to look at her paintings again. While I was doing that I was, the only way I could describe it, pulled into one of the paintings. I knew that I was in a different time period. My feet were on grass. I could smell the night air. I could smell the blood, the burning flesh. I could hear the screams.

"As I looked around my eyes, caught all the activity. I was riveted to the spot. In another direction that I could look, I could see a little girl who seemed to be standing outside. It was almost like a barrier to me because I couldn't get out there where she was. She was painting. I realized that I must be in the painting. This is a lot for my mind to try to put together. I must be in this painting. I felt that this painting was not static, it was dynamic. She was still adding trees. She was still adding creeks. She was still adding rocks. Then I realized that I was nude, and she painted my clothing. She painted me as a gentry. She painted me very well dressed.

"Then I became a vampire. I was not a peasant. I did not have the sticks, the pickaxes and the torches. I could hear the obscenities being yelled at me. I was being dragged out of the house with my family, my women, my females. The people next to me were shifting shapes, becoming black, becoming dark, and becoming wolves. They were trying to kill with a vengeance. I was in the middle of a very fierce battle. There was a growing emotion in me to participate, one I couldn't quell. I wanted to protect the women. It was imperative that I protected the family. I lusted after the blood scent. I wanted to help the men. I wanted to take a shape. I wanted to kill. I wanted to rip veins. How dare they do this to me. How dare they interrupt our home, these peasants. I could feel it surging through me. My blood was racing. People were dying all around me. I was beginning to get in the position where I was going to kill someone. Then I was outside of the picture.

"This was too much for me. I left on all fours. I managed to get out of that room, out of the wine cellar. I ran upstairs, passing three or four people that I think were the four people that had helped me in my attempt to catch Charlotte and got in my car. I don't know how I managed to drive home. I locked my doors and my windows. I have been here ever since. It was two or three days before I would even accept a phone call. I spent a lot of time trying to make sure I was in my own surroundings, that this was my house, checking my clock, checking my calendars, turning on the television to see that I was looking at the news. I have been doing things to verify where I am and trying not to think about anything that happened to me because I can't. I was a coward. I know it was cowardice. I was hoping that they would not find me.

"This went on for weeks, and finally David broke through with some wild information. He talked to me. I don't remember half of what he told me. He always tries to give me enough information to help me, but I really did not want to think about it." At this point, he says, "Well, I did not want to think about it. But in recounting it, it makes it seem a lot less harmful. But I know that it happened, and I know that these people were not ghosts. I know that I was not in the twentieth century when it happened to me."

Robaire interrupts again, "Well, these people seem to be able to do a lot of very interesting things, and you are right, I'm not going to be able to write them off as a typical ghost state. Normally, ghosts haunt a place that has some significance for them, and this place has no significance for them. If these people who are apparently vampires, are who you say they are, and they died in Europe, they should be haunting in Europe. So, what has brought them here, apparently, is Charlotte. Do you think this is some sort of poltergeist?"

Otto Weinberger laughed. He says, "Well, maybe we should end this interview. I'm starting to get tired, and you are not listening."

Robaire says, "Please, please, listen to me. I'm not trying to give you a bad time. I am only suggesting things that I am somewhat familiar with."

Otto Weinberger relents and says, "Okay, we will continue with this."

He says, "Given your hypothesis, what it is that they want? Why haven't we seen a massacre? You say they don't need bodies, why haven't they taken bodies? They could do that. Couldn't they do that? They seem to be able to do everything else."

At this point, Otto stands and turns in front of the fireplace, "Given my hypothesis, they do not want to take a body. They do not want to displace a soul. I don't believe that they are permitted to do that. The reason that I don't believe they are permitted to do that is because they were killed in the accepted vampire manner. They have immortality because they have participated in the blood feast. But they had limits, and they knew they had limits. But what I believe they can do, and what is horrifying also, is reincarnate. That is their plan. Charlotte is their vehicle. Charlotte is the channel, and Charlotte is the perfect channel because the thing that you don't want to understand, and that David doesn't want to believe, is that Charlotte is a vampire."

Robaire takes up a light posture. It is hard for him to believe. He has walked with Charlotte. He was talked with Charlotte. Charlotte has yelled at him. She has called him on the carpet. But she is Yvette's friend. She has been Yvette's friend for years. He just doesn't buy it. He has seen her in the daytime. He has seen her eat. There is nothing suggestive about her that would make him think that she is a vampire, that she is going to take a shape, or she is going to need blood or any of this. He is trying not to express ridicule, but a little bit is starting to come through.

Otto Weinberger continues in this stern tone that he is now taking, "Charlotte is a vampire. The telekinetic and the telepathic things that you have seen her do she has done because she is a vampire, and not because she has a normal sort of ESP. You should understand that, if you don't understand anything else. And you should try to help her to understand it, and you should try to help David to understand it, because I do not know where it will go.

"I'm tired right now. You can come back and talk to me again. I will talk to you again. Maybe after staying two or three more nights, your perspective will change. I hope to God that no one must go through what I went through, but I know why this happened to me. I suggest, for your own safety, you find out where the private detective is. I'm sure he has not met a good end, but I don't know exactly what has happened to him.

"I caution you to remember that David loves Charlotte, and that Charlotte loves David, and I am uncomfortable that they have started to withhold information from me. I know that one of the reasons you came to talk to me is out of concern. But possibly, you should realize that David may, and Charlotte will, withhold vital information from you and Yvette. So, keep that in mind. Just watch your step. Don't try to do anything that in any way could be perceived as a threat because these entities will protect her to the fullest extent that they know how."

Robaire slightly sarcastically, but not too sarcastically because he is too sensitive, says, "Okay. I understand your hypothesis that they are dead, that they somehow remove people magically into another century where they were vital, killing them there, putting them back here, and that they could do that at will. I understand that I can't think of a defense against it but be assured that they haven't done it randomly. You probably have little to fear from them at this point, because you've made no more action, and you've had no more actions toward Charlotte. I assume that is another reason that you haven't gone toward her house."

Otto says, "Even if my mind were clearer and I were in a better state, I think I would stay away from her right now until I had a better defense."

He says, "The position I think I'm going to take is to be very observant. I hope that you feel that you can always trust me, and if there is something that I don't tell you, it will probably be for your own good. I hope that I'm able to remain there under the pretense of the wedding. I'm going to take this tape back and analyze it, and I'm going to take the other instrumentation that I have set up here down and analyze it. That may give you some comfort since you will be hearing from me very shortly on that information."

He thanks him very much for letting him come in and go through this. He asks him if he has any idea of when he will be able to return to work or to something useful. He says, "I'm not concerning myself with that right now. There is something in my community not too far from me that is overwhelming. I just want to relax and use my mind because I think that I have enough information, I've made enough travels, and I don't have to go anywhere else. I just want to relax."

Robaire collects his equipment, excuses himself and lets himself out. He tells him, "Don't worry, I'll keep in contact with you. If anything shows up here that might harm you or might become harmful to you, I'll let you know. If it's not something that is just too far out, I'm sure that you could even stay at the house with the rest of us so we could watch you."

Otto Weinberger passes that off. It is just not an acceptable solution, but he thanks him. Robaire returns to the house. He puts his materials in the room. He doesn't go to them immediately. He begins to look for David. He finds David, as usual, attempting to talk to Charlotte. This time, they are laughing, and they are talking about the wedding. He is telling her about his brothers and sisters, the difference in their personalities, and the things they used to do as little kids.

Charlotte is really in a different mood. She is really cheering up and she is laughing. Because this is an experience that he has never seen her have, he is hesitant to interrupt her. But as they see Robaire approach them, they invite him over. He gets involved in the family history and he recounts his own experiences with his own siblings. They continue to laugh.

Yvette comes along and suggests that they start thinking about dinner again.

She says, "Well, that's a good idea. Maybe we will go out for dinner tonight."

Everyone is surprised that Charlotte wants to go out for dinner. Yvette immediately says, "Oh yes. Well, let's dress up. Maybe we can even drive and find us a very nice place. Let's go through the phone book and find a nice place where we could go. We can actually dress up and maybe take in a movie." They decide to do this. The women go off to get the information. David is alone with Robaire.

Robaire says to him, "I have just left, as I told you I would, Otto Weinberger. I did, I guess what you would call, an interview. And at your leisure, I would like to play the tape for you as soon as I'm sure that my other instrumentation is clear. The one thing that he seemed to want to caution me about is that you are not fulling disclosing things that you have learned, and that there is some person or private detective that used to be around. Did you just dismiss him? Was he fired? What happened to him?"

David says, "Oh, I guess you might as well know. That is the reason that I was talking to Yvette about her increased powers. We know that he was removed from her room. We found out later that he was found dead in his apartment in New Jersey someplace, and that the police don't think that there is any foul play because he died of a heart attack or suffocation and a heart attack. Whatever happened first. Figure he had a heart attack and then he suffocated. So, as it stands right now, that is all we know."

Then Robaire says, "Charlotte can probably tell us what happened. You saw him leave a room, just leave a room and he didn't go through the door? Am I correct?"

David says, "Yes, you are correct. He seemed to disappear."

"Was he alone when he left this room?" Robaire wants to know.

He says, "No, he was not alone when he left the room. He left the room, through contact with the four monks, or what I assumed to be four monks. They were dressed as monks as far as I have seen in television and in books."

Robaire says, "Give me some more information about the clothing. Maybe I could trace it. Did it seem to have come from this century? I'm using those terms now because I've just left Otto Weinberger, and he's telling me about century changes."

He says, "Well, I don't really know what century they came from. I didn't see any faces, and I didn't see any limbs. They were completely hooded, and their sleeves covered everything. They had the traditional rope at the waist that dropped from the waist. That's all I know. There was one in each corner of her room as I was coming through her double doors, and I watched her throw him into a wall. He collapsed back from the wall. He didn't appear dead then, but he could have been from the impact of the throw. Then he was gone. But I clearly saw this. They were almost translucent, but they were there. Then they were gone, and he was gone at the same time.

"To be honest with you, my attention was directed at Charlotte, and Charlotte by this time had collapsed on the bed. I had been badly beaten by this very same person. The nanny is in by this time because it did make quite a bit of noise. She was surprised to see me there. I had to explain my presence and tell her that I wasn't the source of the noise. Then she called the doctor and a whole series of events happened. It was quite some time before I found out, three or four days, maybe even weeks, exactly that he had died."

Robaire says, "Well, this is probably all very true."

David says, "It is true. I wouldn't bring you this far to play games with you."

Robaire, not being quite upfront, suggests, "Perhaps the private detective thought you were playing games with him."

David is quite angry at this point, "The private detective broke into my home. He found things that I did not want him to see, I was not ready for him to see. I may never be ready for him to see these things. He is an employee of mine. The information that he gathered and brought back to me was all that he was entitled to. He was not entitled to a full disclosure from me, and that was our arrangement to start with. He decided to change that arrangement. And on top of that, he decides to try to kill me and decides to try to kill my fiancé. I know he's dead. I didn't kill him. She didn't kill him. Whatever killed him did it very thoroughly. That's all I can tell you."

Robaire says, "Well, I believe that over all you could tell me, but I think Charlotte could tell us what happened in between. Are you willing for me to have Charlotte tell us what happened in between?"

David says, "I assume there must be a physic communication between herself. In fact, I am pretty sure that there is physic communication between Charlotte and the vampires because there seemed to be a concerted effort to remove the private detective from the room definitely, and a concerted effort to continue Charlotte's initial thought, which was to murder him, which was to kill him to stop him. That was her initial reaction. And whoever it was that I saw suspended above her in four corners of the room, I believe carried out her thought pattern. I know that no words were spoken, and even if words were spoken, these had to be supernatural entities."

He is suggesting to Robaire very strongly, "This is again an example of her telekinetic and telepathic abilities. I have reason to believe that she has had more than one conversation with them, or she might communicate with them even more frequently than either of us could imagine. When I have pressed this issue, she has only responded either sarcastically or with tears. She had to be sedated after the first incident, and she had to be sedated after this incident. The vampires have not told her what has happened in between. You could attempt to get this information, if you could explain to me why we are going to risk our lives trying to make her tell us about it.

"If they want to keep if from her, then they have good reason for it. I don't know if you are going to be able to get it or not. And I don't know if, in the process of attempting to get it, you are going to get us both hurt. But if you talked to Otto Weinberger, you know that what happened to him probably was not very nice, and she has no idea what happened to Otto Weinberger.

"I'd like you to think about it. I'd like you to talk to Yvette about it and see if Yvette could approach her. Give her some time. I would love to give her some time. Give her two or three days to come back and see if she could give you that information."

Robaire is saying, "Well, I was thinking more in the terms of a hypnosis. I wanted to know if she had to be informed of these transformations, or if she is conscious of them all the time."

David says, "I told you she is not conscious of them all the time. She was in the room with me, and I was having bandages put on me."

Robaire says, "You're not aware that it is possible for her to be in communication with them and still be in the room talking to you. This is not an idea that you have accepted yet? This is the woman that you plan to marry. Let me put this object to you so you can think about it. It probably is very possible that she could be in communication with them and sitting in the room talking to you at the same time and be very concerned about your state of health. It is probably very possible that she can know what is going on when they seem to have completed her action. Her line of thought was that he should be walled. From what you say, they found mortar dust on his body, and he died of a heart attack or suffocated. He probably was put into a wall somewhere and released after he died, which is exactly what she intended to happen, even though it was in anger she intended it to happen. But how and when it happened, I would like to know. You should know if she could find these things out."

David says, "I'm going to think about it. I'm going to think about it before I even ask her. You should think about it before you talk to Yvette because there is only so much that Yvette is going to be able to take before she is going to become a little bit frightened. So, I think we should give all this a lot of thought. Then once we decide we are going to approach her with it, we are going to ask her about it. I don't recommend hypnosis, but I do recommend that you ask her the question and give her some time to get back to you about it because she is already very sensitive about it. From what I have seen, I don't blame her."

So, they agree that it is vital to find out if she could put in that section that she has not seen. It is vital to find out why they want to shield her because they shielded her from the actual horror, the actual death that takes place, and they can retain more influence over her. And if she sees the whole thing happen, maybe they could get a little bit more of her back. This has not occurred to David. This he likes.

"You are right. If we can do it and we can do it without shaking her up too much, bothering her too much emotionally, yes, she should know. She should see everything that happened. We know that somewhere in her mind she is seeing some of it because she is painting it. But it is not coming frontal, and she needs to be more aware so that she could see that this is a horrible thing to happen to a human being. You're right. Then maybe we will have a little bit of the Charlotte that we know back. But I think that we had better bide our time and I think that we had better concentrate on wedding plans, on the surface anyway."

So, they agree to do that.

By this time, the two women are back, and they suggested a place that they could all go out to. Yvette and Charlotte went to make reservations at a nice restaurant and to see if there are any local plays or any local movies that they might want to take in just to get them out of the house. While they were doing that, Robaire and David were continuing their conversation about what had happened to the private detective. When that conversation was terminated, Robaire went up to examine his equipment. He puts the tapes in his pocket because he didn't have time to listen to them, and he didn't think he was going to have time to listen. He puts them away to take away with him. He examines the equipment, which he claimed would show the presence or activity of other entities or other physic activity, immediately and found that nothing was present in the room with himself and Otto Weinberger.

He calls Otto Weinberger, "As far as my equipment could detect nothing else was present in the room in the house. The house seemed to be clear. You should try to relax and try to get some sleep, basically try to calm down. We are going out to dinner. I haven't had time to review the tapes, but I am going to take the tapes with me. I have spoken to David about the mistrust that has developed on your side. I explained to him that there was a considerable amount of mistrust on his side too because he is very protective of Charlotte, and he didn't want anything to get in the way of Charlotte's happiness. From my point of view, the mistrust was justifiable because they have just been through this terrible incident with the private detective.

"But I don't feel any personal threat. I feel you should feel no personal threat because David and Charlotte are still very good people, and Yvette and I are very comfortable there. It seems that we are going to be permitted to stay. I'm going to continue with my investigation. Should that change, or should you decide that you feel well enough to become involved in the situation again, I welcome you."

Otto Weinberger says, "Yes, that's all very well and good. I am very happy to hear that. I hope that you do stay because they do need someone there. But you still have to remember that with the one exception of the private detective, and I'm not all together sure what happened there, none of the atrocities were committed by either David or Charlotte, and if they still appear to very normal and very human to you, that's good on the one hand. On the other hand, keep that other piece of information in mind."

They signed off for the night. David proceeded to get dressed to go out. Robaire proceeded to get dressed in his room. The girls traded things back and forth. They are close in size. Charlotte realizes that she hadn't been shopping in months. She is rather embarrassed because she does really love David, she is conscious of whether she has washed her hair or not, if this dress looks nice, and if he likes this perfume. Because of all these things that have been happening she hasn't even taken much of this into consideration.

Yvette was very tactful. Yvette says, "Well, look at this. This is a nice new sweater that I picked up in San Trope. This is a nice skirt. I have a pair of jeans."

She just basically went through Yvette's wardrobe which reminded her that she was losing grip in a lot of ways, and that this is a way that she did not want to lose grip. She was subtle and kind of covered it up, but it was obvious to Yvette. She knew Yvette was going to be nice about it. They went through each other's wardrobe. They traded clothes, jewelry, and everything else until they both felt confident coming out to meet the two men.

The men were waiting for them in the library. They were having a before dinner drink. It was a little bit awkward for Robaire because he realized, when he sees Charlotte coming down the stairs and when Charlotte's eyes fall on David, that they are very much in love. He is just taking Yvette, his friend, out. These are all the emotions that were running through everyone's mind. It was kind of an awkward situation. As Robaire was thinking about this, he also realized that it was very good that these feelings were still present. That meant that these two were still reachable.

They all get into Charlotte's Volvo, with David driving, drive themselves into town and have dinner at a French restaurant. Charlotte is vibrant. This reminds her of Europe. She and Yvette exchange stories of the happy times that they have had in Europe. Charlotte eats everything on her plate. She eats all her dessert. She requests more dessert. Everyone is so happy that she is even eating that they are laughing about it. It has become a point of humor. So, she says she hadn't realized that anyone was really that conscious of the fact that she wasn't eating. She laughs too.

They decided to walk up and down the street a little bit because there were no movies that they really wanted to see and there were no small-town plays. They walked up and down the different streets and took a little stroll. They walked backed to their car and got in without incident.

Both Charlotte and David are fully aware of this. We've come out. We've gone into town. We've had a nice meal. We've walked down the street at night. It is dark, and nothing has happened. Nothing has gone wrong. Nothing abnormal or unusual has happened. They both are kind of giggly about it, and it is almost an inside joke between the two of them.

Robaire says, "Let me in on it. What's so funny?"

They say, "Well, it's just that, that's what's so funny, that absolutely nothing is going on." They drive back to the house. By this time, it is about one o'clock because they had a late evening meal.

Robaire excuses himself. He wants to get to the tapes right away. Yvette excuses herself because she wants to give herself a manicure and a pedicure. She asks Charlotte if she wants one. Charlotte says, "Not today, but definitely tomorrow." So that leaves Charlotte and David. David excuses himself because he wants to reflect on what has happened this evening, and he doesn't want to blow it. He tells her he is tired, and he is going to go on to bed. That leaves her to walk around her house which is almost three-quarters of the way decorated. She is very happy. She realizes that she is very happy, that she is very lucky, everything is hers, and that soon he will be completely hers too. Just for a moment everything else seems very far removed, very far removed.

The nanny approaches her and says, "Well, I think those two visiting you have been very good for you. And you know I don't normally say much, not since you have been a little girl and you have been out to Europe and you have done all these things, but I think it's a really good idea that you keep these two here. I've seen several changes in you to the good, to the bad, and now back to the good. I'm very happy about it. I think it's also helped David a lot. I think David is a very sincere man. I'm not trying to get in your business, and I don't want to even suggest anything out of the way, but I'm also very happy that you are engaged. I hope that everything works out for you."

She begins to cry. Then Charlotte begins to cry. They are both crying because the two of them have known each other the longest, though a lot that was going on was unspoken, a lot of emotion, a lot of things that the nanny realized that she didn't have to verbalize. Charlotte was very glad that she verbalized this, because her sentiments were the same. She felt just the same. They spend some time talking and walking around the house, going into different rooms.

Charlotte says, "Well, you know, I never asked you what you thought about my interior decorating. I'd like to know what you think about it."

The nanny very wisely says, "The house will be what you make of it and the people inside of it make of it. Everything is quite expensive, and I'm sure done in the very best of taste. I'm sure you had your reasons for picking the types of decor that you chose. I haven't been to Europe. I have no art background. I don't know what basis you use, but I trust it will all work very well in here. It seems to be very nice to me."

She lets it drop like that because she has noticed that things have tended to darken up, and she, of course, has noticed that Charlotte was a lot less active in the daytime. She is too honest of a person not to mention it, so she says, "I have noticed that you are a little bit less active in the daytime, and it seems we are a little bit closed in here. I have attributed it to the fact that you are tired. The other servants don't seem to question it, especially now that Yvette and Robaire are here, and you are up and around. So, I'm sure it's just that you were tired, and you have just been through too many terrible experiences, and I know that that is the way the other servants feel also."

She suggests to Charlotte, "Charlotte you went out to dinner, and that was good for you. But, you know, we have a very nice cook, and I noticed that it was fun for you and Yvette to cook for the young men, but I think now, for a couple of reasons, maybe you should have a more formal dinner. The cook gets a little bored, and he shouldn't. So, let him show you a little bit of what he can do in the kitchen."

Charlotte agrees that it is a wonderful idea. "And maybe you should invite some other friends, some of the people that attended the art gallery opening, so they can see you. You could introduce these people to Yvette, your closest friend."

Charlotte thinks about this and says, "Yes, that is a good idea because we haven't been very social. This will give me a good idea of what we are missing in the way of basic china, and maybe even manners, because I hope to have the wedding guests stay here for possibly even a week prior to the wedding, and I want everything to be very comfortable for them."

The nanny says, "Yes, of course. And we need to go over a little bit of etiquette to make sure that everything is just right." So, they agree that this is a good way to practice and to start on that. It is too late to go and talk to the servants about it, but they make a pact to do it first thing in the morning. The nanny is going to do it when she gets up, and when Charlotte arises, they will go in together and explain to the servants what they have in mind.

Charlotte is getting ready to retire. The nanny tells her, "Good night. Have a good night's sleep, and don't be afraid. There are a lot more people in this house and a lot of people who mean you good. Try to relax. You just have had a run of bad luck, a very bad run of luck. Just get a good night's sleep." The nanny goes to her room.

The only one who hasn't finished preparing for bed and awake at this point is Robaire. He is listening to the tapes and going over what Otto Weinberger was telling him. He's still having trouble imaging what Otto Weinberger went through. He didn't pick up anything on his machine, so he doesn't understand who and what could have created the time warp or the illusion of different centuries and places. He doesn't know if this could have been hypnosis, or just under this stress and pressure Otto Weinberger had snapped. He would have to rule that out immediately because obviously Otto Weinberger was not in a very good state of mind. He thought to collaborate his story he needed more than mangled bodies and the accounts in the newspapers because that could have happened a lot of different ways.

Once again, he felt that he needed the only other eyewitness he knew of, David, but the best witness to what was going on there was Charlotte. He thought he should go for permission from David to hypnotize her. He hoped that if these entities existed, he had the permission from them also.

So, Robaire went over the tapes again and again. He had brought some books with him, and he couldn't, in his mind, recall any time when this kind of phenomenon had taken place. There was nothing, that he could really relate to in anything that he had learned. He tried to look it up under various categories and it didn't really hit. It didn't have any of the markings of a haunting and it didn't have any of the markings, if you would even think of demonology, of that or poltergeist. There didn't appear to be any cold spots in the house. Otto Weinberger said himself that the house was always very comfortable to him. There is nothing that seemed to menace him, or he has no premonition that he should not be there, or any kind of forewarning that this event was going to take place.

Also, it just didn't seem malicious mischief in general like you would find in poltergeist. It wasn't a poltergeist occurrence or something that you could put in the poltergeist category. The likely candidate for that would be Charlotte, but not this sort of thing. This did have some various revenge overtones, but it seemed complex and so complicated that he, himself, is not sure that it was coming from just one source. So, he arrives at the conclusion that he hopes that he can hypnotize Charlotte, and that Charlotte can tell him what it is that she knows without interference from these entities that he keeps being warned about but cannot track.

He is a little disturbed of these tales of early childhood paintings. He is also disturbed with the paintings, but he knows some children have obsessions with various superheroes or fairy tales. He cannot help but think of this continuing painting all through to adulthood that only stopped apparently when she was away at boarding school. He doesn't know what she did in France, and he's going to talk to Yvette about what she was creating in France. That bothers him. He still thinks that Charlotte is definitely the source of whatever is wrong, but he has not turned a deaf ear to what Otto Weinberger has told him. He is weary of something that he can't touch, see or feel and they have not bothered to present themselves to him yet, and when they do present themselves usually it is fatal.

He has a lot to think about when it comes to how he can approach Charlotte with this hypnosis, and if giving her full consent will mean anything after being briefed by David. But neither one of them seem to have control over what happened. It would be a gruesome thought, but it did occur to him that this is a gruesome thought, if something would just happen in his presence, then he would have some idea of what everyone else is talking about. Because he is proud of himself for having a little bit of sensitivity. He didn't think that he was a medium. He thought that the concept of having to be a medium was a dangerous one, and most of the people deliberately set themselves up for that way. But he didn't know that he had a natural sensitivity or propensity and that is one of the reasons that he is in this field. He sensed nothing. He sensed a lot of sadness and guilt in Charlotte, and he wasn't sure that it was properly placed. He sensed sadness and guilt in Otto Weinberger of a different sort, and he tried to eradicate that because he wasn't sure that it was properly placed. He also sensed general frustration in David.

He went over again through the tapes. He thought he would try the two approaches of going for Charlotte, and then maybe hitting a little bit more of the history of the house because up to this point, no one has really brought up the relic to him yet. He doesn't really know about the relic, but he does think that if there is a haunting or something like a haunting in the house, maybe it comes from the house and not anybody else in it. He jots down all the related possibilities, and he tries to find ways to omit and eliminate them. With that, he goes to bed.

The next morning, they are all at breakfast. They are all quite cheery because they have resolved something to do. Yvette, the nanny and Charlotte have discussed the possibility of the dinner party, the reason for it, meeting some of the notables in Mendocino, just getting their manners down right, and finding out what they have and what they don't have on a small scale. They decided that the wedding will probably be somewhat large, but there will be some intimacy to the after affair. Charlotte is very happy about it.

Yvette is really elated because she hasn't even seen the art gallery yet. She tells Charlotte, "First thing this morning, after breakfast, I'm pulling you out the door so that you can show me the art gallery. Let's open the windows and see what's going on. I haven't even met your secretary."

Charlotte says, "Oh, that's right. Jennifer hasn't been to the house, and Jennifer has just been kind of holding down the fort. I guess Jennifer really is a jewel because she hasn't been asking too many questions either. But maybe she realizes with the first set of murders that it would take me a little time to recuperate, and since she is still being paid, it is a rather safe situation. Maybe I'm even lucky that I keep her."

Charlotte and Yvette go off to the art gallery. The nanny starts to make what arrangements she can make for a dinner party. David attempts to contact some of his prior freelance employers. Since everything seemed to be going so well, he decides that he should probably drive into San Francisco and keep touching bases with different people. He goes off for the day. Robaire, of course, wants to get back to Otto Weinberger, see what Otto Weinberger has on the history of the house, and what the local Mendocino newspapers and the library have on the history of the house. That is what he plans to spend his whole day, and maybe the next day, doing.

Charlotte and Yvette go out with the resolution that they are going to take Jennifer to lunch because she has been sitting there all by herself and they think that she is a trooper. They call Jennifer beforehand. Charlotte drives, and Yvette rides in with her. She shows Yvette the art gallery which is pretty much the way she left it. There is some decor that is standard interior decorating. There are some display cases for the people that would have been displayed there, but right now they are empty.

Jennifer is upstairs. She is taking inventory on some of the work that had been left by the last person that was there so she could get it shipped back to him in increments. She is also answering letters from people who would like to show in the art gallery in the upcoming season. She tells Charlotte that her vacation was wonderful, she went to Bermuda, and she was very well rested. She is very cheery. She is glad they came in to take her out to lunch because everything is starting to get to her. She has been looking at all these boxes, even packing with the help of moving men and going through all these letters from people. She knows that she is going to end up having to ask Charlotte what kind of reputation they have as artists and if she wants to exhibit them. Just being able to call Charlotte sometimes and not get through to her or sometimes being told that Charlotte was unavailable to talk was getting a little frustrating. Jennifer is happy to see that Charlotte was in good spirits, that she had all her health and apparently all her mental facilities, and she had some good friends with her.

Charlotte and Yvette say, "Well, we just had breakfast. We're going to look around. Maybe you could tell us where some of the people are that have written to us to exhibit." Of course, Charlotte makes interjections about Yvette and Yvette's background. She explains that Yvette has had almost equal training in art, and that Yvette's comments would be very welcome. Charlotte and Yvette go downstairs while Jennifer continues her work. Yvette thinks the art gallery is beautiful, isn't it a shame that Charlotte hasn't immediately found the next person for the season and that it is not the furthermost thing on Charlotte's mind.

Then she says, "Well, I guess I should say the foremost thing on your mind is your wedding. So maybe that's not so bad after all."

Charlotte says, "Well, the two of us both know that neither one of those things are the foremost thing on my mind, and I have to keep those two things on my mind."

She looks around. She is amazed because there is a lot of open air, and there are a lot of graphics used. Charlotte renovated a building for the art gallery. There is a lot of solarium type places where sunlight falls, and there are other places where direct sunlight cannot be permitted to fall, but whenever it could be used, she did so. The art gallery is almost in direct contrast now to the home that she is living in. Yvette noticed this. She commends her, "Everything is beautiful. This is lovely. Everything is just wonderful. You did all this by yourself?" In the back of her mind, she is thinking, *But why is the house so dark?* She just happens to mention it to Jennifer later when they go back upstairs to talk to her.

Jennifer lays out two or three people that she thinks are most promising. The only way that Jennifer can tell is because they have listed in a resume, and of other places, they have exhibited, and she has heard of these other places. Some of the people she just puts aside automatically because they don't have the credentials. She takes the cream of the crop and shows them to Charlotte.

She says, "Well, this set of ten right here that we've gotten in so far seem to be available during the time period that we need them, and they seem to have the right resumes. But you must look them over to see which ones you would like to show, and which order you would like to show them. If they have enough work, you might want to show one for the whole season."

Both Charlotte and Yvette were impressed at the kind of responses Charlotte was getting in Mendocino. They were pleased that people were coming across country and from other places to exhibit their works. Part of that reason that she was getting this kind of interest was, once again, the kind of help that her family could provide. Also, everywhere David went he would try to put in a good word for her and advertise the art gallery, and he had a few connections. So, it was just a matter of sitting down and looking through it. She is amazed. She thought she would have to try to get the people there in time. She had already determined that she would just let this season pass and work on the wedding, then maybe next season go back to the art gallery.

She picks out two or three of them. One is a sculptor, one does watercolor with oils, and the other was in metals. She says to Jennifer, "Write back to these three. Ask how much of their work they willing to commit, for what time period, what they want to ask for them, and if they just want to show or if they want to show and sell also. Find out if they want a reception at every showing, or an initial reception, or initial and ending reception. We also need to know how they would like their work presented."

Jennifer jots down the notes. That is enough for her to do probably for the next three or four weeks. By this time, three hours have passed because it took her quite some time to show off her art gallery, to see what Jennifer was packing up, to help give instructions to the moving men, and to look at and decide on who was going to be exhibiting work. It is about lunch time, so Charlotte, Jennifer and Yvette all decide to go out to lunch together. They have lunch at an outside café.

Jennifer is still a little bit concerned because she was sent away several times with pay while things were happening in Charlotte's life. She was sent away about the time they sent the nanny away. She thought it was Charlotte, or it was Charlotte but at Charlotte's and David's suggestion, but it really wasn't. She was sent away again immediately after the murders. She knows why she was sent away that time. Then she was sent away again about the time of the private detective's disappearance.

She is happy that she has this job. It is a wonderful job and Charlotte is a wonderful person. It seems that she has good friends, and she loves the Mendocino coast. But she is getting a little nervous about always being sent away with pay, these multiple vacations, and especially with the murders that have happened. She has been wondering if she was going to have to leave her position at the art gallery because she senses that there is something wrong here. She voices it because it has been bothering her.

Charlotte looks at Yvette, and Yvette looks at Charlotte. Charlotte says, "We know. As far as we have been told, the police have taken care of everything. We were told the same thing you were told. Has anything happened that made you feel uncomfortable? If it has, I will hire a guard, and you could either shorten your daytime hours for now so you can get home before dark, or I can always have you escorted home."

Jennifer says, "Well, I'm probably just being silly, but those two things kind of bothered me. But I thought I should say something about it because a lot of people had advised me to quit immediately after the murders. Since then though, I haven't heard anything about it one way or the other. So, people must have been satisfied. But right after the murders, everyone says, 'I would never work there'. But, of course, I wouldn't leave you because I knew that you had nothing to do with it, and I knew it would be a bad time to leave you. Then you gave me a paid vacation. But I'm still a little bit uncomfortable, and I thought I should tell you especially since I'm in here by myself a lot. I was wondering, were you going to continue with the next season? And if you weren't going to continue with the next season, were you going to terminate me? All these things have been running through my mind."

Charlotte tells her, "Oh, no. I'm perfectly happy with your work, and I'm perfectly happy that you stayed."

Jennifer says, "And I'm happy that you decided to pick this season to exhibit. This has been a little bit much I think even for me, even with pay, but I just think we need to keep working."

Yvette says, "And that's exactly what I was telling her this morning. I was also telling her that she has to get her mind off this wedding."

Jennifer says, "What wedding?"

She says, "Well, haven't you noticed the engagement ring?" Then Charlotte shows Jennifer her engagement ring.

Then Jennifer says, "David?"

Charlotte says, "David."

They all laugh. Jennifer says, "Oh, that's what it is."

Yvette says, "Yes, that's what it is."

Jennifer immediately relaxes. She goes into peals of laughter. She is so happy. She is so congratulatory. She is hoping that she is going to be invited to the wedding. Charlotte says, "Yes. Of course, I need you to help me with it. We're all making plans for it. Yvette came over, and I'm still choosing my designs and my dresses and all the other things. We will keep in touch with you about it."

Jennifer relaxes, and she proceeds to enjoy her meal. She's bubbly about the different things that have happened to her, the phone calls that she has gotten and the people that she never thought she would get to meet. Even though she hasn't had the kind of training in art, she did recognize some of the names that have called through there.

After lunch Jennifer, Charlotte, and Yvette decide to stay in the streets and window shop. They look at the local arts and crafts that are out on the streets. They go down by the docks and look at some of the ships. They relax and talk girl talk. Jennifer was saying that she didn't realize that Charlotte and David were so involved, but she could tell that David really cared about Charlotte. This kind of talk goes back and forth.

Jennifer mentions who she went to Bermuda with. Yvette mentions that Jennifer had to meet Robaire, who was staying at the Von Shillingsfurst Estate.

This continues for a while. Jennifer felt much better and much more relaxed because Charlotte seemed a lot better. She hadn't voiced that she might be quitting as much as it really was apparent to her, but now this has changed it for her. She was going to go right back to work, but not that day because Charlotte had told her to take the rest of the day and the rest of the weekend off and pick up on this on Monday. Charlotte also had asked her to make contacts on Monday and get back to her.

They dropped her off at the office so she could get her car at the art gallery.

Charlotte and Yvette proceed home to see what's for dinner. They also want to take a bath and nap for a little bit. David is still in San Francisco. Robaire has gone again to see Otto Weinberger. He tells Otto, "As far as I know, the house is cleared. But I sense some other source active there. But it hasn't made itself apparent to me. In a lot of ways, I'm glad that it hasn't." He runs the idea past Otto Weinberger about hypnosis.

Otto Weinberger tells him, "You're on your own. I would have to tell you what David tells you, and that is I couldn't be responsible for what happens to you. But you could try it."

Robaire says, "You know, you've done a lot of research, and it will save me a lot of legwork if we compare notes on the history of the house. I have been wondering if there was something inherent in the house that is wrong, since you yourself admit that Charlotte has had no problems prior to this, and David has had no problems prior to this. Yvette can vouch for that. The problem that I have is that the only person that has really voiced a supernatural experience to me is you, and you, yourself, at times have doubted your sanity. I don't mean to offend you or to shatter your self-confidence. It's just that I have to look at this from every angle."

Otto Weinberger says, "Fine. This is everything that I figured out. I did some jottings, and I took some very good notes. In addition, I collaborated with the private detective that David hired. So, I pretty much found out what he found out up until the time that he disappeared. He knew what my experience was, but I don't know what happened to him up until the time that he disappeared. You're welcome to that. And I suggest that you check the Mendocino local register and the local records to find out what you can find about the house that predates the house. You may find something significant. The one thing that I can tell you, I don't know if anyone has brought this up, is the reason I got involved is whom the architect that Charlotte hired uncovered something that looked to us like a coat of arms.

"We could not place it as something from a Russian family, we didn't know of any Russian nobility in this area or any Russian excursions that were financed by nobility in this area. Then we thought it would have to be an Indian relic, but it wasn't. It seemed to have been authentic. It is in David's possession, so you should ask David to show it to you. This is what I have up to now."

He gave Robaire all his jottings and notes. A lot of the things that he had been written down were just pure speculation, a lot of it was visual observation, and some of it was the conversations that he had had with the coroner after the first death. He gave him everything. "This is all that I have. I suggest you read everything, and that you look at everything before you make one step. I suggest you do this before you even suggest to either David or Charlotte that you're thinking about a hypnosis. The entities, as you want to call them, are probably already aware that this thought is there. You may be in more danger than we realize. Then again, you might not be. But I will give you everything that I have if it will help you."

He gives him a huge stack of things that he has compiled. It was obvious to Robaire that some of it had come from him, and some of it had come from the private detective. He says, "Do you know where the private detective lived? Possibly we could put a phone call into him and see if he has any relatives."

Otto Weinberger cautioned him against doing that, "If the private detective's disappearance is somehow connected to all this other business that's going on, then I wouldn't advise you to put in a phone call anywhere. Take these things home and read them carefully. Go back over the tapes. Ask David for the relic after you do these things. Then see if you want to become further involved. See if you want to leave Yvette in the house any longer."

He proceeds to tell Otto Weinberger, "Well, we've been out to dinner. The girls are out right now visiting the art gallery because the first thing Yvette wanted to know was where the art gallery was and why she isn't planning for the next season. That's what they are doing right now. So, things are really, from our point of view, not so bad. They are planning a dinner party for some of the people in Mendocino. And one of the reasons that they are going to have this dinner party is because Charlotte needs to do an inventory and get her manners and various other things together prior to her wedding guests' arrival. They thought that this would be a good way to play act it out. I'm sure you're on the list. Maybe you should come and see that there has been a great change from what you have been telling me and from some of what David has alluded to."

Otto Weinberger says, "Fine, but do these things first. Go to the library. Visit the art gallery yourself. Then let's talk about it."

Robaire says, "I have no problem with that. I really believe in doing my research. I know I'm new to the situation, and I know that some very horrible things have happened here. I'm just hoping that I can give a reasonable explanation because basically that's the way I like to look at things. Nine times out of ten, everything has a logical reason for happening, and I always come from the position that I will eventually find it."

He excuses himself and once again Otto Weinberger tells him, "You are free to come anytime you would like to. And if I sense that it's dangerous for anyone of us, I'll let you know."

Robaire says, "If I sense that it is dangerous for either one of us, I will also voice that opinion."

Robaire returns two or three hours behind the girls. He decides that it is too late to go to the public library, so he is just going to go library in the house and read the books that have been given to him by Otto Weinberger. The nanny comes in and asks him if he would like an afternoon snack, some tea or a coke. He tells her, "Yes, I'll have a slice of pie and a glass of milk." He proceeds to eat that while he is going through these manuscripts.

David has been up in San Francisco trying to find out what is going on in New Jersey and, still, if any suspicion has been cast upon him. He is also talking to various churches. He has narrowed it down to the Catholic church. He wants to know if he gave a description of these monks, if someone could tell him what order they belonged to. That's what he decided to spend his day doing. As it turns out, the monks were so nondescript, and for the time period that they were, they really couldn't place them as being anything other than the monk of probably some trier. It could have been a Catholic trier. It could have been a denomination. So that is a dead end. He has a few names and a few contacts that he is going to try to talk to when he gets back home. He decides that since it is getting late, he had better start his drive back to Mendocino.

He arrives about dinner time. He is exhausted. He wants to shower and go to sleep for at least three hours. They decide that they just might as well have a late dinner because Robaire is very much into his reading. The girls decide to go and start their list of people who they might want to invite. They also figure out who would be a bridesmaid, and who will just be out in the audience.

Everyone is busy. They decide that they will probably have dinner about ten o'clock or eleven o'clock, and they will have it out on the terrace. They inform the housekeepers of this. The housekeeper and the nanny had already eaten their meals.

Yvette says, "I'm very happy with Jennifer. You didn't really mention Jennifer to me before. I kind of wondered how things were going, still operating and what was happening. I guess I just kind of got the picture that everything had just stopped dead."

Charlotte says, "Oh no. Jennifer has been with me since the beginning. She went with me to the city planning meeting. No. I hired her very early. I was very lucky to find her. She is out of New York. She's mostly familiar with imports, cataloging imports that come in off ships. But she has had some art background, and with the attention to detail that she has and the cataloging experience, I thought was invaluable. She was ready to make a change since she was answering an ad that I had placed in San Francisco. She thought that this was a lot less hustle and bustle and that she would settle right in. So far, she has. She's been just perfect. I thought after the first set of murders that she would quit, but she didn't. I gave her a paid vacation and told her to come back when she felt that she could, and of course I came to you. I think maybe that's what kept her on."

Yvette says, "Well, I think that's a good idea, and I think it is also a good idea that you spend a little bit more time with the art gallery because look at you. You are a lot less hurried. You are almost right back to your old self, the person that I've known all these years. You were quite different when I arrived."

Charlotte says, "Well, I guess you're right. I guess I am back to my old self, if that's a good place to be. But let's go on with making the list."

In the back of Charlotte's mind, Charlotte knows she is not back to her old self. She knows that things have happened to her that she will never be able to erase. She is happy that it's not as apparent anymore to Yvette. That is a victory, because then maybe she and whatever family she produced could survive, and maybe what her ancestors have been telling her has been true, and that is she will be able to cover this up and she will be able to pull this off.

They go down for dinner. The men are already in the library having a before dinner drink. Everybody is relatively casually dressed. David is aware that Robaire has been back to see Otto Weinberger. He is a little bit relieved because this is a path that he doesn't have to beat anymore, and it's almost as if he's got his private detective back. He is relieved that he has somebody that is a little bit more sensitive, and who at least seems to know that he must proceed cautiously. He hopes Robaire is a much better friend. He is happy that he has gotten all this information from Otto Weinberger. Now he is going to take the time to go over it.

He shows him the relic. He tells him about the monks again, and that he went to San Francisco to see if he could try to place the order. He says, "I didn't get very far, but I got a few contacts that I came back with. Maybe between the two of us, if it's even important, we will find out what was going on here."

Robaire says, "I have a feeling, and I don't know where it's coming from, that that isn't important. It's not as important as you think."

David says, "I just spent ten hours driving time back and forth to San Francisco asking people about monks' robes, and you're going to tell me now that it's not important? Do you know how much attention I've drawn to myself?"

Robaire says, "Well, it's not that it's not important or it has no significance. If you come up with something, maybe we will be able to use it. The reason that I'm not going to have you focus on it is because I have three theories right now since reading this information from Otto Weinberger and studying the interviews that I have done with him, the observations that I have made in the house, and things that you've told me. Either the house itself is haunted or it has nothing to do with anyone here, and maybe even predates the financier and the ship captain, or someone or something, more than one thing from your own admission, has decided to protect Charlotte and has drawn lines around her. Charlotte is the reason that these things happen.

"It doesn't matter what you see if whatever it is that is harming Charlotte is stopped. I'm further exploring that line of thought because of the way Otto Weinberger had his experience. He admits to having provoked the action. But what happened to him didn't have any real significance other than to stop him from continuing his action, and to let him see, if he could be the lead, how a vampire feels. That's the two things that came out of that. He doesn't want to come anywhere near this house. He is hoping that no one will bother him in his own house. He had a very good feel for what it feels like to be a vampire. But he didn't get sympathetic with it, or there's no empathy in him for it. He just knows what it feels like. Maybe it was just to show him the power of it, versus trying to get some sympathy.

"It is not a typical haunting. There are no cold spots in this house. There is no sad story about some girl who has hung herself, and we keep seeing her walk down the same hall in a wedding dress. It's not those repeat types of things."

David says, "Well, that's kind of the conclusion that I have come to." He doesn't actually say that he knows that this is true, but he says, "That's somewhat of the conclusion that I've come to. But please feel free to explore the possibility of just the house itself being haunted."

Robaire says, "Of course I will. I'm going to review the information that was provided by your private detective and by Otto Weinberger about the local area, and everything that they have on Charlotte's history and the history in general. Then I'm going to go to the public library and see what I can find out myself. But there is still that one thing that is bothering me. You said you answered it before. I still don't know what provoked the private detective, who you told me yourself was your friend or somewhat of a friend that you hired on more than one occasion over the years, to try to beat you to death and rape your fiancé. You haven't given me a good explanation for that.

"Either he was a shady character to start with, and I believe that you would have told Charlotte that he was a shady character, or there is something you're not telling me. Did he snap in a way that was different from what I've seen in Otto Weinberger? Otto Weinberger has snapped. You're aware of that, aren't you? You realize that somehow, we must all bear some responsibility for that. And I know you love Charlotte, but you have got to start talking to me because from your own admission probably three people have died and one of them in a very bad way. That's what you brought me here for. You said I could come. I realize that I came at my own risk, but you did want help if you could get it. And I need to understand again what your relationship was more clearly with the detective because apparently, he was trying to help too."

He says to him, "The private detective broke into my house."

Robaire says, "I know. You told me that he broke into your house and that he beat you up. Why did he break into your house and beat you up?"

David says, "It didn't quite happen in that sequence. He was in my house when I arrived. He had broken into my darkroom, and he had found some things in my dark room that I didn't want him to see."

Robaire says, "Yes, you mentioned that before, but I need to know what those things were."

David says, "I left Charlotte to go on assignment because Otto Weinberger had assured me that she would be quite safe. And she was very upset with me.

She didn't want to let me into the house. So, I went to Europe. I somehow got this fabulous assignment Morace. Then I took the opinion that it would get me closer to knowing what she's about. When I came back, Jasper had decorated the house, but the decorations were very dark, very heavy. The tapestries were heavy. The house was not black, but if you draw the drapes during the daytime, no sunlight will come in. And Charlotte was in a reverse schedule where she was sleeping in the daytime, and she was only seeing me at night. And I can't swear to it, I guess I can't repeat it, I wouldn't put my finger on it, but it seems to me that everybody in this house was operating off some kind of unknown telepathy and Charlotte was controlling it.

"She was mistress of her house. I panicked. It didn't change until you and Yvette came, and I don't know what will happen when you and Yvette leave. But I couldn't break her out of it. So out of the panic I went through the newspapers and looked up the old papers to find out where her parents were buried, and what had happened in the accident. I exhumed the bodies."

By this time, he is crying. Robaire says, "If you don't want to talk about the rest of it right now, maybe I pushed too hard. The girls will be down soon, and this would be difficult to explain."

David says, "No. I want to tell you all of it now. If we must move, we can go outside so they won't find us. We'll have to do that. But I exhumed the bodies. The private detective helped me, and some other people that I knew who wouldn't talk if I paid them. I was the only one that got close enough to see what was inside, and I photographed it.

"I guess you know that her parents died in a car accident, and that their bodies didn't burn completely. And what I found inside was not totally human. It was two charred bodies in separate coffins. And we opened them both. I asked the men to back up so that I could get a better fix and a better picture. It was because I had already spotted that something was different about the hands. So, I got a good close view of the hands, and I clipped the hair from the hands because the hands were not human hands.

"The hands were paws on both parents. I clipped nails from the hands. And up under the nails were fragments, it turned out to be, of the roof of a car. I put these things in a zip-loc bag. I put the hair and the nails in one bag, and I put the metal fragments, which is another reason I went up to San Francisco, in another bag. Then I noticed that this relic, what we have been calling a coat of arms, matched her parents' two rings. One ring appeared to be a regular wedding ring. The second ring appeared to be a replica of the coat of arms. I wasn't sure because it was small. It was miniature. So, I took out the coat of arms to put it closer together, and the bodies transformed. I photographed that too. Their clothing was no longer burned. It was no longer tattered. The people were beautiful. Charlotte's father and mother were beautiful. They looked like they were between thirty-five and forty-five. They were unscathed. They didn't get up. There was no life to them, but they were just beautiful. I put the relic away, and I closed the coffins.

"Then I asked the people to come back and help me cover them up. I dropped the hairs off at some local veterinarian, and I told him that I had gotten attacked by a wolf. He believed me at the time. I told him that I didn't know what it was, that I thought maybe it was a cat, I wasn't sure because I was drunk, I had run off the road. He told me that whatever the story was he would examine it and tell me what kind of animal it was. I told him that I was concerned about rabies shots or something at the time, and I needed to know right away.

"I developed the photographs, and they came out very good, just the way I thought. That's what the private detective found. He also found the veterinarian's report that explained that the hair was the hair of a wolf, and the nails were the nails of a wolf. He saw the paws and he put two and two together and decided that this was too horrible to live, as far as I can gather. So, by the time he had seen all this, I was walking into my apartment. He began to yell at me uncontrollably, 'I figured it out and, you haven't paid me enough'. I offered to pay him more. He said, 'You couldn't pay anybody enough to deal with whatever this is. This should not live, and you may be one of them. You should not live'. He proceeded to beat me to death because I had wrestled his gun from him. He left me for dead. He thought I was dead. I wasn't sure I wasn't dead with what had happened. I managed to get up because I knew that he would be heading for Charlotte, and I got there just in time to see what I had told you earlier. I didn't know for at least two or three weeks where his body was until I got a phone call from the publisher who originally recommended him to me, and he told me that he had died of a heart attack. As far as I know, that's all that you didn't know."

Robaire says, "Well, that's pretty significant. Yes, you should have told me about that, and I would like to see those pictures. I would like to see those pictures as soon as possible."

David says, "Hold on. The more you know, in a way, the more danger you put yourself in. The thing that I have been telling you is that I didn't kill the private detective. She didn't kill the private detective, and neither one of us intended for him to die. Yes, I will show them to you if you want to see them, but I can't guarantee your safety."

Robaire says, "That's what I'm here for. Calm down. It may not be as bad as you think it is. I know that's a horrible experience to go through even if you had found nothing, and it took a lot of courage really for you to do that. And you must really love her to even risk that. That's the way you must look at it. Just calm down. I'm sure we will find a way out of this because that gives me a lot of information, a lot of directions that I know not to go into now."

By this time, the girls are downstairs. They are talking about the art gallery, about Jennifer, and they are talking about the wedding. There is an uneasy quiet between the two men. Only Charlotte notices it. Yvette is not as perceptive.

Dinner goes quite smoothly with just small talk. Both men now make sure that it stays small talk.

They retire for bed. They play backgammon before they go. They take their baths and go into their separate rooms. Then the nanny tells everyone good night. She especially comes in and checks on Charlotte to make sure that Charlotte can sleep and takes her medicine. It is lights out for the night.

The next morning everyone arrives for breakfast. Breakfast goes without incident. The girls plan to put in a call to Europe to see if they can contact the designer that Yvette had do the drawings for the wedding dress and some of the people who were producing the fabrics. They thought that that would probably take them most of the day, even with the time lapse. The men express a feeling of claustrophobia and ask just to be able to get out and drive around the countryside, because Robaire hasn't seen any of the countryside, and this is his first time in this part of the United States. They really plan to go to David's apartment and look at the photographs and all the other documentation that David has in his apartment. The girls say fine, and they proceed with the things that they had to do.

The gentlemen take David's car into town, which is about an eighty-minute drive. Along the way David, once again, tries to explain to Robaire that the more involved he becomes the harder it would be to extricate himself from this situation, he'll just be pulled in deeper, and that they can't guarantee his protection. Robaire says he has been in situations, that he can't say are similar, but that have been dangerous, and he will just have to go along and see. When they arrive at David's apartment, it was still a mess. David has done what he could to straighten it up during the time that he could leave Charlotte and fix it.

He had a housekeeper that came in on a twice-weekly basis, but he suspended her when he realized the situation and what he had in his apartment. He goes to the dark room where he has things pretty much locked up and brings out the photographs that have been developed and affixed for Robaire to look at. As he shows him the photographs he explains to him again the scenario, the explanation, what he originally saw, who he believes were the only people that were privy to this information, the only people that actually saw this and why he kept them away. He related to Robaire how something told him to just ask them to stand back, that there was a possibility that there would be something to be seen that he didn't want them to see, and some of the people he doesn't even know how to find now. They were just paid to do this, and he hopes that they will keep their mouths shut.

The first series of photographs show the bodies in full view, full-length pictures. They don't pick up the detail of the hands. There are several of those. It is not a pleasant thing to look at, but it is not unusual for someone who had died in a car crash. The next series of photographs zero in on the hand. The couple are taken from an odd angle because the hand kind of popped out of the coffin. That is how David noticed it. He clicked the minute that it came out that way.

He is explaining these things to Robaire, "That's why they were taken at that angle because it scared me. I was shocked when it came out, and I didn't immediately notice it. Once I did notice it, then I changed lenses and started to pick up more detail and got my lighting and everything proper." He shows the pictures to Robaire with commentary. "I saw the paws at the different angles, and I decided to take close ups of the hands. The hands were the hands of a wolf. They had been burned."

The pictures supported his story, and the pictures didn't appear to have been retouched. Robaire wants to know if he could have some negatives so that he could check it out because he has methods of checking out these sorts of things.

David conceded. Then he showed him the next series of pictures. He says, "I had discovered the rings and the various jewelry that was still left apparently unscathed by the fire. The parents were buried in it. That's what gave me the idea to bring the relics up closer to one of the rings, which was clearly not a wedding ring. I wanted to see if the two matched, or if there was a difference, to try to note the difference. When I did that, the next series of pictures show the transformation."

Robaire is in awe, but he had to have professional skepticism. He says, "This is amazing. I can see why you were amazed at what has taken place, but I still need to look at the negatives to make sure that nothing has been retouched."

David agrees, "I don't know why you would think that I would want to make this up but do whatever you can to ensure that this is not so." Then he gave him the veterinary report. Robaire read the veterinary report. It wasn't very extensive. He understood that the hairs and the clippings that came from the source that David says was the tombs of Charlotte's parents were the hairs of a wolf. The only other way he could verify that is to go and repeat the examination. He wasn't quite ready to do that.

He says to David, "Before I can verify this, we'll have to assume that everything is just as you're telling me. Try not to be offended by this. I'm coming from a different point of view than Otto Weinberger. I didn't come here looking for a vampire. I didn't come here looking for a werewolf or a ghost. I came here from the point of view that probably something here very normal and natural has gone on, and because of the stress of the situation and other things that have happened and different people's imaginations, the ordinary has appeared extraordinary. So, bear with me. Now when you saw these bodies, you say you noticed nothing different than charred bodies?"

David says, "Well, wait a minute. I'm not used to looking at charred bodies. I'm a freelance photographer. I don't normally follow a coroner when I freelance. I do all kinds of things, but murders are not things that I normally do, or fires. They're not things I normally do. The whole series of murders that I got involved in before I met Charlotte was unusual because I had not been used to doing that sort of thing. I would have had enough sense to know that someone would probably track me.

"I could have anticipated some of the things that were to follow, but that was the first and last kind of assignment that I would take like that. I'm not used to looking at bodies. I'm just normally an observant person, and I knew that when I went in there to exhume these bodies that I had better be observant. So, I saw charred bodies at first, and I saw normal hands and feet, and I thought. It's not an easy thing for me to look at because it's not something that I'm used to doing."

So Robaire says, "Hold on, don't get offensive. I understand what you're saying. I just want to make you aware that these things are also true. You are not used to looking at this, and even for the average person, even if they're of sound mind and very practical, there is a little bit of the supernatural that's surrounds a cemetery and a grave anyway. Will you concede to that?"

David says, "Yes, of course I will concede to that."

"Will you concede to the fact that you probably were terrified for reasons other than the fact that you would get caught in a criminal act. You were thinking that if you went to exhume a body that you would have a lot of emotions running through your mind about what you were doing, probably resulting from childhood fears and other kind of fears that people normally have if they go near a graveyard. Is that right?" asks Robaire.

Robaire says, "Well, hold on. That's exactly what I'm trying to point out to you. Now, you took these pictures, and you admit that when the hand came out, the hand startled you. You admit that you were nervous throughout the whole procedure for a lot of reasons."

He says, "Yes, I was nervous throughout the procedure for a lot of reasons. That's why I'm glad that I'm not coming back to tell the story without evidence. I'm glad that I have photographic evidence of what took place and I have the veterinarian report. Now unfortunately you are not going to be able to go back and see those hands because those hands are no longer there. But it may be evidence enough if you want to re-exhume to find that these bodies don't appear to be bodies that have burned in a fire any longer. These bodies will look like the bodies in the third series of pictures, and that would be totally different from the description given by the coroner at the time of the murder. But I caution you that I don't know what happened when I brought these two objects in contact to cause this transformation. I personally would not try to re-exhume knowing that some change has taken place."

Robaire says, "Well, all this is noted. I hope I don't have to do an examination either. Go ahead, tell me some more. Let's back up again and tell me, you clipped this hair from the father's hand?"

He says, "Yes, from the father's hand. The mother's hand seemed to be in a similar condition as demonstrated by the photography. But to pick up one hand and clip the hair from it was a lot for me to do. I knew that if I got in there that I would have to have enough stomach to do that much, so I did that much. That seemed to be enough proof."

"Then you also," Robaire asks, "clipped the nails. What made you decide to clip the nails?"

David responded, "Because obviously the nails and the photographs demonstrate something very unusual for the hands of a human, and they didn't seem to be human nails, first of all."

Robaire asks, "Is there something else that made you clip the nails?"

He says, "Yes, I found particles of metal embedded in the nails, and I saw particles of what appeared to be upholstery embedded in the nails."

Robaire says, "What did you do with that? That's not mentioned in the veterinary report."

"I explained to you before when we were talking in Charlotte's library that I separated the two out because I suspected that they probably would call for more of an explanation to the veterinarian, if I had to explain these fibers and these particles. I didn't want to give him that much information. I just wanted to go in and tell him a story about running into an animal at night that I could not identify, that didn't really scratch me, so we wouldn't have to worry about having rabies shots. I told him that I was just concerned about the contact." That was David's story.

Robaire says, "And the veterinarian didn't ask you how you had time to clip his nails?"

He says, "Well, fortunately he didn't. You're right. He didn't buy much of the story. The reason that he didn't buy much of the story was because the hair, he said, was over forty years old or at least somewhere between thirty and forty years old. He wasn't sure where it was placed or how to place it. He thought perhaps I had run into something that had been hanging off someone's wall. That was his suggestion. He made light of the whole situation that maybe it was something that had been shot and stuffed, and that would account for the appearance and the consistency of the hair. Fortunately for me, he laughed the whole thing off. He identified it as definitely being the hair of a wolf, but other than that, he couldn't believe that it was a live wolf that had attacked me within the last twenty-four or forty-eight hours."

Robaire says, "Well, it is a possibility. You could have found a stuffed animal, and you could have cut the hair off a stuffed animal and cut the nails off a stuffed animal."

David says, "If there's a lab that you trust, you're welcome to take these specimens, including the metallic specimens. I dropped some of them off in San Francisco, and I am having them analyzed now."

Robaire says, "Well, what story did you give them?"

David answers, "I didn't have to give them a story. I just asked them for an analysis. I paid them, and I'm waiting for the report to come back."

Robaire says, "I think that's probably the best approach. We should limit these fabrications that you have to give people because eventually, it's a small world is what I'm trying to tell you, and one might run into the other. And there are three people dead!"

David says, "I realize that there are three people dead. That's why I took these into San Francisco, and I did the other specimens locally. I'm really getting tired of having to go through the third degree with you because you asked me to explain to you what happened. You started out saying that you assumed, until you could prove different, that I was telling you the truth. So, if you want to hear the story, let the rest of the story come out. Then when you want to channel the questions or play devil's advocate, I would appreciate it if you did it then because this is very real to me.

"If you could believe that this has happened to me, then you must understand the kind of stress that I'm under and the kind of stress that Charlotte is under. I know that you must play the skeptic, but I would ask you if you could just go on and leave me alone right now. I'm not happy that I exhumed my fiancé's parents and that they weren't totally human."

Robaire says, "Yes, I guess that is a difficult situation for anyone to take. I will, with your permission, take some of the negatives. You have enough negatives here that I could take a few frames, and you will still retain a few frames of each incident and have them analyzed. I'm going to send them to Europe or maybe carry them back myself. I'll take the clippings that remain when the other specimens are sent back from San Francisco and any other things that I can. It's possible that I can get someone to identify and date the relic, if it's even possible, if it's old enough for that. I'll try to do everything I can to substantiate this."

David says, "What if everything we say is true? You have hard cold analytical facts, which would be pretty much the approach that I took. But I was hoping that I would find something different, that this is the hair of a wolf that has been dead thirty years, that these photographs have not been retouched. I am confident that the relic we have may date back to the tenth century. Then what do we do?"

Robaire says, "Well, if we know that all of that is true, then I simply have to wait for another visual occurrence that I can be an observer at, and hopefully be an unharmed observer. At that point, I will probably have several suggestions about what we can do. In the meantime, since we all seem to be aware that the planning of the wedding and Yvette's presence have made a marked change in Charlotte, let's just work on that positive because that's going. We seem to have some time to resolve this."

David says, "That's just what bothers me because I don't believe that we really have time. I don't believe that these other things, or entities, have just gone away. I think they are constantly around her to make sure that she is all right, and they are permitting this to happen, at which time they are going to pull it back or turn the course. I don't know how I would want to put it. I don't know."

Robaire says, "Did Otto Weinberger tell you the rest of his theory of why you have not been harmed. You realize that everyone has been harmed but you?"

David says, "Yes, but I have no intention of harming Charlotte."

Robaire says, "You have no intention of harming Charlotte, that's true. I have no intention of harming Charlotte. Otto Weinberger had no real intention on harming Charlotte. But there was some process that he believed to be going on that he would like to have prevented from happening, and they harmed Otto Weinberger. You don't believe Otto Weinberger was going to harm Charlotte, do you?"

David says, "No, I don't believe that. Otto Weinberger was trying to help her."

Robaire responds, "All right. Well, you know he was trying to help her. How was he going to help her?"

David answers, "Well, obviously he was going to stop the process of vampirism."

Robaire says, "Well, seemingly that's enough to get you harmed around here, if I buy everything you say and everything is true, and if I buy everything that Otto Weinberger says that he believes to be true. He admits that at this point he may not be the best source of information, but a lot of times, even in the ravings of someone who might be slightly mad, from time to time there's a little bit of truth. They have plans for you. They want you to continue with the wedding, and they want you to marry Charlotte. The two picture perfect pair that you photographed, Charlotte's mother and father, maybe you can put them on her wall because she doesn't have any photographs of them. It's very possible that if what everyone thinks is true is going on, then you will be part of that picture-perfect pair also. I think that's the plans that they have for you. Have you thought about it? If you haven't thought about it, you had better think about it. I don't even know if I set myself up by saying what Otto Weinberger is sure is a reality."

David says, "Some of it I considered. A lot of what I've had to do because I've had to do it alone and under confidentiality, I have been reacting. I have always been reacting. I haven't had a lot of time for long term plans, except for the wedding or for sometimes quiet thought. I'm either driving here or driving there or reacting to this or reacting to that. Some of this has occurred to me. How I will offset it has not occurred to me. The only thing that really seems to be foremost in my mind is that I don't want to lose Charlotte."

Robaire says, "You tell me though that she has a definite telepathic ability, and this telepathic ability extends beyond communication to control, or you feel control. Do you think perhaps she is exerting this on you? And please don't get upset with me. Have you evaluated your feelings for her? Do you think that your feelings for her are genuine?"

David says, "That's the one thing I am sure of because those feelings came long before I began to detect this in Charlotte."

Robaire says, "Yes, it came long before you began to detect those things in Charlotte, but all the time there was a supernatural presence. But we should probably start driving home to be there for lunch, or we might arrive late and arouse some very natural, very real, anger."

They go to the apartment. Robaire gets his samples, the samples that are available to him. They take the forty-five-minute drive back to the estate where the ladies are waiting. They are pretty much excited because they have gotten a commitment from someone to do her dress. They are still deciding on color schemes and fabric, but of course they don't want to reveal that too much to the gentlemen because that is bad luck. When this statement is made by Yvette, David and Robaire just look at each other.

They all sit down to have a nice lunch that has been prepared by the servants.

They decided that it's time to go horseback riding. They know that they have all been inside too much, and it is time to go horseback riding altogether for the rest of the afternoon. They ride over a good portion of her land of her estate. Charlotte owns ten to twelve acres. They go down to the sea because Yvette hasn't seen any of it and Robaire hasn't seen any of it. They take paths down to the sea. They take paths up and around the house and all around the area.

Charlotte tries to explain to them what she knows of the area and that is that there is this beautiful coast, and just about five or ten miles, which is the area where her estate spans, is the redwood empire. They ride through the redwoods.

Yvette and Robaire are very impressed by the beauty of it all. They can understand now why anyone would choose to pick this location. They realize how lucky her family was to have found this house that was situated right between the redwoods and the ocean.

They ride the complete perimeter, which takes them all of four or five hours. There is the much discussion of the wedding and the wedding plans. They are joking back and forth and just having good natured fun. It is very relaxing for everybody.

They stop, get off their horses and walk a little while. They sit down and talk. Most of the conversation is on the wedding. Most of the conversation is conducted by the females. It would appear to be introverted, but it is just between the women. There is a silent bond between David and Robaire now, and there is a lot more on their mind. They don't want to be as obvious that there's a lot more on their mind. The women talk about who they want at the wedding and who they don't. They do a lot of reminiscing, once again, about who they knew in school and who should come in what capacity. They try to make the men familiar with this person's and that person's personality, and why they want this person to be a bridesmaid. They ask their opinion on the color choices. The men give standard responses, but they are not really thinking about the conversation. It doesn't really matter because the girls are so involved in it, they just overlook the fact that the men are not as involved in it as they are.

This conversation continues sporadically for about two hours. The women end up making the suggestions and answering their own questions. They are thinking that everybody is in full agreement with it because there's really no argument.

They return to their rooms, change clothes, shower, and come downstairs.

Of course, the men somehow seem to arrive in the library first. Robaire says, "I am going to get the specimens off right away. I have decided that I should not leave and take them in myself, but I have ways of getting them to some people in Europe to see. I'm not going to wait for the analysis from the lab on the metals and the upholstery. When I get back, I will either take it on face value or I will send it back to you. Since no one has the car, it doesn't really matter that the analysis comes back describing it as upholstery or that is fifty years old. At least I think no one has the car."

He says to David, "I'm still very much concerned about Otto Weinberger, and I have very gray hopes that Otto Weinberger's story is wrong. Maybe this whole thing was too tiring for him. He's been back and forth to Europe several times and he's also been a party to two very horrible murders. He had to sit around and try to hunt a vampire that may or may not have existed. So, let's start from the premise that possibly he had an altered state of reality, that he didn't see quite what he thought he saw, and he didn't experience quite what he thought he experienced. The best thing that we can do for him, since the psychiatrist hasn't been able to do that for him, I'm going to suggest that the psychiatrist that you mentioned visit him for two or three days before I do and consult with him, if he will permit it.

"Then I would like to put Otto Weinberger through a series of hypnoses with the psychiatrist present. I say Otto Weinberger because Charlotte seems mentally to be a lot more stable and not as critical right now in terms of priority, and because I can't see why they would object to that. If we can confirm that he is seeing these things, then once again I will have to take another look at what's going on here."

David says, "Then will I be next because I told you that there are certain things that I have seen?"

Robaire says, "You also told me that at the time you saw them you had almost been beaten to death, and since then both you and Otto Weinberger say that before that happened and since that happened you have seen nothing, and no one has attempted to do anything to you for any reason. So, possibly you'll be the next person if all goes well with Otto Weinberger, and possibly we'll go straight to Charlotte, if hypnosis will work in this instance. Tomorrow morning, because I think it is probably too late to do it now, I want you to make the introductions for me to the psychiatrist that you have had involved in this and let me talk with him. I would like to visit him at his office."

David says, "That means driving to San Francisco."

Robaire says, "Well, when will your specimens be ready?"

David says, "I can call and find out if they will be ready tomorrow. If they are, we can go and pick them up and talk to the psychiatrist. I believe that he will be available for us during the day, as long as we let him know that we are coming."

Robaire says, "Well, that's good. That's no problem. But what will the ladies be doing?"

David says, "They seemed to have had quite a good time visiting Jennifer when they went out to the art gallery, and I think Yvette's idea of bringing her back to the business world is not a bad one. I'm going to suggest, even if I must call Jennifer, that they go in and check on the instructions that I know from talking to Charlotte that she has left. She should follow up on that to make sure that Jennifer does everything asked of her. She doesn't have to follow up on that by phone. They could drive into Mendocino and make another day of it, have lunch. That way, Jennifer won't be so alone or by herself the whole time that day. That's what I'm going to suggest they do."

By that time, Charlotte is downstairs. She tells him, "Yvette is still fussing over her hair. I think that I want to have a haircut, but I'm not sure. We can't make up our minds. I advised her to leave it as is because once you cut it, it's decided. I told her that if you haven't made up your mind, maybe you should let somebody professional cut it."

David says to her, "Didn't you leave some instructions for Jennifer to choose some people or to write back to some people who had asked to be exhibited in your art gallery in the upcoming season?"

Charlotte says, "Yes, I did. I told her that I would get back to her by phone to see if she had any more information."

He says, "Isn't it about time to be having a response from them? Did you telex them?"

She says, "I don't know if she telexed them or if she wrote them."

He says, "I think that you should be paying just a little bit more attention to business. I think that I should too because even though we are making wedding plans, we should still generate some friends around here."

Charlotte says, "Yes, you're right. I do have a business, and I should be paying more attention to my business."

He says, "I think that you and Yvette should go into Mendocino tomorrow and spend a little bit more time with Jennifer because I know that you sent her off on these vacations. But as you said before, you sensed that she would feel a little bit more comfortable if she had more frequent contact with you, and according to you she just loves Yvette. So why don't you two spend the day following up as much as you can on what you've asked her to do with recruiting new artists for the exhibit. Maybe you could take her out to a nice lunch. Do a little window shopping or whatever. Make a day of it. Maybe go to a matinee, the three of you. I think it would be good for all three of you."

She says, "You're probably right because we been spending too much time on these dresses, and it has gotten little bit frustrating."

He asks her, "Why is it frustrating?"

She responds, "Well, it's not something that you normally discuss with your bridegroom, but it's just frustrating because I can't make up my mind and Yvette doesn't want to dress me. She wants me to make up my mind. I can't make up my mind to exactly what I want. She brought me some very beautiful choices. There are just too many beautiful choices, and I can't wear everything. I want it to be significant. I can't make up my mind."

David says, "Well, since we haven't even set an exact date, you should take that pressure off you. You have plenty of time to decide which one you want to wear. Maybe one of the fabrics you will want to use at the wedding, and the other fabrics you could use at the reception and make evening dresses out of them. We could bring them along on our honeymoon."

She says, "Our honeymoon? We'll be leaving the estate?"

That brought out a deadly silence. He is thinking, isn't it obvious that we could afford to go on a honeymoon? Why shouldn't we go on a honeymoon? Why is it that she doesn't want to be too far from her estate? He is thinking, maybe I'm just interrupting this wrong, so I'll just put the question to her. He asks her, "When are you planning to exhibit? I thought that you were planning to exhibit far enough in advance. And if you kept up with the business like I am suggesting you do, we'll have plenty of time to be away from both of our businesses for a while when it's time for our honeymoon. Where is it that you wanted to go, or have you thought about that? Have you talked to Yvette? Have you thought of a place that's special to you?"

She says, "Well, I have never really thought of leaving the estate. just thought the estate was so beautiful that we would just stay right here."

He says, "That never occurred to me. I thought perhaps we would go to Bermuda or perhaps we will go to Hong Kong. Have you ever been to Hong Kong? I know you spent a lot of time in Europe, but we could shop for jewels in Hong Kong, and Hong Kong is very romantic. We could take junks in Hong Kong harbor all evening, or even live on a junk for two or three weeks. There are a lot of different things that we could do."

She says, "I guess you're right. There are a lot of different things that we could do."

He says, "You were planning on evening dresses and other kinds of clothing to go away for at least a month, weren't you?"

She says, "No, I hadn't planned on that. I thought that we would invite a few friends here, we would have the wedding, and we would have a reception. I really hadn't thought much past that. I hadn't thought about us leaving." He didn't press the issue, but he thought that it was quite significant that she didn't think they would go on a honeymoon and that she was fighting the idea. without bringing out an obvious argument. He let it drop, but he noted it.

David puts his arms around Charlotte, and he walks her out toward the terrace so they could have a little privacy. He shuts the doors behind them. He says to her, "You know, we have got to have some time away by ourselves. I don't know why you haven't thought about this. We both have been through too much. And I care too much about you to have you not be able to rest, and I think that you cannot rest well here."

She says, "I think you have it backwards. I will rest better here than any place else. Don't you know that by now."

He says, "You don't want to go on a honeymoon?" As he is talking to her, he starts to lower his voice. He is trying to get her in a much more romantic mood.

She is not really avoiding it. It is just that she's a little surprised that he still doesn't understand. He gives her a very long deep kiss. To him, he has won the argument. She kisses him back. She wants to kiss him back. She is glad that he wants to kiss her. But he hasn't won the argument. He whispers in her ear, "I would love to be on a junk in the middle of Hong Kong harbor with you. Just take two or three days, a week maybe, or three weeks, just alone, the two of us. We would have so much fun. Can't you imagine what it would be like?"

She says, "I have some idea that it would probably be a nice honeymoon."

He says, "What about Bermuda? You swim like a fish. Wouldn't you like to go snorkeling? The weather is always hot there, and we could—"

She interrupts, "I live near a beach, and there's no better scenery than there is here." He is trying to get her to commit herself to thinking about a honeymoon, a honeymoon away from the estate. He becomes very physical with her. He kisses her and whispers in her ear. He pulls her very close to him.

She is fighting none of this. She finds it very enjoyable. She kind of melts into his body, kisses him back, lays her head on his shoulder, and listens to all his arguments about why they should leave the estate for at least a month, maybe even two. She thinks that he still doesn't understand, but there is time to convince him, and she won't argue with him about it now. She'll just let him make plans and think about it. He says, "I'll pick the place, and I'll pick the length of time," because he is feeling sure of himself, "I'll make the arrangements."

She says, "Fine," knowing fully well that she isn't going to go.

They continue their embraces out on the terrace. Coming down one of the garden paths are Robaire and Yvette looking for David and Charlotte. They pretend to be embarrassed and turn around and try to pretend they are sneaking away. Of course, they are called right back. They are told that they aren't interrupting anything. They say, "Don't expect us to believe that. We are going to go ahead and go right on to dinner because they're serving dinner now."

David says, "We're going on to dinner too. We might as well all go in together."

They all go into dinner, at which point they begin to talk about their honeymoon. David announces that he is going to decide where they are going and how they will get there, if they would go by cruise, or by boat, or probably do a combination of both. He makes it clear that he isn't very interested in going to Europe because he knows that Charlotte is very familiar with Europe, and he wants to show her something that perhaps she hasn't seen. He didn't think that she has been to the Orient yet, so he suggests going to Hong Kong or perhaps the Caribbean.

Yvette says, "I think the Caribbean would be wonderful. You could go there almost any time of the year and have a good time. Maybe you could do both because you can almost go to Hong Kong any time of year and have a good time. How lucky you are, Charlotte."

David says, "I am very familiar with both places. I have good friends in both places. I know some of the most scenic spots in both places."

Whereupon Charlotte says, "Well, when you went to those places before, were you always alone, or are you going to be taking me some place that you've taken someone else to?"

He says, "Oh no. Of course, I wouldn't do that. There are places that I have taken other people to, and there are people there that I have been intimate with prior to knowing you, but I wouldn't take you any place like that." She was still uncomfortable with the idea. She wasn't as uncomfortable as she appeared, and she wanted it to appear that she was jealous. She was just hoping that she could use that as more of an edge to stay home, which is really where she wanted to be.

Robaire picked up on this and decided that it was time to announce that he was going to attempt to put Otto Weinberger under a trance state. It just came out in the middle of the conversation because he knew she was hedging, or he felt he knew she was hedging somewhat, and he felt that David hadn't picked up on it. So, he decides to go to the heart of the matter, change the subject quickly and watch her reaction and see if she would be guarded about that. She turns to him and says, "What do you mean a trance, are you some kind of a medium?"

He says, "No. As we've discussed before, I'm just kind of an investigator in two-way paranormal. And oftentimes, people feel they've had a paranormal experience, and they're equally as relieved as you are to find out that they haven't had one. So, you do what you can to assure them that there isn't one, or if they've had one, that you know how to terminate it and to make sure it doesn't reoccur. And one of things you could do is put them under hypnosis and see what it is that they remember."

She thought that was a very good idea because she hadn't seen Otto Weinberger, though she wasn't very familiar with him. The only news that she ever heard of him was from Mr. Smythe, and Mr. Smythe was never very verbal about his friend. He was friendly and chatting, but mostly about the decorations and the landscaping. The last conversation she said she remembered them having was did she want any real hard construction done or did she just basically want to stick to landscaping and interior decorating. She told him that she hadn't really decided, and that since she was getting married, she was going to leave some things up to her husband to decide. Of course, David felt wonderful with that.

Again, Robaire sensed that she was hedging. He was uncomfortable with this because this was almost a deception, and in the beginning, Charlotte was much more open, much franker, and now she is starting to not out and out lie, but to almost manipulate. He knows it is not necessary to manipulate David because most of the time David does what she wants him to do, and she always picks the position that he could forget it. He is not sure where this new mood is coming from or why. He backs off the trance conversation.

David is very surprised that he even voiced it in front of her because he thought that they had agreed not to have this conversation. He thought that they had agreed not to let either one of them know that this was going to take place.

It didn't really matter because right in the middle of dinner, shortly after this interchange, Jasper Smythe is admitted into the dining room. He wants to talk. He doesn't wait to pull the gentlemen aside. He wants to blurt it out that he is very much concerned about his friend, and he was wondering if they had any ideas, or if they would just speak to him a minute about it. David and Robaire jumped up, and they insisted that the two young ladies continue their dinner. And of course, the nanny insisted that they do as well. They took him out on the terrace.

Jasper told them, "I have been visiting Otto Weinberger, and I feel that Otto Weinberger is taking a turn for the worse and he isn't coming out of it. I feel that this irrational fear of whatever it was that had happened to him, could happen to him at any minute again. No one can quit that fear. I invited Otto over to my house for a special occasion, and he attended. Usually, these kinds of activities would bring him out because he doesn't have a family and he can mingle with the children of all ages, my extended family. It would make him forget any problems that he was preoccupied with. He was very good with the children. And they noticed that he did a lot of talking to himself, and he was very unsure of everything. He was always looking over his shoulder, and he was just almost very difficult to deal with. He wasn't sure of anything or of anyone, and he almost had to leave just out of embarrassment because he couldn't keep his composure with all those people. The more people that arrived, the more upset he became instead of it calming him down. These were people that he knew, and he was used to seeing over the years. The more of them that came in, the more noise it was, the more it seemed to distract him, the less he was able to concentrate. And he left just so that he could leave without, what I would describe as, a breakdown. This happened yesterday. I have continued to call by phone to try to talk to him, and I'm not getting anywhere. I don't feel comfortable leaving him there. I won't be able to get him to come away or to have anyone else stay in the house with him."

Robaire says, "This means that I better go over there. We better call in the psychiatrist now and proceed with this after he has been sedated and had a good night's sleep. I will stay with him tonight, and, Mr. Smythe, I suggest you stay with him tonight because you're a person that he is familiar with. In the morning, if we have the permission of the psychiatrist, we'll begin with hypnosis."

They call the psychiatrist from the estate. He agrees to meet them at Otto Weinberger's house. They leave for Otto Weinberger's house immediately.

David tells the women that he would be back, and that Robaire would be staying with Otto Weinberger.

Charlotte expressed, as what could only be taken as very sincere concern, and with somewhat of a tinge of guilt, that she felt there was nothing that she could do about the situation, and it was better to let them go and try whatever it is that they were going to try before she attempted in any way to intercede. David, Jasper Smythe, and Robaire drive in Jasper Smythe's car over to Otto Weinberger's house. They know it's going to be four or five hours before the psychiatrist will even arrive.

They get him to admit them into the house, which is not the easiest thing to do.

Otto wants to know what they want. He says he has talked to them repeatedly and he has told them everything it is that he knows. He really does not want visitors. He is nervous, very nervous. They had decided on the way over to let Jasper do most of the talking because Otto has known Jasper the longest.

Jasper starts out telling him, "We are very concerned about you. This has gone on too long. You must fight it. And whether you like it or not, we are not going to leave you alone."

He says, "That's nonsense. I am used to living by myself, and there was no reason why I can't live by myself."

Jasper says, "You're right. There is no reason why you can't live by yourself. But for some reason you are very jittery and very nervous, and you're just not yourself. We have called for Dr. Andrews, and he's driving down now."

Otto says, "For me? You've called this Dr. Andrews for me? The one that we had working with Charlotte?"

He says, "Yes, we have because we don't think things are going quite right with you. We think he should sedate you because you don't look like you've been sleeping. We think that a good night's sleep or a couple of good nights' sleep is what you need. You know that we will watch you. We will know that you're all right. When you're well rested, we want to talk to you again. So, do you trust us enough to permit this?"

He says, "Yes."

They were concerned about what he had been eating, because they didn't think that he had been out shopping. Jasper checked his refrigerator and there was not much there to eat. So, David leaves to go and purchase some food, and Jasper and Robaire stay with Otto who hasn't shaved or done much of anything. He just seemed to be totally unaware of or totally out of contact with reality.

They talk to him. They encourage him to shave, change his clothing, get into some nice comfortable pajamas, and just take a good look at himself. When he went to look in the mirror, he, himself, was shocked at his appearance. He was also shocked that he had been over to Jasper Smythe's house the day before in that condition. Robaire convinces him to clean himself up, and they are with him most of the time while he is doing it.

By the time he had completed dressing for bed, David was back with food. They made him some hearty soup. David had also bought some pot pies, fresh bread, butter and fresh fruit. He didn't want to get him any wine because he didn't know what the doctor would sedate him with, and Robaire had suggested that Otto should avoid coffee and tea. He eats, and he has an appetite, a definite appetite. David eats little parts of it with him to reassure him. It tasted like good food. He ate just about everything they put before him. That made him drowsy. He began to sleep. He slept for about two hours before the psychiatrist arrived because at this point about four and a half hours had passed.

The psychiatrist has decided to give him an injection to sedate him to make sure he really goes to sleep. They promised him that at least those two would always be with him until the next morning. The psychiatrist decided that he wasn't going to leave either since he had come this far. Otto Weinberger's house is big enough that everyone could have a room, but Jasper and Robaire decided to stay in that very room and watch him. The psychiatrist decided to take the room next door, and he had brought an overnight bag.

Robaire asks David, "Would you go back to the estate and with Yvette's assistance, pack something for two or three or maybe five nights. I'm not sure how long we will have to stay here. Maybe you could grab something for me to read. That will give me something to do while I'm here."

Otto Weinberger slept. He slept a good twelve, thirteen hours. By the time he awakened, it was about one o'clock. The psychiatrist puts him through a series of tests, and he felt that more rest was called for since we now have a much clearer thinking Otto Weinberger.

So once again, they made meals for him and reminded him that he should go on and continue with his hygiene regiment. He sat and talked with them about various subjects mostly relating to projects that he had going in school. He was careful not to discuss anything that had to do with what was happening at Charlotte's house or any of the other research. He talked for three or four hours. Then they decided it might be a good idea for him to get dressed and walk around outside.

He went outside with Jasper and the psychiatrist. Robaire stayed inside to see if he could notice any changes, and there weren't any apparent changes to him. They walked him around outside for three or four hours. They took a nice good long brisk walk and by the time he got home he was tired and wanted to sit down. Robaire had made a fire for him. Jasper suggested that they play chess, which is something that they usually do. He tried to play chess, and they tried for two or three hours. He remembered the game, and he understood the moves, but he was just not the competition that he normally is. By this time, it was time for him to have another meal and then to go back to sleep.

They were preparing the meal while he was playing chess with his friend. He had started to relax a little bit because he had started to trust Robaire and the psychiatrist. Once again, he had a nice hearty meal. He was sedated without any argument because he could see that he was getting a better grip on things. He went back to sleep for another ten to twelve hours. While he was asleep, they discussed that probably what contributed to his problem, whether he had this experience or not, was lack of sleep, and then compounded by whether he had no desire, or it just didn't occur to him, to eat. The doctor also insisted that he take vitamins along with his meals because he was sure that would put him in the right frame of mind.

They had one more night like this. Then the psychiatrist felt that it would be a good time to go ahead and do the hypnosis. He was familiar with hypnosis and so was Robaire, so they did it together. Otto Weinberger understood the necessity for it. They explained to him that if he would recount the same story under hypnosis, it would tell them one thing and if he recounted a different story under hypnosis, it would tell them another. It was understood by Otto Weinberger and Jasper Smythe that if the story is true and these entities are interceding, then this would be the mildest way to find out because the next subject was going to be Charlotte.

They sat him down and began to go through the hypnosis. They were sure that he was in a deep trance because they also used medicine in addition to voice suggestion. Under hypnosis he recounted the same story, but this time with more clarity, more detail, and more terror. They had to bring him out of it before he could complete it. They let him go on and sleep after that. They suggested that he had memory of it, but that he understands who he was with now, and that the likelihood of this repeating again would not occur.

They let him sleep for another eight hours. Robaire is now exhausted. They decided since they got that much out of him, and it brought that kind of response that they really didn't need to go any further with him. They thought it probably wouldn't happen again with the post-hypnotic suggestions that they made. They wanted him to remember his constitution, his character, the person that he was before this had happened. They hoped that worked. But they could see how he could be terrified.

Jasper agreed to stay with him. By this time, David has found someone to do the housekeeping. She would come in and out to help Jasper. Jasper also had other relatives, younger nieces and nephews, that knew him very well and that he didn't have to explain anything to and they would take turns with him. It was pretty much decided that Otto Weinberger was not to be left alone, and that they would handle him like this.

Robaire and David return to the estate. The psychiatrist goes back to San Francisco feeling that Otto Weinberger can stay on an out-patient basis, unless he hears something different from Jasper and as long as he is able to sleep and eat, and if he could do some reading in his field, that no one should push him any harder than that. Charlotte, because she has a basic human concern, is anxious to find out the results of the hypnosis. Not so much the details as to what happened to him but if he was all right.

Robaire was anxious to see her paintings, but he wanted her to show them to her. He and David return to the estate. Then they needed to sleep, and they needed to relax. Charlotte and Yvette, during the day, spend half a day at the art gallery and the other half of the day planning the wedding. They are getting the names together. They are trying to set a wedding date because they hadn't set an exact date yet. But it was difficult to set an exact date because they hadn't got the bridal attire together. They were also projecting for the next showing.

David and Robaire slept for about two days because they had missed a lot of sleep. When they awaken, Robaire asks Charlotte to show him her paintings again, and asks her would she mind answering any questions about them. He deliberately leaves Yvette out of the situation. She takes Robaire downstairs to her room. She shows him the paintings. He asks her would she mind putting them in chronological order for him, if she could remember that. She attempted to do that. They were mostly done on large canvasses. She said she had started painting when she was about thirteen or fourteen and that she didn't paint when she was at school, she would paint when she had come home for various short breaks. He asks her, "Did you ever paint while you were at finishing school?"

She says, "Of course. When I was an art major, I did all kinds of paintings."

Then he asks her, "What are your subjects? Were they the same subjects?"

She says, "No. I preferred to do still lives of inanimate objects and I kept the same medium, watercolor."

He says, "Do you know what the subjects of these paintings are? And do you understand that all these paintings seem to have the same subject?"

She says, "I do now. I understand now what the subject of these paintings are."

He says, "What do you mean by now?"

She says, "I really would rather not discuss this with you."

He says, "Well, you trust me, don't you? You trust Yvette. And you know Yvette trusts me, and Yvette would only send you someone who would try to help you."

She says, "I believe that to be true, but I do not necessarily believe that you can help me. I do not believe that revealing this information could help anybody. And I do understand the subject of the paintings."

He says, "What do you mean revealing this information won't help anybody."

She says, "It's not really a question of revealing the information to help someone. It's a question of revealing the information not to harm someone. It's a question of privacy, and a question of loyalty to my family."

He asks her, "Is this your family?"

"I am not familiar with the people in the paintings."

"They are people and they seem to be very old paintings of different centuries, not anyone you could have possibly met. What prompted you to paint this sort of thing? What made you visualize this? Did you take it from a photograph, or did you just pick places with a scene that you had seen somewhere? I don't understand. There is a consistent theme running throughout these paintings. Did you just make this up?"

She says, "Once again, I would rather not talk about the paintings. I don't see any good reason to do anything more than evaluate them from a position of color and a position of an artistic point of view. Have I mastered my brush stroke? What kind of emotions did they evoke in the persons who looked at them? Did I do what I attempted to do in painting the pictures?"

"Well, what was it that you attempted to do?"

"It depends on one picture to the other. They're all depicting different scenes, and each one should create a different kind of feeling in the person who is looking at it. That's what art is all about."

He says, "You're hedging." He knew he was treading on uneven ground. "You're hedging. If you felt that, do you think that this is good work? I really don't know because I don't know anything about art. Do you think this is good work? Yvette tells me that you do reasonably good work."

She says, "I don't think that it's anybody's masterpiece, but it's not a bad piece of art."

"Do you plan to exhibit it in your gallery?"

"I won't exhibit this. I probably will exhibit the still life or other still lives that I have painted before."

"Well, why not?"

"I think it will reveal too much of my heritage." That came out before she knew it.

He says, "That's exactly what I'm getting at. Why is this part of your heritage?"

"I don't want to have to lie to you. You're a good friend of Yvette's, and Yvette is a good friend of mine. I would rather discontinue the conversation about these paintings."

He presses on, "I don't think you know why you painted these things in the first place. So, I don't even think that you could lie about it."

With that, she just turned around and walked off. She begins to look for David. She finds David not too far outside. He was close because he knew this was going on. She began to complain to David, even though she knew that David was not going to be a source of help. She says to David, "Robaire is questioning me."

David says, "Robaire is a friend of Yvette's, who is a friend of yours."

She says, "Well, I've noticed the camaraderie between you two since he's been here. He's been here almost two weeks. You can't tell me that you don't know that he's asking about those paintings, and you can't tell me that you don't know why I can't answer him."

By this time, Robaire has walked up. "And I would repeat that I know why you probably cannot answer me."

She turned around to face him and says, "And I think you know a lot less than you think you know. Now, I don't wish to discuss this anymore. And if you two have decided to do this together, then I'll have to take it up with David privately. I don't mean to hurt your feelings, Robaire, but I've got to settle this with my fiancé. Then I will talk with Yvette about you."

Robaire walks off. He had been dismissed. David stood there. Both knew that she wasn't going to say anything to David right there. There was kind of an uneasy silence. She glared at him. Then she left to go to her bedroom to lie down.

Robaire decides to talk to Yvette. At first, he comes back to talk to David because he knows that he is not too far away, and he knows that David is alone. He says to David, "I'm in a very bad position because I don't want to talk to

Yvette too much, although I know that Yvette is a very good friend of Charlotte. And I don't want to talk to you too much because I know that she has ways of getting things out of you. So, I'm going to have to think about what I can do. But I need some help with this. I think she needs to be put under trance, and I don't know if we could risk that. She seems pretty sure about what she said about knowing more about it than I thought she knew about it. So, I think what happened is that earlier on she didn't know, but she does know now, and she knows that she knows now."

David says to him, "That's kind of what I've been trying to explain to you. That was the change that I noticed when I had come back from my last job that prompted me to exhume her parents' bodies. There's a definite change in her, and she only shows it when she must. But she knows that there are certain things that she does not have to put up with, and she does not put up with them. She has a different sort of, I don't know how to describe it. When I first met her, it was total innocence, and now that is almost gone. Something or someone has filled her in. She's taken a definite position, and she's decided to guard that position.

"One of the positions is that she must protect her family and another one of her positions, which I understand very well, is that she must survive herself. But there's an intermediate position, or a third position, that I'm not quite sure about and that's got me uneasy. That is what has Otto Weinberger uneasy, and I think that is what has you uneasy, if you believe Otto Weinberger."

So Robaire says, "Yes, you're right. It's the third position. The first two are obvious. You want to protect your family name, and she's been through enough to suspect that oftentimes her life might be in danger. But there's something else that she knows, and she knows very well that she knows it. She's covering it up. I don't think she sees any reason why I should ever know. I think at a time when it's right you may find out some of it, but then again, I don't know if I will be able to communicate with you at that point."

With that, he walks off from David. David is back in the same position that he was in before, and David knows it. Robaire stays in his room for about two days. He doesn't come down and doesn't eat. He listens to the tapes over and over again because he is confused about what happened at David's apartment. He has some idea of what could have happened, but he is not sure. He decides that before he should even guess at what happened and be wrong, maybe he had better keep listening to the tapes. He does this. He tries to write notes from every angle to see if there was anything that he could have missed that Otto Weinberger was telling him because he feels that Otto Weinberger is very observant. He had to give him credit for being an observant person. He assumed there must be some merit, though the conclusions that Otto Weinberger has drawn don't have to be one hundred percent correct, his observations still have validity.

He goes over the tapes repeatedly. He concludes that he has overlooked another direction that he was going to go in before he began his hypnosis session. He realized that Otto Weinberger's state of mind, his fear for Otto Weinberger's wellbeing, and his mental disposition, has made him rush to do something. He did it in an order that he normally would not have taken had he been given more time. His next step is to get more of the house, more history of the surrounding area because Otto Weinberger had mentioned the relics to him, and because when he was in David's apartment, David displayed apparent willingness to show he was not trying to keep anything from Robaire that would harm Robaire.

And Robaire learned about the photographs, the veterinarian report and the transformation that the relic caused. He decides that the way to proceed is to find out some more information or any kind of information he could find out about the relics because when he starts to involve human beings in trying to relate their experiences, it doesn't work out well. He got enough information from Otto Weinberger to tell him that Otto Weinberger believes that the occurrences happened. But the cost to him was that Otto Weinberger was under a great strain and under hypnosis Otto Weinberger recalls for himself, from his own memory, in greater detail than he remembered in his conscious mind.

The only conclusion that he can draw is that something blocks David. David related seeing one happening and something blocked them. If the other stories about Charlotte are true, possibly it was Charlotte. Maybe Charlotte was right. The clarity in what David had seen, he should not remember as well as he should remember other things, or he might have ended up in Otto Weinberger's position, and obviously the psychiatrist, though he is very well credentialed, is not in a position to evaluate this. Robaire knows that he is not able to evaluate this. He is sending these thoughts through his mind. He is losing a lot of his anger.

He has decided that maybe right now his investigation should not be so personal and that the history of the books and the inanimate objects that he has should give him some information. He is thinking about Charlotte's paintings, how she described painting attacks by villagers, peasants, or also by clergy. Possibly there is something, protective about the relics, as David suggested when they were in his apartment. He has got to find out why that relic is protected if it was not a curse, and maybe he will be permitted to do that. If he is permitted to do that or if he tries to do that, then probably he will only be risking his own life and his own sanity.

That's the direction that Otto Weinberger started in, and he didn't seem to get into trouble until he left that direction and started heading toward Charlotte. So, he is going to work on the theory that maybe he will be permitted to do that, and possibly he could do it and be up front about it with David and with Charlotte. He doesn't know if Charlotte knows anything about them, if she understands anything about them, or if he just comes right out and asks her, will she tell him. But if they have the kind of power that David said they have for the family and possibly for herself, then he should know more about them. Then he realizes that if they were, he wouldn't tell either. But it is the only line that he could pursue, and he needed something, somewhere to go. Otherwise, he is spinning his wheels. He needs direction.

He goes downstairs after the second day. No one has bothered him. David has been sleeping. Yvette and Charlotte have been working on the trousseau to work out their own anxieties and their own frustrations. Charlotte is worried about David and the whole thing in general. Yvette is worried about Robaire and, again, the whole thing in general. The ladies are simply having conversations about dresses because it is a more relaxing thing to think about.

They are somewhat displeased with each other. There are words that don't pass between them because this almost puts them on a different side from each other. It is not something that they are used to. Yvette is thinking that maybe if Charlotte would be a little more cooperative, Robaire wouldn't be this angry. She doesn't want him to do something rash and get himself hurt in the manner that she understands that the other people have been hurt. She is hoping that this is the Charlotte she has always known, and that Charlotte won't be a party to anything that hurts him. Charlotte is wishing that they would come here and do what they had originally stated they would do, and that is help her plan her wedding. She is hoping they will stop looking any further into what is happening to them because she has a certain kind of calm, or a certain kind of assurance that if there are no more attempts on her life, there won't be any more of these horrible occurrences, and if there are attempts on her life possibly she could intercede herself now. And because she is exercising this ability, she doesn't seem to have lost anything of herself in this exchange. Also, because she trusts her family, she feels that they will act sensibly and with restraint in most cases. The more informed she gets, the less, in a lot of ways, they will have to act because a lot of things she will avoid herself, and a lot of things she will try to head off herself. It may be a real chance that she'll she able to resume a normal life. She knows that she is going to have a real serious in-depth talk with Yvette. But she is not ready to do it yet. She knows that Yvette is not ready to handle it yet because Yvette needs to hear from Robaire.

When Robaire comes downstairs for lunch, all three of them are there. He is almost apologetic. He states to everyone, "I slept very well, and I needed some time to be by myself. I appreciated the fact that Charlotte was still gracious, even with my ill temper. I hope that David is as understanding. I realized that David was really trying to cooperate, and I also hoped that Yvette would give me some time to talk to her alone."

Yvette says, "Sure." She was happy that he wanted to talk to her. "If you aren't quite ready to talk to me now, I'll wait until later in the day or another couple of days. It's also good to give things time because they look different to you initially than they may look to you later."

He joins them for lunch. They have a very relaxing congenial lunch. He realizes that there has never been much hostility amongst this assembly, David, Charlotte, and Yvette, and that he shouldn't bring any there because it just isn't there. He realizes that if he is not getting exactly what he wants, the way he wants, then he is going to have to examine his own approach first before he considers that somebody is playing a game with him, withholding from him, or doing something that is deceptive.

He realizes that he is enjoying the lunch. He is very much enjoying Charlotte's house. He is a guest in her house and his attitude toward her was unfair for a lot of reasons. The world looks a lot different to him after two days. He decides not to rush lunch and to talk about things that don't have the burning importance to him that they should like the trousseau, and the different places that David has investigated for the honeymoon. He makes suggestions himself because he has traveled the world a little bit. He understands that they probably don't want to go into Europe, but he has been to some of the islands off the British coast. He has also been to some of the islands off South America.

The climate there is very nice also. He hasn't been to the Caribbean, so he has nothing to offer about that. But he suggests, from experiences that he has had, these other islands as possibilities. He also suggests some inns that they might go to that he stayed at, and people he can give as contacts.

This is what they discuss for almost two hours after lunch, even after they have left the table and they are outside walking through the gardens. He permits this. Though he's anxious to redirect the conversation, he doesn't. As they walk through the gardens, he and Yvette fall back. David and Charlotte take a faster pace because they realize that he needs to talk to Yvette. Yvette knows that he is not a very aggressive or hostile person normally, so she waits for him to initiate the conversation in the direction that he wants it to go in.

First, he is very ashamed of his behavior with Yvette. He knows that he left France with someone who he knew very well, someone who could not have possibly done anything to affect the course of events one way or the other, and he knew she should not have been the source of his anger because she was doing exactly what he told her to do. He apologizes to her, "It is inexcusable, Yvette. My tone of voice that I have taken with you and the things that I even suggested that you may be a party to is inexcusable. I'm very sorry about this. It's just that I'm at a loss. I'm a little bit overwhelmed. I didn't have a clear direction to go in. Instead of admitting that and stopping for a minute and reflecting upon it, I was angry. I think another reason that I didn't handle it the way that I normally do."

Yvette interrupts, "Yes, I know, because I didn't expect that kind of response from you knowing you as well as I do."

He says, "I think it's because I've been up too much. I haven't slept as well as I should. I was trying to make sure that Otto Weinberger was recuperating and rehabilitating. I know it's not a good excuse to be rude to a good friend. But I think that that's why when I started the session with David, I was probably too frazzled to do it. And if I had thought that it was getting a little bit clearer, I wouldn't have done that at the time. It was necessary to do it immediately for Otto Weinberger because he needed some reassurances. He needed some mental intercession because otherwise his anxiety was heightened, and I don't know where it would have gone. But these interviews are not leading me in the right direction.

"The bottom line is that Otto Weinberger believes Otto Weinberger, and the bottom line with David will be that David believes Otto Weinberger, and unless I'm shown some other kind of phenomena that I cannot discount on mental grounds, then the only reason to do these interviews is to chronicle events, and not as a source of proof. There is another course of action that I had originally decided to pursue and that was to find out a little bit more about the land and the house and to go to the local library to find out if this had been an old burial ground or something."

Yvette says, "Well, I can help you a little bit with that. And possibly you could have more concrete proof because I know that Charlotte must have some deeds of trust that show at least one prior owner. You can go to the court and find out other previous owners. But from what Charlotte has always told me, it was originally land on the coast that was run by a sea captain. He bought ten or twelve acres, and he built some sort of house on it, but it wasn't the most elegant. He basically wanted a place off the coast with a good docking area, so he could leave his house by small boat and get to his ship. That's basically what he used it for because most of the time he was at sea. He was unmarried and had no children, but he did have several servants and housekeepers.

"Then the property was sold by the State. I'm not sure he was even alive at that point. It was sold to a financier from San Francisco who wanted it as a summer home, as a place to get away, bring all of his friends, and have a nice party every now and then when he wanted to get out of the city. The financier renovated the house. He almost built the house over again. He expanded the wings and added more rooms. He turned it into an elegant show place because he was very much involved in the upper crust in San Francisco. He gave it the kind of elegance that apparently Charlotte's parents found, and Charlotte would return to when she didn't go on spring breaks with me."

Yvette continues, "I have never come here before. I don't know why. When we were in school together, it seems that either she came home with me or she went home alone. It didn't seem to be significant. I don't think it really has any significance. It seemed to be more fun to go into Europe and have ski vacations or something of that order, than it was to come out here, though Charlotte always did seem to love this place, and it was always my idea to get her to come home with me. Well, anyway, her parents bought it in the fifties.

"As I said before, it wasn't utilized daily as a normal home. But it was very elegant. That's one of the reasons, supposedly, that they bought it. They didn't have a chance to do any renovating because they died immediately, which was very sad for Charlotte because she was only two years old when they died.

When Charlotte finished educating herself and preparing herself in only the way Charlotte would, if you know Charlotte she always wants to make sure she has a solid foundation for things, her big project was to come home and to live in this house that her parents must have loved enough to buy. She planned to renovate it, and she did have the funds to do so. Her other project was to start her art gallery.

"That's where Mr. Smythe comes in, and apparently Mr. Smythe found something he thought was alarming here. He actually breached, what I consider, a confidence in that he told someone else outside what was going on, whatever it was he thought that was going on or could be going on in Charlotte's house, which I don't think it could have been that much. But he brought Otto Weinberger in and now Otto Weinberger is in whatever condition he's in. All of this is a little bit hard for me to understand because I was Charlotte's roommate, and I don't understand anything that that's horrifying about being in Charlotte's house or being anywhere near Charlotte's house. And we've both been here now for almost three weeks. I realize he is seriously in this state, but I'm a little bit annoyed. I am a little bit annoyed that Charlotte is being looked upon as a ghoul or is being blamed for his condition."

Robaire says, "I can understand your side of things, and I can somewhat understand his side of things. But, still, things definitely have happened here that are out of the ordinary."

She says to him, "Well, I've known Charlotte since she was maybe eight or nine years old, and they are out of the ordinary for Charlotte too. That's what I don't think anyone understands. I'm not just defending her because she is my friend. I'm defending her because I'm real close to her, and I know her. It is out of the ordinary to have two people die in front of you that are trying to kill you, and you don't have a weapon, and you don't even know these people. Just because she's alive and they're dead and there's no real explanation for what happened in between, she must be a monster? And when this private detective gets out of line, you've been hired to investigate things before, you know you have some ethics about what you can do what you can't do. And one of the things that you don't do is beat up your employer.

"The second thing you don't do is break into people's homes with the intent of sexually molesting them. And he somehow dies of a heart attack, and once again she's the monster! It's just not adding up. I'd rather get on with the wedding. If she's having ESP experiences, I hope she develops them because it looks like she needs them. I had hoped that you would come here with that kind of an attitude. I didn't think that you would come here with a preconceived notion about Charlotte. But neither one of us has seen any signs of anything else."

Robaire is reluctant to tell her about the photographs. He realizes that he is only going to do that because he wants to be right. He decides not to inform her about these photographs because he wants to win the argument, and it is not going to serve any useful purpose at this point because she is not in any danger, we have not seen any signs of this in Charlotte, and it wouldn't be good to change her perspective of her friend, if it even would. So, he bites his tongue.

He says, "I understand. I thought I was going to be talking to you. It seems that you have been talking to me, and I've been listening. I still want to see what I can find out about these other two things, if you think that it is all right."

She says, "Yes, I think you should look into the house because maybe the house is haunted. I don't know, and Charlotte's hasn't been here enough to have it affect her. I would hate for you to talk to the servants about the possibility of a haunting since they haven't seen anything either. And it might get to the point where she won't be able to keep anyone here working for her. And as you can see, everyone seems to love to be here, and they follow her directions explicitly without any question. Do you want to talk to the nanny that she has had since she was two years old? Maybe you should talk to her.

"I know you deal all the time in the paranormal and people that really have extraordinary problems. Maybe you should go and talk to the nanny. Sit down and have a nice little teatime with Megan Hampton. Just bring yourself down to earth and relax a little bit. You can continue your investigation. If there is something here that might be poltergeist or haunting, I'm not discounting that. I'm just saying try not to take it to the other extreme. I have no idea what happened to Otto Weinberger. But we've done the human thing, all of us. David has done his best to keep in contact with Otto, and Charlotte has done her best to see to his wellbeing.

"All of us are aware of this, and all of us have been touched by this. But you must remember that he brought himself into this circle. And I think it just shows what a good person that Charlotte is, and that David ought to be continuing to look after him. That's the way that I look at that."

He says, "Well, maybe you're right. Maybe I should go to the library and find out what I can about the surrounding land. But before I do, I should ask the nanny if she has time to have tea with me because I'd like to talk to her and ask her some questions."

Yvette says, "Well, that's fine. But what excuse are you going to have for probing the nanny? You're going to have to have a good one. She thinks you're here with me. So why would you want to talk to the person who raised Charlotte? You would have to have a good reason. And I hope that you don't have to lie to her."

He says, "I'm going to tell her that I'm a writer of sorts. And I am because I have written papers on things that I have seen. I'll tell her that I was just interested in the background of the house and the background in general. I will use that to get other things out of her. I won't have to lie to her, and I won't have to press things too far. But we'll just see what she has to say, if she'll even talk with me because we know she's very loyal to Charlotte. Maybe, Yvette, it's something that you should do?"

Yvette says, "No. No. I don't want to be bothered. I don't want to be involved in anything that could be perceived as unfriendly or a deception, not anymore. It's not a bad idea, but I say you take that on your own. You're probably better at knowing what you want to ask anyway."

He says, "I think we'd better catch up to David because I'm going to need to talk to David too. And will you do me a favor and distract Charlotte for just a minute because I want to ask him some questions."

She says, "Fine. If I'm able to distract Charlotte, I will. But I think that Charlotte and David are much closer now than both you and I realize. And I had sensed a certain closeness with Charlotte before too. But I'll do what I can to distract Charlotte."

They catch up with David and Charlotte. Yvette asks Charlotte to show her the part of the grounds that she is planning on having the wedding on, if it is going to be an outside wedding. They go off in that direction. It is the part of the estate that is nearest the sea, but on a higher part of the ground.

Robaire says to David that he has finished spending time in his room going over his tapes and asks David more about the relic. David says, "I can only relate to you what I have already related. You saw photographs of it, and you're welcome to see the real thing. But I would advise you at first to do as Yvette had suggested, which you related to me, that Yvette had suggested you talk to the nanny first and you research through all the things that would seem to cause no harm first, before you start to look into something that we know has an obvious deep substance." He agrees that this is probably the way to go. He just wanted to let David know that this was going to be his next move, and if David wanted to go along with him.

David says, "I thought about the library, but I had thought about the library from the point of view of trying to find out more about a vampire. And I realized that the people whose writings were at the library probably had not encountered a vampire and that it would be a waste of my time. But researching the history around Mendocino might be a good idea from that aspect. I don't feel we need to talk to the nanny. I already know where I stand with Charlotte. But it's a good idea maybe to get a little bit more childhood background on her because there are probably some things that the nanny can relate, that Charlotte might not remember. From that point of view, he might be of some assistance in getting that kind of information out of Mrs. Hampton now that she knows that we are well on our way to be married."

He agrees to accompany Robaire and see if they can find out where the nanny is in the house. He finds her in the kitchen. She is giving instructions on dinner because neither Yvette or Charlotte has decided, and she thought that somebody should do it since it is after lunch. They ask her if they could speak with her a minute. She steps outside the kitchen. David says, "Mrs. Hampton, because I'm planning this wedding, there's still a lot of little things that I don't know about Charlotte and probably some things that she can't remember herself about when she was growing up. I kind of wanted to include these in the wedding, maybe some little funny stories that you can remember or some incidents that happened as Charlotte was growing up."

She says, "Oh yes, I have seen weddings that have been done that way. I've seen weddings where each side tells little stories that they have gathered from the parents or the brothers and sisters of the other side that predate their relationship. That's always quite interesting, and it's always quite entertaining for the audience."

He says, "That's exactly what I had in mind. I was hoping that sometime after dinner you would be willing to sit down and talk to Robaire and I because he's going to be doing some of the photography since I'm going to be involved in the wedding. I'm going to set things up, and he's going to help me, along with some other people. He's also going to do some of the painting. So, we were wondering if you could tell us about some things, and we could figure out a way to arrange it in the wedding while the girls are working so hard on the trousseau."

She says, "That seems like an excellent idea. I think it would bring a lot of joy to Charlotte. So, yes, I'll be very available after dinner. I'll just bring my crocheting into the library, and we could discuss it. I'm sure we could find an excuse to have the girls off somewhere, so it will be a surprise to them. In fact, I was going to suggest that Charlotte do a little baking after dinner because we used to do that when she was younger, and I was wondering if she was losing a little bit of her skills. I know it's silly, but it's doesn't hurt to be old fashioned. There's a torte that Charlotte likes to bake that she had found a recipe for. I think it relates to her family. It's of German origin.

"I think she also wanted to surprise you with it, David, and she wanted to ease some of the tension because I understand that Mr. Decarte was upset for some reason with his friend Yvette. That's all I know about it. But I think this would be a good thing to do, and I was going to suggest that she go ahead and do this. We'll have time to talk after dinner. That will give me time to reminisce and get them all together for you, as many as I can think of.

"If you could think of any other ways to bring them to mind, I'm fully willing to cooperate because I think that it will bring an added dimension to the wedding because not many people around here know Charlotte and she doesn't have many relatives. It almost makes her sometimes seem too much of the orphan child. This will give her side of the family a little bit more depth."

They agree. They thank her. They were surprised that she would have this much perception. But they were happy too that she did. They told her that they were going to go into town to look around Mendocino a little, and that they would see her after dinner. She agreed to that.

The two gentlemen go off to Mendocino looking for a library and trying to find out if there was a main library here in the city, or should they go to a county library. After talking to the librarian, they decide that it was a good idea that they do both.

They find out the basic facts of Mendocino from the town library. Then they go to the county library to find recordings of deeds and facts about surrounding land. The way that Yvette and Charlotte had both related the story about the transfer of deeds and the ownership of the house seemed to be very accurate, and there doesn't seem to be anything out of the ordinary. There is no other person. The family seemed to have settled on this parcel that armies or Indians have ridden across. But no one seems to have made any other use of it than the three people they already know about.

They decide, with the information that they have about the surrounding land and about Mendocino County, they are going to go home and try to decipher that. Then it wouldn't be a bad idea to go to San Francisco and see if they could find out more about the financier and find a way to get more information about the sea captain. David decides to take on the financier because he is much more familiar with America in general, and the West Coast and San Francisco. He decides that would be his task, and Robaire can stay locally to see what he could find out about the sea captain, and he needs some maritime information. He might have to get it out of San Francisco anyway. They weren't sure. They decide to divide the work up that way. They also decide that it would be better to do it as soon as possible so they could start eliminating possibilities and sources. They don't think there is going to be anything there, but they want to ensure that they have every fact in hand and that they follow it through.

This takes them almost until dinner time. They return home and they prepare. Since they know that Charlotte is going to do this special thing, they decide to bring both the ladies roses. Charlotte prefers red, and Robaire knows that Yvette prefers white. They give Charlotte a red bouquet with ferns, and they give Yvette white long stem roses with baby's breath with the thought that they would go in each of the women's bedroom.

They also decided that they were going to dress for dinner because Robaire knows that Yvette has evening clothes and that she has brought with them, and if she is going to make a torte, the rest of the dinner is going to be formal too and they're going to be ready for it. They decided that they were going to dress formally for dinner and present the roses, and this would really break a lot of the ice that has been around the house for a long time.

They arrive. They bring the roses with them instead of having them sent because they can't get anyone to come that far at that time of night. They take them to their rooms. They have been prepared for that since they don't have to be placed immediately in water. They go about their grooming and dress for black tie.

They pull the nanny aside and have her suggest to the ladies without any explanation that they dress formally. The girls are very excited. They know they are having dinner at home, and that they have a little surprise on both sides of this. They go ahead and dress formally because they were getting tired of the jeans and the various standard everyday dress. It is almost kind of like make believe. They have no quarrel about dressing formally.

They all arrive at dinner. The table is beautifully set. It is going to be a formal serving. The ladies are dressed in their evening clothes, and so are the gentlemen. The gentlemen present their roses. Both Charlotte and Yvette are very surprised. They are happy. They though it was a nice touch that they thought about them. It broke a lot of the ice. Immediately they take them up to their rooms. The nanny says not to bother with them, that she'll send servants up to have them arranged and put in vases.

They go back down to continue dinner. The dinner is nice. It is an eight-course meal. Everything is very properly prepared. Then Charlotte comes out with her surprise. She brings this out herself because she has made a torte. It is mostly chocolate, but it has whipped cream, strawberries, and continuing layers of good things. She serves ice cream and additional fresh whipped cream on the side. They eat it and think that it is wonderful.

It relaxes everyone. They have coffee. Robaire requests expresso, and they can provide it. They have their coffee and their desserts at the table. They all compliment Charlotte because no one knew that Charlotte could cook like this.

David was really pleased that she would take the time to do such a domestic thing for him. He was dreaming about the whole situation. They wanted to have their coffee and liquors at the table because they already had plans to talk to the nanny. Charlotte said that was fine because she and Yvette had to go on and continue with some other baking. These are some skills that she should brush up on, and the nanny had reminded her it was something to do. They had recipes for different cookies and knickknacks that they were going to practice on.

They went back after dinner, and after they changed, into the kitchen to make cakes and cookies.

The gentlemen head straight for the nanny, who was waiting as she had promised in the library with her crocheting and warm milk. They take a seat. They, of course, greet her and tell her that they had a wonderful dinner, that all her suggestions so far have worked well, and they are very happy with the way things are going so far. She says, "I am too because there have been several times since Charlotte has met David that I have been quite worried about her, though I know it is not his fault." She describes that things have taken on a different tone, and that they are going even keel now, Charlotte seems to know where she is going with her life. She is happy that she is getting married, she has a career, she has been educated, and the world is essentially hers right now.

They ask her, "Were there times in the past, before she met David that you were concerned about her?" She is not quite sure where this question is coming from because she thought things were going to take a little bit of a lighter tone.

She said to them, "Well, Charlotte, from time to time, has been given to having nightmares. She has awakened in her sleep. She has tried to tell me about it, but it didn't make a lot of sense. I think one of the ways she worked them out was the paintings. But I don't understand art, so I never bothered with them. I only made sure she turned out to be a very nice young lady."

Then they ask her, "How long have you been employed by her family? You seem to have a New England accent. You apparently did not come from Europe." They already know but they ask her anyway.

She says, "No. I was retained by the family, I guess in pretty much the way that Jennifer was. I was already on this side of the coast, though I do have a New England background, and I read an ad in the newspaper. I was also contacted by some people who were working for them through another method, and I came in for an interview with several other people. For some reason, they decided to employ me. But they unfortunately didn't live long enough for me to get to know them very well. And I also feel that they seemed to be two very attractive people, and they had a beautiful little girl that they loved very much, and she loved them very much. That's why it was so sad the night that they didn't come home."

Robaire says, "Explain to us, you were here on the night that they didn't come home."

She says, "Oh, of course, because I was hired full-time to be a live in and my commitment was extensive. They wanted to make sure that they didn't find someone that wanted to leave after the child was thirteen or fifteen. My commitment was extensive. I was to stay here for as long as they chose for me to stay here. In one sense that commitment is unusual, but in another sense it's like a lifetime job. The place was so beautiful, the valley was good, and the people were so easy to get along with that somehow, I didn't mind making that kind of commitment, though it was unusual. After that happened, I realized that I had to hold up my end of things. Now I'm hoping that I can help to raise

Charlotte's children. I don't think I'll be around for her grandchildren, but at least for her children."

They say to her, "Yes, it is a very unusual commitment. But you were here the night that Charlotte's parents died?"

She says, "Yes. I was the one who opened the door for the highway patrol. I was the one who took the information. I let Charlotte sleep. I didn't waken her because it happened in the middle of the night, well, not in the very middle of the night, but past Charlotte's bedtime. By the time they were found, and the details were related to us, we were sure what we were dealing with. They didn't ask anyone to come down to identify the bodies because of the nature of the accident. That would be a waste of time. But they were very careful in checking and double checking the identities before they came here to tell us what had happened. I was the one that they told. Of course, I was horrified. I hadn't known them very long."

Robaire asks, "How long is very long?"

She answers, "Well, I had known them about a month or a month and a half living here because it took them about two or three weeks to decide upon the final employee. So, I was back and forth. We had short trial periods, both for me and both for them. But living here, maybe about a month and a half. They went off during the evening. It seemed during the day they were too occupied, or they were possibly having trouble with the time lag. But they often ended up going out during the evenings to do their work. The people that they dealt with apparently received them after six or seven, and they would go ahead and they would go to the movies, or they might go out to dinner."

Robaire asks, "Did you notice, did they go out during the day at all?"

David throws him a look. "You don't want to ask these kinds of questions."

She says, "During the daytime, I was pretty much occupied with Charlotte. That was what I had seen as my job, and most of the time there was something that they were doing or someplace they were going. That is one of the reasons why I was here to keep up with the child. I can't remember every day where they were, but I know they were always doing something."

Robaire and David once again exchange looks. Robaire says, "Tell us more about that night. We know that this is difficult for you."

She says, "Thirty years have passed, and Charlotte doesn't seem to have been badly affected by it as I thought she would be maybe because, thank God, she was so young. But the highway patrol came to the door and told me that they had found her parents, dead, in a car accident, the car had burned, and there was very little left of the bodies. They wanted to know if I knew a person to call to claim the bodies and make the funeral arrangements. I told him yes. I had been introduced to most of the people that handled the business, the trustees, and that I would get on the phone to them right away, which is what I did. They took up the details of the burial. The will had requested that there not be a formal funeral. They were buried. They had already picked out the area where they were going to be buried. And they were just taken care of. But we explained to Charlotte that they were dead when she was old enough to comprehend that."

Robaire asks, "Well, what happened when Charlotte woke up the next morning, even though she was two years old?"

The nanny says, "I would have almost sworn that she knew, and somehow she had excepted it. She didn't ask where her parents were. She kind of made the statement that she understood that her parents would not be coming back, and that she wanted to have breakfast. So, we proceeded with breakfast and dressing her in her normal clothes and the education structure we were starting her on. And she didn't normally see her parents in the daytime anyway. I was concerned at night that once again she would ask about them. But she didn't. She just took her hot chocolate and went to bed. The next day, it was the same. And the next day, it was the same.

"She was about seven or eight and it was getting time to send her off to school when I broached the subject because I knew that it would come up at school. She told me she understood why her parents didn't come back, that it would be all right, and not to concern myself about it. So, I left it at that, waiting to see what would happen at school, would I get any feedback from people or is she really accepting it as well as she seemed to have. I knew that there would be psychiatrists at school and if there was any trouble or if anything came up, I would be the first to know about it. Nothing did come up except for the occasional nightmare, and they didn't seem to be related to anything that had to do with her parents.

"An occasional nightmare for a child is not unusual, so I thought nothing of it and the school thought nothing of it. As she grew up and got into her teens, we began to discuss a little bit more because she had a good concept of death at that time. We discussed that her parents had died, and she had been left in an orphanage at a young age. And she had met other children in school whose parents had died earlier, whose parents had died while she was in school with them, and she knew it wasn't a happy thing. She accepted it like other people have. She has learned to accept it. And I thought then that I handled it the best way because it doesn't seem to have harmed her at all. She has grown up to be quite a nice young lady."

Robaire says, "Back to the things that you think happened that might be entertaining."

She says, "Well, one of the things that comes to mind is riding lessons. She had to have riding lessons. She never really did like the horses until she became older. One of the things that we had to get her engaged in riding to get her on the horse and to stay on the horse, was to have her instructor go around the estate with her. She wasn't happy about that. And a couple of times, she fell off. She would make excuses about why she didn't want to go out there.

"I guess to other people they aren't that funny. But to me, it was hilarious watching her every day when she would come home from school. She would be off during summer break, and she didn't have a problem going to Europe with Yvette to go skiing which she didn't mind. It was the horses. She didn't think they smelled very nice. A couple of times she tried to perfume the horses. She tried to tie bouquets on their tails. She would try everything to see if it would help. She got to the point where she wouldn't go in the stables. They would have to bring the horse out. If the horse used the bathroom or if the horse had to do the things that come naturally while Charlotte was riding him, then Charlotte would get off and insist that she had to walk back home. These things we thought were very funny. It wasn't until she was fifteen or sixteen that she was able to get over her attitude about the horses, and that's why she doesn't have any dogs."

David says, "I want to have dogs, and I was thinking the dogs would be very good to have out on the estate."

She says, "I'm sure that if they are kept outside, you won't have any problem with Charlotte. But that was one of the things that I and the servants used to laugh at it whenever it was time for her to go riding because she tried to avoid that."

They ask her if there were any other things that she could recall that wouldn't cause Charlotte too much embarrassment and that people would think would be kind of funny. She says, "Once Charlotte and Yvette wanted to attend the school prom and Charlotte hadn't really been asked because she went to an all-girls school. When it came time to intermingle with her male counterparts, Charlotte always made sure she didn't have to do it. It was time for she and Yvette to find someone to go out with, and Yvette didn't want to have to bring someone from Europe."

The nanny begins to relate the story of the prom date. She says, "Well, I don't know is this is fair because this isn't something that I saw, but Charlotte and Yvette called me up to tell me about it. At any rate, they decided that since they didn't have prom dates, they were going to quickly acquaint themselves with somebody so they could get somebody to take them to the prom. They met two guys, and the guys asked them. That was like a relief. First it was like what are we going to do? We don't have anyone to take us to the prom.

"Then they found two guys from the all-male school who they could go with, the male counterparts. They had to go with someone from there. It was a joint prom. They found two guys to ask them that they said didn't look too bad and seemed to have a reasonable amount of manners. They knew that they would have to be well behaved because of the school rules. The girls were going in limousines that Charlotte's trustee had hired. The dates picked them up in limousines. They got in the back seat of the car. Things went well.

"But it seems that the guys got a little bit out of hand. They thought that they were just going to be escorting them to the dance, and they were going to dance with them so they wouldn't have to sit there. They would interact with whomever else was there, even the people who had dates. They were hoping to meet someone that they hadn't seen before and find someone they liked, even though they were going out with another girl. The girls put up with as much as they could on the ride over there. The chauffeur was, of course, very stern. But he couldn't follow them into the dance. It turned out that the tuxedos that the two boys were wearing shrunk in one hour. They probably had been cleaned and pressed at the same place. They could barely keep them on. They had to leave because now they weren't properly dressed.

"So, the limousine took them home and returned to pick up Charlotte and Yvette who stayed the full course of the dance. The other people who had seen the situation, of course, came up to them. They met a lot of different people that they normally would not have met. It also got them out of a sticky situation. They were careful not to laugh in front of the boys. But they were rather relieved to get rid of them because they didn't like what had taken place on the way to the prom. They said that the prom turned out to be much better because they had more of a choice of the men to dance with. The women saw what happened to them, and they almost had to lend them their dates so they wouldn't be wallflowers the rest of the night. And the gentlemen were very polite, and, of course, they wanted to assist these two ladies that were in obvious distress. They had a wonderful time. They evidently did meet some people that they exchanged phone numbers with."

She continues, "That's another one I can think of. I'll have to think some more on this. I don't know if that's the one that you would want to use, and I don't know if she would be happy that I told you that. But I'll have to think of some things that will really entertain the audience. But I thought that was rather funny myself."

David and Robaire, once again, look at each other. They are wondering what happened to these peoples' clothes. This seems to be too much of a coincidence, but they didn't say anything about it. They laughed with her. They told her thank you and excused themselves for the evening.

This discourse took about two hours. They didn't want to press it because really what they wanted to get at was what could she remember, if she could remember anything significant about the parents before they died. Robaire asks, "If you don't mind, is there anything else you can think of about Charlotte's childhood?" He wanted to learn all he could about her childhood without drawing too much attention and pressing too hard.

She says, "No. I don't mind this because I really have felt left out, and I wanted to get to know you two a little bit better. I know Yvette quite well. This is a good chance for me to sit down and talk to you and get to know you two a little better. Anytime, maybe after lunch tomorrow or whenever we have time and you want to sit down and talk to me, I'm usually available. I am going to go on to bed now because I have a lot of things planned for in the morning."

Then they ask her if she had seen Charlotte's trousseau yet, and had she made any comments or was she involved in the decision-making process. She replies, "No. I have felt a little left out of that too. But I understand that I am a little bit older, and that this is one of the things that is better left between Charlotte and Yvette. I'm not too worried about it because I'm not sure I would have the best advice on that anyway. Yvette seems to be right on top of the fashion situation, and she wants Charlotte to always look and be her best."

They excuse her, and she goes on to bed for the night. Robaire says to David, "Well, she doesn't have too much knowledge of what happened in the family, but she might know where some files are kept, or some paperwork is kept. Maybe we can even get to the trustees."

David says, "But if I start heading toward the trustees before I'm married to Charlotte, or even after I'm married to Charlotte, it's going to draw a different kind of suspicion, especially with the kind of problems that Charlotte has been having lately.

"That's one of the reasons that I have not gone in that direction. I have some money of my own, but I don't come from a background that is as wealthy as Charlotte's. We were middle class, and I earned my money on my own in an adventuresome way. I could see how this could be looked upon as not a good situation, especially since Charlotte has been under such distress to the point where she has even had to be questioned by the police because she knows me. So, I have avoided the trustees. I know that they are paying the bills. And I know that they must have been watching Charlotte and me as much as they could. I have no idea why I haven't been contacted by them sooner. I know what you're thinking, and it is a very good idea, but I don't think I could do it now. I don't think I could do it until I'm officially Charlotte's husband. Then I would like to ask a lot of questions."

Robaire says, "Well, I think that you are marrying someone that you don't know too much about their background. I've been permitted to investigate her and how much of this investigation they're aware of I don't know. Let's assume they're aware of none of it. Let's hope they're aware of none of it. Let's assume that you just want to ask them questions about the girl you're going to marry. Let's assume that you would like to know the extent of control that they have over her resources, and at what point will they be turned over to her."

David says, "I haven't even asked Charlotte these questions."

Robaire says, "Well, maybe you should. Then after you ask Charlotte, see if Charlotte will introduce you to her trustees. She must know who they are."

David says, "I have the resources to take care of all her needs. So, I didn't see any reason to do this. But, okay. It really puts me in an awkward position, but I can see where they may be a source of information because they must know the parents. But for some reason, maybe it's just that I don't want to appear to be a gigolo, I don't want to go in this direction."

Robaire says, "I have an uneasy feeling too. I have an uneasy feeling because I'm afraid that these trustees are a little more entwined than we know.

That may be one of the reasons why they have not interceded. But I think that's another thing that we will have to do very soon."

David finds Charlotte in the kitchen with Yvette wearing an apron. They are trying to make something out of flour. He tells her, "I want to talk to you about some business now that I should have talked to you about before. How long are you going to be doing this?"

She says, "Well, cooking is very tiring. I intend to go to bed after this. When we are finished cooking, we both intend to go to bed."

Yvette says, "Yes, because we have had it."

Charlotte says, "But, I'll be up first thing in the morning. I will talk to you about whatever it is that you want me to talk to you about."

He says, "I hope you're up early because I have to go into San Francisco."

She says, "Again? For what? Is Otto Weinberger having a problem? Are you going back to the psychiatrist? Why are you going to San Francisco?"

He says, "There are some things that I need to look into there. You know, I did have an occupation prior to this, and I do need to keep the doors open, even though I'm not actively engaged in this, and I won't be until after the honeymoon. I still need to keep my avenues open." That makes sense to her. She doesn't pursue it. She is too tired anyway.

She says, "All right, first thing in the morning, about eight o'clock, let's go for a horseback ride and you can talk to me then. Then you'll still have time to drive to San Francisco. Is Robaire going with you?"

He says, "No. I think Robaire is going to stay here, and he's going to probably go to the library. You know how he is. There's something that he's still working on from France, and he just likes to keep up on things. So, he's probably going to go back to the Mendocino or county library to see what information he could get there."

Yvette is pretty much aware of what he is getting at. But she doesn't ask him any more questions. It seemed to have satisfied Charlotte because she hadn't raised the issue again. He retires to bed because he knows he has got a long drive in the morning, and he has got to get up early.

The two women continue their baking until it is time for them to go to sleep. The next morning, Charlotte keeps her appointment with David. He greets her in the morning. He kisses and hugs her. They haven't had privacy in quite a while. They start heading for the stables so they could go horseback riding. During the horseback ride, he tells her, "You know, there's a lot about each of our finances that we don't know in terms of net worth. A lot of things you just kind of take on face value. Do you have any questions to ask me about the kind of money that I've amassed, or any kind of assets I have, or whatever it is that I might happen to own?"

She says, "No. I'm not particularly interested in that. For one reason, I'm sure my trustees will investigate you extensively as soon as I let them know that I'm getting married. That was one of the dictates of the will."

He says, "Oh, I didn't know that. Are there any other dictates of the will?"

She says, "No. Only that everything was left to me, and hopefully that I find a suitable mate. But they will look into it."

He says, "What if they don't like me? What if I'm not acceptable for you to marry?"

She says, "That clause isn't put in the will. I don't think that was their concern. They know that I will find an acceptable mate."

He says, "How much of your fortune do you control?"

She says to him, "I never really thought about it. When I need something, or when I want to do something like when I opened the art gallery, I just went ahead and did it. I tell them about it, and they provide the funds that I tell them I need. I'm not really interested in trying to invest or control or doing those things myself. They had to give me reports as soon as I was old enough to understand it. The rules said when I turn twenty-one and if I was still in school at that time, not to bother me until I was ready to deal with it.

"So, by the time I came back from Europe and got ready to set up the art gallery, they started giving me quarterly, yearly, and semiannually reports to tell me what they were investing in and what my assets were. I really haven't had time to think about how they handle my tax work and everything. I know I'm not broke. I know that they're not doing anything that's illegal because they are a very reputable firm. They're not going out of business. I have just been trying to redecorate my house and work in the art gallery. I bought the building that the art gallery is in."

He asks her, "Do you have a deed for your house? Have you ever seen a deed of your house that says your house is yours?"

She says, "I haven't seen the deed to the house that says the house is mine."

He says, "You never thought to ask about this?"

She says, "No. I didn't think to ask about it. It doesn't concern me as a practical matter. I've had a lot of other things to do."

He says, "Other people have to start businesses and remodel their houses, but they still have to know about deeds. They still know their net worth, and there are other things that they must bother themselves with."

She says, "I know that you are right. And I know that I should start asking some questions about it."

He says, "Well you should at least tell them that you are getting ready to get married so they can start asking me some questions, and I can meet them. Then I can find out a little bit about what's going on." She is not upset about this at all. She doesn't take it in the wrong way. She knows exactly what he needs. She doesn't think that he is a fortune hunter.

She says, "Okay. I will arrange a meeting with you and the trustees, after I tell them that I agreed to marry you. I will let you know sometime within the week when they will be available to see you. But you were also supposed to give me an itinerary of the honeymoon so that Yvette and I can plan the trousseau."

He says, "I'll have that ready for you tomorrow."

By this time, they have ridden two or three miles. They started to head back to the stables. She decides that she is going to talk to some of the stable hands for a little while. He goes on into the house because he must get ready to go into Mendocino. She tells the stable hands that she thinks one of her horses needs re-shoeing, that she noticed when she was riding him that he seemed to be uncomfortable, and she wants to have him checked. The stable hand says, "Fine."

She goes into the house. She showers. She is tired so she lies down for two or three hours. David is off to Mendocino. Robaire is off to the library as soon as he can get out. Yvette knocks on her door and wakes her up. "What do we have planned for today? Maybe this is a day that we should go into Mendocino and check on the art gallery again because we haven't been in a while. We could see how Jennifer is doing."

Charlotte says, "That's probably a good idea."

She gets dressed and calls ahead to let Jennifer know that she is coming into Mendocino and that she is going to take her to lunch again. She tells Jennifer that she will want to find out if they have gotten any answers from the people that they want to exhibit later. They pick up Jennifer and take her to another restaurant outside of Mendocino. They talk. They find out how she is doing.

Charlotte asks, "Has everything been boxed and sent back from the previous exhibit? And have we received any responses yet?"

She says, "It's been boxed and sent back. I haven't received any answers yet, though I'm sure we will soon. That's all I'm waiting for."

Charlotte tells her, "We are working on my trousseau right now, and that's taking up all our time. One of the things that is slowing us up is that David hasn't told us which patch the honeymoon is going to take and where we will be at what time. We need to know what the temperatures will be so we can finalize the designs."

Jennifer says, "I can see how that could make things difficult, but I'm sure David will do them in the next few days if he said he would. I'm anxious to see what the dresses will be like."

Jennifer is mainly expressing wonder because she has never really met anyone who had taken their own clothing from the designer stage, having had designs made up for them and materials matched on through to actual completion of the dress. She is very impressed by this. Even coming from New York, she hadn't really seen anyone take this much care in their wardrobe. She was interested to see how it would come out. She was also surprised that the designers let Charlotte and Yvette have such freedom with the fabric.

Not only did they just give them designs, and they were permitted to select fabrics, but they then agreed to put them together in whatever manner that Charlotte and Yvette decided. Jennifer just thought this was wonderful. She also thought this was probably very expensive. Charlotte assured her that it was, but you only get married once in your life and this is well worth it. Yvette says, "Of course it is. If it hadn't been for my contacts in the fabric and design industry, even Charlotte's money wouldn't have gotten them this opportunity."

Charlotte says, "That's quite right. I am happy that Yvette made this opportunity available to me, and that she is going to continue to avail herself of it as time goes on."

Yvette says, "I do it only for important occasions, when things come up when I am in Europe, and I want to be dressed just right. I have noticed that often other people were green with envy because they didn't know how I pulled it off. But I just have a few friends in the right places who will do these things for me and still leave their name on the label."

They assure her that she will be able to see some of it, and that she will be invited to the wedding. They explain to her that they can't really make her a bridesmaid because Charlotte has friends from school that she is obligated to ask. This is an awkward moment. She is not really concerned though because she knows that she will be at the wedding. "I was hoping that I could at least see some of the trousseau because I won't see it. I'll probably never see it because I won't be on the honeymoon with you."

Charlotte says, "I think that could be arranged. You probably have some useful ideas too. When we have it more finalized, we will come into town and pick you up and bring you to the house. Then you can tell us what you think about it." She thinks that is pretty good. She is ready to go back to work. They drop her off at the art gallery.

They walk around Mendocino for a little while discussing the wedding. Yvette is deliberately staying off subjects that might upset Charlotte or cause worry. Then they go back home. By this time, it is almost dinner time. Neither one of the gentlemen have returned. They decide that they will check on their baking because they made the dough, but the servants put them in the oven during the day because it was too tiring for them to stay in the kitchen the night before. They compiled the recipes, had put together some of the things, and put them out to rise. They wanted to know what was going on with them. They went into the kitchen.

The cook says, "They are going all right. You could probably serve them tonight. The others could be served earlier in the afternoon in case anyone wants tea or something to nibble on." They are both still very tired because they both worked late into the night. They decide to rest in their rooms until dinner.

Robaire arrives at home first. He has found something of interest, but he is waiting for David to come in so he could explain to David what he has found out.

David, too, has found out something interesting in as far as he has more leads. David is not really used to doing this legwork himself. But he has had such bad luck turning things over and delegating duties to different people, so he has decided that that is not a good idea. He knows that when he enlists outside help, he loses privacy.

He walks in and immediately begins to look for Robaire. Robaire is sitting out on the terrace. He is looking through his note pad where he has made notes about the sea captain. The sea captain is nondescript. There is not a lot said about him anywhere except that he does own this land, and that he had bought this land. The transaction was described as a cash transaction. When he died, he had no surviving relatives, so the land went back to the state. Then the financier bought it from the state because they didn't decide to make a national park or historical monument out of it. It, fortunately, had no other real significance. That is all that he could find out about the sea captain. All he could find out about the financier was that he was buying the land, and some mention was made of it in the local newspaper at the time it was happening because it was quite a large parcel of land to be acquired.

David says, "I went into San Francisco and the financier, as he is referred to, is actually an investment banker. He was wealthy, in the category of a millionaire, and seemed to have rubbed noses with the mayor and various city officials. And he decided, as a lot of people did around that time, that to be in San Francisco all the time was rather dull, and he wanted to do something novel. He thought it would be good for business because he wanted to get these people to invest. Some of the people that knew him are still alive, and I managed to get them to talk. He would give these lavish parties out here, not that he didn't want to have fun, mostly with the idea of relaxing the people and befriending the people and getting them to invest. He wanted them to use him as a broker. He was quite successful at that.

"And the reason that he finally sold the property was that it was too far out for most people, and as it was getting in the fifties there were things happening across the East Bay. He decided to go into that direction and more into Main and Sausalito. Though he's dead now, that was before he relocated. He started doing things in the Oakland hills and Sausalito, which then became the in place for people from San Francisco. That's why he sold the property. Why or how Charlotte's parents stumbled upon the property is not clear. It seems that they were referred here by another investment broker, and he apparently remains in their employ if he is still alive. That information was unclear. You would have to find that out from Charlotte. But they were kind of directed right here. They didn't do a lot of other looking in other places."

That he found interesting too. But he didn't have any explanation for it. Robaire says, "Okay. Let's compile our notes. It seems that the sea captain just bought the land and used it. He doesn't seem to figure in any of the problems and he doesn't seem to be haunting this house, if anything is haunting this house. The financier, as you said, died somewhere else and apparently had no special attachment to this house. Was he married?"

David answers, "Yes, he was. He had a few children, but he married after he sold the house. That doesn't seem to be contributory either. There was no reason for him to be hanging around creating any disturbances at this point. At least we can almost rule him out. But Charlotte's parents, on the other hand, lived in only one place, found only this house, and moved only here. It was almost as if they had other information."

Robaire says, "If you believe that vampire story that the vampires have already planned this as a result of multiple purges in Europe, which seem to be what her pictures are describing, then you could see why they seem to have been guided exactly here."

David says, "I'm still not quite following you."

Robaire says, "Well, it's obvious that's what Otto Weinberger was saying and what got him into trouble. She has been somewhat chronicling her family history in her portraits. And her portraits seem to indicate, and everything else seems to indicate, that not only do they want Charlotte to survive, they want their way of life to survive, and some essence of them are still obviously here surviving. So, when her parents escaped, and I can only call it an escape after looking at the pictures many times, it seems that they did meet lots of resistance in every country they have been in in different times.

"So, her parents escaped here to a country where this is relatively unknown and probably would not be believed. And with the help of these entities you, yourself, say seem to have control that you don't fully understand. Perhaps they somehow have a network with the real estate broker, and they would know intuitively if nothing else. You'll have to bear with me here because this is new to me. I've told you before I can't place this type of phenomena, but I would surmise that they simply picked an area that they thought would be best for their family and the rest of their family to eventually survive. Why they picked this area is probably obvious. It's not as populated. It is in state a where this would not be as believable, or the supernatural is not as a part of history or a fact of life."

David says, "What do you mean it is supernatural. No one is really going to believe the supernatural that quickly."

Robaire says, "In some parts of the world, it's far more acceptable. It is an easy conclusion to reach if you were in some of the islands or if you were in Salem. I have done some work in Salem. I have some familiarity there. If I were a vampire trying to hide the fact that I might have a tendency toward some supernatural or some dabbling in witchcraft, I wouldn't settle on the east coast. As you remember anyone with the least suspicion were burned or drowned. Most of these people in the records we reviewed from centuries past have done nothing. They just looked wrong.

"And the town legitimately, through a legal process, did away with him. So, these ancestors or whoever these people are must be fully aware of that, so they wouldn't place them anywhere in the east coast. There are probably just not enough resources and sophistication in the Midwest. The people who would be least likely to believe it would probably be right here in sunny California. That's the impression we Europeans always get. Why they didn't take them into the southern part of California, I would just guess that there's a lot more privacy up here.

"Also, I suspect that the way the money is being transported has something to do with why they are in Mendocino. But then if you realize in this area, Mendocino, Napa, and Sonoma, there are a lot of families that have European backgrounds, foreign sounding names. They are not so necessarily immediately American stock. They probably would welcome rather than fear someone who simply came from Europe and had a background such as Charlotte has. So, for a lot of reasons this is a logical place to put this family, even if this family were just hiding from some other kind of scourge for whatever reason. The people here would probably take a lot less notice of the Von Shillingsfursts. Not only take less notice of them, but also welcome them, which seems to be what had happened.

"In the face of everything, when Charlotte's parents died, we have no accounts of any unusual happenings or anything that someone thought would have been unusual. If they had settled somewhere else, maybe those accounts would have occurred. And since Charlotte has been here, she has been welcomed with open arms by the city council, publicly. So, I think this was a well thought out plan. I think that they meant to carry it all the way through, and I think we are just seeing the first stages of it. Any maybe what you are wondering is how and if and should you want to fit into this plan."

David says, "That's quite a mouthful. And I can see the reasoning behind it. On the one hand, if this is all done ultimately to protect Charlotte, I cannot interrupt it. On the other hand, I cannot go along with a plague or an infestation of vampires."

Robaire says, "I'm not sure because as I have said before, I have not dealt with these phenomena. I have never really run into someone who was legitimately practicing witchcraft. I've been to a few seances and most of them I have been able to show were hoaxes. I have been called in on a few cases where there was something going on and the people didn't know what it was, and some of those turned out to be supernatural happenings and some of them didn't. I simply recorded the information and left because it was a private matter, and it was not my position to attempt to exercise. I just have a feeling that this is the intent, this is maybe phase one or phase two of the plan, and that Charlotte is obviously very important to these people. I don't know if we are just perceiving an overly extended family love, or if we're perceiving also that she has a very practical usefulness. Charlotte could probably tell us that better herself."

David says, "I can't argue with you on any of these things. I just hope that we come to a logical and rational conclusion, and that we can keep Charlotte in the same frame of mind as when I met her because I know that she too will want to arrive at a logical and rational conclusion."

Robaire interjects, "But you have to remember she has been terrified. She has been terrorized. She has no reason to suspect that anything will ever protect or save her but these people."

David says, "That's true, and probably a lot of that is my fault."

Robaire says, "You always arrive at that conclusion, and even if it is the correct conclusion, right now it is not a helpful conclusion. We will have to find ways to deal with this, rather than trying to lay blame. And we always will have to find to what extent these entities, if they exist, and I'm ninety percent sure that they do exist, what extent will they go and what are their capabilities? What do they really want?" They leave it at that and go to their rooms.

Charlotte is very forceful in her encounters with what she would see as the public or the outside as being David and somewhat, Robaire and Yvette. She tries to project a confidence and a sense of assurance about what she is saying, and she intends to back everything up that she says. But she has a little self-doubt. The basis of that self-doubt, once again, is that things are taking place and she doesn't know all that happened. She saw one portion of it, and she knows it ended in death. She didn't see what happened in between. When she goes to bed that night all her thoughts are on what could have happened to the private detective, but not because she particularly liked him. She has gotten over her initial, natural, her glad, her who cares what happened to him attitude. She is a little worried because she knows that this is still very much on David's mind.

When she goes to sleep that night, she has a dream. In her dream, she is outside of a monastery. She sees mortar and stone. She is conscious that she is walking up to what looks to be a big old building. Everywhere she looks around her is nicely kept grass. There is one road leading away from this building. She walks through the arches. On the side of the arches is a plague that reads, "This is a monastery. The monks here have taken their vow of silence. This is the year of our Lord 800 A.D." She continues to walk through. She is not at all afraid. She doesn't know why she is not afraid. She is aware that she is dreaming. She is also aware that she is not having a normal dream, or a random dream that other people have. She is having a dream and answering her questions. She walks down the hall of the monastery. She sees no monks.

The place is totally vacant and there is nothing but solitude and quiet. She is not afraid that she is alone. She walks down toward the end of the corridor, the same path that the private detective took. She sees the light. She is drawn to the light, not in the sense that he was. That was the only source of hope he had. Because of the light there, she wanted to know what was in that room. Once again, she has no fear, no disquiet, no discomfort. She just wanted to go and look in that room.

In that room, she sees the private detective alive. He seems to be very afraid, but she doesn't see what he is afraid of. He seemed to be gesturing. He is saying something, but what he is saying isn't audible to her. He is afraid. He is terrified. There is no one else in the room. He backs into the corner that he is standing in front of and the wall separates. He goes into the wall, and the wall folds over him.

She watches all of this with a relative amount of calm. She understands in her mind that this is going to kill him, and that he is behind the wall dying. But she is not disturbed by this. It just answers her question.

She walks back down the hall, out of the room. She comes out of the monastery and stands on the grass. There is a nice cool breeze blowing in the night. It seems almost as if she were working for a moment because once again, she sees her room, and she realizes that she is in her bed. She continues with her dream. She is in his apartment. She is walking around his house. She is looking at him and he is dead. It is not an unpleasant death, but he is dead. She knows that he is dead. She knows that she is in his house and that his house is in another state. She also knows he died probably of a heart attack. She takes all this in. Once again, she is conscious in her bed. She awakens.

She turns on her light and sits on the side of her bed. She reflects on this dream because she has had this kind of a dream before. It is this kind of dream that generated her paintings. But she doesn't feel any urge to paint. The next thought that comes to her is that David is going to submit to hypnosis probably tomorrow. But she is not going to be able to permit it, and she will intercede. She isn't worried about Robaire or the psychiatrist trying to initiate a trance because if they do it to her, she would be able to control it. She is sure that she can intercede when they attempt it on David, though David would volunteer.

David would be very honest in his attempt to give them all the information he has. But he knows too much, and she will have to intercede. She is close enough to him that she will intercede with love. She won't permit him to be harmed, either mentally or physically. And he will be aware of her interception. She goes back to sleep. She has a normal sleep.

The next morning when she comes downstairs, Yvette is out looking for wildflowers because she thinks it is a very nice thing to do. She wants to gather some up and put them on the table.

Robaire and David are downstairs. They have already decided that David is going to go through the hypnosis and tell them what he had seen. Robaire wants to prevent them from approaching Charlotte because he can't guarantee what's going to happen to them if they do. He is going to help them confront this so that they can stop looking in that direction. The two men have agreed to do this with the psychiatrist at his apartment away from the estate. They suggested that Yvette try to find a way to keep Charlotte busy. It won't be a difficult thing to do because they are now deciding on her fittings and taking her measurements.

Yvette will tell them that she hadn't decided if she wanted to be the same size at the wedding that she is now and that they have plenty to discuss around that. She thought that she could keep Charlotte very busy and keep her full attention for at least four or five hours. That would be all the time they needed. They wouldn't need any more than that.

David greets Charlotte, "Good morning. Did you have a nice sleep? You look very well rested." Of course, he gives her a good morning kiss and hugs her. She hugs him back very normally. She seemed to be very happy, very pleased.

He tells her that he has some business to conduct with Robaire because he doesn't want to lie to her, and he has an underlying feeling that lying to her doesn't do an awful lot of good. He tells her that he has some business to conduct with Robaire and he would be away for four or five hours. He hates to be away from her. He has had to be away from her so much because of this incident with Otto Weinberger. He is concerning himself with the fact that they will have a lot of time alone after the wedding.

She says, "I understand that you have things to do, and that you had a life before me. I had a life before you too. We must go on conducting our various businesses, and besides Yvette and I really have a full day. That's why I was hurrying around to finish breakfast so that I could get started with Yvette."

He is taken aback by this because he was hoping he would meet some resistance. He has a feeling that she has got to know that they are not just going off duck hunting. She has put up no resistance, and he doesn't know why. But she's very calm, very sweet, very relaxed. Though he likes this, he doesn't know how to explain it. Robaire, of course, is taking it all in. He is hoping that this is a sign that they can expect no violence. He relaxes.

The men go off. They are a little nervous because they don't know if what they do will generate or provoke violence, or what kind of violence. And if what had taken place in those paintings is true, they don't want to meet up with any of those people. This has taken quite a bit of bravery on their part.

They drive on to David's apartment. The psychiatrist is there. They tell him that they hope things go well. They alert him to the fact that it might involve some danger. They don't tell him too much because he can always turn them over to the police.

David starts to sit through a trance. He knows Robaire thinks that he is blocking to protect Charlotte, but he wants Robaire to trust him and to know that he would not set Robaire up for the kill or withhold something from Robaire or Yvette that might mean their lives. He wants to be honest. He agrees to the full regiment for hypnosis. He agrees to the medicine and to be taped. So, he is ready.

They begin their sedation, and their verbal suggestion. They put him in the proper frame of mind and tried to go through certain levels to make sure that he was cooperating in telling them things. As this is proceeding, Yvette and

Charlotte are taking measurements of each other. But Charlotte is totally aware of what is happening where David is. She can do this without appearing distracted because Yvette is not aware that Charlotte is doing two things at one time. Charlotte is watching the progression of the sedation, the deepening of the trance state. She is watching David recall childhood instances and various things to ensure that he is responding and not faking. She permits this. When it gets to the point where they start to ask questions about her family, the personal things he knows, or what happened with the psychiatrist, all he can do is describe what has taken place in Charlotte's bedroom at the very moment that Yvette is measuring her.

Robaire is asking him to begin where he was badly beaten, when he opened the French doors, and he entered Charlotte's bedroom. In his mind, he does open the French doors and he does enter Charlotte's bedroom. But he doesn't see four monks in the corner, and he doesn't see the private detective. It is daytime and he sees Yvette measuring Charlotte. He sees Yvette choosing and holding up various pieces of cloth. He can describe the fabrics, the textures, the colors. He begins to relate the conversation between the two people.

Robaire realizes that he is out of control and he doesn't know what to make of it. The psychiatrist doesn't know what to make of it. They are afraid that something is happening that will have him end up as Otto Weinberger has ended up. Immediately, they try to bring him out of the trance. They try to abort. They don't try to tamper with whatever Charlotte has done because they don't understand it. They are afraid to use any more medicines on him. They don't want to do anything else with suggestion in his mind because he has opened the door to the room, which was what they asked him to do. But what he was seeing is not what they expected him to relate to them, and what he is seeing is apparently going on right now.

Robaire is on the phone to Yvette. Yvette picks up on the extension in Charlotte's room. He asks her what she was doing. She tells him, "I don't understand. I thought that you wanted me to distract Charlotte." She is trying to say this without Charlotte hearing her. Charlotte is turning her back to take off her slip. She is trying to act like she is not interested in the conversation that Yvette is trying to hide. Robaire wants to know what they are doing now in the room. Yvette whispers, "Well, right now I'm holding a piece of pink fabric." This is exactly what David was describing to them. He makes her tell them now. Robaire is asking an awake and very alert Yvette what is happening in the room. She tells him. So, all he can do is hang up the phone.

Yvette hangs up the phone. She is irritated and she is frustrated. She doesn't know what is going on. Charlotte smiled. It is not a nasty smile. It is a mild smile. She goes on with, "What do you think? Should I wear this to the reception, or should I save this in case we go on a ship?" She goes on with the conversation.

Since Yvette is in the middle of a semi-deception herself, she must go along with the conversation too. "Well, it depends. What you have got to do is disturb David to tell you exactly what kind of honeymoon you are going on and what you're going to do first, if you're going to go to Hong Kong first, or if you're going to go a warm place first. Then we can decide what evening wear is most appropriate. But right now, all we can do is take your measurements. Then we can decide what style would be best suited for this fabric."

They put out some more designs. They continue with this for about two hours.

In the other part of town, Robaire and the psychiatrist are trying to bring David out of Charlotte's trance. Robaire realizes now that David is in Charlotte's trance, so he is immediately relieved. He is released faster than the medicine should have left his system. He has no ill effects. He feels fine, and he would like to know what happened.

The psychiatrist and Robaire look at each other. But the psychiatrist does not know what Robaire knows about what Yvette is doing at that very moment. All he knows is that they didn't get a horror story, they just got a story of a man who apparently is over occupied with his fiancé. He is a little dismayed by this.

Robaire tries to pull it off because he knows there is more to it than this. He says, "Well, apparently, we didn't get a deep enough suggestion place. Maybe he's not a good subject or maybe his concentration is too directed on something else, and that's natural. Either we will try it another time or not try it again at all. I don't think that we should continue with this. Thank you for coming down for this. I'm sure you will analyze it from your point of view, and I will analyze it my point of view. It still might be fruitful."

The psychiatrist agrees that it still should be fruitful because he knows that his medicine was potent, he knows that he has the ability to put a person in a trance, and he did get information out of David to know that David was in a trance.

Robaire doesn't feel it was a waste of his time. He is happy that he hasn't had a horror story. He now must compare this and look at this in a new light in conjunction with Otto Weinberger's story. Robaire realizes the position that this has left Otto Weinberger in because he is now the only one who has related what he believes to have been a horror story.

This is all running through Robaire's mind, but he thinks he will have to deal with this later. He understands now why David has often been in a position of smoothing and covering things up. He tries not to seem too rushed to get out of the situation, but he tells the psychiatrist that David is fully alert. David agrees, "Yes. I am fully alert, and I would like to know what happened. And your answer that nothing happened is not enough."

They say, "But we left you with a post hypnotic suggestion that you would recall what you told us." They use those catch words that will bring that recall to him. Now he remembers what happened in the session. He immediately has enough sense to know that he should shut up. He agrees with Robaire that the psychiatrist should get back to San Francisco because it would be too late for him to be out, and having to drive alone that late would be asking too much.

They thanked him for his time, and they hoped that he would communicate back and forth with them. So, he departs the apartment. Robaire and David just sit there. David is not unhappy; but he is not happy because he knows that someone has interceded on his behalf, and he knows that someone was Charlotte. He knows that he has got to go back and face her. Somewhere inside of him he knows she is going to laugh, but it would be a playful laugh.

Robaire is highly irritated. He is not only irritated at Charlotte, but he is also irritated at Yvette. He would like to be irritated at David, but reason tells him that would get him nowhere. He breaks for time to be alone.

They drive back to the estate. David is uncomfortable. Robaire can't wait to get out of the car. He wants to walk around the estate and think. David lets him do it. David goes into the house and immediately wants to go to sleep because he is under sedation. Charlotte wants him to go to sleep too because she doesn't want to go through a question-and-answer period with him right now. He goes to his room and goes to sleep. He sleeps off the medicine that should have taken affect two hours ago. He sleeps until dinner time.

Yvette and Charlotte continue their measuring and comparing. They plan what they are going to do and when they are going to do it. She has a whole list of questions for David when he comes down for dinner, the questions that he wanted to talk about two days ago. She says to David, "Where are we going? When are going where? I'd like to know because you wanted me to have evening gowns, and I must have other attire to wear. I'd like to know what the climate will be like, and will we be on land or at sea or in airplanes?" She has a whole list of items that she wants to talk to him about without revealing too much about what she's going to have on. David is furious.

Robaire has still not quite calmed down, but he is going to sit there and have his after-dinner drink and retire to his room to think it over because that is the way he would handle it. Robaire is not the kind of person who would normally get very angry, but he is very irritated by this.

Yvette, in all innocence, wants to continue with this conversation. She has a whole list of colors, color matches, and fabric. She wants to know because she could do this with it, or she could do that with it. This is what she has had to think about. She wants a little help from him so he can have to think about it too. David knows that she is doing this with almost a tinge of sarcasm, but he also knows that she is very relieved that he is still David intact, and that she was permitted to handle this without any other kind of intercession. He is taking all this in.

He tells her, "Let's go to Hong Kong first because I would like to get you some jewelry. Hong Kong is relatively warm in the summertime, but sometimes the nights get a little cold so if you design evening dresses to go out, you should either design jackets or think of light furs. I don't want you to buy the furs because they have nice furs in Hong Kong, and if that's the case I'll just pick you up a coat or several coats. Depending on how well you like it, we could spend two or three weeks there in that area. Then we should go into Bermuda, and it will be very warm. We can do a complete tour of the Caribbean. We can go into Jamaica. Montego Bay is nice that time of year."

They go on out to the terrace. Charlotte expresses a desire to wear velvet and satin sometimes. She says, "I know that this is not always appropriate, and sometimes it can be too heated, but sometimes I just feel like having nice satin or nice silk near my skin, and I'm trying to find a fabric that will be light enough to do this." He agrees that maybe that is something that she could look in to. But he assures her that she'll have no problems staying warm if he is around, and he will take her only in to the warmer climates.

Yvette pipes up with, "When you get on a ship sometimes, even though you're in a warmer climate, breezes could come up, and you do need jackets and you do need sleeves on your jackets." Charlotte agrees that this often happens.

David says, "Well, then I should tell you how much my land, how much by sea, and how much by airplane, if I can figure it out. Give me about a week, and I will tell you that information. I will also have the probable temperatures for the time period. That will help you. I want you to be comfortable. I want you to be relaxed. I want you to have a lot of fun. Of course, I take the point of view that if you don't have something, we could always pick it up there. But I know how important it is to a woman to be able to create her own wardrobe at a time like this, so I'll let you know within a week exactly where and when we will be and what the climate will be like."

Yvette and Charlotte decided this is fair enough. They let that issue rest. Yvette has been trying to approach Robaire who is obviously in a very bad mood. The mood is one that she has not seen before. She has not seen this black mood before, and she has not seen it directed toward her. Since Charlotte was extremely playful, and this playfulness was contagious, she is in a very playful mood. Robaire is not ready for it. Robaire has had it.

When she approaches Robaire with this attitude, he snaps at her. He reminds her that she brought him all the way from France with a very serious matter in mind. She answers with, "I'm also here to help lift the mood of my friend, and if I can lift the mood of my friend why does that anger you?"

He doesn't have a reply for that because he knows that she is right, but he knows that he is right. He tells her, "Something happened today that has upset me. I must think it over before I speak to you about it, and I must think it over before I discuss it further with David. I have been thinking about it since we returned from David's apartment."

She says, "Yes. I know that you had asked me to keep Charlotte busy until you finished your hypnotic trance session with David. How did that go? Did you achieve hypnosis? Did you achieve a trance state with him? Did he refuse to cooperate? I don't understand why you are upset with me. I think I do need to know. Did any of those things happen?"

He says, "Well, yes. He fully cooperated with the trance state. That is about all I can tell you right now. We do believe that we achieved hypnosis. I'm going to review the tapes because I taped the session."

She says, "May I come along?"

"No. I don't think that you should come along right now," he snapped. His tone of voice was so harsh that it hurt her feelings. He could see that it had hurt her feelings. He is immediately sorry.

She says, "All right. I guess I will talk to you tomorrow or the next couple of days, or whenever it is that you get over this feeling that you're having. But I hope you continue to communicate with us because I don't understand what is happening. David seems a little pushed out of shape, but no one is taking things as hard as you are."

He says, "Just give me some time to think about it. That's all I ask for. Please, just give me some time to think about it, and I'll let you know. I'll be happy to discuss with you most of what I've found out." So, he goes upstairs to listen to the tapes.

Since it is later in the evening, she decides that she is going to go to her room and watch television because she is a little embarrassed. He is, after all, her friend, and she brought him here telling everyone that he was her friend, and that they were very close. Then he made this public scene, and if you were close enough to hear everything that he had said, you knew that he was upset with her. So, she goes to her room. She wanted to be by herself because she is embarrassed.

Charlotte picks up on this, but Charlotte still wants to talk to David to find out if David is all right because she is concerned. She has put together what happened in the monastery. She knows some of what happened to the monks. She doesn't know why he backed into that wall, but she has a pretty good idea, without having to visualize it, that it had something to do with the kind of forms that she painted. She knew that he was clearly terrified, and she did not want anything like that to happen to David. She just wanted to talk with him and make sure that he was all right.

He was very much all right. He wanted to take her out on the terrace again and have quiet moment with her. He wanted to tell her how much he loves her, and that he was sure that everything would be all right. She said she knew all along that things would go well. She asks about Otto Weinberger.

He says, "The last thing I heard, Jasper Smythe had called right before dinner, Otto was not getting better, but definitely not getting worse. He is eating and doing his basic care of himself. So that, at least, has been a gain. Jasper said that he wasn't nearly as fearful. He was never left alone, which was a major concern. He apparently has gained a little trust in humanity in general because of the people that he has always been around, like Jasper and Jasper's family. They have been taking turns to make sure that he isn't alone, and they make sure that he eats three meals a day. He has been permitting this and enjoying it. Jasper said that he was getting to the point where he as playing chess again with some of the nephews that came over."

She was happy to hear about this. She knew that had put David in a better frame of mind because she knew that David had harbored guilt that she didn't want him to have about the private detective. She didn't know how long it would last or if it would ever go away. But she had hoped that none of his friends or anyone that was close to him would be in that position again. She knew it was still somewhat on his mind.

She says to him, "I have noticed an interaction between Robaire and Yvette that doesn't seem quite right. I know Yvette hadn't said anything, but Yvette was very embarrassed, and her feelings were hurt. She has gone to bed early. I'm going to go to bed also, but I'm going to stop in and talk to Yvette, if Yvette is willing to talk, about what was happening between she and Robaire. I know that Robaire meant a lot to Yvette. I hope nothing that has happened in this house has caused another friction or crack in the relationship."

He appreciated that she had that kind of perception and that sensitivity. He thought then maybe I am overly concerned, maybe I should let things rest a bit and let them take their course. She kisses him good night. She goes upstairs and knocks on Yvette's door. Yvette is reluctant. She is hoping it is Robaire, but it is Charlotte. There is visible disappointment in her face when she discovers it is Charlotte. Charlotte says, "I understand that you were hoping it is Robaire, but it is me. I want to talk to you. May I come in?"

Yvette says, "Of course, you can come in. I'm always happy to see you. It's just that I guess you know he's upset with me, and I don't know why. He's very upset with me."

Charlotte says, "It's probably more my fault. As he thinks about it tonight and in the days to come, he will realize it."

Yvette says, "Well, I don't want him to put the blame on you because I don't know what happened. I don't want him to be mad at anyone."

Charlotte says, "Don't worry about it. I think it will work itself out. I know you're very upset, and I don't want anyone who has come a long way to feel uncomfortable staying in my house. I'm a better hostess than that. I will try to talk to him too, if he will talk to me. And I want you to feel very welcome and very comfortable in this house and know that I will try to do everything I can to make him feel very welcome and very comfortable. I will again speak to David in the morning to see if he could find something for them to do together to have him work this out because it seems that Robaire, I don't know him very well, but from the time that he's been here it seems that when he gets into a problem or something seems to overwhelm him he becomes introverted and maybe a this time it is not a good time. David is good at pulling people out of things. Let's hope that David can help him with it."

Yvette says, "Maybe that's a good idea. You're right I should not worry. I'll just go ahead and rest."

Charlotte goes down and knocks on Robaire's door. Robaire is listening to tapes. He calls out a very secretive, "Who is it?"

She says, "It's Charlotte. May I come in? I'd like to talk to you. Are you dressed? I'm alone. Yvette is not with me. David's not with me."

He says, "Yes. I have not undressed." He turns off the tapes and hides the machines. Then he opened the door and he let her in. She came in to sit down and talk to him.

She says, "You seem to be unhappy. And I'm not trying to get involved with your relationship with Yvette, I know it's none of my business, but once again I hope you understand that you are welcome in my house and that I will do everything I can to make you comfortable in my house. Also, Yvette is very concerned. I'm not going to intercede any further. I just wanted to let you know that. I hope you have a good night's sleep. If there is anything that I can do, please call on me." She is very nice, very sweet and very sensitive.

He, of course, can see why David is in love with her. But he is still a little upset about what happened. He says to her, "Goodnight," and he thanked her.

She offered to have one of the servants bring him up some hot chocolate because she says that has often helped her. He thought that was a very good idea, hot chocolate. She said she would take care of it immediately. She rings one of the servants from the phone in the hall, after she says good night to him and leaves his room. She suggests that he bring some hot chocolate up and maybe a biscuit or something for Robaire. She goes to her room, and she retires for the night.

She sleeps without incident. She is very well rested. David also has a very uneventful sleep. The house is quiet for the night.

The next day, Robaire and David run into each other outside. Robaire says, "If you follow this vampire theory, then there is someone that has to move about in the daytime for them. We talked to the nanny. She didn't seem to find it significant that she never saw the parents during the daytime. You said yourself the thing that alarmed you and made you exhume bodies is that you thought that the servants were acting in a trance-like state. I haven't noticed that, but then I don't see a lot of differences here either. Also, she's not on the reverse schedule that you had described to me when I first came. You have seen her exhibit telepathy. I suspect that she's exhibited telepathy, and that's why we couldn't continue the trance."

David says, "What do you mean?"

He says, "Well, I think she interceded and that's who blocked the trance. Have you ever thought about that?"

David says, "No. Well, in all honesty, I did have a sense of Charlotte being with me, but it wasn't a disquieting sense. What I saw is what I told you I saw."

Robaire says, "Yes. I know. You saw what she was doing at that time, and she was the one that let you see that. I think she interfered because she didn't want anyone else to have to. It is good to know that she can, but we don't know how far that's going to go. Anyway, if this is true, then they must have had a network of people who would work for them and do things that had to be done between nine and five and no one would ask any questions. This network must have started in Europe, and there must be some fragment or extensions of it here in America. I think that's how they found this house.

"The trustees that are working for them now may not even be aware of it. They probably have very sedate lives, they go to work, whatever. They could be yuppies for all we know. They go to work every day, and they come home at night and do whatever it is that they're supposed to do. At certain times, they end up doing exactly what Charlotte's family wants them to do. I have been thinking about your job in Europe. That seems like that was so convenient. Don't you think that was a little bit too convenient?"

He says, "Well, actually I hadn't really thought about it."

Robaire says, "But when you came, she was quite different from when you left. Haven't you wondered what happened in that time period?"

He says, "Of course I wondered what happened in that time period. I tried to ask her, and she hasn't given me an answer."

Robaire says, "I think that was an arranged job. I think they arranged to get you out of town, and they knew that Otto Weinberger was not going to be a problem."

David says, "Once again, who is 'they'?"

Robaire says, "They must be whoever it is that has done these other things that you say you haven't done, we know that you haven't done, you say that Charlotte has done, and we know that Charlotte hasn't done."

David says, "They can't be that powerful. So, what you're suggesting is, or what your hypothesis is that they have always lived this way. You are telling me that they have always had people do things for them that they could contact and control telepathically, that they didn't have to do things during the daytime?"

Robaire says, "That's the only answer because otherwise they couldn't die and exchange land, they couldn't keep their wealth. A lot of things they must do, and they must do in an accepted manner. They must have lawyers. They must have different people working for them. Otherwise, how did they just come right here without looking at other places first? They must have had more than a hunch. That's probably why no one is bothering you. You seem to be very acceptable to these people who can give them more than a hunch. That's probably how they've been able to make sure that the trustees did not know the extent of your investigation because anybody would have fought you from trying to prove that she was a vampire, if they knew that's what you were doing. They would be horrified. The nanny would be horrified.

"But somehow this information is blocked from them. Also, they have not decided to kill you. They let you proceed. If you didn't bother Charlotte, they didn't seem to care. The more you know it seems the better. I think that's why I couldn't complete my trance because you know far more than Otto Weinberger. That's what Otto Weinberger was trying to tell me. And you will know much more than you know now. That's why Charlotte keeps demanding your loyalty."

David says, "I must think about this. I must go somewhere and put this all together in my mind. You are right. There has been a lot of times where if there was anybody to intercede, they should have interceded. And you're right, I have not been horrified. They let me get beat up though. But I have not been through some of the experiences that I think would have made it difficult for even me to come back."

Robaire says, "Of course not. That's the other thing that Otto Weinberger was right about. They do want you here."

He says, "They really don't need to be concerned about that because I want to be here. The other thing is that I do think that if I'm going to be here, I should be loyal to her family or I should leave."

Robaire turns this over in his mind. He says, "As long as innocent people are not getting hurt for no reason. And if innocent people are not getting hurt, that's the posture that I will take. I'm sure that is the posture that Yvette has already taken. If her parents are practicing vampires, were there any deaths here during the time period that they were alive? If not, why not? Is there a certain time period where they don't have the need for blood? We have too many questions that are unanswered. We know why Charlotte isn't doing this, but we don't have any answers about them."

David says, "Maybe we shouldn't look for any. Maybe she should just maintain the status quo, and that is not a problem now. That's what I had decided to do when I asked Charlotte to marry me. It's not a problem now, and when and if it becomes a problem, I'll have to deal with it. But I don't think that it will become a problem. I'm concerned about this expression of telepathy and telekinesis. If it's something that she can control, I'm not going to concern myself about that. A lot of people must live with it. Just as long as it stops right there."

Robaire says, "Then you have defined my job for me, exactly what you want me to do better. You want me to make sure that it stops right there."

David says, "Yes. I want you to make sure it will either stop right there or it's something that she can control."

Robaire says, "I still need to find out more about the relic."

David says, "No argument here, if they are going to let you do it." They agreed again to keep with their line of questioning of Mrs. Hampton because they need to do this, and this has not been interrupted. This is not seen as a threatening move. They are going to proceed with that.

They proceed with their interview of Megan Hampton. She has little to offer in the way of deeds and anything other than how Charlotte was raised during the time periods that Charlotte was home. She does have some insight because of the communication from the psychiatrist. But she does remind them that she too worked for the trustees, and she is close to Charlotte, and what she would reveal to them would be the most intimate things that happened to Charlotte when she was growing up, and somehow, she feels that's unfair to Charlotte.

In the meantime, once again, David has not forgotten his conversation when about how he should meet the trustees. Charlotte had promised him this introduction when he went riding with her.

The trustee, who was head of the firm that has invested and looked after Charlotte's affairs, Mr. Leopold, has an assistant who has been with the company twenty-five years, Mr. Simon Schnell. Mr. Schnell is going to take over when Mr. Leopold retires. When Charlotte requests a meeting, it is a rather informal meeting so as not to put anyone on guard because she knows that David is very aggressive about it. She wants to tone this down when she has the trustees over to her home, even though she herself is not very familiar with her trustees because she has always been away at school. She has Mr. Leopold over for dinner, expecting Robaire and Yvette to be there.

Mr. Leopold says that he must bring Mr. Simon Schnell because Mr. Schnell will be taking his place when he retires, and he needs to be fully informed of what is happening to Charlotte. He agrees to go ahead and bring Mr. Schnell to dinner, which is going to be followed by a little conversation in the library between Charlotte, David, and Mr. Schnell.

Unbeknown to Mr. Leopold, Mr. Schnell began embezzling from Charlotte's account at the time of the first disastrous love affair. He has since embezzled numerous times, one time being after the first set of murders. He has essentially decided to make Charlotte his own personal gold mine and keep the other accounts in the firm very above board. He is patient. He plans to continue to embezzle and invest her money in his name over two to three decades. He is a very trusted employee because he has been with the firm twenty years, and he has worked his way up through the firm. Because of his longevity with the firm and his closeness to Mr. Leopold, he has been fully apprised of the paintings and the incidents at school.

The psychiatrist's reports were, of course, sent directly to him and Mr. Leopold to review. He was banking on the conclusion that she would be a crazy old maid, that she would never marry, and she would have a limited need for funds because he projected how much her art gallery would need, and if it did well at all it would generate money. He also projected what she would need on a personal basis to keep up her house and her servants in the style she was living now. He even made allowances for her, trips to Europe, or whatever it is that she might want to do. What he hadn't accounted for was family and more family, and a husband that might have a background that would discover or uncover what he had been doing.

He arrives at the Von Shillingsfurst estate. The butler takes their coats. They have a before dinner drink where he is introduced to David, Robaire, Charlotte and Yvette. He hadn't met Charlotte formally before. He is very comfortable. He is confident because he thinks he has things well in hand. He has been slow and very meticulous about his embezzlement, and he thinks he is going to have time to cover most things. The one thing that he does have in his favor is that all of any paperwork was always kept in the hands of the trustees because they were dealing with a two-year-old child and a nanny.

He is relaxed, congenial, and as conversational as his personality would permit him to be. Running through his mind all the time is that he must stop David's inquiries because he understands now that David has prompted this meeting and possibly, he will need to stop David's marriage. The tactic that he has decided to take is one of distraction until he can find out exactly what he is dealing with. The firm, in general, has always kept track of Charlotte so he has known pretty much what Charlotte has made. He is counting on the fact that David has had a history of being a playboy, and he knows David's background all too well. He didn't expect David to take to Charlotte. And the more trouble that seemed to follow Charlotte in the last two months, the more likely he thought it would be that David would take a different direction. He was wrong about that. He cannot imagine how he had come to this wrong conclusion.

He is invited, along with Mr. Leopold, by a very stable Charlotte to a renovated house to have a meeting. He is presently going to have to discuss with David some of Charlotte's affairs at Charlotte's request. Robaire and Yvette are present at dinner. Mr. Leopold and Mr. Schnell acknowledge the fact that they are aware of Yvette, that they are very happy to meet such a very beautiful nice young lady, that they had often taken care of the arrangements so Charlotte could visit with Yvette and her parents in France, and they were happy to finally meet the lady.

Yvette returned the compliment because Yvette herself does not have trustees since both of her parents are alive. She makes most of her money on her own, though she has money that she will inherit and that she has access to while she is alive. So, this is a situation that she has heard of before, but it is not one from her personal experience.

Robaire is very much intrigued by both the trustees, but he is quiet. He takes an observant posture because he is not exactly sure what is going on here and somehow, he just doesn't quite like it. He understands why neither he nor Yvette have been invited into the private discussion in the library. He is not at all taken back by that. He doesn't feel snubbed. Robaire and Yvette decide that backgammon is for them tonight and possibly some walks around the garden. They announce these plans early to relieve anyone's anxiety that they are going to be obviously and deliberately excluded from the meeting in the library.

Once again, the talk at the table is about the upcoming wedding. This is where the wedding is announced. Charlotte says, "I accepted David's proposal almost two months ago. There is so much on my mind, I didn't think to tell both of you about it. Yvette and Robaire have been here for almost two months now trying to get our invitations out, and the wedding has been all encompassing. I'm very tired. Yvette has been very good and very patient with me and she is helping me go through the trousseau, and Yvette will be solely responsible for the clothing that I have on my back because she brought all of the designs and all of the fabric from Paris. She has been in constant contact with the designers, and they've gotten the measurements from everyone including the bridesmaids. Things seem to be proceeding quite well. We expect the wedding to take place within the next month."

Both trustees are shocked at this turn of events, but Mr. Leopold is very happy. He wishes her well. He tells her that he hopes she has many little Von Shillingsfursts, and he can only hope that they grow up in a house that is full of laughter and full of joy. She thanks him for this. He says he hopes he receives an invitation to the wedding. She says of course he will. Mr. Schnell, of course, voices his desire to go to the wedding. He is told also that of course he will be at the wedding. They explain to them some of the details of the wedding.

Charlotte says, "We plan to have the wedding outside. Jasper Smythe, whom Mr. Leopold hired, is now altering the landscaping in the area where we are going to have the wedding so that we will have a trellis or archway over the area. And with the archway we could have the wedding whether it should rain or whatever the situation is. He is planning for that. We expect most of the guests will have to travel a long way. Charlotte, once again, thanks Mr. Leopold for having such a good taste in the architect because he has done exactly what she has asked him to do pretty much without question."

Mr. Leopold says, "I took very good care in selecting Jasper Smythe. I knew that to come home and for it to really be home for you, might be a more painful experience than you would anticipate because you were the only family that would be here. Out of all the architects I interviewed, Mr. Smythe seemed to be congenial and the most flexible. There was no other choice. I hope he comes across that way to everyone else."

She says, "That's why I'm so happy with him. I, myself, had anxieties that he was going to make me do this or do that because I was a young female in charge of the house. But he let me do exactly what I wanted to. He relaxed me immediately. Any time I question, he was always there ready to answer it."

Robaire and Yvette look at each other because they are hoping that this line of conversation doesn't keep going in the direction of Jasper Smythe so that Otto Weinberger is not brought up.

Fortunately, David intercedes by saying, "I am very impressed with the interior work that Jasper Smythe has done. I am also overwhelmed with the way he set up the outside so that there are various places to sit along the walk. The redwoods tend to cast shadows in unlikely places, and I have found those to be very romantic as I was pursuing my courtship of Charlotte." Yvette and everyone smile. Charlotte blushed.

Yvette took up the conversation, "Robaire and I both have found the gardens and the landscaping just wonderful. Most of the time we have enjoyed the outside because it is so beautiful. He has picked plants that have the best scent, and they seem to have a year-round growth period. I didn't know that an architect could encompass all that. I didn't know his field was that wide."

The trustee points out, "A good architect always hires and delegates his duties. He brings in experts in different fields. What you credit him for is his ability to recognize those expert contact and get them. He probably isn't aware of what happened with the landscaping, and he probably isn't aware exactly how well everything has turned out. But he has, of course, made some yes or no decisions as plans were being presented to him."

At this point, Robaire and David look at each other because they know that Jasper Smythe must have stayed very close to the project, close enough to find the relics that he had discovered. David says, "Yes, he definitely was an on-site architect. He's not one of those architects that just puts his name up and sends his workers out because you could find him around the house most anytime of the day. And he still comes from time to time." Charlotte had to admit that this is true.

By this time, a servant interrupts with another course. Dinner proceeds quite smoothly with more small talk. Charlotte and David retire to the library with Mr. Leopold and Mr. Schnell. They close both library doors. Yvette and Robaire decide to take a walk out in the garden. The servants bring them in after dinner liquors. Mr. Leopold chose to stick with hot chocolate because he knows that he has a long drive. Mr. Schnell says he'll go along and have some creme de menthe. For Mr. Schnell, this is quite an unexpected turn of events. He never expected Charlotte to get married. He did not expect to be faced at this very moment with a very beautiful, calm and clear-headed Charlotte, seated next to her fiancé who seemed to be equally as alert. In him rises a quiet panic.

While they are having their conversation, he decides that the best way to deal with David is to pay someone to tamper with the brakes on his car. But he tells them, "I'm very glad that you called this meeting because I was going to have to ask you to come to the office. I was going to ask both of you because the parcel map of the land is being contested. And the land as it stands and as it has been described in county records is apparently, from what some sources are saying, not properly drawn. It includes land that is not Charlotte's and excludes land that should be Charlotte's."

Mr. Leopold is shocked at the revelation because he hadn't been informed.

Mr. Schnell said it came across his desk that very day, and he didn't want to bother Mr. Leopold because he knew Mr. Leopold was getting ready to retire.

Mr. Leopold kind of shot him a glance. Neither David nor Charlotte quite understood, but there seemed to be a little bit of shock in that. Mr. Schnell carries on with the conversation by saying, "I will, of course, do everything I can to look into this because we were party to the initial transfer of the deed. As far as I know, the deed was transferred properly. The land the financier bought was also the land that Charlotte parents bought, which was also the land that was originally mapped out by the sea captain. But, of course, this is going to take probably several months work to clear this up and deal with the county about it. I've certainly got my hands full. I hated to bring you this bad news because I know that you are getting ready to leave on your honeymoon. But I thought that you should be the first to know because if someone decides to build on that land, you could run into some real trouble. I don't think that this land is not unclaimed. This land does have an owner. I hated to tell you this right before you were getting ready to leave to go on your honeymoon."

Charlotte and David are at a loss for words. David feels like a complete idiot. He doesn't know anything about what a parcel map means. He has done some investments. But he has moved around so much, he hasn't even bothered to buy a house, a simple house. He realizes that he has insisted upon this meeting, and he is not equipped to be there. A lot of things run through his mind, and Charlotte picks up on this. She turns the conversation by saying, "I'm very glad that you have made us aware of it, Mr. Schnell, as soon as you found out about it. Is there something that we should do? Should we retain other attorneys? Or how is this handled?"

He says, "Don't worry. This is something that our firm basically will have to deal with because there are attorneys, accountants and various other experts, of course, that work for our firm. We will simply have to handle this matter. From experience, I know that these matters don't correct that quickly, and every bit of know how is needed to resolve this problem."

In the back of his mind, which is very conniving, he knows that this is strictly a diversionary tactic which may later be used as a method to murder David, and David only. He knows that if Charlotte dies, the land will either go to charity or to the state, and he still won't be able to do his skimming off the top. So, what he has managed to, which took some quick thinking because he really didn't know what he was being summoned out here for, was to turn the topic away from investments and liquid assets to the very house that they lived in. It bought him some time.

Charlotte looked at David. David looked at Charlotte. They both knew they should get a little more informed, a little more educated, on the subject before they can come back and talk it again. Charlotte was forced to dismiss the assembly. She did so politely and asks them if they would like to have their desserts now with any kind of cordials. Mr. Leopold looked at Mr. Schnell, and he didn't seem at all sure.

Mr. Schnell says, "Of course we will," because things are going partly his way. He has a relaxed look on his face. All throughout dessert and the sipping of the cordials, he assures Charlotte that he would personally look into the matter, and that he would take great care that nothing should happen to her ancestral home after she had gone to so much trouble landscaping and renovating it. He sipped his sherry.

They all commented on what delicious desserts they were having.

David is upset for a lot of reasons. But he has been in business situations before. He realizes that these are guests in Charlotte's home, so he goes along with the program. He eats his dessert and drinks his cordial, and he pays attention to his fiancé hoping that they will leave soon. After they finish their desserts and have a little bit of coffee, Mr. Schnell doesn't show anxiety or any rush to leave. They give him his tea and they give Mr. Leopold, at Mr. Schnell's suggestion, coffee with cream and two sugars. They finish that.

It is after ten o'clock before they leave the house. Charlotte and David say their goodbyes. Robaire and Yvette have peeked in from the garden, but they understand that the situation is not over. So, they only wave and go back outside. As soon as the doors are closed behind both trustees, David turns to Charlotte and demands that he see the deed. This catches Charlotte quite off guard. Charlotte is almost in tears. She is about to possibly lose some part of her home. She doesn't know what this means. She was two years old when her parents bought this home. She has never seen any paperwork on the home. She was just getting around to asking for it. It has always been in the hands of the trustees because a two-year-old girl could never have handled this.

She doesn't want to threaten his manhood, so she lowers her tone of voice. But what she doesn't realize is that she is crying, and she is sobbing. She is shaking a little bit because this is a direction that she didn't expect anyone to come from.

He takes her in his arms. He begins to kiss her neck. He tells her, "I love you no matter what happens, and I don't give a damn about the land. It's just that if the land is yours, I don't want to see anybody take advantage of you." They were trying to calm each other down, but he has some idea what it means to her, what it means to them both. They feel ignorant and helpless.

She says to him, "I don't know if you understand that all the important papers have always been with the trustees, not with the nanny, not with me, not with any of the servants, with the trustees." Then she goes on to remind him that he cannot go into their office demanding anything because he is not married to her yet, and legally they shouldn't reveal anything to him.

David calms her down by kissing her, whispering in her ear, running his hands through her hair, and assuring her that if this means that she has nothing, it doesn't matter to him. He says, "I'm very angry and I need to get out of the house. I need to go for a long ride so I can think about this. It's difficult for me to think clearly when you are crying. It's difficult for me to handle this, and this should be something that I we can handle together."

He takes a long ride. Charlotte goes to bed. She cries herself to sleep.

As David is riding in his car, he sizes up his position. He is not her husband. He is asking questions. He suspects that something may not be kosher. But he realizes his position. He does not have the kind of wealth that Charlotte has that they talked about in that room. He may get it in his lifetime, but he didn't have it when he was two years old. Maybe to them, his motives were always suspect.

He decides that the best approach for him would be to research the county records and see what the county records say. He is not sure how to go about doing that. He wonders if he should hire a lawyer, and if he does hire a lawyer, is that procedure a threatening move because these people are supposed to work for her. He wonders how he can hire a lawyer to research information on something that basically doesn't belong to him. He turns all this over in his mind. He decides that maybe he'll just try to find out how to research county records and boundary lines and read parcel maps on deeds, which he suspects is not going to be that easy with ten to twelve acres. Then he will try to see the trustees in their offices again.

He goes home and takes a long hot shower. It is all that he can do to stay out of Charlotte's room. When he finishes his shower, he gets dressed in his robe and comes down the hall and knocks on Charlotte's door. Charlotte opens the door. He wants to come in the room, so Charlotte lets him in the room. She asks him, "Did your drive help? Did it help you at all? You have awakened me. I was getting some sleep." He apologized for that. He can tell that she has been crying. He says that he really feels inadequate, and that he has never wanted to sleep with her more in his life than he does right now.

Of course, she tells him, "This cannot be done. Not in this house. Not in this hall. My nanny is one door down, and I hope you have some- thing on under your robe." Then he begins to kiss her, and it is very difficult for her not to respond to his advances. She permits him to kiss her, and she kisses him back. She holds on to him and he hugs her. She starts to cry again. This is just too much for him.

She says, "I'm going to call one of the servants and have them bring me up some hot chocolate. I want you to go back to your room, and I want you to get some sleep. If you don't do this, I'm going to have to ask you to take your residence outside of the house again." He relents, kisses her good night, and leaves the room. He looks back at her and she looks beautiful. She is wearing a long aqua marine gown with long sleeves that fall a little off the shoulder. It is floor length. It seems to have lots and lots of material, but it is very light. Her hair is up.

He had to force himself out of the room.

He goes in his room and goes to sleep. There is a knock on his door. One of the servants says, "Charlotte, has recommended that you have some hot chocolate, and it has been spiked with some sherry. She thinks it will help you sleep." He accepts it and has a very good night's sleep.

The next morning, they are all downstairs again. David and Charlotte are exceptionally quiet at breakfast, but obviously a lot closer. A lot of chemistry and a lot more electricity is passing through him. Robaire and Yvette can't make up their minds if they should ask questions yet. They decide to just be there in case they are needed. Robaire is good at that, and Yvette has learned that from Robaire. Most of the time is spent very quietly.

The two girls have gotten back to baking because Charlotte has discovered that this is a restful thing to do. The men take the horses out for the whole day.

In approximately one week, Mr. Schnell calls the house and asks to speak to Charlotte or David, if David is now acting as Charlotte's representative. Charlotte has caught on to this. She told him, "You can talk to me because I'm still the person who, as far as I know, is the legal owner of the estate. Either we can meet if necessary and David can be present, or I can relay the information to David because I see him all the time." He announces that Mr. Leopold has already retired and is no longer at the firm, and that there should be a letter in the mail coming to Charlotte announcing the restructuring of the firm.

There is mail on the table by the phone and Charlotte opens it up and reads it as she is talking to Mr. Schnell on the phone. The letter is from Mr. Leopold announcing his regrets that he has to end their long association now, but he has had plans of retirement for a long time, and he has been in the firm prior to taking on the accounts of her parents, which she had to remember was thirty years ago. It said that he was happy that he had been permitted to see her grow up to be a nice young lady. Her house seems to be very comfortable now, he's read all of the reviews about the art gallery, and he was present. He thinks that her future is very bright. David seems to be a good young man for her, and she can expect full cooperation from the new head of the firm, Mr. Schnell.

Mr. Schnell is waiting as Charlotte is reading the letter so that she now knows the position of the man that she is talking to. He lets that sink in. He tells her, "I am still in the process of investigating this new problem. I must get some surveyors to confirm things. I think this is work is better left for David. I want to make a site visit. Maybe David should meet me at the site in question with the surveyors and get a good look at what we are talking about. Then I can explain some things to David because David said he was very confused about the parcel maps. I wanted to explain exactly what I think is going on. I have to take the surveyors out there anyway, so David might as well participate in the survey."

She asks if she could be able to go. He says, "Of course you're welcome to go or anyone else that you might want to bring along. You're welcome to go, but I was under the impression that you wanted David to be fully in charge, and that David needed to handle this."

She says, "Yes, of course, I was insistent that David be fully informed."

He says, "Even though you are not married yet, you have made this very clear to the firm. And we want to respect your wishes, even though we are aware that his resources don't come up to yours."

She says, "For sure David will be there. Which day do you want him to be there?"

He says, "I have it scheduled with the surveyors for next week. He should come early in the morning because you know how construction workers and surveyors are. They get started between six-thirty and seven. He should be there at six-thirty or seven."

The real reason that he wants him there this early is that he wants to make sure that he uses his car for nothing else than to drive to the survey site. He knows that Charlotte's Volvo won't make it, and David's vehicle is more suitable to rain so David will have to take his vehicle. He has already arranged to have the brakes rigged the night before. All he must do is wait there with some very unsuspecting surveyors who will be the witnesses that he to David's accident.

David is going alone. He is going to find out what is going on here.

Robaire continues his congenial reminiscing with the nanny in the hopes that she has some clue as to what was happening with Charlotte prior to leaving for school. He doesn't know why he wants to go back. It is a hunch that tells him that he should go back over that night that Charlotte's parents died. He has to do it in a very low, very roundabout way. It is something that the nanny really doesn't want to talk about too much, and she doesn't remember it so well. She can't see the significance of it. She doesn't want to do anything to bring anymore gloom in Charlotte. Robaire begins to ask her again what was it that made her think that Charlotte was aware of the accident, "You had mentioned to me that Charlotte was aware, or you felt that when Charlotte was awakened the next morning, that you didn't have to tell her that her parents were dead."

She says, "She has always had, which probably Yvette will tell you, a sixth sense. I have attributed that to that. I have not been one to believe too much in such things, but I've had a few hunches myself."

Robaire says, "Before the accident, were there any other visitors to the house? How long were they here? You say they were here at least a month, possibly a month and a half. Were there any visitors from where they came from or any visitors from town?" She says the only visitors that she knows of that came, and they usually came in the evening, were the trustees. He asks if she overheard any of the conversations.

She told him, "No. Never would I do anything like that. But I knew Mr. Von Shillingsfurst was slightly upset with Mr. Leopold one evening. But it seemed to have been smoothed over well before the accident. I don't know what it was about, but I did get that impression."

Robaire says, "Did you overhear a conversation that made you get that impression?"

The nanny says, "I cannot remember. It was thirty years ago. But somehow something had irritated Mr. Von Shillingsfurst, and I know the source of that irritation was Mr. Leopold."

He says, "Where were they coming from when they had the accident?"

She says, "They were coming from Mr. Leopold's."

He says, "Coming from Mr. Leopold's office? Why didn't Mr. Leopold come here? It seems that they were very important clients, and I would think that, unless it was something that involved a notary or some other thing, he would have come here. Do you know the nature of business they were conducting?"

She says, "No. I never know what the nature of the business is that they were conducting. But I know usually, you're right, he does come here. But this evening he apparently insisted that they come there, and Mr. Von Shillingsfurst was only too anxious to get there."

Robaire asks, "What was his wife's attitude?"

She says, "Well, as I recall, she was a little bit more cautious. But she went anyway. She was, in general, a very soft-spoken woman. She was very beautiful, and he adored her. She could have put her foot down, but she chose not to. So, they proceeded to go and visit Mr. Leopold. They had the meeting with Mr. Leopold, and in returning from the meeting they had a car accident. That's the extent of what I know about it."

Robaire says, "You called Mr. Leopold to tell him that they didn't make it home from visiting him?"

She says, "Yes. That is what I called Mr. Leopold for, to tell him that Charlotte's parents didn't make it home, and that the highway patrol was at the door."

Robaire has gotten this information. He has decided that since the trustees have arrived now, and it is obvious to everybody that Charlotte is upset about this, and he knows that the nanny is a barometer for when Charlotte is upset, and that David is upset about this, he had better leave this topic alone for a little while.

He thanks her for her attention and for talking to him about it. He excuses himself and says he must go up to his room and listen to some tapes and send some telegrams back to France.

In the meantime, he turns his attention to the coat of arms since he has one of them now. He sees in the coat of arms, again, what is obviously the symbol of nobility, the swords, the shields. It is apparent that this coat of arms was designed before guns were in place because there was no gun on this coat of arms and this coat of arms has not been changed. But there is a very unusual looking wolf. Robaire also notices that the wolf has very prominent upper canine teeth, and that it conveys hostility and ferocity. The bat also conveys hostility and ferocity, and he is thinking that a bat is a very strange thing to put on a coat of arms. Usually, a hawk or an eagle is used. He can see why Otto Weinberger and Jasper Smythe arrived at the conclusion that this is the coat of arms of someone practicing supernatural powers because it came across to him that way. Even though there was limited information in the space that was involved, that is what this represents.

He decides that he needs to talk some more with David about this coat of arms because he is not used to researching it. He has gone over the research that Otto Weinberger had given him. It seems to be accurate, and it seems to add up. But why are they here? Why are these things here? And why have they been found in the ground?

He puts that aside also because he thinks that he should spend more time watching Charlotte and Yvette a little closer. He has uneasy feelings about the trustees, and he knows that he is picking up uneasy feelings because of Charlotte and David and something that the nanny said about the car accident. But he is not real sure. He makes sure that when Charlotte and Yvette must go somewhere, he takes them and brings them back. They are happy for the attention.

Things go very lightly and very joyfully because they are finalizing Charlotte's trousseau. She has been given the exact itinerary for the honeymoon. They are finalizing Charlotte's wedding dress, which is beautiful. It has a high collar that comes around the back that frames her face. It shows cleavage. It has a hem that splits and divides in the middle to show a little of the low mid-calf and then flows out around the back to meet the train that comes off her head piece. Her head piece is simply material with a band around it. The band is made of ropes of pearls, and the ropes of pearls are so close together, they are stiff. They closely approximate her head size. Her hairdo will be tresses around her shoulders falling softly in the front and toward the back behind the hat. Everything is just beautiful. The dress is done in layers of satin, crinoline, and chiffon. It has real pearl accents all over it. The pearl accents run as a trim on both sides coming from the empire style of the dress, down to the bodice, all around the hem. She will only be wearing pearl jewelry. It is almost angelic.

Yvette is very pleased with what the designer has sent back, and she is happy that Charlotte had not had to go to Paris for any more fittings. Charlotte, because of the stress, has lost a little weight. The colors of the wedding are going to be green and white. The maid of honor will be dressed totally in green. She has a dress like the bride's in that she has the empire style with the revealing skirt underneath, and she has a pearl trim on her green background. It is a beautiful deep forest green. Her sleeves, like the bridesmaid's sleeves, fall away and hang almost in a long triangle from the elbow. They are very loose sleeves. She is wearing a very soft hood. Her dress is made of a very soft, very thick satin. She has braided green ropes around the bodice and down the back of her dress.

The bridesmaids also will be in green. They won't have the pearl accent, but where the pearl accent is flowing along both sides of the underskirt that is being revealed from the bodice, they just have ropes, the braided rope trim and the braided rope around the bodice. They don't have the high collar. They have very loose sleeves that fall from the elbow. They, like Yvette, have a dickey in the same green so that their bodice is not revealed. They have no hairdresser, but they are to wear the braids in their hair.

The girls spend a lot of time trying to see what the hair length was and if everyone could wear it down in multiple braids or if they could wear one braid down the back and have the rope braided into their hair on either side. That seemed to be the easiest and most uniform thing to do, so they decided to do it that way. Since Charlotte's hair is covered, they just want to make sure that her tresses fall properly. Yvette's hair will be braided with the green braided rope also.

David keeps his appointment to go to the site in question at six thirty in the morning, which he thinks is an ungodly hour. But he wants to go along with this before he really pulls the guy on the carpet. Charlotte does not interfere with this drive, basically because it is six thirty in the morning and she is asleep. But as she is asleep, she is dreaming that his car is not in control. She can't help but keep thinking that his car is not in control, and there is something she has to do about it. She has got to stop this car. She can't stop this car. She has got to stop this car.

David is driving in his car and the way the road winds around the cliff, if he is not careful with his turns, he could end up in the Pacific Ocean. He starts to brake as he comes around the curb, and he has none. Then he begins to try to master the curves just by driving. He is trying to brake, and he is trying to pull up the parking brake. He is trying to turn off the ignition. None of these things are working. He swerves off to the side of the road. He gets into dirt and swerves back onto the road. But somehow, his car seems to be a little bit slowed. Now his wheels are not turning. It takes him awhile to realize what had happened when he went off the road and got back on the road. The car just wasn't moving the same way, and he realizes his wheels are not turning and something is jammed in both of his axles. The car is skidding. It is now rolling. He is going downhill. He gets to a point where he must go uphill, and the car just grinds to a halt. He immediately gets out of the car. The car slowly goes down the hill skidding because the wheels are not turning.

The surveyors, because he is almost at the site, have witnessed this as they were supposed to because that was the one thing that they were there for. Mr. Schnell had really hired them to witness this accident because there is nothing wrong with the way the land has been divided. Everyone, including Mr. Schnell, must run to the scene of the accident. They are very relieved that David is on the other side of the car and clear of it as it overturns. It doesn't catch fire. He has one of the men send for a tow truck and to let Charlotte know what is happening and that he is not going to be back right away. He wanted her to know that he is all right.

Robaire drives Charlotte to the scene of the accident. It is a nightmare for her in more ways than one. She keeps asking Robaire the whole way there, about a fifteen-minute drive, "Are you sure that he is alright? Are you sure they said he was alright? Are you sure they said he was alive? Are you sure he's unhurt?"

Robaire says, "Yes. He would have made the call himself, but it would have been faster to get you the call from the towing station. He's all right, and he's not hurt. I know what you are thinking. It's not a repeat scene of your parents. It's okay."

Once again, she is crying. She has had it. She has learned to cry very easily now. It is not such a bad thing to have to do. He tells her not to worry, she should go ahead and let it out because it is a hard thing for people to have to take. She regains her composure when she gets there. Robaire and she demand that the car be taken to the stables immediately.

The axles are examined by Robaire. The relics are found jammed in the axles in the front and in the back so that the wheels could not turn. He removes these in pieces. Once he relates the information to David and Charlotte, they agree that the car should be scrapped, and no report should be made, and no investigation take place. But Charlotte now has a very good idea of why he needed to be there at six thirty in the morning and why he needed to be there alone. She wants to deal with the trustee.

The vampires intervene.

David, because he has been shaken up, wants a nice hot bath. He wants to go to sleep for a little while. By the time they get the car off the road and examine the axles, it is well past dinner time and it is time for everyone to go to bed. Charlotte goes to sleep too. She is almost tempted to go into David's room, but she knows that she shouldn't. So, she goes into her own room and goes to sleep. When she goes to sleep, she has another physic interaction with the vampires who are ready to talk to her.

In her dream state, and she is fully asleep dreaming, the vampires want to let her know what has been going on. They feel now is the time that they tell her what they have been trying to keep from her for a long time just because she has had enough things to worry about. She receives the information in the form of a dream where she is having a conversation with two or three people that she has already been introduced to before when she was in Italy with her family. She recognized them immediately, and she knows them by name. They ask how she has been, as if time is really passing for them. She tells them that she has been fine and that she is planning for the wedding. They say, "That is good."

She says, "But you must know that."

They say, "Yes, we are aware of most everything, but it is often nice just to have conversation about some things in general."

She agrees with that. One of them says, "Well, once we have gone through with finding out how you are and just giving you that proverbial hug and hello, we have some news to tell you that is very important. We want you to listen very closely. Just because we must reach you in this manner, it does not make us any less loving and does not make us any less concerned about you. We always want to be able to extend a greeting to you, as we would any of our relatives."

She says, "What is it?"

They tell her, "Mr. Leopold killed your parents. We tried to keep this from you because we still had to work with him. You must wonder why he is still alive, and we can assure you that we have a very good reason for it. It was difficult to keep this kind of a network going in Mendocino, and you know why we had to be in Mendocino because if we were in larger cities, in more populated areas, we were more easily discovered. So, we had to deal with Mr. Leopold in another way, though it causes great pains to know that he had murdered both of your parents who he thought were human beings and that he had total care and say over a two-year-old child. But we watched him very closely.

"Mr. Leopold has expressed great remorse after we dealt with him. We have no worries that Mr. Leopold will do anything to harm you or will do anything but further you in your career because he wants to make up for what he has done. Mr. Schnell has evidence that Mr. Leopold killed your parents. He has been blackmailing him since he joined the firm. That's one of the ways he worked himself up in the firm. This network is too valuable Charlotte for us to let it go. We must keep it. We will even have to keep Mr. Schnell."

Charlotte interjects and she realizes who she is having a conversation with, "Is he going to have to end up like Otto Weinberger? I don't understand. Why hasn't Mr. Leopold ended up like Otto Weinberger?"

They tell her, "Because it is the way we handle Mr. Leopold, and we will handle Mr. Schnell the same way. But you have got to think Charlotte. We know that your first response would be to even turn him over to the police or to do something yourself or to tell David. None of these things must you do. This is something that you are going to have to keep to yourself. We had to keep it to ourselves. You have got to interact with Mr. Schnell like you know nothing as we made sure you were able to interact with Mr. Leopold. We made sure you knew nothing."

Charlotte says, "And every day, he was so nice to me, and every birthday he didn't forget. Every Christmas, I had a special present. And he killed my parents? You let him live?"

They say, "Yes. He did all those things because he had a great remorse. He was very remorseful. And we saw to it that he had a very great remorse. We didn't try to make him kill himself. We just pointed out to him what he had done, and how he had left a two-year-old girl parentless. Because he was a man of conscious, he was used to stealing, but he wasn't used to having to kill, and your father was a vampire. Your father had much more intuition than Mr. Leopold expected. He knew every thought that went through Mr. Leopold's mind. So, the night that your parents drove to see Mr. Leopold he was furious. He was so furious that he didn't notice that he shouldn't have had to drive to Mr. Leopold, but Mr. Leopold should have come to him.

"Once again, Charlotte, we would like to remind you, we have a wide range of knowledge, but we too are not insoluble. That was how Mr. Leopold set him up and set the car up. The car went off the road out of control just as David's did. We were unavailable to stop it in time. Your father was very head strong. Your mother couldn't talk to your father. He was a very interesting man. Someday we will sit down and talk to you about both of your parents."

Charlotte says, "Tell me, how did you deal with Mr. Leopold?"

The vampires tell her, "Right now, we would like you to concentrate on your wedding and to go on as if things are normal. David may not buy the accident but try to smooth it off without letting him think that something negative is coming from your side. And we will deal with Mr. Schnell as we have dealt with Mr. Leopold. Mr. Schnell will continue to work at the firm. He will continue to handle your account. He will never interfere with you or David again. And he will put back any money that he has taken from you. This we can assure you."

Robaire now has three relics, and David shows him where he could find a fourth. They take a walk out by the path where David's horse stumbled on the other coat of arms. He shows him where it is, but he decides not to remove it from the earth. They both conclude that there must be many more of these, enough to enclose the perimeter.

David and Robaire drive out to the site of the accident in Charlotte's car. They try to figure out what happened from the skid marks. It is obvious that David went off the road into dirt, and these things are not buried in cement. And you can see where there are holes where something has left the ground. These holes are about ten feet apart. The holes have almost the same dimensions as the coat of arms. Robaire and David take one of their intact coats of arms and set it down in the hole. It is a perfect fit. So, he knows where it has come from, why it came and what it did. He wants to know now if Charlotte did this or did this come from another source. But he is at least very happy about it, he thinks he should be happy about it.

They both agree to say nothing else about the coat of arms because not only has it protected Charlotte and her parents, but apparently now also David. It is much too valuable a thing to ever reveal. They can't help but have an interest. Even though they agree not to say any more about it to anybody, that would be doing any kind of investigatory work, they still retain definite curiosity. They hope that Jasper Smythe and Otto Weinberger have lost their curiosity about it. But David realizes that he, Charlotte and Robaire have many years to look into all of Charlotte's past at their leisure, and possibly after the second or third child she'll feel like going into the part of Eastern Germany where they come from or maybe she will leave things as they are. He knows now that this is not a pressing issue. He also knows that the division that he has always felt that either she could place there or seemed to be there, has now been removed because something or someone has chosen deliberately to save his life. He is very pleased about that.

The wedding plans are still in the works. Reservations are made for Hong Kong first for ten days. David did it that way thinking that he could get an extensive amount of jewelry for Charlotte in Hong Kong, and the Orient is the best place. She would be quite ready after all the shopping to have a nice relaxed twenty-one-day Caribbean cruise in the sun. He especially wanted to do this because he didn't know if he could keep her from reverting to her previous cycle and he didn't want to have to drag Yvette, Jennifer, Robaire, and all the other people that seem to keep her cheerful along with him on his honeymoon. He was hoping that just he, himself, would be enough to keep her the Charlotte that he first met.

The trousseau is complete. All the invitations are sent out. The bridesmaids are sent their gowns by the designer directly from Paris. They are to have their final fittings by their local tailor, one of their choice. The grounds are prepared by Jasper Smythe for the wedding. He has done a lot of things with different plants and flowers that grow out of the ground. He has done some potting in the area of the wedding. He also plans to have freshly cut flowers, some bouquets and other different arrangements. He has contracted this out to a florist. He is very happy to be involved with the wedding. He is also very happy that the wedding is proceeding. He could come back and tell Otto Weinberger that there seems to be nothing but happiness in the Von Shillingsfurst house now, and that there is nothing out of the ordinary there at all. There are just four very happy, full of life young people. They accepted him, they even invited him along on some of their trips to the movies. He has had several dinners with them. He can't think of a nicer group of people.

When he relates this information to Otto Weinberger, Otto Weinberger is quite pleased. He is still not quite in the state of mind that he should be in. He is not nearly as afraid anymore. He has reasoned out what has happened to him and why. And in this reasoning process, he has concluded that, if he does not do these acts again, then he won't receive that kind of response again. That has taken away a lot of the fear. Even all the post-hypnotic suggestions, all of the visits or babysitting, all the turns that Jasper, who is really good support and his friend, had his family making sure he had three meals a day, that he had someone to talk to, they could keep his mental agility there by playing different games with him, none of that was as helpful, though that strength gave him more fortitude. None of that was as helpful as just getting a little of his reasoning process back and knowing that his was a cause and affect situation, and so he would be able to keep his reality. He realized how precious his very own reality was. Right now, that meant more to him than anything in the world. His sanity meant more to him than anything he could find out about, any investigation he could uncover, anything. His priority was just being able to keep and be in control of his reality. Of course, he has had many conversations with the psychiatrist about this.

The psychiatrist simply relates to him, "Otto, this is the conclusion that other people with what we call shattered personalities or altered realities come to. If they ever come out into what we call the range of normal, and you know that is a very wide range, they have that same great appreciation for reality, for the reality that everyone else exists every day. They are appreciative that they are not on the fringes and that they're not even further outside on those fringes."

Otto Weinberger had volunteered to get involved in someone's business. He does a lot of soul searching. He is not married. He has no children. He is somewhat in Charlotte's position. He does have extended family in Germany, but he hasn't seen them in years, and he couldn't swear to it that they would really want to see him that much with open arms. He would assume they would. Maybe he went a little too far. Maybe he made too much of an identification with Charlotte herself. He is thinking that he doesn't really have a lonely life because it's filled with things for him to do, but he doesn't have the constant love and support that he thinks he has. These are the conclusions that he is coming to now while he is at home alone and while talking to the psychiatrist.

Jasper talks to the psychiatrist. Jasper is very intuitive. Jasper is really Otto's friend because he likes Otto. He has sensed that these are the conclusions that Otto is coming to, that it is good to put these happenings off to the very normal, and that he is going to take the blame for it. He is thinking that he is going to just decide that he went a little too far and probably he should have taken some time to examine his own background, and perhaps he lived in that proverbial glass house. Jasper wants to head this off. He talks to the psychiatrist at length from his home because he has always known how to reach him. "He is not a psychiatrist. He is not a parapsychologist. He has had no training in this area. He is just a good friend, but I don't want Otto Weinberger to walk away with any kind of guilt. At first, he was carrying one kind of guilt, and now he is carrying another kind of guilt. I don't think any of it is quite fair, and I don't know exactly what I am going to do about."

He has several conversations with the psychiatrist. The psychiatrist tells him, "It may just work itself out. It is something to be watched. I'm glad that you have been perceptive enough to notice it, and you are keeping informed of what is going on. Keep me informed if he stops eating or he stops sleeping, or if he looks any more anxious than he is now. And for your own sake, remember that Otto Weinberger could not have had a better friend at this time."

Jasper thanks him and decides that he had better get back to Charlotte's house so that he can finish up his duties because he still has quite a bit to do before the wedding. He is very excited about the wedding. He is also hoping that things will be smoothed over well enough so that Otto Weinberger can attend the wedding. He is driving up to the Von Shillingsfurst estate with these thoughts on his mind. He didn't want to bring it up because he knows that they have helped Otto an awful lot. He realizes the position that everyone had put Charlotte in, and how unfair it had been, but he still couldn't help thinking about how much different his friend was, different to the point where he could no longer function in his chosen field. He would be happy if he could just get him to be able to function in his chosen field.

He is giving directions to gardeners now because the land is in the proper condition to start potting plants that he knows will bloom within a month or month and a half. Jasper comes up to the estate. He parks his car in a safe place away from everything. He goes over to talk to the gardeners. Charlotte comes out and asks him, "How is Otto Weinberger doing?"

He says, "You know, that has been on my mind for months now. I knew that I shouldn't talk to you directly about it, but now that you have mentioned it, I'm very glad you brought it up because I've often wanted to say more directly to you about it. He's much better in that he is sleeping now. He is eating three meals a day. My family sees that. He's a lot less fearful. But he is still quite not himself. He has not gone back to work. I don't know when he will be back to work. It's not a monetary thing for him. He's not under any financial distress. But it's good to see him have enough healthy mental activity that he can carry out all of his duties and anything that he should choose to do."

Charlotte says, "Yes. Of course, I understand exactly what you're getting at. He doesn't need the money, but he should be able to go and continue teaching at the university should he choose to or do any research that he would like to pursue. I was wondering if you think it would be helpful if I went to see him. I have a free morning and afternoon. I can call him and ask him if I could come over and visit, and just sit and talk with him for a little while."

Mr. Schnell says, "Don't worry. With the kind of business that your wife's family has done with the firm and with the length of time she has been with the firm, that is nothing. I've watched Charlotte since she was seven. In fact, it was Mr. Leopold's idea. He's watched Charlotte since she was two. And to give her this gift, it would be almost like he would be there to give away the bride. It would be the kind of gift that you would get from your parents."

David says, "Is he going to be back in time for the wedding?"

Mr. Schnell says, "I don't know. I think he is going to try. It's important to him. But, of course, the stress of this job has gotten to him, and his health is also pretty important to him."

David asks, "Is he in ill health at all?"

Mr. Schnell says, "He has had a few episodes that he doesn't like to become public." This is not quite true. But in case he needs it to be true, Mr. Schnell has already planted that seed in David's mind.

David says, "I'm very sorry to hear this, and I hope he does relax as long as he needs to. But I also hope that he's here in time for the wedding." He says goodbye and hangs up.

Robaire says, "My goodness! Do they want to give you a boat? Is this a bribe? I guess it couldn't be a bribe because you wouldn't want to trade your house for a boat."

David says, "No. Because of the amount of money that Charlotte has with them and because of the longevity of their relationship, Mr. Leopold thinks that this is a very meager parting gift. Mr. Schnell says that it was Mr. Leopold's idea. Whether it was or not, we won't know until we see Mr.

Leopold. But I have a feeling that when we do see Mr. Leopold that everything Mr. Schnell says, he will agree to."

Robaire says, "I kind of got that feeling too, even though your conversation in the library was private. Through the interaction that I had with him at the table, it seemed that Mr. Schnell was running things before Mr. Leopold had left, and not in the sense of learning the ropes either."

David says, "I know what you mean. I know exactly what you mean. But Charlotte has asked me to stop thinking about it, to let the matter drop. And that's what I am going to have to do."

Robaire says, "I guess you are because you don't want to start a fight this early in the game."

He says, "No, you don't ever want to start a fight with Charlotte." They both think that this is rather humorous. They decide that it probably is a good time to go horseback riding, that will relax them.

In the meantime, Yvette, Charlotte, and Megan are in the library. Megan has her pencil and note pad. She is thinking of things that are traditional to list in the bridal shop. Yvette is calling Jennifer asking if she wants to go into the caterer in Sonoma with them. Jennifer is at the art gallery, and she says, "Yes. It would give me a break. Can I have the rest day off?"

Yvette says, "If it doesn't take us all day, yes, of course, you could have the rest of the day off." They also tell her that they are going to San Francisco in two days and asked her if she would like to go there.

She says, "Oh yes! To get out of Mendocino, it's not like Mendocino is so terrible, but I was starting to get claustrophobia. Yeah, I'd like to go with you. Just tell me when and where to be."

Yvette says, "We'll drive through and pick you up."

Jennifer says, "Fine, what time?"

Yvette says, "For the caterer about eight. For San Francisco about seven-thirty in two days."

She says, "That will fit great in my schedule. I get two days off with pay?"

Yvette says, "You get two days off with pay."

She, of course, is very excited about that. She says, "I'll be thinking of some things too that I've seen at weddings to add at the menu because I know you guys are probably drained. Charlotte sometimes gets drained thinking about ideas for this and thinking about ideas for that when we were opening the art gallery. So, I'll bring a list along of possible edibles. I'm pretty good at that."

Yvette says, "I bet you are because we watched you eat when we went out to lunch with you." Then they all laugh at that.

Jennifer says, "Thanks for including me. I'll be sure to be ready. Goodbye."

Yvette says, "Goodbye."

Charlotte is relieved that that's done. They both turn their attention to Mrs. Hampton. Mrs. Hampton suggests, "It is traditional for the bride to ask for, whether or not she has it, crystal in the way of glasses, china, silverware, and bedding. People would like to know the size of your beds, towels. They want to get things you can use together, and things that you will share together. And you try to make sure that you don't get duplicates, though you know you are going to get duplicates."

Charlotte says, "Yes, I've been to weddings, and I have seen that happen. I have seen where there are ten tea sets. And we already have everything we need."

Mrs. Hampton says, "You don't know. You might decide to build a summer home, or it's just always good to have a complete backup. Anyway, people are going to give you a wedding gift, unless you insist that people not give you a wedding gift. And then people are going to offended about that. So, it's just better to go ahead and make the list." They start with china. Then they go on to crystal, linens, etc. This takes at least an hour.

At this point, it is almost dinner time and Yvette would like to know about dinner. Mrs. Hampton says that she believes the main course is roast chicken, and she doesn't know what the other courses are, but that they're having some vanilla bean ice cream for dessert because she saw the cook making it. Yvette says, "Vanilla bean homemade ice cream!"

Charlotte says, "Vanilla bean homemade ice cream!"

Mrs. Hampton says, "Yes, I know, it's your favorite." She hugs her. It was almost as if she was thirteen or fourteen years old again.

Mrs. Hampton smiles. She says, "This is something that we haven't really talked about, but I'm not sure exactly what it is that I'm to do when you return from your honeymoon."

Charlotte says, "What do you mean you are not sure? I hope you are going to be right here and comfortable."

She says, "You are going to be a married young lady and you do not have any children. I don't know when you are going to have children. So, you don't really have a need for a nanny. I could go back east because I have relatives back east that do need some looking after. I could take a break and take a vacation because all I have ever had to do with my money was save it. I would be quite comfortable. I don't have to be employed here."

Charlotte says, "But I don't want you to leave. You're the only really family that I have."

Mrs. Hampton says, "You will have real family now. You'll have David. You'll hopefully have children."

Charlotte says, "That's exactly the point. I want someone here that has raised me to raise my children. I couldn't think of a better person. It hasn't ever occurred to me that you would want to leave because I'm getting married. I can understand if you want to go back and take this opportunity to visit some of your family for a month. I'd love to have you do that because that's only fair. A month or two months, if you would like to."

She says, "I think probably two months would be better because I haven't seen them in a while, and you need to settle into your house with your husband. It's going to be hard enough for him to settle into your house. And this is another subject that I haven't brought up to you because it seems that you are handling it fairly well." Yvette agrees with her on that point.

The nanny says, "I'm not trying to get into your business, but I am giving you a little womanly insight because your mother is not here to do it."

Charlotte says, "Well, okay. Two months, three months, whatever. But I would like you to come back definitely with the idea that you are a permanent part of the family, that this is your home, and that you will help raise my children."

The nanny is starting to cry. She is tearful. She says, "You know, I've watched you grow up from two years old, and in some ways some of the worse circumstances. But you've turned out to be a very nice young lady, and I do take some of the credit for that, a very nice young lady." By this time, they all three are crying because it is very sad.

She says, "I didn't know what you wanted, and I don't want you to think that I have to say here because I do have other family. But you have been so close to me. You're the daughter that I never had. I just want you to understand that I don't have to stay here. I can still visit you from the east coast when you need me, or I can visit you when you do have children like a lot of mothers do."

She says, "No. You were here, Meggy, when I wasn't, while I was at school. In some ways this is more your home than it is mine. I want you to stay here, and I want you to stay here in comfort and know that you can stay here the rest of your life if you need to. You go visit those other people on the east coast, the ones that I don't know about because as far as I concerned you belong to me."

Yvette says, "I know she feels that way because that's all she ever talks about."

The nanny starts drying her eyes. She says, "I'd better go and make sure dinner is going to be ready on time."

Yvette says to Charlotte, "I never really thought that she was thinking that way. So much has been happening, I didn't know that she would think that I would want her to leave so that I could be alone with David. That would never occur to me. The house has got to have servants. All kinds of people will be in the house. And she has been more like my mother." Yvette says, "Yes, but she has never been one to take anything for granted, and that is why she has been so good at what she does. She's very tactful and she does know how not to intrude."

Charlotte says, "I guess you're right, but I didn't ever expect us to even have to have this conversation."

Yvette says now, "Now that it's out, it has cleared the air, and you know what has been on her mind. That must have caused her a great deal of anxiety, especially if she doesn't want to leave you, and I don't think she wants to leave you. Now that she's assured that you want her to stay, I think you should have a conversation with David about it, so that he doesn't do anything that could be misconstrued as him wanting her to leave."

Charlotte says, "Yes, I will. But right now, what I want to do is have a long hot bath and go to sleep for about two hours."

Yvette says, "That sounds like a good idea to me." They both go upstairs with that in mind.

As Charlotte is drawing her own bath, she is wondering, once again, what her children will look like. Will they have her gray eyes, will their eyes be blue like David's, and since neither of them are blond, will they be dark haired, will she have a boy first, will he mind if she doesn't have a boy first, and the idea of a summer home? The idea of a summer home had never crossed her mind. She is permitting her mind to wander into dreams about all the things that she thought were inaccessible to her before, because for most people where she lives right now is a summer home, but since David likes to travel they could build a house in Bermuda or some other place in the Caribbean or in Canada near where David's relatives are.

As she is thinking about this, David is downstairs on the phone to his mother's house. It seems that he has caught them at a time when most of his family is there. They are jumping up and down, because they have gotten a phone call from David, and they have been wondering how he was doing. He calls them with the news that he is getting married. This is a big shock to everybody. Everybody is on the extensions listening. His brother says, "We never thought that you would. Who is the lucky one, or should I say the unlucky one?"

The sisters are saying, "We're very happy for you, David. We're glad that you are settling down. You be nice to that young lady."

The mother has taken much the same tone, "But tell us a little about her."

He says, "You'll get to meet her pretty soon because we are having the wedding out here, and you'll all have to be flown out here. You'll see that she has a beautiful home, and I think that I will live in this beautiful home with her. She's a very attractive young lady. She's about thirty-two years old, and she is an artist."

His mother says, "Artist! Oh no."

He says, "That should be the furthest thing from your mind when you think of an artist. I know what's coming to your mind, and she's not like that at all. She has opened an art gallery in Mendocino, and that's how I met her." David was never one to give a lot of explanations about what he has done or what he is doing, so they are just happy that he is alive, well and all right. They are also happy that he is settling down. They are anxious to meet her.

He says, "I'll be sending you all of the details as soon as I get more of them. I love you all." They said they loved him.

He asks, "By the way, how did I get everybody at home at once?"

They say, "We were having a barbecue. That's why everyone came over." He could hear some of his nephews and nieces in the background.

He says, "Sounds like you're having a lot of fun."

They say, "Yes, we are. We are having a good time."

He says, "How's the weather out there?"

They say, "We've had a break in the cold spell, and that's why we are barbecuing."

He says, "Oh. Well, enjoy yourselves. I'd almost want to say that I wish I were there, but that's not quite true because I'm so happy right here where I am now."

His whole family is happy for him. They say, "Then it's a good thing that you knew to stay out there. We've never seen you stay on that side of the coast that long. I guess we should have known something was keeping you there." They say, "Goodbye."

He says, "Goodbye," and hangs up.

This phone call is made from his bedroom. He decides that he wants to rest too after his horseback ride. He takes a nice hot shower. He lies across the bed. There is a knock on the door. He is hoping it is Charlotte, but it is Robaire.

Robaire says, "I have some friends in the same line of work that Mr. Schnell is in. I know that Charlotte said not to bother with it, and I'm not going to bother with it, but I just wanted to remind you that that's the case. I wanted to give you the addresses so that you could reach them when you come back from your honeymoon because Yvette and I are going back to France."

David says, "Yea, I guess you're right. You are going to have to leave us, and we're going to miss you. I've been talking to you, and I have been throwing ideas off you. You've made quite a difference in our lives, both of you, and I appreciate it."

Robaire says, "Well, I miss this country too, what I've seen of it. It is quite beautiful. Yvette and I may take a small vacation on some of those islands that I was telling you about because we need to relax a little bit too. This has been a little bit harrowing for us. The only other thing that I am going to do, for my own sake, for my own peace is mind, is make sure that Otto Weinberger is all right."

He says, "That's a good idea. You should do that before you go back home to France."

Since David has not been able to get enough sleep before dinner, because dinner will be happening shortly as he is notified by servants by telephone, he decides to go and knock on Charlotte's door, still in his robe. She is emerging from her bathtub. She grabs a robe thinking it is either Yvette or Mrs. Hampton who has forgotten something on the list. She says, "Come in." He comes on in.

She realizes that it is David, and that David once again has only a robe on, and that now she only has on a robe.

He says, "Please don't throw me out. I want to talk to you for a minute."

She says, "Okay. Just for one minute we could talk. What's wrong? Has something happened?"

He says, "No. I just had some questions about the car accident. Mr. Schnell called while you were in the library with Megan and Yvette." As he is saying that, he can see that she is very angry. He is happy that she is registering this emotion because he doesn't understand why if they both suspect they must suspect that he is trying to kill her. But she keeps insisting that she let this go. He says, "He called while you were in the library, and Robaire and I were at the phone in the hall. We were just getting ready to go horseback riding when he called. The servant said that he would like to speak to either you or myself. So, since you were very busy, I told him that I would take the phone. I hope that's all right with you."

She says, "Of course, that's all right, David. Any time from now on apparently my business is your business, and I hope that your business is my business, if it is something that I am interested in."

He says, "Anyway, I took the phone call for you. Mr. Schnell wanted you to know he had spent two or three thousand dollars surveying this land, and it might go up to five. He wasn't sure, by the time he got drafting and the other stuff done. He had to do it to have his own map."

She says, "What did you say to him?"

He says, "I said to him I was sure you were going to say that that will be fine."

She says, "You're right. That will be fine."

He's irritated about this, but he lets that go. He says, "He said also that the firm is giving us a boat, I'm not quite sure what size boat, that we can use off our dock, your dock, our dock, down off the shore, and that this was Mr. Leopold's idea."

She says, "That is awful nice of Mr. Leopold. But isn't that a rather expensive gift?"

He says, "That was my response. I thought it was a rather expensive gift. But he says with the amount of money that they are handling for you, the kind of investments that they have made, the longevity of your relationship, and the fact that Mr. Leopold has known you since you were two years old, he says

Mr. Leopold feels more like the father that you never had. And since he can't give away the bride, he has decided to give away the store. This is coming from him and the firm with good wishes."

She says, "That's really nice. Is he planning to be at the wedding?"

David says, "Well, that was the other thing he brought up. Mr. Schnell is definitely going to be at the wedding to represent the firm, but he wasn't sure Mr. Leopold was going to be there because Mr. Leopold is in ill health."

Charlotte says, "Ill health? He seemed fine when we saw him. What was it, a week ago, week and a half ago?"

He says, "Yes. He didn't show any signs of being sick. In fact, I would describe him as being robust."

She says, "Yes. That would be my description of him too."

"The other thing I was noticing Charlotte, did you notice that it seemed that he, I know Mr. Schnell is taking over the firm, but it seems that there's another kind of relationship between he and Mr. Schnell where Mr. Schnell is the person who gives the instructions, and Mr. Leopold follows. I don't understand that."

Charlotte says, "It's probably Mr. Leopold's attempt to let Mr. Schnell exercise his muscles and really take full charge because it's a lot of responsibility."

David just kind of looks at her again. He doesn't say anything. He moves to put his arms around her. He starts to kiss her. She kisses him back. He starts to go for the belts on her robe. At this point, she stops him and says, "That all feels very nice. But you will have to stop now, and I would like you to go back to your room."

David says, "I'm not really sure why you are proceeding this way. We've never quite discussed it because so much was always happening. At first, I attributed it to trust or rather mistrust. And I know that you've had some bad relationships, and I don't want to get into prior relationships because I don't want to have to discuss my prior relationships, but I don't understand why you are behaving this way now. Have you any doubt that we are going to get married?"

She says, "No. I really have no doubt that we are going to get married."

He says, "Well, do you doubt that I love you?"

She says, "No, I don't doubt that you love me. And I do love you, which is going to be the next question. But I am not your wife. So, you should go back into your bedroom David, and I'll see you at dinner."

At this point, the phone rings. It is the servant telling her that dinner is ready. He asks if she wanted dinner held up or would she want it served on time. She says, "Serve it on time because we will all be there. Are Yvette and Robaire ready?"

The servant says, "Yes. We called them, and they are coming down the stairs now."

She hangs up the phone and says, "So you see David, we really don't have time. You should go get dressed for dinner."

There is nothing for David to do but leave. In the back of his mind, he is going to continue this conversation after dinner even if he must force the situation.

She gets dressed for dinner. She is very pleased that he has made these kinds of advances. She knew that she had to stop it, but she is very pleased that he made these advances. She is humming to herself as she is applying lotion. She is putting on extra special perfume and things that are softer, the more sensual of her wardrobe, so that she can downstairs to dinner. She is doing this consciously. In the back of her mind, she is in a playful mood. It is kind of funny to her because if he thinks about it, in her mind, he should understand. But once he sees how she is dressed, it should be crystal clear to him. She is the last person to come downstairs.

They are all at the table, and they are waiting for her to come downstairs so they can begin serving. She is in cashmere, a very form fitting cashmere slacks and sweater. And she is wearing a very sensual perfume, and she has taken extra care with her hair. Once again, David compliments her on her appearance, and so does Robaire. Yvette just smiles. Yvette never knows what is going on in these rooms but knowing Charlotte she has a pretty good idea of what tried to go on in the room. She is starting to see things from the position that Jennifer does, but she is a little older, so she doesn't burst out in laughter.

Charlotte comes downstairs and takes her seat at the table. David is sizing up the situation, and he is realizing that his moves or his advances did have a proper affect. She has, in one sense, let down her hair, and she must have been pleased by this. She was consciously putting on clothes that would be far more, and he even hated to use the word with Charlotte, but sexy. He is taking this all in. Robaire, of course, is taking this all in as well. Neither one of them say anything. They proceed with dinner. The servants have taken it all in, and Mrs. Hampton has noticed it.

The conversation at dinner is about the menu, and if the men have any preferences. She turns to David and deliberately asks him about his mother and his sisters, and if he knows of any special foods that they like to eat, if there is anything that is particularly Canadian, and if so, if he has a menu for it. If it is not something that is commonly known, she would like to have it because she wants to make sure that both sides of the family are represented. She knows they'll have a lot of desserts and other dishes from Germany, but she was wondering if he would even, since she hadn't met his mother, if she could maybe even talk to his mother or if he would talk to his mother and get some ideas before tomorrow. She knows it is the last minute, but it just occurred to her that this is something that they should do, and there is quite a bit of time before the menu is prepared.

She says, "Will that be fine?"

He says that he has just talked to his family today. She says, "Oh that occurred today too?"

He is a little embarrassed. "Yes, that occurred today too."

She says, "You talked to your mother and sisters, and they are all fine?"

He says, "Yes I did." But he had time to regain his composure, and says, "Yes, and I talked to my brothers too, and they were fine also." He knew exactly what she was getting at. What she was getting at was that he wouldn't have wanted his sister up in that room under these circumstances. She put it that way, and she didn't have to say any more about it.

As he was regaining his composure, he realized that she was just that shrewd, and that this had taken place earlier prior to the art gallery opening, and several times during the relationship, that she had just kind of handled it that way. He says, "I will be happy to call them again. They are three hours ahead of us, but I'll be happy to call them again tomorrow morning, early before you leave. I'll probably reach my mother and I can get this information from her if she has any special dishes."

She says, "It might even be better to surprise her. Offhand, you know your mother well enough to know if there's some things that she likes."

He says, "You're right. It probably would be a lot better to surprise her."

Yvette agrees that that would have a much nicer touch especially since this relationship has gone on so long and they've never heard of Charlotte, and that might smooth over some ruffled feathers if there were any, and they hoped that there weren't any. He says, "I will think of some tonight, and I'll let you know first thing in the morning before you go into Sonoma with Jennifer and Yvette." That is agreed upon.

The rest of dinner goes rather smoothly. Dinner is good. That is what is occupying everyone's mind. Dinner is quite delicious and very simple. David asks Charlotte if he might see her alone again after dinner, or did she have other plans. She said that she would enjoy spending two or three hours after dinner with him because there were some things that she thought they should talk about too. Yvette and Robaire say that they wanted to go to a movie that the local movie house in Mendocino was playing. It is something that they wanted to see because they had been in France. They hadn't seen any movies yet in America, and it would be new to them.

They wanted to know if they would be able to borrow the car and would they have problems with driver's licenses. Charlotte says, "Have the chauffeur take you so that you can get there and get back without any problems." That's what they decide to do. The next showing is going to be at eight o'clock. They decide they better go and get ready.

Charlotte and David leave the table and go out on the terrace. David says, "I still would like to know why I got the response that I got earlier this afternoon. It's not something that makes any sense to me."

She says, "I don't really think that it needs much more explanation. If you thought about it, I am living in my parents' house. You're living here. Originally, you were living here because it became difficult for you to stay in your apartment because of the whole series of misadventures that we have had, and that's why we are all here. But I'm still living in my parent's house under the jurisdiction of my parents, though they are dead. That would not take place in my parent's house with a man that I was not married to under any circumstances."

He says, "But this is your house. It's as if you have an apartment and you live alone. Are you trying to tell me that this other relationship that you had in France was never this involved? And you know I would have never asked you this before because it doesn't matter to me."

She says, "It is something that must probably matter to all men. But okay, we will go with the premise that this doesn't matter to you. So, if it doesn't matter to you, then I don't need to answer that. And if it does matter to you, I don't need to answer that. I just don't need to answer that."

He says, "I don't think that I'm getting across to you."

She says, "You're getting across to me, and I think I'm getting across to you. It's just that you're not going to accept this fact right now. And I don't understand what your time frame is because I will be your wife in probably less than three weeks. So why are you pressing the issue?"

He says, "I'm just trying to get, I guess, maybe a little bit of a handle on, is this a question of morality? Is this a question of religious morality?"

She says, "Well, wait a minute. What do you mean is this a question of religious morality? I think I see what you're getting at. We are going to be married by the justice of the peace. You know I have never been baptized. You know that I practice no known religion. You have some ideas about my family, and you know that we have probably never been able to practice in any known religion. This is what you are going to use to try to get into bed sooner than we are officially man and wife? That's a little bit lower than I expected from you David."

He says, "I don't care how you want to look at it. I want you to address the situation."

She says, "I have addressed the situation, and I want you to think about what you are saying and who you are saying it to because this is unfair to me in a lot of ways. And I don't think that this is a ground that I should have to defend. I also thought you had a lot more sensitivity."

He says, "Is this something that I need to go and talk over with Robaire?"

She says, "Well, have I ever had to go and talk over something that is happening between us with Robaire? Where is this coming from? I mean, there are facets that are in Robaire's personality that are not in your personality, and there are facets to Yvette's personality that are not in my personality. There are facets to Jennifer's personality that are not in either one of our personalities. But I am marrying you, and you're marrying me because, supposedly, we love each other. But the issue is you are saying something else, and I told you something, I think it was about two or three months ago, that if you were to become a member of my family, that you would have to remain loyal to my family. And you understand my family very well."

He says, "But everyone has morals. You don't lie. You don't steal. You don't kill. Everyone has basic morals. Is your rejection of me based on these morals?"

She says, "I don't know if this justifies an answer or not. I don't understand really what your problem is because whatever it is that you are waiting for, you will get soon enough when we marry. And I, myself, am looking forward to that. Also, it's a question of what you would have me teach my daughter should we have one."

He says, "Well, I hope that you teach her to pick a man that she can trust and that won't hurt her. Then she should do what she thinks is right for the situation."

She says, "Now how am I going to tell her to make sure that she has picked a man that she thinks is right and is not going to hurt her. This is not something that I will be able to do. And you know it's not something that I'm going to be able to do, and you know that it's not something that you are going to tell her either. So, I don't think that we should have any more of this kind of conversation because I will start to take it wrong, and I'm trying not to be too sensitive about the issue. So, why don't we just let it cool out for a little while, give it two or three days, and possibly we can talk about it again if you feel that we need to."

He agrees to that. He wants to get away from the terrace. He wants to get away from the house. He wants to walk her out so that they are a little bit more private.

This is fine with her. She is anxious herself to spend some time alone with him. She takes his hand, and They take a walk. She talks about being very anxious to see the Caribbean and asks him to describe the Caribbean to her. He tells her, "The Caribbean is an awful lot like this area except for I don't remember seeing any redwoods in the area. The Caribbean is very humid. There is a lot of moisture in the air, and it is very hot. In certain places in the Caribbean when you swim, if you look down at any point from a boat or if you are standing up, you can see the ocean floor. Oftentimes, that is where people snorkel because the water is so clear, and it is very beautiful. I'm sure Charlotte that you have heard this before.

"The water in the Caribbean is very beautiful because it is so clear, and depending on the time of day, it turns beautiful shades of blues and greens. And you're never afraid to swim because you can almost see for ten to fifteen yards any direction ahead of you, and there is nothing coming at you. The people there have a zest for life. It's almost as if every night is a festival. The food, of course, is very good. It is difficult, oftentimes, to sleep when it is very hot and very humid, so you find that you are up a lot longer and you don't sleep as well. But you don't really want to sleep because there is always something to do twenty-four hours a day.

"But if we are on ship, we'll just go into ports. We'll go into ports for two or three days. We may stay in hotels on the port if we chose, or we may stay on ship. It depends on what want you to do. When we are back on the ship, the atmosphere will be more like it is here, and it might get colder. Then you will be able to sleep better. But if you are on land and in a hotel, it gets very muggy, and it's very uncomfortable sometimes, and it's very difficult to sleep. But it's so beautiful, you just ignore all of that."

She says, "Tell me about Hong Kong."

He says, "The reason I want to take you to Hong Kong first is because I want to buy you some jewelry, a lot of jewelry. Not just the wedding ring, but a lot of different kinds of jewelry. And that's the best place to get it."

She says, "Oh, you mean pearls? I always thought it was Japan for pearls."

He says, "No. No. It's Hong Kong."

She says, "Is there some special place you know that you always get jewelry?"

He says, "I know where that question is leading. Who was I buying the special jewelry for at this special place? Yes, there is a place that I've heard of and that I have bought jewelry from, but you should not concern yourself with that."

David is walking along the ground with Charlotte. He has his arms around her, one arm around her shoulder, the other arm around her waist. They are walking very slowly. She has one arm around his waist. She is wearing cashmere. He has flannels on and a nice sweater with a shirt underneath it. They are walking along the grounds. He is telling her that she will love Bermuda and all the reasons why she will love Bermuda, and if she doesn't like Bermuda, then immediately, if he has to abort the cruise, he will get her to another port which she will enjoy even more. He tells her that they'll just explore every little island of the Caribbean, and he hopes he will have time to explore her as thoroughly.

She says he will have time to explore her, and she hopes that she will get to know him in the way that he is getting at.

He says, "But, if we go into Hong Kong I would like to, in fact I've already planned to, rent a private junk. And I have acquired some house staff on the junk, so we won't have total privacy, but we will be able to achieve total privacy by closing a few doors. We'll just go up and down Hong Kong harbor most of the time. Then some of the time we'll get out and do some shopping. You could either have some more clothing made, and I will probably have some more clothing made, or you might wish to shop for furs and jewels. I'm very much concerned about the jewelry because I notice that you don't wear much."

She says, "I don't wear much, but my mother had quite a bit of jewelry. Would you like to see it?"

Once again, he feels a little bit upstaged, but he's getting a little bit closer to the family. He says, "I didn't realize that you knew where your mother's jewelry was."

She says, "But you remember I put you in my father's robe after we were attacked by the private detective. So, I do know about some of their personal things. They had clothes hanging in the closet. They had jewelry out. I know my father smoked, because he had a cigarette lighter. The cigarette lighter is engraved. I know that he wore cuff links and stickpins for his tie."

He says, "Where are these things?"

She says, "They're in my room." She cut him off before he could go any further, "You'd like to come up to my room, and you want to come up to my room for the purpose of looking at this jewelry?"

He says, "Yes, I would."

She says, "Fine. Let's do that right now."

This, of course, was another humorous episode because she knows he is uncomfortable, and this is very awkward for him, but she knows he is also very curious. He was hoping that this is one thing that he could show his wife. He realizes now that this is not something that he could show his wife in the sense that he wanted to do it. He says, "Yes, let's go see what this jewelry looks like."

They go up to the room. The servants, of course, are aware of every move.

She goes to a very large chest. She opens the chest, and inside the chest are several layers of drawers. David is amazed that the chest is not locked. So, he is thinking that these things can't be very valuable. Out of the chest come several sets of pearls with different links and different diameters. Some are made with other jewels, and some just are plain. There are also emeralds, diamonds, rubies, and topaz. Some of them are solid gold. It is obvious that the settings and designs are very old, and they should possibly be remounted.

He's amazed because it is almost like going into a treasure chest. He asks her, "Why haven't you worn any of these things?" That's the first question. The second question is he remembers the jewelry at the grave site and that the jewelry there resembled the coat of arms.

She says, "I don't know why I've never worn any of these things. Maybe it was too painful for me to wear them. When I was younger, they were just not suited for me. But something told me that I probably shouldn't put them on."

The pearls were obvious and very simple. After seeing the settings of the emeralds and the diamonds, because they were set in gold, he started to see the pattern of the coat of arms. Then he knew why her intuition told her to keep it off. He went back again to look at the pearls, and on the clasp of the pearls is also the coat of arms. He is hoping he is not participating in some kind of ritual or something that might be black magic, but he suggests that she put it on and wear it, and if she wants to have it updated or redesigned that he can find some people that will do that confidentially, but he wants to show her this insignia on the back of her jewelry.

She was unaware prior to this that it was there. He says, "We can have this jewelry updated because it is your mother's jewelry, and it is of heredity. It's something that you have inherited. I can find someone who will confidentially update it so it's more modern, but I still think you should keep your insignia."

This she is amazed at because she thought he would fight that at every turn, but he hasn't. He uses this moment to tell her, "This particular symbol is being repeated. Do you have any idea what it means?"

She says, "No. I know that it somehow identified our family."

He says, "Yes, it identified your family, but it's not visible. It's almost as if at one time you did want it to identify your family, or your ancestors wanted it to identify your family. Then at some other point, they decided it was too risky to use this emblem."

She says, "I'll have to think about it some more before I get some answers for you."

He says, "I have one more question for you, and you can think about this and get an answer for this. What interrupted my axles on the car?"

She says, "I think I did partially, but I don't think I did totally. I wanted to stop the car."

He says, "You were aware that I was in the car and the car was out of control?"

She says, "Yes. I was aware that you were in the car and the car was out of control."

Then he says, "Did you interrupt my trance, my hypnotic state with Robaire?"

She says, "Yes, I interrupted your hypnotic trance with Robaire."

"Then I have one more question. Why were your parents unable to prevent their accident?" David asks.

She says, "Because they were too far from the estate, and that should be obvious to you now. But I will go on the honeymoon with you if that is what you want me to do."

It slowly begins to sink into him that she probably didn't do it all by herself, that if he hadn't gone off the road the way he did, or maybe he was even pulled off the road at that point the way he was so that these things could jam his axles, he would have died as her parents did because it was that far out of their control.

He says, "When you tell me you have to come back with another answer, or you have to think about it, or somehow you have to go away and return with more information, where are you getting this information from? Is this in any way connected to the pictures that you are painting?"

She says, "The pictures that I painted are the pictures of my ancestors, which you should be well aware of by now since you told me you exhumed my parent's bodies, and you have some pictures of your own now. When I was painting them as a child, I was painting from dreams. My understanding is that this was the best way to communicate this information to me over a period of years. So, now when I go back and look at it, it tells me in awful lot about my family because I have no one else here to tell me, no one physically here to tell me."

He says, "What do you mean you understand? Are you still in communication with a ghost?"

She says, "They're not ghosts. My understanding of a ghost, and Robaire would probably be able to define it better, but I think I heard him define it this way once before, a ghost is someone who was once human. By the time my family began to die, they were no longer human. They had a certain limited immortality. And you know the story about the vampires. I don't have to relate that to you as if we're reading yellow journalism off a newsstand. You know exactly what it means. You know the source of death to my parents was a car crash, and why burning was sufficient."

He says, "You're now ready to acknowledge that your parents apparently practiced vampirism?"

She says, "That's what I've been told."

He screams, "Well, who is telling you this?"

She says, "My ancestors."

He says, "Your ancestors? Which ancestors, and how long have you been having conversations?"

She says, "Various ancestors. Sometimes they identify themselves by name, by century and by blood connection, and sometimes they don't. I always recognize immediately who they are. Most of the time it is revealed in a dream. I was sleeping when you were driving down the highway to meet Mr. Schnell. Sometimes I'm wide awake. Oftentimes, recently when you have pressured me, I have mentally thought them out so that I could have answers for myself. Up until now, it hasn't mattered. I knew that I was painting a certain subject, the same subject, but it didn't bother me. It didn't matter."

He says, "So you're able to contact them, and they will talk to you when you want them to talk to you?"

She says, "No. I didn't say that they will talk to me when I want them to talk to me. What I said was that I have been able to talk to them, and that I have been able to occasion when I initiated the contact. But the last few months have been extremely traumatic. If they hadn't been extremely traumatic, I probably wouldn't have been permitted this contact because they want me to deal in the real world. They don't want to interfere with my free will. They don't want to interfere with your free will. They don't want to interfere with the free will of our children. They have made that plain to me. That's why my nanny was able to raise me.

"And I am not a practicing vampire. I have some remnants of a child who was born in a womb of a woman who has spanned the supernatural. I don't know how far it will go, but I've been told that I will remain mortal if I don't participate in the blood feast. I think you are aware of what the blood feast is, and I have no desire to do that. It has also been explained to me that my children will remain mortal and generations to follow, if there is no participation in the blood feast, and that is a factor of environment, upbringing, that morality that you were getting at before.

"So, I guess we can't wait a few days. We must talk about it now. I don't intend to raise any children that are going to have to eat off jugular veins. I don't want to eat off jugular veins. I don't know what conditions brought my ancestors to this. After what I have seen and after what I have experienced, I don't even feel worthy enough to ask them. But they have always been there to help me when I needed them whether I knew it or not. And apparently, they were there to help you when you didn't know it."

David says, "This is quite a mouthful. These are some of the things that I was hoping that we would get to on the cruise or during the honeymoon, when I thought that possibly because I was your husband, I would have your complete trust."

She says, "There's certain things that I probably will never reveal to you because they are a violation of a trust that I have to keep with someone else. I think that you can understand that. And there are things about your side of the family that you probably will never reveal because they are a violation of a trust which you must keep with someone else. They know that if their activities were recognized or even suspected, it will be worse than the witch hunt in Salem, whether they are guilty of these things or not. That's why we had to keep moving through Europe from the east into Western Europe. That's why I'm Von Shillingsfurst now, when my ancestors were probably called something else. And Mr. Weinberger could probably tell you what they were called formally, and he could probably tell you what they were called informally.

"But the fact of the matter is, we amassed quite a bit of wealth and we didn't steal it from people. Most of it was given to us. We amassed lands, and most of them were taken from us. So even in my ancestors, there is a certain amount of bitterness. So try to get this, if you are as you say still in love with me, in bits and pieces because that's how I'm receiving it because if I receive it any other way then we'll have to have more of those scenes in the alley. We'll have to have more of these incidences like the private detective. And there will have to be more occurrences like Otto Weinberger. So, the least I know, except for the things that I can avoid, and they will tell me things to avoid trying to head off situations, we tried to head off situations, but there was no way that what happened in the alley could be avoided."

He says, "While we're at it, explain to me why this could not be avoided."

She says, "You know perfectly well why it could not be avoided. I couldn't go to the police and tell them that some person who has been dead two or three centuries told me, which they didn't at the time, that you were being followed by someone who wanted to kill you and decided to kill me first. Was I going to be believed? No! I couldn't even alert the people back east who were carrying on the investigation and have them believe that someone wanted to kill me because you had just met me. So, the only recourse they had was the one that they took, or I wouldn't be here now. And you saw the private detective, and you know who took him away. So, you know who they are."

He says, "They were dressed in robes. I went up to San Francisco looking for monks, thinking they might have been Catholic, or Lutheran, or God knows what."

She says, "In one sense, they were monks. But I doubt that you would find that they are Catholic or Lutheran."

He says, "Tell me what it is that you know about that. You know more than you have told us. Why did you block what little information that I could give them?"

She says, "I blocked it because I felt that recall of the memory after what happened to Otto Weinberger."

He says, "Oh, you know that too?"

She says, "Yes, I know that too. It would have been too stressful and too painful for you because he almost beat you to death. And to have you recall that under hypnosis would have amounted to a second beating. And hopefully a post-hypnotic suggestion would have alleviated some of this, but I didn't want to have to count of it. Secondly, it dispelled a lot of the rumors that redirected a lot of the people. The psychiatrist was happy with this kind of response. Robaire is an in-house person, and he knows what the truth really is. So, it wasn't really a deception, and we have helped Otto Weinberger back to health. He doesn't want to go back to his teaching institution with headlines or papers that he has participated in a type of weird seance, or he found the vampire he was looking for.

"I think if he thought about it, he would appreciate me for it because he could not do this successfully and stay in this community. And he could not do it with the confidentiality that you can do it in Europe because America is a different place and people are a lot more skeptical. He would have been raked over the coals. I would have been raked over the coals. My parents would have been officially exhumed, and I could not permit that to happen."

He says to her, "I can't argue with that. I had some understanding of it. Some of it I didn't quite have the depth of understanding that you did. And I'm glad you interceded at that point. But I still would like to know if you can tell me what happened with the monks."

She says, "Because he was your friend, because you felt guilty because you had worked with him on a friendly basis, and even though you saw what he was trying to do to me and even though he beat you almost to death, you still felt that he wouldn't have responded this way if you hadn't brought him into the case. And you can remember the time when you did things side by side, buddy, buddy, so I tried to find out what happened to him when he left here. If you can just let me tell you things without asking too many questions, I will let you know. When he left here, he was taken to a monastery in the 1,000th century. The monastery was apparently run by my family or even constructed, borrowed and used by my family. He was permitted to look around for a while to assess the situation, to get his grip on reality, realize he was on the top of a very steep hill, that there was one road down, and that it was twilight. He couldn't see the way down.

"And monasteries, as usual, are in the most inaccessible points, and he went in to look for help. But the help that he received put him into a wall and he suffocated in the wall, and as a result of his suffocation he had a heart attack. He then was redeposited back in his home in New Jersey dead. That's why your paper accounts say that he was a little dusty when they found him. And that's all I was permitted to see. I don't know what made him want to go that close to the wall."

David is just sitting on the edge of the bed, and he has his head down. He feels bad. She says, "I don't know what happened in the first two murders. All I know is what I told you. And after finding out what happened to the private detective, I really don't think I could stand to find out. But I know what the private detective had planned for me. I saw what he did to you, and I know what would have happened in your car."

He says, "If you know what would have happened in my car, then you know for sure that Mr. Schnell was trying to kill me."

She says, "Yes, I know for sure that Mr. Schnell was trying to kill you. He jammed your axles because he couldn't stop the car any other way, and it was the quickest thing to do. Not only did I find out while I got complete verification that Mr. Schnell is trying to kill you, I got a full disclosure on who killed my parents."

He says, "Oh my God. But it couldn't have been Mr. Schnell because he wasn't in the firm."

She says, "It wasn't Mr. Schnell. It was Mr. Leopold."

He says, "How long have you known this? You didn't come to me? You didn't need to talk to me? You didn't need to get this off your chest?"

She says, "I did talk to someone about it, the person who told me about it. And I've known about it for about two weeks."

"So why has Mr. Leopold survived? Explain this to me. I don't understand."

She says, "Well, I can relate it to you simply the way that it was related to me, and there's some things about it that I still don't understand. My father had a young chronological age, and my mother had a young chronological age. How old they were I don't know. How they aged, I don't know. But they were approximately thirty-five. My father had suspected Mr. Leopold of embezzling shortly after he had retained the firm. He was furious because he knew his hands were tied because they apparently were fleeing a purge in Europe where several of our family members had been caught and massacred, immediate cousins, aunts, uncles. The survivors decided to split up and go in different directions. I don't know. They won't tell me that much because they don't trust me to have that information. It could me someone's life or death.

"So, at any rate, my parents came here. They weren't looking for a big city. They were looking for a quiet town that tended toward shadows with the redwoods, and they were directed here to Mendocino by a network, a very extensive network that we've had to develop. Mr. Leopold's friend was on the tail end of that network branching into America. It turns out that Mr. Leopold is not of quite the same stock that his counterparts are in Europe because he had decided to steal, and my father found out about it. And to have the discussion, Mr. Leopold had the appointment in the evening at his offices. And my father, being very headstrong and very anxious to get on with it, and not having the same mobility that Mr. Leopold had in the daytime, was forced to meet Mr. Leopold on his own terms. My mother had asked him not to go, but if he had to go, she was going to go with him."

She continues, "I can remember, even though I was two years old, that she kissed me good night and hugged me. It was a very different kind of hug and a very long time she spent with me. She insisted that he come in, and he said I'll see her when we get back, and she insisted that he come in now and talk to me. And he loved me, so he did. He picked me up and he played with me. He tickled me and he brushed my hair. This is very clear to me now. It wasn't clear to me before, probably for twenty or twenty-five years, but it's very clear to me now. My mother said we must leave you now, and there were tears in her eyes.

"My father was still saying, 'Well, you know it's not that much money. I'm just mad that he has done this, and we need to straighten him out about it.' My mother was, of course, saying, 'Don't discuss this in front of Charlotte, let's just go.' She hugged me again. She looked at nanny, and she tells Mrs. Hampton to please make sure that she always, always takes very good care of me. That was a very unusual way to put it. But I know now that my mother knew they wouldn't be coming back. So, they got in the car. They drove to Mr. Leopold's office. And at Mr. Leopold's office the car was rigged so that it would go off the road. It went off the road before they made it back to the estate. They were totally out of control.

"The only thing they could do, because they weren't within their perimeter, was what you saw happen, and that was an attempt to get out of a burning car any way they could. Apparently, they attempted to shift shape to rip the roof off and get out of the car. It wasn't fast enough. It wasn't quick enough. And they perished, which is what you saw, which is what everyone saw. As the newspaper accounts read, there were no known suspects because the only person to inherit was a two-year-old girl, and she could have hardly killed her parents. But the trustees at the time were somewhat under suspicion, but since they were a very old reputable firm, it was immediately dismissed, and there was no investigation made into the matter.

"Mr. Schnell gets wind of this, and when he comes on to the firm five years later, he is fully briefed. He comes into the firm with the intention of blackmailing Mr. Leopold. Now something happened to Mr. Leopold in between now and those five years that my ancestors know because they were aware of the murder. And they would have killed Mr. Leopold, but he was too valuable. So, they chose to handle him another way, which is what I keep trying to tell you, Mr. Schnell must be handled another way. He must remain alive. He must remain competent, and he will run the firm, and he will take care of business because Mr. Leopold did. Don't you agree?"

David says, "Yes of course I agree. I would never have known that Mr. Leopold killed your parents. I never would have expected it. He treats you like you're his daughter. He seems to have genuine affection for you. She says he does, he's also carried an extreme guilt. But what has offset his guilt, because he was a thief, he was not a murderer, is that when Mr. Schnell came on board five years later, I guess I was about seven years old, he began to blackmail Mr. Leopold. That's how he worked his way up in the firm. He wasn't really blackmailing him for fun, because fun could be traced. And Mr. Leopold was perceptive enough to find anything, even an adulterous affair, to say that this is the reason he had to give this person this extortion money or to outright kill him.

"But what he was blackmailing him for was a position in the firm. So, Mr. Leopold didn't know which way to turn because he knew that my family was aware of what he had done, and they made it very plain to him that they wanted him to stay out of the business of murder. He decided also on his own, because he was a man of conscious, that he wanted to stay out of the business of murder, and that he wanted to do the very best he could by this two-year-old girl. He had been doing it for five years until Mr. Schnell intervened. He didn't know that Mr. Schnell was embezzling from me."

David says, "Mr. Schnell is embezzling from you?"

She says, "Of course he's embezzling from me. He's taking liquid assets, and he's playing around with my investments, liquid able assets. He is playing around with my investments. And when we called him in here to talk to him about those things, because that's what you wanted to do, he had to turn the conversation. It was strictly a diversionary tactic. He created this whole parcel map scene. He created the whole thing. He made it up. It was a lie to give him time to cover his tracks in case there was more of an investigation. But what I didn't understand is that he was as lethal as Mr. Leopold.

"I also didn't understand that whatever it was that my ancestors did to Mr. Leopold had the effect that they wanted, and that is he had extreme guilt. He had remorse, and he wanted to make it up to me. So, he has genuine affection for me, but it also, I would say, broke his back. He became somewhat more susceptible to being manipulated, and when Mr. Schnell came along with this information he almost just gave up and became what you consider spineless. From then on, Mr. Schnell was really running the organization. My family was aware of this too. But he was skimming small amounts apparently, and they knew they could make him put it back at any time if they needed to, and there were other things much more important going on. We didn't know that he would resort to murder. His problem is he never expected me to marry. He thought I had enough problems.

"He was aware of the incident in Europe with Jean. He thought that I was sour on men, and that after the murders a basket case. I'm sure if you were to look at his accounts, that every time I had a crisis his stealing increased. So when he finally gets introduced to you, and you seem like serious business, and you can bet he has investigated you very thoroughly, he's apparently decided that you do love me and, you're not going to harm me, so he's going to have to kill you. And the whole set up with the surveyors, that was just so that they could be good honest witnesses to your car accident."

By this time, she is really crying because this is the second time this has happened to her. She looks at him and says, "These people that we are, we managed to keep your life intact." She turns her back to him, and she asks, "Please leave the room because I need some privacy."

He leaves without saying a word.

She gets dressed for bed and goes to sleep immediately, a very deep, a very sound sleep because she needs it. David, on the other hand, can't sleep. He is thinking over all the things that she said, the comments that she's been making all along, why don't you go to the zoo, you must be loyal to my family. He is beginning to see a little bit more of her position, and the victimization that is taking place on both sides, which is what Otto Weinberger discovered in a more horrible way. He also is aware that he has got to be man enough to be her husband, or he should leave her alone. He had already decided a long time ago that he was man enough to be her husband, but the important thing to do was to get her to talk to him about the things that he should know because otherwise he could become harmful not knowing about this and not knowing about that.

Apparently, the ancestors had very clearly and properly handled Mr. Leopold. But Mr. Leopold had a different mentality than Mr. Schnell, and he assumes that since this time period has past that, they're sizing Mr. Schnell up and that they will, as she says, handle Mr. Schnell. His is aware that they don't want another murder, that they don't want another basket case, and that they need him to work in that firm.

He knows that he had better get to sleep early because he had already promised to call his mother to talk to her about recipes. Then he remembered that he was just going to make a list. He proceeded the rest of the evening to make a list of his mother's favorite recipes, and made a note on it to Charlotte and Yvette that if the chef doesn't recognize the one that they decide and doesn't know the ingredients or how it's to be prepared, then he will call his mother or one of his sisters and she can tell him. Then it can be a real surprise for his mother. He also decides that while they are out in Sonoma that he is going to get Charlotte some chocolates and roses because she has had a very hard night. He goes to sleep.

The next morning, Yvette and Charlotte get in Charlotte's car and drive into town to pick up Jennifer, who is wearing a very cute little crinoline sleeveless dress. She has a sweater in case in gets cold. The weather is beautiful today. She is babbling because it seems that her friend in San Francisco has gotten more serious, and she has an engagement ring. So the conversation all the way into Sonoma is about how she didn't expect him to propose, that he has proposed but that it's not going to affect her position in the art gallery because he now loves Mendocino, and he thinks that he'll be able to drive from San Francisco into Mendocino. Charlotte says, "What does he do? We really don't want to lose you at the art gallery. We want this next exhibit to go within two months of returning from my honeymoon, and I don't want to have to worry about this."

Jennifer says, "And it's such a great job, I don't want to lose it, and he knows that I don't want to lose it. He knows that I really like you guys. He's a merchant seaman. So, he was working off this coast and it was easier for us to see each other this way. And the times that I told you that I really need to see him because he had called, I did really need to see him. But he will be in and out quite a bit, so I will have definitely enough time and no distractions so I could work in the art gallery."

Yvette says, "That sounds just wonderful. We must have a celebration. We must congratulate you. When is the date set?"

She says, "I think that I am going to wait at least a year because of his job. He's been in and out so much. It's not like we've been constantly dating. I've explained this to him. I have accepted his proposal because I am pretty sure I'm in love with him, and I'm pretty sure he is in love with me, but he has many ports of call. I can wait it out a year and see if he still wants to walk down that isle with me." Yvette and Charlotte are amazed because they thought Jennifer was a little bit more immature than that. They tell her that it is a pretty good move.

By this time, they are at the first caterer. They get out of the car and go in. The premises look very clean. It looks like it is going to be French, so they let Yvette take charge. Yvette goes through the logistics again of what they need and when they need it. She would like to see their basic menu, which they are only too happy to show her. Then she wants to know how they are going to be able to deviate from the menu, if they're going to be permitted to deviate, and if it's possible that they might even serve food that isn't French. The cook is horrified at this. Yvette begins to speak to him in French, and Charlotte begins to speak to him in French. But he doesn't speak French.

They get back in the car and they decide to go on to the next person who is on the list. This is also considered French cuisine, but it's American. This is now a woman. She has her basic menu for weddings. She also will do the cake. They hadn't even thought about the cake, so they looked at each other and say, "We hadn't even thought about who was going to bake the cake, but you will bake the cake?"

She says, "Yes of course. I will bake the cake. How many tiers do you want on the cake?"

They say, "What about eight? Let's put eight tiers on the cake."

She says, "That's an odd number. So okay, we'll put eight tiers on the cake."

They say, "But wait a minute. Let's decide on the menu."

They look at her basic menu. Her basic menu seems to be very good. She includes a lot of finger foods and a lot of very rich kinds of snacks. They were not thinking of potato chips and dips. She says, "Oh no. I would be horrified at potato chips and dip. They go through the menu, and they think that this seems to be just about what we would like, it has somewhat of a French flavor do it, it has a continental flair."

She says, "I intended it to. Then it has some basic American additions."

Charlotte says, "Speaking of additions, would you mind, my fiancé's mother, we would like to have some special things that she likes to eat. Would you mind if we gave you the recipes, or you may not need the recipes, but if we gave you the recipes and had just a few dishes so that she would feel very much welcomed and very much at home because she has never met me. He and I have been engaged for almost two months, and prior to that we had been dating for two or three months, and she's never met me. We don't want her to feel left out."

The proprietor thinks that this is just a sweet idea. She says, "Normally I wouldn't, but for such thoughtfulness, if it were my son, I would have wanted him to do that, I'm going to go ahead and make this exception."

They said that money was not an object, and they would like to pay her for this. She says, "Okay. Then we have no problem." They ask her how many staff normally accompany her.

She tells them that for seven hundred people she would need at least between five and ten. They tell her that they can accommodate her at the mansion, that if it's all right with her she can stay overnight at the house, and then she could begin to cook in the kitchen if she needs a day in advance. She says, "That sounds fine. You sound like wonderful people, and I'm looking quite forward to it. If I get any new menu suggestions off the basic, I'll let you know. Can you tell me a little bit about your background?"

Charlotte blushes because she still doesn't know that much about David's background. All she knows is that he is from the Eastern Canadian border, but he comes from, by comparison, a large family and that there are at least four children in it. She herself comes from Germany, and she left there when she was two years old. She doesn't remember much about it, but she has been practicing on some of her recipes, and she would love to have some desserts from that area if not some meals from that area.

The caterer, whose name is Josephine, says, "I think that this will be no problem. I can handle a very interesting meal for you. I will send you the menu within the week, and you can have it approved by your fiancé. If you have any additions that you haven't gotten to me before, then I can always add them later. But I will need to know if we are talking about three weeks from now, within a week, no later than a week and a half so that I can make sure that I have everything in stock and that everything is going to be fresh. And I will be there two days prior to the wedding."

Charlotte says, "This sounds fine. Can I take a vote?"

Yvette and Jennifer say, "Yes. Let's go with this." Charlotte makes her deposit. They tell her that they will send someone out to look over her kitchen and see what she could serve with what she has there and see what they will need to bring with them. The china may not match, but the grade will be the same, and the silver may not match, but the grade will be the same. And if necessary, they may use none of her things, but they will make sure that her guests are treated in a style that they are accustomed to.

She says, "Thank you. That's pretty much what I had in mind. We'll be getting back to you and keeping in touch with you by phone." She takes her card and they decide by being in that store they are famished. She asks them did they want to sample some of her cooking. They take the opportunity to sample various pastries and pates. She suggests that they sit down and have tea with some of their food, or mineral water. Jennifer and Yvette opted for mineral water with the mouse and pate. Charlotte opted for 7-Up.

They speak with her for about an hour about the project and try to describe some of the scenery in the hopes that she could reflect the surrounding area in some of her cooking. She says, "The basic theme I understood was it was to be a wedding. But it's also nice to know that you are close to the sea, and that there's redwood around because you could do a lot of things with shells and various other things like that."

She was glad that they gave her those ideas. They said that was pretty much what they had in mind because it would be hopefully the first and last time that she got married, and she would like to have some uniqueness in it. Josephine says, "That is exactly what I had in mind. And you could be assured that my food is an art form. I have been told that Charlotte is an artist. I take my work seriously too. Do you want ice sculptures and fountains flowing with champagne? There is a lot of things that I can do creatively. We could set them up along the grounds. I would also like to come out there, if you have officially decided on me, within the next week so I can get a better idea of what I am working with."

Yvette says, "Oh yes, that's wonderful. And the ice sculptures and the champagne fountains all over the grounds, I think it would be beautiful, maybe with some orchids or some other things in there. So please come out and get a feel for it. And, yes, do a lot of things with shells. And the fact that we're near the redwoods, I could see that a lot could be done with that. It would just be beautiful. Also, our colors are green and white, and it's a forest green. You might even want to do a Robin Hood theme around that."

She says, "The style is a little old English, so maybe even showing you some of the bridesmaids designs would help you with the cake." She says, "Most definitely because we want the bride and groom on top of the cake. I should be out there within the week."

They agreed that this is probably the best idea, and as much as they hated to leave her kitchen because the food was so good, they should get back into Mendocino. They said their goodbyes and left for Mendocino. The trip back home to Mendocino was uneventful. Charlotte took her time because she wanted to be relaxed when she got there, and the other girls wanted to be relaxed when they got there also. They were too full to take a more formal lunch. They did stop off in Sonoma for some other light kind of refreshments, something very cold to drink and some cheeses. Then they sat on the grass across from the cheese factory in Sonoma in the main square. They laugh, talk, and exchange stories.

Jennifer is asked what made her decide on this young man. She says, "I had been dating him back east, and when I came out to San Francisco, I had always wanted to come to San Francisco anyway, I was fully aware that he was here, and I just established a closer contact. But then I moved on into Mendocino, and he was more than willing to come and visit me in Mendocino. We just kept this relationship going back and forth from Mendocino to San Francisco instead of from New York to San Francisco. And it seemed that he was as interested as he said he was, and he proved it a couple of days ago by giving me an engagement ring."

They ask her if she had told her family yet. She says, "I only have two sisters, and a mother and father. And immediately, I called my two sisters and they screamed on the phone together. Both are already married, and I was the last one."

Yvette says, "Well, it looks like it's just me then because I'm going to be the only single one."

They say, "When you get back to France, you'll be so busy, you won't even have time to think about it."

She says, "I don't know. All of this marrying is kind of becoming, I'm catching the fever."

Charlotte says, "That's not the reason to get married. You have to find that very special person." Charlotte looked at Jennifer and Jennifer looked at Charlotte, and they kind of winked.

Yvette says, "Well, we better get back to Charlotte's very special person because I somehow get the feeling that he likes to know where she is most of the time."

They start the drive back from Sonoma to Mendocino. They ask Jennifer is she wants to come home with them or if she wants to be dropped off at her house.

She said that she would rather be dropped off at her house because she was expecting a call from her now fiancé, she had to correct herself, from San Francisco, then too she had to get ready for work in the morning. Charlotte asks her how she was handling the business alone, was she going to be able to carry on for the next two months without Charlotte's guidance. She says, "As long as you select the exhibitors before you go on your honeymoon. I don't think I'll have too much trouble getting the exhibits in and cataloging them. And, of course, I don't do any placement of the exhibits until you come back. But I will have the announcements ready to go out. I will try to have the same set of caterers that we had before because it seemed that they worked out pretty well, and the first few showings you had decided you wanted to go to be fancy about it."

Charlotte says, "That's right because I want to establish a reputation. I will select the exhibitors before I leave, and if you compile a list for me tomorrow and call me with it over the phone, or you could either come out to the estate, either one, or we come into Mendocino, I'll pick from them. Then you could write them and get a definite yes or no before I leave. Then once they come in, just leave them in the storage room until we have time to figure out what we want where. And make sure that they send the photographs of each exhibit, so we won't have to open the boxes."

Jennifer says, "Of course, I remember that because that's too much of a hassle."

They drop her off at home, and Yvette and Charlotte proceed to the estate. All the way there the talk, pretty much, was about Jennifer's wedding and how it was somewhat of a surprise. Charlotte says, "Well, it wasn't quite to me because she seems to always have the personality to interact very well with men, and she was always giving me that little extra push sometimes when I have doubts about going out with David. I guess she would be the one to get married next. I'm glad she's decided to take it a little bit slow as far as having the wedding date so far in advance, and that's always a good idea. I'm wondering if we're rushing things."

Yvette says, "No. Not under your circumstance. I think the closer that you let David, the more legitimate control David has, the more things will change for you. Your relationship will change when he's your husband. He's going to change too, but I don't think he'll change in a negative way, and I know you've always heard that people change when they get married. You will change and he will change, but that's because there's a lot more commitment there. And I will feel a lot better when this happens."

Charlotte says, "I guess you're right. I am kind of looking forward to it because I'm kind of tired of having to keep making excuses and putting him off."

By this time, they are up to the drive. It is obvious that the men have been playing tennis. The girls get out of the car and ask the men, "Since you seem to have been the first ones to try out the new tennis courts, how are they?"

The gentlemen says, "They're just great. They work pretty well."

David says, "Robaire beat me pretty badly. But next time I play, hopeful we'll play doubles and I'll have some help," and he puts his arms around Charlotte and pulls her in closer, and says, "Wont I?"

She says, "Well, I guess you might. But I wouldn't count on me because Yvette is pretty good too. Yvette used to beat me all the time."

They go on into the house. Robaire says, "We didn't wait lunch for you. I hope you don't mind. But I'm sure there is something still left if you are going to eat."

The two girls look at each other and say, "No. We nibbled all the way through Josephine's kitchen."

David asks, "Who is Josephine?"

Charlotte says, "Josephine, we decided, is going to be catering the wedding. You should be meeting her shortly, maybe tomorrow, maybe the next day. She wants to come out and see the facilities. She seems to be an excellent cook, and she also thinks that she'll be able to do those recipes that are special to your mother."

He says, "That's good. I'm glad to hear that. I think that the list I have is very simple, and even if it's not exactly her recipe, she would recognize the dish, and the idea that they were included I think will have the desired effect. It's better than spoiling it by asking her exactly how she wants it made. And besides, professionally they might handle it differently anyway."

Charlotte says, "That's what I was thinking. So, I just gave her the list of dishes you gave me, and she said she didn't think she would have any problems with it. The other thing is, we still must drop the bridal registers off at the store. So, I was wondering if you had any preferences in stores other than the one I picked, and if you wanted to go over the list with Mrs. Hampton to find out if there is anything you wanted to add."

He says, "She has already approached me about that, after you left to see caterer. So, I told her that after we showered from tennis I would come down and talk to her, and if she didn't mind, I would like to include Robaire because he might remember some things that I might forget." She says that is perfectly fine.

He says, "So we have to go up now and not keep her waiting, Charlotte, and get ready to go through that." They depart. They go upstairs presumably to clean up so they could come back down and finish the bridal registry. Yvette and Charlotte decide to get on the phone and double check with the bridesmaids that everything is all right with their clothing. They have decided on four bridesmaids, so they call the four of them. They are lucky because they can catch them all at home, even with the time differences, and there are no problems. The bridesmaids are all very pleased with their gowns, their gowns are beautiful, and they can't wait to see Charlotte's home because most of them have never been there. All of them are very excited about the wedding, and they can't wait to see David.

Charlotte and Yvette also wanted to know if they had received their invitations because if they had gotten theirs then maybe all the other invited guests have received theirs by now too. They said that they had received their invitations, all just about a week within each other. Charlotte and Yvette signed off, and they looked at each other. They were kind of relaxed and it seemed that things were going along well, they hadn't forgotten anything.

They decide, once again, to go downstairs and look at the grounds that Mr. Smythe was working on. He was there again, and they were coming along beautifully. Yvette had learned from what he had done with the house and what he had done with the rest of the grounds, not to interfere, and to just admire his work. She told him, once again, that she was very pleased with what was happening. He says, "Thank you. I think I have in mind what your exact concerns are that you would be able to stay out in the weather. A wedding in the rain, I think, would be one of the most beautiful things that could happen."

She explained to him that she was going to have some champagne fountains in several places, and she was going to float orchids in them. She tells him that she was also going to float orchids in the pools and the fountains that they already had. She wanted to know if he had any ideas about that and about getting more flowers and keeping them fresh. He says, "I think I can handle it. How many fountains did you expect to have?"

She says, "No more than ten around the grounds."

He says, "I think I can handle that. And I know the number of freshwater pools we have, so I will be able to make that quite fragrant."

She says, "And the caterer is going to do her theme around this scene, so she's going to be doing a lot of things with shells. Maybe you could add that also."

He says, "Yes, I guess I can. Then mine will match hers."

Charlotte says, "I just wanted to let you know that we had decided on that, kind of a mermaid sort of thing."

He says, "That sounds like that's going to be beautiful. I'll get to work on that right away because I haven't added anything to the structure that I have erected except for the flowers that I had started to grow along the side of it."

Then the girls went on to talk to the cooks in the kitchen and tell them that sometime this week a new caterer named Ms. Josephine would be coming in from Santa Rosa, and that they were to hopefully have the kitchen as spotless as possible. Charlotte asks them to give her every courtesy in showing her where things were and making sure she was aware of everything so she would not come here and find out there was something she thought was here that is not here. The servants said they understood exactly. They wanted to know if they were going to be able to help in the preparation of the meal of the wedding.

Charlotte says, "That would be left up to Ms. Josephine, if you wish to help. As far as I am concerned I would rather have you in the audience as an invited guest of the family. But if you want to help you can also talk to her about that."

They were very pleased that they were going to attend the wedding. They say, "If she has enough people, then we would actually rather attend the wedding and not miss anything."

Charlotte says, "I thought that you would prefer that." She wondered what was for dinner.

One of the servants answered, "We're having sole and vegetables because Mrs. Hampton said that things should be kept a little light for a while. Well, she said she hopes that you will still fit in your wedding dress, and she wants to help you along with your diet."

Charlotte says, "That was very thoughtful of her. And that's true, I don't need to be eating very heavy things because the dress is made to strict measurements. We shouldn't have to go letting it in and letting it out. So, filet of sole will be fine."

They leave the kitchen and decide that they are tired from the drive. They have about two hours before dinner, so they are going to go up to their rooms to relax a little bit. Yvette said she has still some reading to do that she had started on the plane, and she might as well finish that book. Charlotte said she just probably needed some quiet time to herself. They parted ways.

David interrupted Charlotte's quiet time by insisting that she talk to him and try to recall everything that she could about her family. "I didn't realize that you still had clothing, and you still had jewels. Try to think because you might have something else. Where did you put this clothing? And where did you put these jewels? Well, I know where you put the jewels, but where did you put the clothing? It wasn't difficult for you to find your father's robe."

She says, "If you recall, I didn't find my father's robe. Mrs. Hampton found my father's robe, and she has put most of the clothing away. I've often wondered where some of my mother's dresses were because I'm sure they are beautiful. Somehow it was too much for me to go and try them on, but if you're going to go with me, we can go downstairs and ask Mrs. Hampton where these things are."

They both go downstairs. Mrs. Hampton is in the kitchen again checking on dinner. They ask her would she mind showing them where she had put Heindrick's and Ava's clothing. Her eyes got a little misty, and she says, "What brought this on? Why is it you want to look at these things? You have every right to know about your parents, but isn't this kind of a bad time, and couldn't you have happier thoughts right now?"

Charlotte says, "Don't worry. It's not what you think. It's not bad at all. I've always wondered what my mother's clothing was like, and David just has a little bit of interest too. In fact, I don't have any idea which rooms they slept in."

Mrs. Hampton says, "They slept in the other wing. If you want to see now, I can take you into the other wing. I'm not very familiar with the other wing because I was not the servant who saw them directly more closely. There were two servants that did that."

Charlotte says, "There were? Where are they?"

She says, "They might be dead by now. They looked to be a little bit older than I am."

David says, "Well, were they American?"

She says, "Yes, they were American. They were hired over here, but as I recall the rule called for them to be dismissed immediately if anything should happen to Heindrick or Ava. And they were dismissed immediately. They were paid off. And I believe it was one day I was off with you, Charlotte. When I came back, they were packed and gone. I think it might have even happened before the funeral took place."

David says, "Didn't you think that was odd instructions that these two particular servants should be dismissed? Were the other servants dismissed?"

She says, "No. Servants have come and gone. For the most part, we've been lucky because they are happy with the house, and most of the people have stayed on. Some of them have even had generations come on here and stay on because they liked Charlotte so much. Her coming back kind of brightened up the house. So, we didn't really have trouble keeping servants. It's just those two, and I don't believe they really wanted to leave. They didn't say much about it one way or the other, and they seemed to fully understand that they had to go. But they left immediately."

He says, "Do you remember who they were?"

She says, "No. One tended particularly to Mrs. Von Shillingsfurst, and the other one tended to Mr. Von Shillingsfurst."

Charlotte says, "If that's the case, are there any papers of them being hired or anything like that?"

She says, "Well, Charlotte, just like everything else, that is probably with the trustees."

So once again, David and Charlotte know they have run into a dead end, but maybe they at least could go into the rooms and see what is happening. So, Charlotte asks, "Did they sleep in separate rooms, or did they have one room?"

Mrs. Hampton says, "I believe they had individual beds with connecting doors. That is how the master suite was built in that wing."

Charlotte says, "You don't even know for sure?"

She says, "No. There was no reason for me to go into anyone's bedroom. And I was never invited into anyone's bedroom, so I never have gone into either of their bedrooms."

David says, "Has Jasper renovated this part of the house?"

Charlotte says, "I really don't know if he has because I haven't been on that side of the house. I've been in my wing and in the main part of the house mostly just as you have. I hadn't really noticed that there was this section. I guess I had noticed it from the outside. But so many things were going on, I hadn't paid much attention to it. I just thought he would get around to it. Apparently, this is the most important part of the house, and it's probably the part of the house that we should sleep in after we're married because it seems that I was in the room for guests and children."

Mrs. Hampton says, "Exactly. Your wing was the wing for guests and children."

She asks, "Do you mind showing us the wing?"

Mrs. Hampton says, "Well, we have about an hour and a half before dinner. If we delay dinner that means that the servants must stay later to clean up. So, I think that tomorrow in the daytime you'll have more time to explore. Nothing was given away and there were no other relatives to come and claim things. So, we tried to make sure that things were properly packed, that sort of thing."

David says, "Who is we?"

She says, "Well, we didn't really involve me, though I had some hand in it in that I knew that these people were to be in the house to do this. The we was the servants that had always attended to Charlotte's parents."

Once again, they are back in the same circle. They agree not to press too hard and not to make it too much of an issue. The nanny doesn't understand why suddenly, they want to go through those old dusty clothes right before dinner. She says, "If it's that important to you, first thing in the morning we can look at it."

David and Charlotte say, "I think we have a day in between San Francisco and the tailors, so I guess that would be the best day to go." They agree that the next morning, David and Charlotte are going to look at the rooms. Charlotte suggests they bring Robaire. David was a little surprised at this. Charlotte suggested that Yvette could possibly be sent to accompany Jennifer because she wasn't sure what she was going to find. She frankly was a little bit embarrassed, but she knew that this was something that she had to follow through with.

Mrs. Hampton says, "As you wish, Charlotte. We'll handle it just as you wish. And I suggest that you get ready for dinner."

Once again, they both go upstairs to try to be downstairs on time for dinner.

The dinner goes, once again, without incident. Everyone is looking forward to going into San Francisco. David is telling them that they must see Ghirardelli Square, and that they must do some strolling around the marina. Yvette says, "Wait a minute. It sounds like it's a bicycle built for two and there is five of us actually going."

David and Charlotte say, "We won't get too taken away. We'll just enjoy. But you should see some of the more famous sites in San Francisco."

Most of the night is taken up with the anticipation of what is going to happen two days from now. They play backgammon. Charlotte is very anxious. David has pulled Robaire aside and has told him about the other wing and what they want to find in the other wing. Tomorrow's plans are explained to Robaire. Charlotte asks Yvette if she will do a favor for her, and that is go into to town and check on Jennifer because Jennifer and she seem to get along very well, and she is afraid that if she goes in, Jennifer will talk too much about personal business.

Yvette says, "I know exactly what you mean. I'll be more than happy to do that first thing in the morning. And I know my way into Mendocino now that I have been there five or ten times, so I won't have any problem driving."

Charlotte says, "If you do, we can always send the chauffeur."

She says, "No. I think I can drive in, and I think I'll take her out to lunch. I'll bring back news of whatever is going on at the art gallery."

They all realize that they must be up about eight because Mrs. Hampton does have a tight schedule. Now that she is no longer the nanny, she is responsible for running the whole house when she is not getting up after Charlotte, and seeing what Charlotte is up to, as she had to do when Charlotte was two or three years old. She now has taken on the position of managing the household in accordance, of course, with Charlotte's wishes. They want to make sure that they don't waste any of her time, so they want to be up and ready between seven and eight to go through the rooms. They are very excited that they are going to be able to go through these rooms.

That night, Charlotte does her best to try to get some answers ahead of time to find out what the situation was with her parents, and what she could expect to find in their bedrooms. She does get some answers. She gets answers from an older relative about fifty-five. He is still a very handsome gentleman. He is graying at the temples. He explains to her in his very heavy French accent, "Your parents were two very loving people. They had separate rooms. You shouldn't expect coffins. We have long since discarded coffins. I know that this will be hard for you to deal with. But if you are going to go look, you might as well know. You will find what you found in Italy, and that is the heavy drapery that won't let the light in. And if you look very closely you will find repeated resemblances of the coat of arms."

Once again, she asks, "What's the significance?"

They tell her, "That is the source of our power. That is where all our energies concentrate, where all our consciousness has concentrated over the centuries. So, when one's own energy ebbs, or one is in trouble, that's kind of a central place where you know that you can find help. It's always a source of protection for any Von Shillingsfurst, and it's something that you should never reveal to anyone else. That's why your parents were caught at their weakest moment because they were too far outside of the grounds. And these markings, as you would call them, are all over the ground and in certain parts of the house. And when and if you should be aware of them, you will find yourself being drawn to them. There are certain parts of the house that you will feel more comfortable in than others at certain times. I know that you have already discovered that you feel more comfortable at the estate than any other place you've ever been."

Charlotte says, "Yes, that's true."

He says, "But I don't think you should have to worry about your honeymoon. If you find that you are in trouble you know where you must go."

She says, "Yes, I do. I guess I have an inner feeling that this is where I must go, but I don't understand how this came to be."

He says, "Well, no one likes coffins, we don't like them either. No one likes to be reminded of death. No one likes to have to cause death, or to have to exist because of death. But we all do, humans do, plants do, animals do. And because there are so many of us and because we have such supernatural powers, we can focus them. And we can focus them on these emblems, so that can alleviate a lot of the needs that others of our kind have had."

She says, "What do you mean others of our kind?"

He says, "Well, you have heard before of a vampire, the living dead, the person who exists off the blood of others."

She says, "It's kind of difficult for me to discuss this."

He says, "Charlotte, what I need right now is your objectivity. We brought you this far along, and we've told you that this is not a choice that you have to make, that you can stay in the mortal form if you choose. Most of us have chosen not to. Some of us have chosen to, and they have died. We buried them, as we will bury you. But you are one of the family, and you are the last of the line. One of the reasons that you are the last of the line is that we were purged. Your parents' wishes were for this line to continue. That's why they took upon, what could only be considered, a pilgrimage to a strange land to try to re-establish the seed."

Charlotte says, "I've heard this before. I, of course, want to have children, but I."

He cuts her off, "I know you don't want to have children that will become vampires. So, I'm telling you, as I've told you before, that everyone has free will."

She says, "Why is it not that everyone can become a vampire?"

He says, "A long time ago when we fought in the Carpathians in Poland, people much older than I, conditions were not anything that you could imagine. Those conditions drove some people in some directions just to survive, and other people in other directions. All I can tell you is that this is the direction that it has led us, but we have managed to survive. We have survived with dignity, and we have survived with honor. We bear no ill will toward any human being. And we've tried to teach that to the generations to come, but we must survive. And some of the things that we have learned, we can pass on. It would be foolish not to pass these things on. You do not have to take on all of these abilities, but some of the abilities you have already decided to use."

Charlotte says, "I know I use things, and I use these things without even thinking about them."

He says, "Yes, you did because they were inherent in you, that you should protect yourself first."

She says, "You assure me that it will stop where it is?"

He says, "I assure that it will stop where it is. I cannot assure you that you won't kill someone with your ability, but I can assure you that you do not have to participate in the blood feast."

She says, "Why do you keep calling it that?"

He says, "That's just exactly what it is. To drain a body of blood until it's lifeless, or to drain a body of blood to any point in between."

She says, "Why would you want to take any point in between?"

He explains to her, "I will just tell you what is truthful and try to separate it out from fiction. We have the choice to make the vampire, to make a person one of us, being a vampire, being immortal with all the things that encompass that. We have the choice to simply kill them. As a group, as a family, we have decided never to permit someone who is not one of us to become a vampire. We only kill them when they have attacked us. Then we show no mercy. Otherwise, they are usually left in an intermediate stage, and they have no memory of what has happened to them."

Charlotte says, "Well, David is not one of us. Where does David fit in?"

He explains to her, "David can fit in wherever you chose to have him fit in. He can simply be your husband, which will make him one of us, or any one of those things in between. And because I know that you have humanity because you are one of us, I'm sure he will not be any one of those things in between. It's not a necessity for you. At times, it has been a necessity for us."

She says, "What will I find in my parents' room?"

He says, "You'll probably find some very beautiful dresses of your mother's. She had excellent taste. You'll some nice attire in your father's room. He also had excellent taste. You'll see a lot of darkness, a lot of darkness. But you must understand that even when they lay in the darkness before twilight, they were conscious of each other whether they were in the same room or in different rooms. They were never alone. They were conscious of you, of your wellbeing and everything you were doing, just as we are. Your mother was a very good mother, and your father was an excellent parent. So, you should have nothing but love for them, and they died a horrible death."

She says, "I know that their death must have been horrible, but I've tried not to dwell on it too much. I've tried not to think about it. I have always hoped that I wouldn't have to see, I guess as I am talking to you, their ghost. I think it would be too much for me."

He says, "We arrived at the conclusion quite some time ago that it would be too much for you, and that's why you haven't seen, what you call, their ghosts. David, as he explained to you, restored them to their natural beauty, and we're all grateful for that even though he did it on accident."

She says, "Do have anything planned for Mr. Schnell?"

He says, "I don't know what we have planned for Mr. Schnell, but we will handle Mr. Schnell. Don't worry about that. If you want to find out more about your mother and father, it is your right and we will not stop you. We will try to support you through it, and if there is anything else, we can help you with, we will try and do that also." She thanks him. He says, "Now you'll have to have a restful sleep." Immediately, she does.

The next morning everyone is down at breakfast. Charlotte is very quiet, and David's mood mirrors hers. Robaire is intense. He is crumbling his napkin, dropping his napkin, crumbling his napkin, dropping his napkin. Yvette says, "I've got to get out of the house to go see Jennifer because of the vibrations here. I just can't take it. And it's not even a word I use most of the time, but I want to get in the car and go down the road into Mendocino." So, they let Yvette go.

As soon as everyone else is finished eating, Mrs. Hampton says, "I'll take you into the other wing." It is apparent that Jasper has begun down at the other wing, but he hasn't gone completely into the other wing. At the very back of the other wing, in each corner of the corridor, are huge double doors. Mrs. Hampton says, "The room to your right, Charlotte, was your father's, and the room to your left was Ava's. There is an adjoining door between that wall."

Charlotte says, "I would like to go in and see my mother's room first please." Mrs. Hampton takes out a large set of keys and opens the door. To everyone's surprise, everyone but Mrs. Hampton, there are no cobwebs, there is no dust, there is no stale odor. It seems that the room has been opened and freshened frequently or as frequently as needed. The room is beautiful, but it has a lot of heavy velvets and satins. The room is done in an off-white color. The blinds are drawn, and there is no light that comes from the blinds and into the inside. But it is a beautiful room.

There is a large canopy bed, and it is all done in cream with lots of pillows, lots of comforters and lots of quilts. It has layers and layers of bedding. At the foot of the bed is a nice big oak chest. It is carved, and on the carving is the coat of arms. On the four posters is some fragment of the coat of arms. It has bay windows. This part of the house is slightly above the other wing, although it is not on a different story. It is just beautiful. She has a dresser with three mirrors. There is a front mirror and a mirror that folds out on each side. It is all done in a nice heavy oak with a cream finish.

If Charlotte isn't mistaken, she would swear that she is on a cloud. It has a beautiful, perfumed scent. Mrs. Hampton says, "That smell you smell is the perfume your mother wore. I don't know what it is. I think she brought it from Europe." Charlotte finds herself not wanting to leave the room. It is as if something had been kept from her for years and years, and it was right up under her nose. She just wants to sit down on things, touch things, and lay down on her mother's bed. She wants to open her mother's closet and pull out dresses. She wants to put them up against her waist and try them on and swing around.

David catches her at the waist and tells her, "We should go now and look in your father's room. You can always come back to this room. This whole house is yours."

She says, "Yes, it is our house." She puts some of the dresses away in the closet. She asks Mrs. Hampton not to lock the room.

Mrs. Hampton goes over across the hall and unlocks the other door. David is occupying himself seeing how the two rooms join through the double door, and she opens that one for him too. The father's room is done in green. It is a very deep forest green. It is very much like her bridesmaids' dresses. Since Mrs. Hampton knows what the bridesmaids' dresses look like, and Charlotte knows, she is shocked that the colors are so close. It is very manly, very neat, very orderly. He had a roll-top desk. He had various chests and closets. There is some fragment of the emblem, so apparently some of his furniture was brought from Europe. So, Charlotte asks, "Was this furniture brought from Europe?" Mrs. Hampton says she believes that this furniture was brought from Europe, and that the baby's crib was brought from Europe.

Charlotte says, "Where in the world is the baby's crib, my crib?"

She says, "I can show you that later. It's up in the attic."

David looks around, and he is very much impressed because it seems that things have a definite order, and it is very definitely a man's room. Once again, it has a very distinctive cologne smell, the drapes are drawn, and no light penetrates in the room. But he doesn't get a feeling of claustrophobia at all. He feels at peace.

They close both rooms and lock them. Then at this point, it looks as if she is going to cry, so David takes over and says, "My goodness, what love there must have been between these two people."

She says, "Yes, I guess so."

He says, "Now, I think the thing to look at is the crib. Don't you?"

She says, "Yes, I think we had better go and look at the crib."

Mrs. Hampton says, "My, my, so much in one day and you haven't even had a chance to sit down and go through drawers. I knew you were going to ruffle through drawers and try on dresses and go through slips."

She says, "Yes, I know. But I guess I have years to do that."

They lock up the rooms. All this took about an hour. They went upstairs into the other wing, into another level of stairs which Charlotte had never gone up. There was an attic. In the attic was a crib. The crib was very well covered, so she had to uncover the crib. It again bore the complete coat of arms at each end. There was carving on the railings. It seemed to have the finest of linen on it.

She says to Mrs. Hampton, "And this is the way I slept?"

Mrs. Hampton says, "Of course. This is where you slept every night. And if you adjust the legs a certain way, the crib will rock. I used to rock you to sleep. And sometimes your mother would stop in, and she would sing you songs."

She asks, "Can you remember the songs?"

Mrs. Hampton says, "I probably could have remembered the songs, but the songs were in German. I couldn't retain them because they weren't in English. She just had a great love and a great tenderness for you, and so did your father. It was obvious that they were very concerned about your welfare."

Charlotte says, "Are there any pictures of them in the house? I really wish I had gotten to know them better."

Mrs. Hampton says, "So do I. I really wish I had gotten to know them better too."

She says, "But it seemed like they had they whole life ahead of them."

Megan says, "Yes."

Charlotte drops her head because she knew that their life depended in some ways on the loss or intervention of other human lives. She says, "Maybe in a way, things are for the best."

David looked at her because it was the first time, she had ever said anything that was negative about what she knew her parent's patterns must have been. He put his arms around her and says, "I think we have had enough for today. Let's go downstairs."

She says, "I want to spend a little bit of time by myself David."

He says, "Okay. I'll let you have about three or four hours. Then I'll come and get you, and I want you to take a walk around the grounds with me down to the beach."

She says, "That sounds like a good idea." Mrs. Hampton, once again, locked up.

Charlotte went to her room and put on her prettiest dressing gown, and she lay across her bed. She had an idea now of what kind of woman her mother was, how very feminine her mother was, and somehow, she wanted to live up to that part of the legacy at least. She looked at her clothing. She thought I haven't quite made it. I wonder if we will be able to occupy those two rooms. She is going to speak to Jasper Smythe about it immediately, as soon as she could. She was hoping they would run into him out on the grounds when David promised to come and get her for a walk. She didn't realize that she was tired, but she went right to sleep.

David interrupted Charlotte's rest as he promised and insisted that she get up and go for a walk around the grounds. She knew what he was there for, so she didn't argue about it. She closed the door behind her, went downstairs, out on to the grounds and walked with him. But she didn't have much conversation, and he didn't try to force too much conversation out of her. They walked for a good mile, two or three hours, almost silently. Then they walked back into the house silently.

By this time, it was lunch time. They were hungry. Everyone was at lunch, except for Yvette who was out in Mendocino with Jennifer.

Charlotte says once again she would like some time to herself after lunch. She ate lunch without any comment. The two men have no other choice but to let her go up to her room and spend the time alone. Robaire, on the other hand, had been back in the parents' room. He didn't want Charlotte to know because he thought it would be too close and too upsetting of a situation. He was checking their rooms for any signs of a haunting. He didn't find any so far. He said that he doubted he would find any and he doubted that her parents were about in any form, ghosts or otherwise.

David says, "I'm pretty sure that is the case. But I'm hoping that Charlotte would cheer up because the wedding is coming closer and closer." As soon as some of the guests start to arrive that must come in early, and the caterers and the florists, she should get excited. That was all that they could hope for.

In the meantime, Yvette and Jennifer are at the art gallery. They are trying to reach Charlotte by phone because they want a final confirmation on the next three exhibitors who will be totally watercolor. They thought that this would really cheer her up when she came back from her vacations. They had some pretty good artists. One of them specialized in wildlife and another did scenes of Europe in watercolor. The other one was random, you couldn't categorize him as a painter, but he was a modern artist. They found her in her room. She answered the phone in her room. Yvette tells her, "These three have agreed to exhibit, and Jennifer wanted your permission to go ahead and tell them to start shipping and to pay for the shipping." Charlotte gave her permission. This did lift her spirits somewhat.

Jennifer says, "I know the ropes pretty well. I know that we should do our advertisements and get our invitations out. We can use a somewhat similar mailing list. We'll also have an additional mailing list from the guest sign-in book that we left at the front door. Then too, we have had some contacts within the last six to eight months, and people who have heard about the art gallery would like to be invited to the next showing. So, I had quite a list to work from. I'm going to start the printers on the invitations now, if I can get a firm date from you when you will be returning."

She gave them a date that was about two and a half months into the future. She says, "You can start exhibiting then, and plan for the exhibit to go at least one month. If it's successful, it might go into two."

Jennifer says, "That pretty much answers all my questions."

Charlotte says, "You have a free hand. You watched what happened the first time, and you can just follow through on that. If you have any questions, I'll always be in contact with you from either the ship or someplace. Wherever we are, I'll be calling in to see how things are going. I'll also give you my number so that you can keep in contact with me."

Yvette says, "It looks like things will be quite ready, and there's no apparent interruption in your business considering what you've been through."

Charlotte says, "That's good because the public doesn't need to associate all those things with the art gallery, or it will never function as a very good business."

Yvette says, "And I think that now you can concentrate on bringing a lot more elegance to the business with David at your side and having each showing together. I'm sure he will be at each showing. You must be always exquisitely dressed and jeweled at each art gallery opening."

She says, "I guess I should work on that now since I've gotten the building straight, and there is no real excuse for it. I'm not in school anymore, and with what I'm painting, if I should paint to contribute to the exhibit, then I guess I'm more concerned about my clothing. But you're right. It's time for me to start paying more attention to my appearance and to have the proper appearance to attract the kind of business that I want."

Yvette and Jennifer agree that was kind of tactfully put across to Charlotte because they knew Charlotte could do it all along. It's just that she was so distracted by this and the things that happened in the meantime that it had kind of slipped her mind. Before they hung up, Yvette said that she would be coming home soon, and that she hoped everything was all right with Charlotte because Charlotte kind of had a down tone to her voice. She explained to Yvette on the phone that they had gone ahead and opened her parents' rooms, and that she had never realized that her parents' rooms were in the other wing. She told her that Jasper had not renovated that section yet, and she didn't even see much for him to do except for maybe in the corridors because her mother's room was beautiful. She said her father's room she almost just wanted to leave it just as it was.

Yvette says, "That doesn't sound very good. I was hoping that you and David would occupy those rooms. I'm sure that your parents had wished that you occupy those rooms."

Charlotte says, "Yes, we considered that too."

Yvette says, "When I come home, immediately I would like to see them so I can see if they are in the condition for you to occupy them right after your honeymoon, or if Mr. Smythe should get to work on that so that you'll be able to move right into something very cozy. Are there fireplaces in those bedrooms?"

She says, "No. There are no fireplaces in there now."

Yvette says, "Well there can be fireplaces in those bedrooms by the time you come back from your honeymoon if you let Mr. Smythe do a little renovation. Do they have adjoining doors?"

She says, "Yes."

Yvette says, "I've always thought that was a wonderful idea because there are times when you want privacy, and there are times when you want to have your dress be a surprise to your husband. It generates a lot more mood sometimes if he hasn't watched every move you have made, especially if you don't have to share bathrooms."

Charlotte says, "I know exactly what you mean. I guess my mother and my father understood that very well too."

Yvette says, "I'm coming home, and let's go back through those rooms again. I don't think you should be so upset about it or depressed. I think that's a legacy you should appreciate. It seems that, from what you are telling me and what you have described to me, your mother was a very feminine, very elegant lady. And since there's things that she couldn't teach you that must have made her the apple of your father's eye, maybe we could pick up some tips from her. I know you could use some tips from her to help you out with David because you know marriage is a lifetime commitment. You need to renew and keep things lively. Do you know how long your parents had been married?"

At this, Charlotte kind of flinches because she has no idea. They could have been married for centuries. She simply says, "No. But I'm sure that they were very much in love."

Yvette says, "I can't wait to get home so you can take me through these rooms, and I can see this. We can spend a little time working on this before it gets too close to the wedding, and all we can do is think about the wedding."

With that, she hangs up. Yvette starts to say goodbye to Jennifer who says, "I hope I can see the rooms too before they are occupied."

Yvette says, "I'll make sure that Charlotte leaves word with Mrs. Hampton to let you see the rooms before they return from their honeymoon, but after Mr. Smythe has fixed them up."

Jennifer says, "I can't wait. That should be very exciting." Yvette says goodbye to Jennifer who thanks her for coming out to check on her. Yvette says that's no problem, and either she or Charlotte will always come and check on her at least once a week. They said goodbye, and Yvette goes back toward the estate.

In the meantime, David and Robaire are confirming their appointments again with the various tailors because they don't know which tailor they are going to choose. They still have some contacts in San Francisco, and he has gotten some definite recommendations on one, but he is not sure he is going to go with that. But he is going to see that one first because maybe he could just stop there and not go any further. They are both rather excited that they get to go into San Francisco, and that they can stay away from Mendocino for a while, at least a day. Maybe the ladies will let them stay a whole day away from Mendocino.

By this time, Yvette is home. She goes up to Charlotte's room. Charlotte is still lying across the bed. Yvette says, "I think a lot of things are wrong with you that have absolutely nothing to do with the paranormal. I think that you're just having kind of the willies because you're getting married. That's normal. It's surprising it hasn't shown up in David and if it does, don't panic."

Charlotte says, "Maybe you are right. I am taking a big step."

Yvette says, "It's a big step for anyone to take. There is nothing in your parents' room at his point that could have upset you that bad." Charlotte says she would really rather not discuss it. Yvette says, "I feel just a little bit left out, just a little put off. Well, I guess there are some things even best friends don't talk about, but I didn't think this was one of them. We've always talked about this."

She says, "We will talk about it, but I'm not ready to talk about it right this minute."

Yvette and Charlotte go downstairs. Charlotte has left instructions that Mrs. Hampton is to leave those rooms unlocked and open like the rest of the rooms in the house are. There is no reason to treat it as a shrine or a mausoleum now that she knows where they are. They go right into her mother's room. It was, as was said before, beautiful. Yvette is in awe that this room is just so beautiful.

She says, "Your mother must have had excellent taste. She must have had excellent plans for renovation because I'm sure we'll find that she did this herself, and she did both your room and your father's room because I'm sure the bachelor who lived here didn't do this."

Charlotte says, "You're right. I'm sure he didn't do this. Maybe we could check around town and find out who it was that my mother hired to do this."

Yvette says, "But they are probably long dead. That's thirty years ago. I'm pretty sure they are dead. You can check on it just for information, just to know, and Jasper might be able to tell you because he's been around her a long time. But I don't think they will be around to do anything."

She says, "I know they wouldn't be around to do anything, but I just thought perhaps they can give me some stories about what my parents were like, working for them."

Yvette said once again, "Maybe that's not such a good idea because the kind of stories you want would be of a more intimate nature and with a workman or an architect, Jasper Smythe is the exception because of his personality. Normally, the interaction isn't such that anyone could tell you the kind of stories you want to hear."

Charlotte says, once again, "I guess you are right. That is a little bit ridiculous. But I'm just glad I found the rooms. I don't know why it never occurred to me before. Maybe nanny deliberately avoided the subject or changed the subject if it ever came up and I guess I was so busy being away at school I never thought to ask which rooms were my parents'."

Yvette says, "Now that you have found them, I hope you live in them and use them as they did."

Charlotte again cringes just a little bit, but she says, "I'm sure we'll put them to somewhat of a similar use, David and I."

Yvette says, "Well, what did David think of them?"

She says, "He was very impressed with my father's room. He also wants to use them as our suites."

Yvette says, "Unchanged?"

Charlotte says, "Well, he didn't suggest any changes, and I really have no changes to suggest, maybe just a little freshening up. But other than that, the decor is beautiful."

Yvette says, "It's amazing that a thirty-year-old set of rooms could still be beautiful, comfortable, and very inviting to sleep in but maybe that says something about the nature of your parents."

Charlotte says, "I guess it does say something about the nature of my parents."

Yvette is astute enough to pick up on these remarks that Charlotte is making, remarks and then yet again not remarks. She says, "Aren't you happy with what you found out? I would be very happy if I could open my house at the spur of the moment and find this."

Charlotte says, "I guess you're right. I'm being ridiculous once again, and I should let the subject drop."

As they are walking out of their rooms down the hall, Yvette tells her, "Jennifer is, of course, carrying on very well. You are not going to have to worry about a thing on your honeymoon. You should just strictly enjoy yourself and get to know David. And for God sakes, stop putting David off because David has been through a lot with you, and David was proven that he loves you. Just give David a break. I don't mean to get into your business, but that would just be my going away advice."

They both laugh at that because Charlotte knows that she doesn't mean any harm. Charlotte is headstrong enough that most things go in one ear and out the other, and she truly wants to hear them. Yvette says, "I gave it my best shot. And if David ever asks me, I'll tell him I gave it my best shot, ten or fifteen years down the line and he's wondering why he married you." They are joking back and forth just like they did in school days. Charlotte begins to relax, which is exactly what Yvette intended for her to do.

By this time, Robaire has caught up with them. He suggests a game of tennis for Yvette. Yvette says she is not quite sure she is up to it because, after all, looking and thinking about all those things that must happen at the art gallery have worn her out. Robaire says, "You can't be that tired from using your head. Just go upstairs and get changed, and I will be waiting downstairs for you at the tennis courts."

Charlotte looks at her and gives her one of those do as you say not as I do looks. In other words, you want me to follow the leader, you should go ahead and follow the leader too. Yvette gets the message and goes upstairs trying to set her best example and changes for tennis.

Yvette and Robaire play tennis until shortly before dinner time when they have just enough time to shower and change. They also ask if dinner is to be formal. They've been informed that it is going to be very casual. They leave just enough time to come down with whatever they can find to throw on.

Charlotte is still tired. She goes back into her room. She lays down and starts to do a little wondering and imagining because everyone has told her, everyone being Mrs. Hampton and most recently David, that her parents were beautiful and that her father was very handsome. She wondered if they had a normal courtship. She also wondered about the years, but she decided that she should put the years out of her mind and put those other things out of her mind because after all she has been told she has a choice. She can just imagine them since they are not here anymore as normal people having a normal courtship at a time when romance was very much in vogue.

She is thinking that her mother must have had an awful lot of friends, and that is all she would permit herself to think about. She is thinking how beautiful her mother must have been, how handsome her father must have been, and how educated and cultured they must have been. She imagines what it must have been like on the first date for the two of them. She visualizes her mother to look pretty much like herself, and she has gotten somewhat a description of her father. She understands that she has her father's eyes, and they had explained to her that they believed that she has her mother's grade of hair and her mother's almost heart-shaped face. She is putting all this together.

She thinks when I get more time, I will actually start to look for pictures, but I won't look for pictures now because I'll be very disappointed if I don't find them, and besides, I should spend more of my time on the wedding. But she does allow herself a few hours to wonder what life must have been like for them, the normal side of life.

In the back of her mind keeps entering the thought when it came time to take a victim, how did they deal with that? Did her father procure the victims and bring them home? How was that handled? She couldn't permit herself to even think about that because it was starting to depress her. So, she tried to put it out of her mind. But it was kind of a nagging thought, it just stayed there. Then everything that seemed so beautiful, so romantic, so sweet, just kind of took on a horrible tone.

By this time, David is knocking on the door. She snaps out of her daydreaming and goes to answer the door. David says, "What were you doing in here? I understand you've been alone in here for about two or three hours. What were you thinking about? Were you asleep? Did I awaken you?"

She says, "No, I was not asleep. I was thinking about my parents." He can tell that she is very upset, and she is holding back tears. He can imagine what she is thinking about her parents and that all the beauty they saw in their rooms didn't help.

He says, "Do you want to talk to me about it? I think you should talk to me about it because I think you should talk to somebody about it, and I'm the best person for you to talk to about this sort of thing to."

She says, "I was just wondering about when it came time for them to take a victim."

He says, "Yes, I know. I've had problems with that too. But they are dead now. You and I are alive, and we have not had to function in that manner, and we will not function in that manner. Neither will our children function in that manner. And you're not responsible. I don't hold you responsible. No one will hold you responsible for what your parents do. And even though I know this, it doesn't make me love you any less. I don't know that it makes me love you anymore, but it depends on how you handle it from now on because you have got to get over this. You know it is a reality. I know it is a reality. We both have got to try to be better people because of it. Then we can look back on it in future years and see if we were actually better people because of it."

Charlotte says, "That's pretty much what Yvette was saying, that now that I have the facts in front of me, that I won't really be judged, or I can't really judge myself on what any of my ancestors have done, but what I do now that I know this, and what we do together as a family."

He says, "Exactly, and you know that neither one of us will ever succumb to anything like that."

She says, "You know, I have some kind of an understanding of how they came to have no choice."

He says, "I want you to leave that alone. I don't want you to have a good understanding of how they came to have no choice. I don't want you to empathize with them to that extent. It happened, they lived that way, and you don't have to anymore. You've never had to. They see to that. I will see to that. So, I hope that you do not begin to empathize with them because that's a very negative way to have to live. People are forced to do all kinds of things, but this is not something that you should accept as normal or as a possible alternative when life is not going your way."

She says, "I realize that as well as you do, David. And I still have a hard time with it. I have a hard time with it because they are my parents. I have a hard time with it because it was a way of life for my family for a long time, and I have a hard time with it because it is a way of life that has saved me and you on more than one occasion and will probably have to save us again. So, who are we kidding?"

He says, "Well, I don't know. I don't think you are giving me very much credit. And you did say yourself that Mr. Leopold was not killed, and that Mr. Leopold was permitted to survive. And with what I know, they didn't have to permit Mr. Leopold to survive. You assured me that they would handle Mr. Schnell, and I will have to believe you that they will handle Mr. Schnell. Hopefully, it will not end in any mental harm or a limited amount of mental harm, and any death or any maiming. I know he tried to kill me."

Charlotte says, "No, I've been assured that it won't."

He says, "There, you see. Things have already taken a different turn. And as you say this is now the twentieth century, and life is a lot different. The evil that men face is different now, and so possibly the evil that it brings out of men can be different now. I see none of those evils in you, and I hope that you've seen that in me. So, I think that we have a lot less to worry about than we believe. And just because we know how bad things can get, we will be a lot more watchful than you would have been when I first met you at the art gallery. We'll be a lot more watchful about what we do and what we say."

"That's very true."

"And I'm sure we will be a lot more watchful about our kids, about our children. I'm sure few people have been raised as strictly as you were with Mrs. Hampton and with your private schools. And I don't think that it was any accident that your parents selected her to help them with you. They could have chosen any one of several people, but they chose her. I think they chose her with deliberation. Not only that, but since their death she has been permitted to exercise her morals and her rules around the house, and no one seems to have objected to that."

Charlotte says, "Yes, I guess you're right."

He continues, "And you know, Charlotte, every time we've had one of these horrible occurrences, one or the other of us has been in trouble. And if we hadn't had this kind of intervention, we wouldn't be here talking to each other."

"Yes, that is true. And I guess we should go down to dinner now because I don't really want to think about it much anymore."

He takes her in his arms. He kisses her, and he holds her for a long time as if he never wants to let her go. She says, "But it is time for dinner."

"You're right. So, let's go on down to dinner because we have lots and lots of days to do this." Dinner proceeds without incident.

The day seems to fly, and before everyone realizes it the wedding is about two days away. Everyone has checked and double-checked plans. Most of the bridesmaids have arrived and been accommodated in one of the other rooms in the house. They have all been introduced to David. They are all very surprised and very happy with Charlotte's choice. Yvette is, of course, still close to Charlotte and still very watchful of everything that goes on. The caterer does exactly as she has promised. Jasper Smythe has the landscaping perfectly done, and he assures them that Mr. Weinberger will come even if it is for a little while.

David has retained a local justice of the peace, and no one has questioned that.

Everyone is coming into town. David's family will be coming in tomorrow, the day before the wedding. Charlotte has assured them that they can stay for as long as they like after David and she has left for the honeymoon. Arrangements are made to shuttle people back and forth from San Francisco as they come in.

Hours go by. Minutes go by. Finally, Mrs. Hampton is knocking on Charlotte's door to help dress her for the wedding because now, today, is the day of the wedding.

David and Charlotte are each dressing in their separate rooms. All the bridesmaids and the best man are preparing for the wedding. There isn't a flower girl, but there are enough flowers everywhere that no one seems to notice it. The green and the white make a spectacular view from every angle.

David has gotten several of his friends, not close friends but associates he worked with, to come in and take photographs of the wedding. Charlotte, of course, makes a very beautiful bride.

The wedding goes without incident. The bride and the groom leave and go to their first stop which is San Francisco to Hong Kong. They say their goodbyes.

Mrs. Hampton is almost as tearful as Yvette. They all express that they want to get postcards from Charlotte and from David. Robaire says that he'll make sure that Yvette and he visit at least every other summer. Yvette catches the bouquet.

The bride and the bride groom are off. In the car on the way to the airport, Charlotte says to David, "I'm sure that we will have a wonderful life."

David says, "I will see to it that we have a wonderful life."

In the meantime, Mr. Schnell has returned from the wedding and the reception, which also went very well but the bride and the bride groom didn't stay for the reception. It's about eleven o'clock and he is slightly inebriated. He is pretty happy with himself because he has got the time that he needed with his parcel map diversion, and he doesn't think he is going to have to put any money back because he had some pretty good luck on the stocks. So, he has some extra money, and he will just replace it with that without losing any of his acquired ill-gotten gains. So, he is pleased with himself.

When he arrives at his house, which is in Santa Rosa, he comes in and goes to his bedroom. Sitting on his bed is a woman who appears to be about thirty-five years old. She is dressed in a suit that looks like it was made in the nineteen fifties. She is carrying a purse. She looks like she has been bleeding. She also looks like she has been very badly burned, and he can smell all over his house the smell of burning flesh.

He is a rational man, and he wants to be in control of the situation, and this can't be happening to him, so he turns around to leave the room.

Behind him is standing a man that looks about forty or forty-five years old. He is very distinguished looking. He is graying at the temples. He has severe lacerations all over his body. His clothes are tattered. He is very badly burned also. He extends a hand to stop Mr. Schnell from emerging from his room, and his hand is the paw of a wolf. Mr. Schnell starts to scream. He is now looking at Mrs. Von Shillingsfurst, and he sees that she has claws too.

Mr. Von Shillingsfurst says, "Simon, I didn't tell you that you could look away."

Mr. Schnell turns around, again almost childlike, and says, "Please, please, just leave me alone. Just leave me alone."

Mr. Von Shillingsfurst says, "This is a business matter, Simon. You understand that, don't you?" He is taking a very stern tone.

Simon says, "Yes, yes, I do."

Mr. Von Shillingsfurst says, "I can't hear you!"

He says, "Yes, yes, I do!"

"So now, Simon, don't ever think that you can get away with something like this again. We want you to go to your firm. We want you to stay at your firm. I understand you are now head of the firm. Is that right, Simon?"

Mr. Schnell says, "Yes, I am. Yes, I am."

Mr. Von Shillingsfurst says, "And you would like to keep that position, wouldn't you?"

Mr. Schnell says, "Yes. Yes, I would."

Mrs. Von Shillingsfurst says, "We wouldn't dream of taking it from you."

Mr. Schnell knows better than to look at her, but he is hoping that she is just bleeding on his bed. He says, "You don't want me to quit?"

They say in unison, "Of course not, Simon. We want you to go on and be a very honest trustee."

The next day, Mr. Schnell arrives at his office, and he begins to fix up the books. He removes all notations of any parcel map problems. He begins to slowly, but thoroughly, right Charlotte's account.

The next day, Charlotte and David arrive in Hong Kong.

Printed in the USA
CPSIA information can be obtained
at www.ICGtesting.com
LVHW011735110724
785234LV00001B/79